Winterhaven

Written By Marie Daley

Dedication

3

To My Wonderful Grandchildren: Zac, Kirsten, Jasmine, Savannah, Paulina and Elizabeth
To Our Guys: Bobby F, Gene L, TJ N, Jerimiah D, and Steven M
And Gal: Tammy D
Also to my Great-Grandchildren: Thomas, Zaydin, Addeleigh, Wyatt, Westin, Caraleena, Korbyn, Vayden, Sakura, and Serena!

Yes, we are one big happy and growing family!

The Adventures of Ryes and Garth

Tayna's Dawn

Winterhaven

Table of Contents

6

This page intentionally left blank

Ooops...

Ryes sighed as she sat down in one of the rolling chairs in the computer room. She was bored and didn't want to do any more lessons with the computer today. She craved something different… something more daring. But what? Because it was her turn at watch, she kept an eye to the slowly roving screen that depicted the world outside this safe haven they'd found, but the scene truly rarely changed. The others were all busy, doing other projects or chores and sometimes she glimpsed them on the internally-aimed screens around her. Ardis was concentrating upon the lesson the computer was teaching her at the other console in here. It looked like she was learning how to use the cleaning machines. She wanted to take over the management of them; to use them safely.

"I'm going to get something to eat," she finally said after another hour, just realizing Ryes was in the room with her. Ryes gave her a nod of her head, her eyes going from screen to screen to see if anything was out of order. She sighed.

"I had a bigger than I really needed breakfast," she admitted with a rueful smile, as she turned to look her in the eyes. "You go on and I'll get something later, when I'm hungry." Ardis laughed, nodding her head in agreement.

"I'll bring you back something light to keep you until then," she promised with a smile of understanding.

"Thanks," Ryes replied as Ardis got up out of her chair and was quickly out the door.

Now was her chance to do a little research, her way. They needed more answers than they were ever going to get out of this stubborn machine. She settled down into her chair, getting comfortable. She breathed deeply several times, while relaxing her body. Finally she opened up her Time Walking Talent and cast herself back in time. She searched for when there were people present in this room. She felt a sense of a presence, so willed herself to that time.

It was about halfway through the night and Neil Jarrett was so terribly bored. He hated and loved the night duty watch in the control room. It was normally his chance to catch up on his family mail from Earth, or on the latest flix they'd sent him. But tonight it had been at least a week with nothing coming from home. This wasn't too unusual as there were times when they were busy with their own lives and forgot about him all the way out here at the research station. Even Mom and Dad forgot him sometimes.

He'd just finished running his computer checks, since it was truly one of his main duties. He was one of a half dozen techs in the facility who knew enough of the computer systems to maintain and repair them when things went wrong. Most modules were plug-in and done, but there were times when he had to break out the real test equipment, or diagnostic programs. Everything they were sent from Earth was scrap yard salvage, which was decades old. But since it was all they had, he did his share of the work to keep it running. It was better than nothing. Now, he was bored and craved something more… anything more… And it was still hours before he would be off-duty and he could go get snuggly with Brenda. They both had the next two days off-shift.

Suddenly, as he was finally calling up his favorite game, he felt a horrible wrenching sensation which caused him to choke and sputter. It was like he was being torn apart inside! He pushed back his chair and jumped to his feet while at the same time a native woman jumped out of the same chair, but away from him. She appeared to have been as much in pain from the experience as he. Neil's senses were reeling for several moments and he was breathing hard, as if he'd just jogged a couple of miles non-stop.

Ryes stared at him in total shock. She wasn't wholly pulled into the past, but she was far more substantial than she had ever been when venturing back into time. She was breathing hard, too, as she put a hand over her stomach, as if to make sure her cubs were okay, even if they were still in the future.

"Who are you and how did you do that?" he questioned, more curious than mad. Ryes was flustered. She knew a few words well enough to communicate a little and some simple things, so how was she to form a communication bridge here? She knew she couldn't just will herself to disappear now. She had to get this situation turned around, somehow. She pointed to herself.

"Ryes," she stated. She pointed to the machine console, "Computer," she added, identifying it. She pointed to him, "Who?" He grinned, feeling this was more than he had ever seen from any of the natives they'd captured before.

"Neil," he told her, speaking slowly, pointing to himself. He calmed down and a real smile brightened his face now. "So, Ryes, how did you get here?" She returned his smile, her eyes lighting up now. They were a beautiful green and she had flaming red hair, all braided up.

"I walk back," she replied, hoping his smiles meant the same as theirs. "Learn computer," she gestured with her hand doing a sweeping gesture to indicate the computer console.

"So, you want me to teach you the computer? Why?" he pressed, looking as if he was trying to solve a puzzle.

"You gone. We alone. Need computer," she managed to get out slowly, concentrating upon wording it as clearly as she could. "I walk back learn."

"You mean all the humans are gone?"

"Yes. Empty." she sighed, then smiled at him again. "Need teach plesss." It was Neil's turn to sigh, but his smile brightened again.

"You're really good with English," he noted. "I will teach you, if you teach me, too." He shook his head in disbelief, sure no one would believe him if he even tried to tell anyone about this experience. "How do you walk back? You mean in time?" She blushed furiously.

"Yes. I walk back," she affirmed, finally relaxing a little. He reached over to her then, to try to touch her, but his hand passed through hers as if she were made of air. It stung a little, but she was feeling better now and nodded her head to the surprise in his eyes. "Plesss?" she asked, her eyes pleading. He huffed out a laugh.

"Okay, first item to note. It's please, not plesss," he told her, laughing. "P l e a s e," he repeated slowed.

"P l e a s e," she repeated, grinning. "No plesss." He nodded at this, seeing she did learn fast.

He suddenly grabbed the chair and wheeling it back to the console table, getting an idea. He called up the keyboard and Ryes stepped over closely watched everything he did, playing attention. He was excited about what he was doing, at least. He typed up some bold letters on the screen overhead and she looked at them, wondering. He pointed to each letter, spelling them out for her.

"R y e s," he voiced for her. She grinned, liking the way her name appeared in this foreign script. She wished she could do the same for him in Dolbith, but she was very insubstantial here in this time.

"Yes, me," she agreed. His smile got bigger and she realized she trusted him.

"I'll write a program to teach you English. Type in your name like this, here," he showed her, instructing her. "The computer will then know you. So even if I'm not here to teach you, I can still teach you something."

"Tanks you," she replied, thinking she understood. He laughed at this, nodding his head.

"Thank you," he emphasized in response. She parroted him, grinning.

"I walk now, bye Neil," she suddenly told him, realizing someone was holding her hand.

"Will I see you again?" he asked.

"Yes, see," she promised. After almost being one for a few moments, she knew she'd never have a problem finding him, again. She let go this time and place, letting her inner self endure that wrenching feeling and headed back home, again. But she had found at least one hooman or hueman who accepted her and was willing to help her learn. Soon she was back in her own body, once again. Maren let go of her hand, grinning.

"Off on a short trip, again?" he asked, putting down the bread and meat "sandwich" on its plate on the console table for her.

"I have to learn the computer," she asserted, blushing.

"I have to get back to my chores, too," he replied. "No more Time Walking today," he minded her. She nodded her agreement, so he left out the door.

Once he was gone, she turned to the computer console and entered the letters that spelled out her own name. The main screen before her suddenly went dark and then a few moments later Neil's face appeared on the screen. He was smiling at her.

"Hello Ryes, I'm here to start your lessons. I hope you're ready to learn," he said, appearing happy. She smiled at the screen only understanding a small part of what he said, but she realized she was ready to learn now with Neil as he teacher.

Reunion

Garth bent to finish repacking his pack, while Ryes stood holding onto his spear. She surveyed the lush green, peaceful grassland before her. The apparent peace was fragile with Doran's Valley of Death too close for the unwary. They'd journeyed far from their home dwellings in Matlowe Village, originally leaving on an exploration to see the ruins of Hailys, the greatest city upon Tayna, which had been destroyed almost three hundred years ago by a murdering alien people. On their journey, the pair of them had been caught up in a flood and separated from the rest of their friends, then mislead here to this Valley by Ryes' budding Talent; being sensitive to Doran's lure. But Ryes fought her and won their freedom and finally they found the way back out of her evil domain. Now to find the way back to their friends and family!

As Ryes stood in thought, still exhausted after her ordeal, she felt a strange lurch and a reeling surge of power, as if something within her had been unleashed. Panic gripped her heart as the very air shimmered, blurring all before her eyes into a green and gold mist. Her insides felt as if they were twisted around! Then as suddenly as it happened, it steadied again. Was this some kind of aftereffect from holding and directing such immense energies from the Stone for so long? Her mind was reeling and her heart still beat strongly in panic as she saw what lay before her eyes, once more.

She was standing back in the valley, near the tree they had camped at and the open area around it, which they'd just left behind them. But instead of it being empty, there was a cavalcade of brightly dressed and armored men filling it in front of her. They were almost akin to some of the images captured in one of Darman's old books, which she'd read when she was little! There were at least a dozen soldiers. Their uniforms were red with black and white contrasts. Gold ropes and buttons completed their look, drawing her eyes in with the details they created. The windracers they rode were pure white and tall at the shoulder; more than able to carry some of the heavier muscled men riding them. The trappings on the windracers were extravagant, also a red cloth with the black, red and gold accenting them. They stood in such well-mannered patience, as if long accustomed to such situations. She could feel the power in them as they stood at the ready, to do as they were bid on an instant, both the soldiers and their mounts.

Their leader dismounted and drew his sword as he approached a middle-aged woman, who stood between two willowy trees. Ryes didn't know her, and wondered where she came from?

She thought she'd stopped Doran's calls. Was she one of her Handmaidens, who had just awakened? She was dressed in a softly-flowing green gown, but there was a vagueness in her eyes which looked all too familiar to Ryes. A thousand questions arose in her mind as she watched. Where had these people come from? And so quickly and quietly! How was she back in the valley, when they had finally made it clear of the gully? Was this something Doran or her followers managed to do, to get back at her for her victory?

"I have come for my betrothed," the officer stated loudly, his face diffused with his smoldering anger. He was an older man, who appeared older than Rowan. He was very neat in appearance; every hair in place as if he tamed it first. His ears had strange coloration, as if some kind of special rank. She wondered about such a neatly groomed man. The woman did not respond.

"Release Tyra of House Li to us, immediately!" he ordered, raising his sword to point it in her direction. This was her next surprise. How could he be betrothed to her mother? This didn't make any sense. Tyra was long gone from Tayna now and had been married to Ronn before she died. How could he come here to make such a claim?

"She is sheltered with the Goddess," the woman replied in a mocking voice; a sneer upon her face. "No man may violate this valley unpunished," she stated loudly in return, then turned away, as if dismissing his threat, walking down the path leading toward the temple; the matter dismissed to all appearances. The presence of the armed men were not a danger by her behavior.

"Then so be it! We will take the head of your so-called goddess and still bring Tyra home with us!" he shouted at her retreating back. He signaled his men forward, leading with his drawn sword. A now-familiar, insane laugh filled the air, surprising them. The uncertain men paused, looking around them, trying to find the source.

"It is only someone with strong Mind Voice," he declared, barely glancing back at his troops. "We have a job to complete. Mental barriers up. Forward!" The old officer refused to pay it heed, as the others stood in doubt. He pressed onward, leaving them behind now.

"Watch out!" Ryes shouted in warning as she saw the almost invisible hand of Doran reach out and roughly push the old leader. His face registered shock as he was grabbed and shaken by an unseen force, as if he were a rag doll. His sword was pulled from his grasp and rammed through his chest to its hilt, then run downward, until he was practically cleaved in two. His screams were horrific to hear and died as suddenly as he did. His company stood with terror reflected upon their faces, as mad laughter rang out from the air around them. Doran was daring them to continue and try to take revenge.

Ryes strode forward in anger and slapped aside Doran's grasping hand, as she reached to claim the unfortunate man's soul. There was a loud, shocked shriek at this, which slowly faded. The freed soul vanished to wherever souls fled at life's end. Ryes looked down sadly at the body of the brave officer. Two members of the company dismounted and hesitantly stepped forward.

"Who are you and what do you want?" one of the men demanded, a strange weapon in his hand. It appeared a short barrel with a grip shaped to fit the hand comfortably.

"I'm named Ryes and am the daughter of Tyra Li and Ronn," she answered. She looked back toward the gully, but Garth wasn't standing there, so he didn't know she had been swept off, yet. "We won our freedom from this valley just a few hours ago, but I seemed to have misplaced my husband," she stated with a puzzled frown. The time of the day was even wrong. It was late afternoon, not early morning.

"How can you be the daughter of Tyra Li?" the man demanded, his eyes narrowing and looking angry. "You are lying. Tyra only arrived here two years ago."

"She has no daughters and is far too young to have one as old as you!" a second one agreed as he reached to grab her arm. Ryes felt a shock at his touch, but his hand passed through her arm, as if she were made of air. She was startled by the pain this caused and her insubstantiality. What had happened to her? Why was this happening? The men appeared as surprised as she, when she looked up at their faces.

"I'm more lost than I thought!" she declared, looking to them for answers. They backed away, their fear naked on their faces. Another, older man stepped forward. He was clearly unafraid and had a determined set to his chin. He gestured for the others to secure the fallen officer's body. They reluctantly stepped forward again as a pair of others came over to help. The older officer turned to face her squarely, his face a controlled neutral.

"You are Time Walking," he explained to Ryes in an oddly accented voice. She frowned at this and he glanced back to check on the progress of his command. "No, leave that cursed blade lie," he ordered, as one of the men stooped to retrieve the fallen sword. "It has betrayed The Family and will never again cause another such death."

"What's Time Walking?" she asked, puzzled. The officer's gaze returned to her, looking her directly in the eye.

"Only one of royal blood could fully answer that. I am only an officer of the guard of the House of Oftirrin and have a very base knowledge of the Talents," he told her. He had noted her simple dress and braids, as if she were a puzzle he was going to have to remember later for a report. "Ah, a Forester."

"How do I get back to where I belong?" Ryes pressed, questioning as they prepared to leave, bearing their sad burden. The man's windracer was brought forward to bear his now-wrapped body.

"It is a very rare Talent and none now living are said to have it, that I have heard. And I have never been versed in how it operates. I am sorry," he told her. The old guardsman only shrugged his shoulders, then turned upon his heel, remounted his windracer, and left with the rest of the company. They filed up the gully, disappearing around the bend. She looked down at the bloodstained sword, as a sense of helplessness claimed her. Then she raised her eyebrows in surprise. It was the same sword she used last night to fight her way free of Doran's deadly garden. She shook her head sadly, bewildered.

"At least it served its final duty for me and helped free us of this place," she said into the resulting quiet around her, then sighed.

Ryes turned and walked back toward the gully, feeling very tired and alone. When she reached the top again, she stepped over to the tree she'd been standing near. Even it was barely a sapling! She needed to get back to Garth! She closed her eyes and imagined everything as she last saw it. She strove to listen to the sounds of Garth packing his backpack. In her mind she pictured his face as clearly as she could, putting all her will into the image. Again there was a wrenching feeling within and the air about her caused her skin to tingle. Suddenly she felt his spear solidly in her hands once more, and Garth's strong arms about her. She let herself collapse against him, dropping the spear. She was back and safe with him, again. She began to shiver with an intense cold as tears of relief sprang to her eyes.

"Are you all right, Sweet One?" His voice was tinged with desperate concern. "What can it be? Is that witch making another try for us?"

"No, she can't. I took care of that. And I'm fine now," she breathed, trying to control her shivering, opening her eyes to look into his. A warm smile sprang to her lips. "Let's get well away from this valley. Right now!" He finally chuckled, a smile of his own lighting up his eyes.

"Whatever you wish, Sweet One," he told her. He released her only to pick up the dropped spear and their backpacks, then wrapped an arm around her. They cut across the grassland before them, heading away as quickly as they could manage.

"I feel a million years old," she quietly commented as they began to head southwest. Garth smiled to himself. Ryes was more herself. "And we're going to have to replenish our food supplies soon," she added, her practical side coming out. He laughed heartily and stopped to hug her to him again.

"Of course, Sweet One, whatever you want." There was a lot of affection in his voice and Ryes' heart beat with joy.

"Whatever would I without you?" she asked, as she returned his hug, holding onto him tightly. She needed no answer. She knew it already.

A couple of days later, when the dry rolling grasslands had turned into lush flat meadows, Ryes felt a new stirring within herself, which she didn't understand. She lagged behind Garth all day on the trail, but doing very little of the gathering she usually did. She felt an uneasiness in her stomach and a general feeling of being out of sorts. She didn't want him worried again, so she kept it as much to herself as possible; trying to behave normally when he was near enough to notice. They made an early camp, but discovered she had no appetite for the food he offered her.

She finally lay back and looked up at the sky overhead, through the branches of an old tree they camped under. The sun rested upon the horizon, but Menna at full moon, reflected his glory overhead. She knew bright Shaysa wouldn't appear until later. Even though Shaysa was now waning, she still outshone Menna. Ryes must've drifted off to sleep, because she awoke with a start as Garth lay down next to her. Shaysa was out now, low to the horizon.

"Your color hasn't looked very good, today," he said in a low voice as he settled down, propping his head up on his upraised arm.

"Something's not right," she admitted. "Maybe I'm coming down with some kind of fever?" Garth leaned down to nuzzle her neck.

"No, I don't think so." There was a sureness in his tone, as if there were no doubts in his mind. "Your time has come," he stated, as he touched her body in a light, teasing manner.

"Are you sure?" Ryes asked with a quiver in her voice. His gentle caresses were exciting and energizing her, in spite of her earlier feeling of utter exhaustion.

"Karr looked as you do now, last year when her last season came," Garth assured her. She let out a sigh of relief.

"Then I hope we have lots of fine, healthy cubs," she said as she reached for him, joy singing in her mind, heart and soul. But instead of unlacing her tunic, he suddenly held out his hand before her, palm flat and fingers spread out like a fan.

"I give to you, Ryes, all that I am, body, heart and soul, now and for all eternity," he stated, meeting her emerald eyes with his honey-colored ones, reflecting his truth by the light of their bright fire. He'd given her the opening for the true-mate ritual. He was pledging himself wholly to her for eternity! She was utterly shocked, but suddenly smiled as she placed her hand palm-to-palm with his, knowing he was correct in this. It was what lay within her heart too, even if it was now hammering.

"I give to you, Garth, all that I am, body, heart and soul, now and for all eternity," she said, her love for him in her eyes. He then entwined his fingers with hers.

"And two hearts now joined as one," they both intoned with joy, together. He smiled as he kissed her passionately. He felt complete. Their true-mate vows sealed them together forever, but this was the way it should be for them. They were now truly husband and wife - always! They excitedly undressed each other, now truly eager. A togetherness, a harmony, a knowing they'd always be there for each other, sang in them both as they joined. It was as if it were their first time, all over again.

        "I found them, but I think it'll be a few more days before they'll catch up to us," Sabin told the rest, as he returned to camp, just in time for dinner.
        "Why? The creek can't still be running high!" Shadd asked, her brows furrowed at this news.
        "Oh, they're across the creek and on our side," he assured her with a chuckle. "But they're busy with other concerns right now," he hinted with a wink.
        "It can't be so soon?" Maren questioned, chuckling as he thought he knew the answer to his riddle.
        "What can't be?" Torr asked innocently, looking puzzled.
        "Ryes' time has come," Ardis answered for Sabin, catching on. She laughed merrily, "I think they'll be a little too busy for a while, won't they?" The others joined her in her laughter, as they realized she was right. A woman is only fertile once every three to seven years throughout her lifespan. It was always an exciting event.
        "I left them a small present where they won't miss it," Sabin told them. "After all, I don't think they'll get too much hunting done, either."
        "Since they're busy, why don't we start exploring Hailys? After all, if we don't try to go underground, we should be all right. I'm tired of waiting to see what's lying under all those plants and broken slabs of stone!" Torr asserted, looking restless with this news. He wondered how long it'd be before Shadd's time came? He was having fun with their free-mating, but wanted to start a real family of his own, too.
        "You're right," Maren agreed. "We should know the basic layout and where the ways downward lie, so we won't stumble into one by accident," he stated. "I had Honey out earlier, riding in the meadow nearby, but it isn't as safe as when we camped beside the creek. There's too much loose stone for her to trip over and break a leg! And I've no idea how to replace her shoes like Ryes did for one of them a couple of weeks ago. I should've paid closer attention - just in case of need."
        "You're doing a good job with her," Shadd assured him, smiling to ease his worry.
        "Remember what it's like over at the old mines?" Ardis prompted them. There were nods of agreement as they did remember. "The mines were tapped out and abandoned long ago. The last of their riches were stripped out near the time of the attack upon Tayna. There're shafts which even the elders had forgotten existed, where you could fall forever and die. Ryes said most of this city is underground. We need to know where the shafts lie, so none of us comes to tragic grief."

"You've got the right idea, there," Sabin concurred. "Tomorrow, let's take one of Ryes' blank parchments and see if we can make a map of our own of Hailys, as it is now." Maren laughed as he thumped him on the shoulder.

"We'll make a scholar of you, yet," he teased. "We'll make a map in coal, then one in ink, once we're sure of things. I'll use the compass and get our baselines established, so we'll have our reference points," he said, getting into the project.

"Just as long as you and Torr teach me, so I'll be able to understand what we're creating," Sabin chuckled in return, shaking his head. Maren had really gotten into this map reading, more than he ever thought. He wondered what Garth would say about it? He could imagine him laughing with the rest of them. He hoped they wouldn't take too much longer, but knew better than to bother them, now. He knew they'd get the idea, once they found the food packets atop their backpacks.

"I think it'll be late in the winter, or very early spring," Shadd quietly told Ardis. She nodded her head in turn, agreeing with her friend.

"We'd better find that new home of ours soon," Ardis whispered back. "I don't think mine's too far off, and you were born a couple of months after me. So, yours should come in the middle of the summer. With so many cubs to feed next year, we're going to have to get supplies set aside. We don't want to overburden our men with having to hunt all the time," she returned, smiling as she met her eyes.

"What do you know about preserving?" Shadd questioned.

"I'm sure not as much as Ryes does," she replied, hoping it was true. "I never paid much attention to the home-making skills my mother and sister tried to drill into me like cooking and canning. And now I'm regretting it as I know I need it." She sighed.

"She knows quite a bit about preserving," Maren whispered to the ladies, as Torr and Sabin were looking for the writing supplies in the larger packs Honey usually carried. "She learned it helping the Caravaner women in the winter months. We'll be fine," he assured them. "There's plenty of game around here and if we started gathering some of the wild grains, we could have enough seeds for planting a real crop in the spring. I saw Ryes pack several packets of seeds, so she already has a garden in mind," he informed them.

"That's a relief," Shadd returned, smiling at last. "Thanks, Maren," she said. "You're a good little brother to us all." She hoped he'd find the perfect mate for himself, too. But where were there any women way out here in the wilderness, she wondered?

Three days later Ryes and Garth lay sunning themselves on a wide, warm, flat rock, next to a small lake, which she was sure was the one they were supposed to all meet up at from their previous plans as a group. They hadn't seen any signs of the others, yet. They were a day's walk from the ruins, but couldn't resist the chance the lake had afforded to clean off the dirt from the trail. They'd had a fine time splashing and playing, as if a pair of young cubs, before they'd settled down to lots of serious cleaning of themselves, their clothes and equipment. Now they were napping on the warm rock, waiting for their clothes and blankets to dry. It'd been a pleasant interlude on their travels. But soon the weather would begin to turn and the cold season would be on them. Ryes told Garth they needed to find a place to settle down before the winter snows came. She had only experienced them once in her life and didn't want to face them unprepared ever again. He laughed.

Ryes' mind drifted as she lay on her stomach next to Garth. She felt a sudden splash of icy cold water on her back. She was instantly wide awake, looking for the cause. Maren stood on another rock, above them to the left, with a mischievous grin on his face and a dripping trail cup in his hand. Ryes closed her eyes in disbelief and shook her head in wonder. She lay back down and nudged Garth's shoulder.

"They found us," she said as Garth opened his eyes. She gestured over her shoulder toward Maren.

"Maren?" Garth asked in surprise. "What're you doing here?"

"Came to wake you two lazes up," Maren answered. "Get dressed. We've already got lunch done and ready to eat. And dinner's simmering in the pot." He had a playful note in his voice and a broad smile.

"In wet clothes?" Ryes protested.

"Better hurry," Maren replied as he jumped down from the rocks, grabbed his backpack from where he'd left it, and disappeared through the trees.

"They're almost dry," Garth told her as he handed over her clean tunic. She sat up with a scowl on her face.

"And it'd been such a nice day," she commented. Her face brightened into a merry grin. "Wait 'till I get my hands on my cousin!" Garth laughed heartily in agreement. As Ryes was tying the laces on her tunic, she noticed it was starting to feel a little snug. She frowned and wondered if it should be happening so soon. Garth, seeing where her attention was focused, laughed.

"You're the one who wants lots of cubs. You're going to have to have something to feed them with," he reminded her, still chuckling.

"Do you think they'll notice?" Ryes asked, nodding her head toward the trees Maren had disappeared through.

"They notice everything, Sweet One." Garth laughed again as he handed over her boots and breeches. Ryes blushed furiously, but her eyes danced as she finished dressing, a playful smile upon her lips. They gathered the rest of their things and headed off the way

Maren had gone. Finally, the smells of roasting fish lured them onward more quickly.

"You two made enough noise to wake all the ghosts in the ruins," Sabin said with a smile as he stood to greet Garth and Ryes. The small rock-sheltered clearing near the lake was bright with sunlight. The rock wall afforded them some protection from the elements with a jutting shelf providing a sheltered area for their sleeping blankets. They had collected more stone to form the fire pit for cooking and evening comfort, with logs making seating around it. There was even a pen for Honey nearby. It was the perfect camping place in all their eyes.

Garth smiled and stepped forward to cross Sabin's palm with his. Torr clasped Garth on the shoulder. Ryes went over to greet Honey and to give them some time for themselves, seeing how much they missed him. She gave her some scratches and checked her teeth, ears and legs. Honey nudged her and she laughed, glad she had missed her. Finally, she crossed back across the clearing to stand near Garth, a happy smile upon her face.

"Well, you both look fit. Where have you been hiding? We've searched all over for you and thought you'd never catch up," Torr asked with concern in his eyes.

"We took a longer route than we planned," Garth answered, his smile fading; a seriousness filled his manner as he drew Ryes over to his side. "What's the problem?" he asked Sabin with a direct gaze. There was something bothering him and he knew it.

"Same as always," Sabin replied, his smile now gone, too. "Korman." Garth frowned at the news, his suspicions confirmed. Ryes unfocused her eyes and imagined what she'd like to do to Korman, herself, if she had access to the power that lay in Doran's valley.

"Ryes!" Garth spoke sharply. Startled, she looked up to him and knew. Garth couldn't follow her thoughts, but had felt the strong tide of emotions she'd unconsciously projected to him. She knew that to misuse her newfound abilities would be the first step down the dark path of madness that Doran already tread. She closed her eyes and shivered as a blast from the icy winds of hell brushed her soul.

"Sorry, Garth," she apologized quietly, looking again into his golden eyes. "You're right and I should know and be better than that."

"What's wrong?" Torr asked Garth, a puzzled frown on his face. Ryes hadn't said anything to need such a sharp reprimand.

"Nothing," Sabin answered Torr before Garth could speak. He'd felt it too and wondered why she was suddenly so strong? What were Tyra's Talents, anyway?

"Where's Maren, Shadd and Ardis?" she asked, more herself again and not seeing them anywhere about.

"Maren went to get them. The ladies are out gathering plants and seeds, like you're fond of doing," Torr told her, smiling.

"Come on, let's eat! We can swap stories when we're fed," Maren broke in, just returning to camp. Shadd and Ardis were following, all smiles. Shadd put down her gather bag and ran over, enwrapping Ryes in a welcoming hug. Ardis was right behind her. Garth grinned broadly and nodded his head.

"We heard," Ardis whispered into Ryes' ear. She chuckled at this. They couldn't miss the food packets Sabin left for them!

"It sure smells good," Garth said.

"What? Hasn't the Great Huntress been taking care of you, Garth?" Torr asked in amazement. Ryes blushed as she dropped her pack beside a fallen tree.

"We've had a few distractions." Ryes started to explain.

"Yeah, I'll say," Maren piped in, pointing at Ryes' tunic laces. Ryes scooped up and threw a handful of pebbles at him as he ducked behind a nearby tree. Torr, Sabin and Garth roared with laughter.

"Cut that out," Shadd scolded them. "Men," she commented to Ryes and Ardis, a big smile upon her face. "As we figure it, there'll be quite a few new cubs to have to worry about providing for by next spring. So, we'll get even our own way," she teased.

"Yeah, we'll go out hunting and leave the men home to care for the cubs," Ryes agreed. Ardis looked surprised at this then suddenly smiled, liking the idea. She knew her sister felt trapped, stuck at home with her cub all the time! It was a great suggestion! Shadd was laughing, agreeing with her, too.

"They should be old enough by then," she agreed. The men were frowning, looking like they were wondering if the women were serious. They didn't know much about caring for infants, to begin with!

"Let's eat," Maren repeated, chuckling at the devious plans the women were hatching. He loved it! It was what they deserved, after all.

"You didn't think I was going to leave all the hunting up to you?" Ryes teased Garth, as they sat down with their lunch. The fish smelled great! "If I did, you'd be out hunting every day."

"I've learned a few things from you," he returned, recalling she was even more sensitive to the animals around them, now. "And how could you hunt with your Empath Talent awakened?" he challenged, teasing.

"I learned to block it out before; I'll learn to do it, again," she assured him, her eyes shadowed as she thought upon it. It'd be harder now.

"Don't worry," Ardis told her. "You show us how and where, and we'll take care of things from there," she said. Ryes smiled, liking that idea best.

"That we can do! Shadd, this fish is really good!" she complemented her friend.

"I finally figured out how to use some of your cooking spices," she explained as she passed Torr a second helping. They had cooked up quite a few, which surprised Ryes, but seeing the way the men were scarfing them down, she now understood.

"I'm glad," she replied. "Sorry I wasn't here to help out," she apologized.

"That's all right, we understand," Shadd told her.

Ryes smiled as they all ate in companionable silence, so happy to be among friends out here in this wilderness. Once they finished, she helped gather up the plates while Torr pulled out the map they were making, showing it to Garth. She wanted a look at it too, but thought she needed some time with the women more. The other two women gathered up the cook pots and the rest of their cups and dishes. They went down to the lake and started rinsing and scrubbing their plates and utensils.

"So, what's this about Korman?" Ryes asked, hoping it wasn't true.

"Sabin caught his scent, a few days ago. He seems to be hanging out some distance away; on the far side of the ruins from us. So still a good couple of day's walk away. We don't think he's found our campsite, but we've been posting a watch at night, just in case. I'm relieved he hadn't already found the two of you," Ardis told her as much as they knew, so far. Ryes grimaced.

"He just can't leave things be," she sighed, reaching for a handful of wet sand. She bent to scrub the plates, wondering when they'd be truly free of him?

"So, how many do you think?" Shadd questioned, smiling. Ryes looked up to meet her eyes, then started smiling too. "My sister thought she'd have two and she did! She told me that I'd be able to tell, once I'm pregnant," she related.

"I don't know. I think maybe two," she replied, "but, it may be way too soon to guess," she warned, smiling. "I just feel strange that my tunic's a little snug for the first time in my entire life! This has to be too soon!"

"What's it like?" Ardis pressed, needing to know.

"Different. I felt kind of out of sorts the whole day, and then realized when Garth said I looked like Karr did last year; I realized that's what it had to be. It was kind of like free mating for the first time, all over again," she related, her eyes shining at the memory. "We had a deep need for each other and couldn't get enough!" She didn't want to tell them about their true-mate vows; unsure if Garth would want to mention it first, or not. It wasn't very common for couples, to begin with, and in truth they were both still very young. Shadd sighed longingly at this, seeing Ryes' happiness.

"I can't wait! But, Ardis is a month younger than you and I'm two months younger than her, so I'll be the last one to see what it feels like," she protested, pouting.

"Hey, it's not our fault you're the youngest," Ardis teased, now looking forward to it, herself. It didn't seem to be as bad as her sister said, from the happy, wistful way Ryes looked. And she already knew now that she didn't want it to be anyone else but Sabin!

"Hey, I thought I was the youngest here," Maren protested, sitting atop a nearby rock, laughing.

"Maren!" Ryes scolded. "You're the youngest and peskiest, all at once. Can't we talk without your listening in on everything?"

"I can't be everywhere at once," he protested, a hand to his heart, his eyes merry. "So, did you and Garth exchange true-mate vows, or not?" he pressed. He hadn't heard Garth say so, but some instinct told him that maybe they had... Ryes blushed a deep golden color at this, turning back to her scrubbing with enthusiasm.

"Did you?" Shadd asked, puzzled by her sudden change in behavior.

"It was Garth's idea," she started, feeling like she was fumbling within herself, trying to voice it. "I... just thought he was right. I didn't expect it and he truly took me by surprise when he spoke the words, holding his hand up for the ritual. I didn't know what to do, so I spoke them, too," she admitted, looking up to meet Shadd and Ardis' shocked eyes. Maren jumped down from his rock and came over to her. He grabbed her wrist and pulled her to her feet, serious now.

"You truly did, but did you mean them in your heart?" he pressed, meeting her eyes. She still blushed, but looked at him steadily.

"Yes, I did mean them, every word from my heart," she affirmed. He threw his arms about her, giving her a hearty hug.

"It must run in the family!" he declared, adding in a kiss on her forehead. "Congratulations, cousin!" He merrily laughed as he let her go. She blushed furiously at this, but Shadd and Ardis were embracing her, also. She finally smiled and relaxed, glad they were accepting of the news.

"Has Garth told Sabin and Torr, yet?" Ardis asked Maren, wondering how he knew?

"I think he was trying to tell them," he returned, smiling. "He was having a hard time finding the words when I left. I already figured out what he was saying," he admitted.

"You ornery thing!" Ryes declared, shaking her head. She handed him the plate she was scrubbing, then turned on her heel and left the clearing. "I've got to take a walk," she told them, over her shoulder.

"Men," she muttered under her breath, as his laughter diminished behind her.

She slowed her pace and began to regret her outburst. Maren had only been teasing her, as any friend would have. That warmed her heart. She barely knew anything about her cousins because she'd been in the habit of avoiding everyone in the Village. Maybe it was time to get to know them all much better? She decided she'd find a way to at least come to some kind of understanding with Aunt Tanns, so she'd get the chance. She kept walking, making a leisurely circuit of the lake, enjoying the stirrings of life going on around her and just needing the time to think.

She sat on a rock, soaking up the warmth of the sunshine, her mind thinking on the changes still before her. With these new cubs, it'd be a while after they're born, before she could go on a hunt again. If they ever got back to the Village, she thought maybe she should take up a craft? The metalsmith used to like the small, intricate pieces of jewelry she used to make, every now and then. Even though her hands were skilled, she felt she'd never give up the woods. They, and the life they held, lived in her heart always.

"Ryes?" She startled, turning around to see Maren standing nearby. There was an apologetic look on his face.

"Oh, Maren," Ryes suddenly felt foolish caught daydreaming again. "Did they send you out to find me?" She stood up and smiled, her eyes lighting up with mischief. Maren nodded, his grin breaking out in response.

"Sorry, I didn't mean to upset you," he said, looking like he meant it.

"I'm fine. I guess I've lived too long by myself. There's been so much happening, so fast now," she paused a moment, looking off into nowhere. "I guess I just needed a bit of time alone." She turned and smiled at him again. Maren extended his hand, and she clasped it. Together they turned back for the campsite.

"Well, when do you think they're due?" Maren boldly asked, itching with curiosity. Ryes mentally tallied a few moments.

"Late winter, early spring, or thereabouts," she shrugged, concluding that was as close as she could guess. These were her first, and she really had no idea of what to expect.

"That long?" Maren questioned. Ryes nodded her head, as sure as she could be. "Well, then what took you so long to get here?"

"We went a little further north than we truly needed to go," Ryes answered. She'd wait to see if Garth would tell that tale, and take her que from him. "You can ask Garth about it," she suggested in a lower voice.

"How long ago did you hurt your arm?" Maren asked in a direct way.

He kept their pace slow. He wanted some time to talk to his older cousin, by himself. She'd always been a strange one and he knew her little, even if he was learning a lot about her on this journey, as well as learning a lot from her, too. It was time for him to understand her better and her reasoning. How much did she trust him and the others? He needed to know. He looked at her as she arched an eyebrow in surprise at him. He laughed.

"There ARE healers in our bloodline; remember our grandmother, Jana?" Ryes nodded her head, and smiled at a dim memory.

"I recalled how Aunt Tanns put Rowan to bed once, when he kept insisting he wasn't sick. A fever developed that night which only worsened his temper. But Aunt Tanns had been right and always won out after that." He laughed at this, agreeing with her.

"Even if we can't heal anymore, at least the 'health sense' is still there," Maren said with a sigh. Ryes stopped and faced him fully.

"But we can heal, Maren. I helped my arm and body to heal faster, myself. That's all that I can do, but maybe you've got the Talent for it?" Maren frowned at her statement, not believing her, yet wondering. "It's inside. You just have to reach down hard enough to find it. Try it sometime, Maren. It has to be there. You just have to want to reach it strong enough," she implored. Maren finally shrugged and turned toward camp again.

"Maybe later," he replied thoughtfully, after a few paces in silence. He didn't feel ready to dig for his Talent yet. He felt an awareness of it now and knew it was there waiting, but did not feel ready for it. He wasn't sure he could handle it and the responsibilities that went with such a Talent. He'd seen his mother plagued for years by the villagers - seeking her help. Could he give up his own time for others all the time, he wondered?

Catching Up

They returned to find Garth and Torr stretched out in the sunlight, their empty cups beside them. Ardis and Shadd were sorting their finds from earlier this morning. Sabin was sitting by the fire in deep thought. Sabin's eyes locked on Ryes and she felt a sudden chill travel up her back. In spite of his look, she walked with Maren to stand before him. Sabin stood up, his arms crossed.

"Had to drag her back," Maren teased, holding her hand up in the air to demonstrate; then let it go. Ryes let it drop to her side with a smile. There was a mischievous twinkle in Maren's eyes. Sabin grinned back and gestured toward the seating around the fire pit, appearing unable to hold onto his ire. Getting an idea, Ryes went to her packs and dug in, looking for something. Finding it, she went in search of her and Maren's cups.

Maren sat down and stirred the stew they were simmering for dinner, while Ryes filled their cups from the wine skin she'd brought with her. She'd managed to conserve her meager supply fairly well, she thought. She had wanted to save it for when they found their new home, but thought arriving here at Haily's was a landmark in her life and a reason to celebrate, too. She handed Maren his cup, then passed the skin over to Sabin. He sniffed the contents, then smiled and refilled his own, Torr's and Garth's cup. Ardis and Shadd poured the last into theirs. Once everyone had their share, Ryes raised her cup and said,

"To the future and all that it may hold, for all of us!" She grinned merrily as she spoke in a loud voice for all to hear. Maren and Sabin looked surprised but raised their cups to the toast. Garth and Torr heard and stood up, grabbing their own cups and joined in the fun. Ardis and Shadd appeared delighted with her toast, raising their cups, too.

"To the future," Garth and the others echoed Ryes as they raised their cups to the toast. Then Garth spilled a small amount on the ground before his feet before putting it to his lips, the others mimicking his move. It was respect for those whose hearts would've wished to join them, but were no longer alive to do so.

"Thought you'd left us for good," Torr said after draining his cup, looking at what meager dregs were left in it appearing regretful. Ryes lowered her eyes a moment as Garth chuckled softly and sat down on a nearby log, pulling her gently down beside him. He put his arm possessively around her. Sabin stood, uncertain for a moment, then crossed his arms again and stood before them.

"What took you two so long to get here?" he voiced at last, his disapproval plain in his voice and stance. Ardis tugged at his belt to distract him, but he didn't budge. "The stream returned to a safe level well before you crossed back."

"It's a long tale and needs to be told for all of you to hear," Garth said, gesturing for Sabin to sit. He wasn't bothered by the tone or stance his old friend had taken; though it was plain Ryes was uncomfortable. Torr and Maren pulled over a log for the women and another for themselves and sat down. Sabin, seeing that no tale telling was going to begin until he sat too, finally joined Torr and Maren. The smoldering look in Ardis' eyes warned him to behave.

Then slowly, between them both, Ryes and Garth managed to tell the tale of their separate, harrowing journey. Ryes described the way Doran's strong lure clouded her mind and blinded her senses, until they were suddenly in her valley and in deep danger. They both told of the frustrating invisible wall that kept them in it – captive. And then the appearance of Tyra with her warnings and clues. After that, Garth spoke of the way Doran consumed his soul bit by bit. It was the worst torture he'd ever endured; and how later he spoke with Tyra, himself. Even if he was safe with her, it still unnerved him to be in her presence. There was much about the encounter with Doran that Ryes did tell, but there were things that she couldn't say. For some of it there were no words, and some of it still touched to the quick and she merely left it out. She hadn't even told it all to Garth because she was still trying to understand it, herself.

"And she just let you go after you freed Garth's soul?" Sabin asked with piercing directness.

"She couldn't hold me, Sabin. Her power's gone and I controlled the power streams." Ryes shook her head, running the memories from the rapport through her mind again.

"Then how did you escape?" Maren demanded, Torr nodded his agreement to the voiced question. He appeared to wonder, too.

"First we entered a rapport, one mind touching another..." Ryes shivered at the recollection of that experience, and reached out to grasp Garth's hand. "I found out even more than all the questions I could ever ask, could answer," She looked up to Garth and smiled, "and Doran found out she couldn't control me as she had so many others in the past." Garth chuckled and gave her hand a tender squeeze.

"You mean, she tried again?" Shadd asked, disgusted.

"Of course she did, but I was ready for it and when she attacked me, I burned out her Talents with my Catalyst Talent. I never thought of doing it before, and was surprised I could do it. I wanted all threats she could make against us stopped for all time," Ryes answered with a confident smile. "Her luring others to her service had to quit, as well as her being able to use the Stone of Power. I also turned off that shield generator that kept us trapped in the valley as well as the others like it, too." She didn't notice the utter shock on the faces ringed around her as she looked down into her cup, seeing things again in her mind only she had seen in that temple, then she set the cup aside.

"How did Doran ever come to be there in the first place?" Ardis asked in a curious voice, her face a mix of emotions reflected from her inner turmoil. Ryes' smile faded as she looked at her, and then shifted to the look at the crackling fire. She began the tale slowly, thoughtfully, from stolen faded memories.

"Doran was a daughter of one of the great ruling houses from legendary Kahmarr. She was an oldest daughter and watched her mother, forced by their family, into matchings she abhorred. The last man that her mother had been mated to had treated her cruelly. She finally died from a very bad beating. Doran's mind began to twist with her mother's death and when she came of age, her family began to make demands on her choice of mates. She rebelled and killed the one they'd chosen for her with his own sword. She'd used her Talents to overwhelm him. She tried to rally the support of the other unmatched women of the great families, and what she could from the general population, but the rebellion was suppressed. Because she was pregnant, of Royal Blood and a woman with strong Talents, she couldn't be put to death. If she were banished, it was feared she would continue to raise followers, so it was decided by a great council..." Ryes broke off a moment, still awed by the borrowed memory of the council hall and the great assemblage within it.

"What was decided?" Maren spoke up in frustration. Ryes blinked, trying to bring her mind back to the present.

"I'm sorry, Maren. The hall was so huge and beautiful and the people filling it... there were more than just our own kind of people there," she stopped, wondering how to begin to tell what she saw within her mind.

"What do you mean?" Garth asked curiously.

"There were others who were different of build, coloring and shape and ways of living." She halted, at a loss to describe it to them. "There was one kind of people who were no taller than your waist, Garth, who had large, dark eyes, darkly-tanned skin and were hairless and seemed to wear little clothing, but their bodies were adorned with beautiful tattoos and jewels. They were a very strong-willed people, too." She smiled up at his puzzled expression. "Remember we ARE the `Star People' by our oldest legends and if so, there must be other kinds of people, living upon other worlds. We have other peoples who live here on Tayna, even if the very few to venture into Matlowe have been in the company of the Caravaners. I don't think anyone else ever met them." Ryes looked down into the dancing flames and sighed.

"I met that one blue girl, one winter," Maren ventured. "She seemed mean." Ryes met his eyes for a moment, puzzled, and then shook her head as it was filled with the other borrowed memories in this moment. She decided to change the subject.

"I wish we'd never lost our star traveling ships. I saw them from Doran's and the others' memories. They were fantastic! They moved people from world to world with little seeming effort. Some only shipped goods between worlds, as if traders roaming from port to port among the stars. Some shipped people to `vacation' on others worlds. They went to explore other cultures, or see amazing ruins or different wonders in nature. Others were explorers who travelled to find new worlds and opportunities."

"It was long ago. Now you want to turn back time?" Garth teased. She had a startled look in her eyes at this, which he wondered about, but felt it could wait for later. "What did that great council finally decide to do with Doran?" he prompted to bring her back to the original story.

"Or can we already guess?" Torr added in, smiling. Ryes quirked a smile in return.

"Sort of. Once she had her son, whom she tried to kill, they decided to put her into an endless sleep on a quiet outer world. Tayna was originally a `game preserve' with the population and cities kept deliberately small. She was put here to be forgotten; locked away in a great stone monolith. But after a time, some of her followers came and built the temple and gardens around her. None of them could open it to release her. It took a very special combination of Talents, which none of them possessed. And their great victory was the theft of the power stone for their `sleeping goddess.'" Ryes shook her head as she looked to the others. "It does her no good now, her Talents are gone and she can't tap power streams from the stone. Given time, she'll be no more than a bad memory in an endless cold tomb. Even if this isn't a fate I'd ever wish on anyone, I felt no pity for the creature Doran had become," she finished.

"Who was that old crone who attacked you?" Ardis questioned, feeling a chill over the terrible fate this Doran had before her.

"Doran `lures' women of greater Talents to her service, from time-to-time. I have no idea if she was one of her sleeping handmaidens, or another Talent from somewhere on Tayna. Jana was heading for Doran's valley when Tyra found her and released her from the calling. Tyra had just escaped Doran's keeping, at that time." She shook her head at this, chagrined. "I had hoped to find out where she came from, but this... It was far beyond what I ever expected! She came from Kahmarr, itself!"

"Tyra was one of Doran's followers?" Sabin demanded with vehemence in his voice.

"No," Ryes answered sharply, feeling the sting of his tone as if it'd been herself. "Tyra came here from Kahmarr to escape an arranged marriage. She was of Royal Blood, the House of Li, and had nowhere else to run. She was very young and didn't know what to expect, but took up the offer of shelter from this unknown `goddess,' and was encased in the cold sleep, as were Doran's other, `special' handmaidens. All of them were those of the Blood, who came to her for protection. But Tyra managed to escape Doran's cold sleep after a couple hundred years." Ryes smiled at Maren and shook her head, "I guess after listening to her mad ravings for so long, she didn't think anything of charging Korman with her spear when he killed Ronn and my siblings."

"The mystery is solved!" Torr declared grandly. "And you found out how to escape that place, too. Looks like it runs in the family." Ryes laughed and nodded her head to this.

"I was never so glad as to see Garth!" She wrapped her arms around him in a happy hug, which surprised him. He laughed and hugged her back. "So, my mother ran away to sleep for a few hundred years, to find her true-mate," Ryes told them all.

"Tyra and Ronn were true-mates?" Shadd asked in surprise, "But Rowan didn't say anything about it!"

"No, he didn't," she agreed, "Tyra's ghost told me that, herself. I had a thousand questions for her, but no chance to ask anything if I was to free Garth in time. Most of what I learned about her was from the memories of one of the other sleepers in Doran's temple. They became `friends' after a fashion, while caught up in that mad woman's clutches. By the time I got free of that deadly garden, I only had a yearning for Garth, and to get some sleep. I never got to ask any of my questions before Tyra left us. And I owe her some kind of favor in return for her watching over Garth. I told her she could ask anything, but she said she'd ask it later." She looked up guiltily to Garth. He still had an arm about Ryes, hugging her to his side again, giving her a nod of his head.

"It'd only be fair. I'm sure it won't be something unreasonable; she didn't seem to be like that," he assured her. She let out a sigh of relief and then a yawn snuck out.

Maren had taken their plates and filled them with stew, while Ryes had been telling her long story. They'd all eaten their fill while listening. Now Ryes picked at the last bit of it and while it was not the spices she would have chosen, it was still tasty and filling.

"We need to get our dishes washed," she said, but Garth shook his head no.

"It's too late to be out by the lake tonight for such a chore," he scolded.

"But they'll attract bugs and animals," she protested.

"We'll put them in a wash bucket for now to soak," Ardis suggested, not liking the idea of bugs, nor wild animals in their camp. "And then wash them first thing in the morning."

"They'll be fine. We're posting a watch all night. Nothing big will get into camp," Maren insisted. Ryes appeared to deflate and surrender to their urging.

"It is getting late," Ardis observed, as she yawned. The sun had set some time ago, with all this story telling. They were back to honeyed tea. Sabin stretched as he yawned. She cracked a grin as she shook her head at him.

"I'm ready for bed," Ryes said, standing up.

"You go ahead, I'll join you soon," Garth told her, "I want to talk more with Sabin, Torr and Maren. We still had a lot of catching up to do on what was happening." He especially wanted what news they had on Korman.

"I'm going to bed, too," Shadd told Torr, as she stood and stretched. He eyed her for a few seconds, then realized while he wanted to join her, he couldn't yet.

"I'll be along, shortly," he promised. "Who has first watch, tonight?" he asked Sabin.

"I do, then Maren, but since Garth's here, we can split it up into shorter watches. Why not let Garth take the third watch and leave you the last one?" he suggested, grinning. Garth chuckled at this as he gave his head a nod in agreement. It was only fair, after all. Torr laughed.

"`Bout time you showed up to pull your load, cousin," he teased. Garth chuckled as Ryes shook her head, heading for their alcove. But instead of lying down, she went over to Honey's pen and checked on her, first.

"Pretty girl," she whispered, as she scratched her behind her ears and along her jawline, the way she knew she loved it. "I'll check you over real well tomorrow morning," she promised. Honey lipped her fingers and pawed the ground. She looked happy to see her, too. With a final pat, she went to her blankets. She took off her boots, stowing them away and loosening her breeches and tunic. They didn't quite have as much privacy as they had on the trail, so she was reluctant to fully undress before the others. She saw Shadd and Ardis going to their beds the same way. She fell asleep quickly, even if she was trying to listen to what the men were saying in their low voices.

"It was amazing that you both survived!" Torr stated, giving a nod towards Ryes across the way. "Good thing her Talents opened up when they did."

"I think it was that Power Stone she was talking about that helped the most," Garth stated, his eyes straying over to his wife. "She seems to have several and now I'm wondering how many she truly has to call up at need?"

"You didn't speak your True-mate vows to keep her in check, did you?" Sabin suddenly questioned. Garth smiled at this, shaking his head.

"No," he laughed out. "That wasn't on my mind, nor in my heart at the time. It was real, Sabin. I felt it was the truth from deep inside. It wasn't a shallow sham. But there's something I did want to ask you about," he continued.

"It was him. I know his scent too well," Sabin assured him, feeling sure of what he wanted.

"Truth be told," Maren interjected, "We all know if he's hanging out in a very specific place out here, it has to be where Ronn and Tyra were living. He and Rowan were the only two to know where it actually was set. We can't let him catch any of us off our guard. And if I figured it out, Ryes will too."

"Maybe coming out to the ruins wasn't our best idea," Garth replied, "but, if he's mad enough to follow us all the way out here, then maybe it's time we hunt for him and get it settled," he suggested. "And I think you're right Maren. That must be the reason he's where he's camped. He's expecting her to head to that special spot – where she was born. I'm not letting that happen!"

"You almost had him. All you have to do is make sure he doesn't get his arms wrapped around you, again," Torr encouraged.

"A hunt for Korman!" Maren nodded his head, liking the idea. "A hunt for a REAL animal! If nothing else, we might drive him back to Matlowe. It's time we deal with him, as he deserved long ago."

"At least we know he's not back there terrorizing our friends and families," Torr said.

"That's some small comfort. And at least he's hanging out in an area away from us, overall – for now," Garth said.

"I think he's picked his challenge ground," Torr stated.

"We have to deal with him, or none of our women will be safe out here. Remember that he did kill Tyra, a helpless woman carrying a tiny infant home to what family she had left," Sabin reminded them.

"I was wondering," Garth said, thinking on it. "Tyra was supposed to be a very powerful Talent with several different Talents at her command which she'd been trained from childhood in their uses, but she was helpless when he attacked. Does that mean a woman loses her Talent when she has her cubs?" he asked, meeting Sabin's eyes. He looked thoughtful for a few moments.

"I remember my grandmother saying that hers went away for a time after her cubs were born, but it came back and was stronger," he replied, realizing why he was asking. "She was telling my aunt, as her Visions left her after she had her daughter. I think she was comforting her. I was young, but I remembered it. My mother never had the ability, but apparently saved it for me. Still it seems birth will leave a woman Talentless for a period of time."

"The women in our family always had the stronger Talents," Maren told them, thinking back to his mother and her stronger health sense. "Maybe that's why Korman keeps my mother pregnant, so she's never had more than just a `health sense?'"

"That would be crediting him with brains enough to know all this," Torr scolded, but Sabin suddenly gave him a sharp look.

"Maybe Korman KNEW where Ronn and Tyra were living long before he chose to attack them? Maybe he KNEW when Tyra would be the most weak and vulnerable?" he conjectured.

"It suddenly makes perfect sense and sounds like the truth!" Garth caught a chill up his back at this. "All the more reason to hunt him out now and get this challenge settled. I don't want Ryes left helpless with him on the prowl nearby," he stated with a stern note in his voice. There was an edge to him, which the other men couldn't mistake. He meant business! Anything could happen at any time and he didn't want to chance Ryes being attacked while he was gone, even if only out hunting for the day, as Tyra had been when Ronn was killed.

"You know, this might take more than one challenge," Sabin suggested. "It might take all four of us challenging him to fully defeat him for good."

"I know," Garth replied. "But I get the first chance at him." He got nods from the others around him as he met their eyes.

"Let's look at that map of yours, Torr. If we plan this out, we should be able to find him fairly quickly," Sabin suggested. Torr gave him a nod and went to get it for them. Hunting one of their own was something new for all of them, but this was for the protection of their women and future cubs. If it came down to it, Torr realized, he'd face off Korman himself, if it meant keeping Shadd safe and out of his claws.

Ryes awoke early the next morning, startled to find herself sandwiched between Maren and Garth. She quietly slipped out of the blankets and stretched, once she was clear. She knew in a few months' time she'd never tolerate sleeping upon the ground. She'd have to have some kind of home by then with proper sleeping furs and a real bed. But, the ruins of a great city called Hailys were here, beckoning to her to discover their secrets. She donned her boots and tightened the laces on her breeches and tunic. There was plenty of time to satisfy her curiosity, before they had to find real shelter!

She saw Torr on his feet, leaning against a nearby tree and sound asleep. She stepped over to him and gave him a gentle nudge. He opened his eyes, blinking against the breaking dawn light.

"Go back to bed, Torr Sharp-eyes," she scolded with a smile. He sleepily gave her a smile, then tottered over to his mate and snuggled down into the covers with her. Shadd threw an arm over him in her sleep and they both were quickly out. Ryes smiled, as she shook her head at this. It was funny the way things had worked out for all of them. The other women never looked happier and they'd lived in the house next door to the men for almost two years!

Next, she went to relieve herself in the primitive outhouse the men dug for their use. Then, she restarted the fire from its banked coals and put on a pot of water to make fresh tea. She put Honey's halter on her and opened the gate. She gathered the dirty pots and plates from last night and headed for the lake. First, she bathed Honey and herself in the ice-cold water, feeling more alive than she had for some time. Next, she scrubbed the evening's dishes and pots, setting them out to dry in the early morning sun.

Honey was feeling frisky, so she let her run loose in a clearing next to the lake, as she gathered some fresh tubers and other plants, nearby. She brushed Honey down, until her coat glowed, as she talked to her and gave her the attention she hadn't been able to give her for some time. On the way back, she found some ripe berries and quickly picked them, in spite of the thorny plants they grew upon. They'd be perfect for breakfast! She returned to gather the clean pots and dishes, filled Honey's bucket with fresh water and was now ready to head back. She was relaxed, as she hadn't been since leaving Matlowe.

When she entered camp, Garth and Torr were looking at a map, while they discussed something in quiet voices. Ardis and Shadd were by the fire, cooking something, while Maren was digging through the packs, but Sabin was nowhere in sight.

"Where've you been?" Sabin growled, coming up behind Ryes. She jumped in surprise and looked at him with a puzzled frown.

"I didn't know I needed your permission to go anywhere," she stated sarcastically. She turned to Garth lifting an eyebrow in inquiry.

"Korman's nearby," he reminded her. "He's just worried about your safety." She nodded her head, blushing slightly in embarrassment, having forgotten about Korman already.

"I'm sorry," she apologized to Sabin, meeting his bright, orange-gold eyes. "I wanted to see what was around here and indulge Honey with a bath and brushing. Her coat was looking pretty tacky with all this traveling," she explained. It was a very different-looking windracer she was leading this morning. He had to admit, the animal looked much better for her time and care. He finally gave her a smile and a nod of his head, turning to join Torr and Garth.

"Here," Maren volunteered taking her halter, "I'll put her back in her pen." Ryes smiled her thanks, but thought she needed more room, if they were going to be staying here for any length of time. She'd have to bring it up later, after everyone had eaten. Tara had always said people were more agreeable after a meal.

"Thanks, Maren," she replied, letting him have it, her bucket of water and brush.

"What a pretty Honey," he crooned to her as Ryes shook her head, barely containing her laughter. He was trying hard to win the mare over.

"I found these," she said, joining the women at the fire. She put down the pots and dishes and pulled open her gather pouch.

Inside were the berries, wrapped separately from the other plants she collected.

"Ooooh, I love thorn-bract berries," Shadd declared as she took them and put them on a clean plate. "What do you think of our little oven?" she asked, smiling. Ryes grinned merrily, having discovered it this morning.

"For `roughing it' we sure manage to do things well," she teased. "It's a great idea! Do we still have some flour? I could bake some biscuits or bread with these berries," she offered, wanting to help out.

"How about if we add them to our cooked grains? It'd make them taste so much better," Ardis suggested, instead. Ryes saw she had a pot of cooked grains almost done.

"May I?" she asked. Ardis gestured for her to go ahead, so Ryes sampled it. She obviously, already added honey to it, but it still wasn't right. Part of it was the type of grains they used. So, she went over to her smaller pack and went through her packets of spices. She found what she was looking for and returned. She added a tiny pinch to the pot and stirred it in. After a few minutes of stirring the pot, she tasted it once more and smiled. Perfect!

"Try it now," she invited, as she closed up the packet. Ardis appeared doubtful, considering whatever Ryes added was in such a small quantity, but did and was surprised.

"Wow! What was that you added?" she asked, "It's definitely better!" Ryes smiled.

"Kanta seed. It's tiny, but when it's gathered, dried and ground as finely as possible, it makes an excellent addition to cooked grains and a few other bland dishes. But, it's so strong, you have to use a very minute amount," she warned. "I'll show you the plant, if we find any. They usually grow near rivers, or other running water. My supply could last us the whole winter though, considering how little you actually need." She showed her the bulging packet in her hand wrapped in a heavy brown paper. Ardis frowned at it, but considering the amount she saw her add, believed her.

"How about if we make some flat-cakes with the berries? Those will be ready more quickly and a lot less trouble," Shadd suggested, tasting the cooked grains and nodding her head in approval. "It takes a while for the oven to warm up enough."

"That sounds good," Ryes agreed taking out the rest of the contents of her pouch. "And we could bake these tubers to go with our dinner, but I've no idea what to make for lunch."

"The men have already told us that we're going to be out exploring the ruins. So, lunch will be whatever we find, or trail cakes," Ardis assured her, smiling. "And they'd better not complain about it!" she declared loudly, getting puzzled looks from the men reading the map and a chuckle out of Maren. The women laughed at this, as they bent to their work. "We've been gathering wild grains, setting aside some of the better stuff for spring planting," she told Ryes, in a low voice. "We're hoping wherever we end up, there'll be enough land to grow some real crops."

"That's a great idea," Ryes returned also in a low voice, impressed they'd been thinking ahead, too. "I hope either there's enough rainfall, or access to enough running water to make a good sized garden, too. I brought along some of my best seeds. I thought, since we'll all be saddled with cubs by then, if we can't get out to hunt as often as we like, at least we won't starve."

"That's what we're thinking, too," Shadd agreed, smiling.

"Where's my tea container?" Ryes questioned a bit more loudly, looking through her carry pouch for it, wondering where she left it. Maren sauntered over, handing the tin container to her.

"Your tea's too good to pass up," he told her, grinning. She took it with a smile as she shook her head at his impertinence. "I had some last night when it was my turn for the watch," he admitted.

"Why were you sleeping next to me this morning?" she asked him directly, in a low voice.

"If my father showed up, I wanted to make sure he had to come through me, to get to you," he stated, meeting her eyes. There was surprise in their emerald depths, as she understood what he meant.

"Thanks, cousin," she replied, warmth in her eyes for him. He smiled back and gave her a wink. She was surprised at his willingness to put himself at risk for her, and she had no idea of how to repay such generosity. It deeply touched her heart.

"Ugh, Roots!" Maren exclaimed with evident distaste, as he saw what she'd pulled out of her gather pouch.

"These are sweet tubers," she corrected him with a light laugh. "They're much better than plain ol' roots and they're good for you," she assured him. "What's this about Old Korman?"

"He's definitely in the area. We found fresh traces this morning. We think he's been spying on us and only want to prevent a repeat of a certain part of the family history," he suggested, a serious look in his golden-brown eyes. She sighed, giving her head a nod at this, understanding it only too well.

"Breakfast's almost ready," she said, trying to find something else to talk about; wanting to forget Korman and wishing he'd leave her alone. She would've liked to have led him into Doran's valley. Those two deserved each other! Let them snarl at each other in separate cold boxes for hundreds of years! That thought brought a smile to her lips.

"Why don't we head across the plains, to see if one of the tribes there will take us in?" Maren asked loudly, suddenly jumping up, heading toward Torr, Sabin and Garth.

"The plains are vast, at least twelve hands of days across on a windracer," Ryes scolded him with a laugh. "How can we find any of the tribes, without knowing their boundary patterns?"

"But, maybe... The mountain people?" he started, hoping. "There has to be somewhere we can go to escape my father!"

"How do you look for a pebble on the river bottom? The mountains are said to be vast and their holds hidden from open sight among the rock. Where do we start?" Sabin asked, chiding him. "Anyway, we're not going to be living out on the plains, nor in the mountains," he assured him.

"And I hope we're not going to be settling here in Hailys," he returned. This got a nod from both Sabin and Ryes. "Just where will we be living?" he demanded, looking frustrated.

"When we get there, we'll know," Ryes teased him, smiling. "I've never seen such a place, but it's not something you forget. It has a very distinctive landmark. And we will know it when we see it."

"That's true," Sabin agreed, smiling at their secret. It was fun to tease the others about it from time to time and teasing Maren made it more so.

"Well, it had better be soon," Ardis stated. Ryes smiled as she turned back to helping the women finish their morning meal. She wondered where it truly was, out in the world? She'd never heard the Caravaners talk about it, before, either.

Hailys

"She's not hiding out here! She's not anywhere around Matlowe," Gann told his parents, seeing they'd come all the way out to the river-side homes looking for Mitt. Marla was close to tears and it was tearing up Gann's heart to see her this way.

"Come inside and have a mug of tea," Rowan invited, standing up and gesturing towards his home in invitation. They were sitting around the firepit, which only usually saw gatherings in the winter months. "We'll talk about it." He led the way, hoping they'd follow.

"We don't need tea. We need to find our daughter," Garvin replied, but saw Marla had accepted the invite and was following Rowan.

"Come on, father, let's see what all of us together can figure out," he suggested, gesturing for him to join the others. He appeared to pause for a few heartbeats, as if thinking it over, and then came along with his son. "Besides, it's truly good tea," Gann added with a light chuckle.

They entered the back door and saw Rowan was fetching mugs while Tennan was putting water on to heat on the stove. Dinner had been cooking and the smells were intoxicating. Gann went and fetched the honey pot and set it on the table. He made sure both his parents were comfortably seated, as others from his group started to arrive. They too took seats, as if they had made this their habit for years. Everyone was relaxed but many appeared concerned as they saw the grief in Marla and Garvin. No one spoke until Gann settled and Rowan took the head seat at the table.

"We believe she went after Kovin and Teris, shortly after they left Matlowe," Rowan stated, meeting first Marla's then Garvin's eyes.

"She went out with our hunting party a couple of weeks ago and simply vanished," Kaytas said, pulling her dark hair back from her eyes, as she tried to look steadily into Marla's. "We looked everywhere and none of us are honestly the best at tracking."

"We thought she got either lucky in the hunt or bored with everything and went home. Since we stayed out really late that day looking for her, we didn't notice that she hadn't come back to the Village until later the next day," Leand added. "She has a tremendous head start on us, if we headed out to go look for her."

"Mitt went to join Kovin and Teris, who went to find Garth to warn him about Korman," Gann stated. "I know that's where she went and know I shouldn't have taken my eyes off of her for even a second. It's my fault, father." Marla reached across and squeezed his hand for a moment, shaking her head in denial.

"You know how she is when she gets an idea in her head," she reminded him, finally smiling through the pain a little.

"She's not slow between her ears. She would've caught up to Kovin and Teris, knowing they were her best chance of survival, as quickly as she could," Garvin finally stated with a heavy sigh, appearing to accept the situation.

"How good a tracker is she?" Rowan asked, wondering as Tennan gestured for him to help with the tea. The water was hot already. Tennan had been cooking a soup for dinner, so already had the coals hot and ready when the large pot of water was placed on the stove top. He smiled as he nodded and then stood up.

"Not as good as The Huntress," Kaytas stated, grinning again, "but she's good enough to find their trail. They weren't looking to conceal where they were going." She shrugged. "I'm sure she's safe and they'll catch up to Garth soon, if they haven't already."

"Where were they going? Were they going to explore one of the Caravan routes?" Marla asked, concern in her golden eyes. Rowan returned with a full pitcher and began to fill their mugs. He sighed as he handed them out to the others.

"They were headed towards the ruins," he informed them.

"What?" Tennan asked. She stepped over to the table taking a seat and an offered mug of tea from her grandfather.

"Why?" Garvin demanded at the same time. Gann and Leand nodded, knowing it was the truth. Kaytas merely looked into her mug, as if it held the answers she was looking for within.

"Are you sure?" Marla asked, grabbing Rowan's wrist after he put the pitcher down on the table. He nodded his affirmation in response, but did not shake off her hand.

"They planned out their route carefully on the map and were using it as a starting point for their adventures," he related to the others. "I'm fairly sure Mitt was in on it with them, then."

"And?" Garvin pressed, feeling it in the air. Marla let go of Rowan's wrist, to grab her husband's hand.

"You do know Sabin had more than one Vision before they left?" Gann asked, looking to both his parents. They turned to him, both of them had their eyes riveted upon his face now, giving Rowan a small breather.

"Oh my, his are strong," his mother gasped out, then bit her lower lip.

"They are," he agreed, smiling as he recalled Garth's recounting of it. "And he saw that they're going to find a new home out there – somewhere. And all he would say about it, according to those who were there, is that it was a place he'd never seen before in his life." Rowan laughed heartily at this, raising his mug of tea.

"That leaves the rest of the known world outside of Matlowe," he declared. "To a brighter, bigger and happier world to our children, grandchildren and us all," he toasted. The rest of the company raised their mugs in the toast, most with smiles on their faces now.

"I wonder what they'll find?" Kaytas asked.

"I don't know," Tennan replied, seeming to relax a little. "Just as long as they don't forget us."

"I'll drink to that," Leand agreed, giving her a nod and a smile.

The ruins finally lay before Ryes. There was a tumble of shattered stone and exposed metal beams interspersed with a wide variety of vegetation, which appeared to be attempting to fully retake the city as its own. Ryes had, at first, been a little disappointed, but her curiosity surfaced as she began to ascend a large knoll near the southern edge of Hailys. Maren, who'd been left behind to watch after the women, grumbled loudly at the inanity of climbing a hill when it was almost time for their midday meal. Ardis paused and smiled back at him, a gleam of mischief in her eyes, as Shadd shrugged her shoulders and continued climbing. When they reached the top, there was a huge bubblenut tree, which Ryes pointed out to the women from below. It looked as if there were plenty of nuts to eat, as well as plenty of flowers, which promised more in a few weeks. They started picking the ripe nuts while they surveyed the land about them, opening them and munching them happily.

Garth, Torr and Sabin had gone further north and east of them, looking for underground entrances not already mapped out. Ryes was sorely disappointed in being ordered to stay put, and even more so when Maren was appointed to look after her. She drew a small measure of solace when he loudly protested at being left behind, too. So together they decided to explore a different area of the ruins and as long as they were staying together, they were obeying his orders in spirit. Shadd and Ardis decided this was the best action too, and came along.

"At least the view's worth it," Ryes stated as she stashed several handfuls of nuts into her gather pouch. Some were for later, some for the men, and some were for trying to see if she could grow bubblenut trees of her own, when they found their own new home.

"You're taking quite a few of those," Maren scolded, but noted there were still plenty left - far more than they could possibly eat. As they ripened, the shells turned translucence with the clusters hanging from the branches appearing like soap bubbles.

"They're for eating later and I'm going to see if I can grow a bubblenut tree, myself. I haven't tried to before, but it might be a worthwhile idea," she explained, grinning as she took her last handful and started to crack open the nuts for herself.

"Our own bubblenut trees!" Shadd exclaimed, delighted with the concept. "What a great idea! I hope it works," she added, suddenly frowning, "I wonder what kind of care and watering it'd need?" She started stashing some of the nuts into her gather pouch too.

"We'll see if it works. There's quite a few plants here I'd like to take seeds from to try with, too," she replied, seeing Ardis getting into the swing of it, too, as she gathered some of the nuts to take back.

"Do you know we're on top of some kind of building?" Ardis asked, pointing out pieces of exposed metal, from out of the ground near them. Ryes gave her a nod.

"I've figured that had to be the case, too." Ryes straightened up again, surveying the area. "It looks like it had to have been really big and maybe pretty much demolished."

"Hey, let's see if there's a way inside," Maren suggested, smiling, warming up with a sense of adventure. He had only gathered as many nuts as he thought he would need for a little while, leaving the rest for the women.

"I imagine the air inside would be stale," Ardis pointed out to him. "And if any animals have found ways in, there'd be all kinds of things we wouldn't want to run into inside it."

"Come on," he pleaded as Ardis and Shadd sat down to enjoy their nuts. "Let's try!" Ryes gave him a merry grin, then a nod of her head in agreement.

"You'd probably need a shovel," she suggested, looking around to see if there were any evident features, which might give them an easier ingress into the building. "But, I agree with Ardis, there probably won't be much inside worth bothering with," she warned. She remembered the tremendous heat and wild fires that broke out in that nightmare she had of Hailys before. She wondered, if it had been that way in truth, would anything have escaped the flames? She looked at the exposed metal. Even after what had to be hundreds of years of exposure to the elements, it was still very shiny, as if brand new.

Maren grabbed a stout branch from the tree and pulled with all his weight, trying to break it off. After letting him struggle for a few minutes, she stepped over next to him.

"Why don't you use that?" Ryes questioned as he grunted under the strain. The branch wasn't going to give easily. He released it to see what she was pointing at.

"You could've shown me that sooner," he commented with a loud groan. The women were laughing as he picked up an old branch, which might've been brought down during a storm and started stripping off the smaller branches. They came off easily.

"It's more fun to torture you," Ryes returned, grinning impishly. Maren rolled his eyes heavenward as he sighed. "Come on, how about over here?" she suggested, pointing out a low spot next to some metal beams. "But, one place may be as good as any other."

"This metal never rusted," Ardis commented, examining one of the beams near her. "There's some pitting, but no rust."

"The ancients knew their metals," Shadd agreed, evaluating it too. "If we could get some smaller samples, maybe we could take them to Old Aric to have some good beltknives made?" Ardis' golden-yellow eyes lit up at this in surprise.

"Another great idea!" she declared, smiling with a hand upon her shoulder. "Let's look around," she suggested. Ryes and Maren were clearing away the grasses and small plants, which were growing where they decided to dig. "Keep a look out for some smaller pieces of that metal," she requested. Ryes gave her a nod, as Maren looked thoughtful. It appeared he thought it was a good idea, too.

"Well, you can either help us dig here, or find another spot to try," he suggested. Ardis grinned, standing up.

"The first team to find the metal, or a way inside, wins," she decided. Shadd smiled, liking the idea. It'd help pass the time more quickly!

"What do we win?" Maren questioned, smiling at the idea himself.

"How about two days with no chores?" Ardis reasoned.

"Sounds good to me," Maren agreed, looking to Ryes. She stood shaking her head, knowing it'd be hard for her to sit on her hands for two whole days, but if the others were willing. She just then realized how well she was starting to fit in with this small group of villagers! She slipped off her backpack and gather pouch and put them near the base of one of the bubblenut trees. Maren looked at her with a grin upon his face. He doffed his pack and pouch too, placing them next to hers.

"Yes," she concurred finally, as Shadd gave a nod of her head, in agreement. She added her pack to the base of the tree as did Ardis.

"Wait for us to find our spot and get it cleared, too," Shadd protested right off. Ryes and Maren looked to each other, than nodded their heads for her as they grinned.

"We can do that," he agreed. Ardis found another piece of wood to use for a primitive shovel, and then started looking for a good spot.

"Over there," Shadd pointed out. It was near another line of beams, but looked a little more sunken than Ryes and Maren's spot.

"Great," she consented. The two women quickly cleared it of plants, to get it prepared for the real digging to begin.

"Set, ready and go!" Ardis shouted after a few minutes. Maren grinned as he and Ryes bent their backs into their work, taking this contest in fun, but serious about their efforts. Who knew what treasures, or dangers, actually lurked below? There was laughter from both teams as they started digging in earnest.

Dirt was flying through the air as centuries of deposits were unearthed by their labors. Maren noted the different colors to the soils they dug through, wondering what made them so? After almost a half hour of serious efforts by both teams, they halted, panting heavily.

"This's too much like work!" Shadd remarked, as all four went for their packs and waterskins within.

"At least the soil's soft," Ryes added, after taking a long drink from her waterskin and wiping her hands off on her breeches. "Ahhhh, I miss my old bath tub," she added.

"I miss it, too," Shadd agreed, smiling.

"I vote for a swim in the lake when we're done," Maren suggested. He capped his waterskin and looked at Ryes. "Come on, I think we're getting close." She groaned at this, shaking her head.

"Now who's torturing whom?" she complained, grinning, as she followed him back to their spot.

"Just a return favor," he quipped with a laugh, leading her back. She rolled her eyes as she looked to the other two for support. They both chuckled at this display.

"Let's get to it, too," Ardis agreed, picking up her branch, again. They returned to their digging with a little less reckless abandon, trying to gauge if they were making any real progress. Ryes was keeping an eye to any smaller pieces of metal, wondering if Old Aric could make something of it? She didn't want to find too much; afraid they'd overburden Honey with this project. She worried about her mare. She was a good animal and deserved better than to be left alone in a tiny pen all day. Tonight, she was going to start building a larger one, no matter what the others thought, or if they offered to help her with the project. Honey needed the room to stretch her legs!

"Mother used to worry about you all the time," Maren told her in a low voice as they worked, trying to find a bridge between them. Ryes looked up to him with surprise in her eyes. "She worried that Rowan kept you away from everyone else, too much." She frowned, curious as to why he was bringing this up? What could he want?

"I never knew she cared," she returned, also in a low voice. "She never treated me as if she cared about me. And Rowan didn't keep me away from anyone, I chose it myself. The only thing he's guilty of was indulging me my reclusiveness. And, I never had problems with the Caravaners," she reminded him, realizing she was saying it a little more tartly than she had meant.

"Sorry," she sighed, "I didn't mean to snap at you," she apologized. A gust of wind pulled her red-gold hair across her face.

As she pulled it back into place, she saw Maren with a thoughtful look in his eyes.

"Tennan and I never sought you out, either. Rowan was our grandfather too, and we were jealous that you had him to yourself, all the time," he admitted, meeting her eyes steadily. "We never appreciated all we truly missed out on with staying away. It's funny, but my younger sisters and brother hold you in awe," he grinned. "It's hard for them to think of `The Huntress' as just a cousin. Their friends all love you, too." Ryes was shocked and flattered by this admission. She smiled as she shook her head, blushing.

"I wonder how these cubs of mine will be, with such a colorful family history?" she voiced aloud her uncertainty.

"Just don't isolate yourself and them from the rest of us and the Village, and they'll be just fine," he replied in all seriousness. "I don't think Garth would let you do that anymore, anyway."

"No, he wouldn't," she agreed with a chuckle. They'd gone down almost three feet in their efforts and it looked like more dirt lay below them. "I don't know about our choice of a digging site," she remarked, looking down into their hole, hoping to see something other than dirt and chunks of rock. She had been widening it out a bit, in hopes of finding out more.

"We'll give it another couple of feet before looking for another," he agreed. Suddenly, Shadd and Ardis gave a shout. They looked over to see them waving excitedly.

"Looks like they beat us," he observed, looking chagrined.

"Let's see what they found," Ryes suggested, standing up and brushing off her breeches, arms and face. Maren dropped his digging tool and they strolled over together, both unhappy that the other two got through first.

"Look at this," Shadd urged, pointing down. There was a gaping hole below them and a horrid stench-filled the air, causing them all to back away from it.

"Shadd almost fell in when it suddenly gave way," Ardis said. "I don't know if that stink's from the death dust, or something else," she added, wrinkling her nose.

"Maybe we ought to let it air out for a day at least, before trying to get a look down there," Maren suggested. As he spoke, a huge chunk of earth broke off and tumbled down into the darkness. It took several long heartbeats before he heard it strike something within. It sounded like something metal. "And it looks like we'll need some rope to get down there and a torch, so we can see."

"I think we started some kind of cave in. We should make sure it's done falling in before attempting anything," Shadd stated, looking concerned. Ryes crouched and peered down into the darkness, trying to stretch out with her inner sense. After a few moments, she shook her head and stood up.

"It's been empty for a very long time," she said, in a low voice. "It may only be trapped gas and needs to air out. I don't feel that anything dangerous lurks within." She looked back to the others, grinning at their surprised expressions. "Of course, would my Talent be able to distinguish a death dust as a danger, or not?"

"Are you sure?" Ardis questioned, frowning.

"No, not at all," Ryes returned, smiling merrily. "I'm still learning this Talent stuff. I'm sure Sabin has far more experience on how to approach this. I've no idea what I'm doing," she reminded her. Shadd laughed, agreeing with a nod of her head. Maren chuckled and shook his head.

"Give yourself some time to get to know yourself anew," he suggested. Ryes grinned back at him, giving him a nod of agreement.

"That might be all I truly need. I have to figure out what I can and cannot do with my Talents, first. Let's go back to our site and see if we can make our own breakthrough," she suggested.

"We did win! So, two days of no chores for us!" Ardis declared, as she brushed herself off a bit. She started to dance around in jubilation, which got the others to laugh as Shadd joined her in the dance for a few moments.

"We know," Ryes laughed as she turned away from them. She was curious to know what truly lay below. Her Talents told her it was a great twisted cavity, but there had seemed to be something to that emptiness. She thought it might be a fallen building, but they wouldn't know more until tomorrow.

"Let's go lend them a hand," Shadd suggested in a low voice as the others returned to their dig.

"Truly?" Ardis asked, her nose scrunched up as a breeze brought the obnoxious odor from below her way. She sighed and gave her a nod of agreement. "It will at least get us away from this stink!" She stooped down and grabbed her branch again, smiling to herself as they trailed after them, ready to lend a surprise hand to their efforts.

"Maybe my luck will hold out on their spot too?" Shadd added, grinning mischievously. Ardis merely laughed at hearing it.

"They have to be somewhere around here," Kovin stated, now truly realizing how much ground there was to cover at the ruins. They had come in out of the east and were wandering about aimlessly. He watched as Mitt scrambled nimbly up an exposed metal beam and climb on top of another one it supported, high on top of a huge mound. It held her weight with no movement, nor shifting. She shaded her eyes as she was looking at the area around them, turning around to be sure she covered all directions. After a few minutes, she came back down as quickly as she'd gone up.

"Nothing. No movement other than animals, no sign of a campfire, no sign of a golden-colored windracer and at least no decaying bodies," she sounded dejected at delivering her report. "We could search this place for months!" Teris nodded, understanding her heart's anguish.

"We'll find them," he assured her, gripping her shoulder in assurance. Kovin stooped down and cleared a small patch of some sandy soil. He grabbed a stick and started sketching something on the ground.

"I remember the map they used, a little bit," he told them. "I recall something about a small lake south of the main ruins. If we can find that lake, we might find them. It was the place they were going to head to first before going in to explore."

"I saw a glimmer of water, but it was further west, not south," Mitt stated, starting to smile.

"It might feed into that lake," Kovin suggested, hoping it was true.

"It's a better idea than wandering aimlessly around here and possibly falling into one of those deep holes," Teris agreed. "So let's see this glimmer of water and hope it's going somewhere useful?"

"At least we're not going to starve with all the plants and animals around here to eat," Mitt observed as she fell into step with the men.

"As long as we don't get eaten ourselves," Teris replied slapping a biting insect as it perched on his arm. The other two laughed and nodded in agreement with him.

"It's the bigger stalkers I worry about," Kovin returned after a few minutes. "Did you catch that whiff?" Teris nodded, looking stern.

"What?" Mitt questioned, puzzled for a moment, then caught a faint odor upon a breeze. Her eyes widened in surprise. "Oh!" she added then frowned. "He is here. His body odor is very distinct."

"It's not fresh," Kovin assured her as they wandered around trees, brush and pieces of building, carefully picking their path. "But keep your eyes open and ears sharp," he warned.

"Maybe we can follow him to them?" Teris wondered aloud.

"Then our warning would be too late," Mitt replied grimly. "Let's hurry, as best we can." She pushed to get ahead of Kovin, but he grabbed her arm, pulling her back beside him.

"Watch it! See that drop?" he pointed out, which opened up near where she had been about to rush towards. He turned and treaded a way around it, hoping his chosen path would not drop him into those dark, unsettling depths. Mitt had grasped what was happening immediately and waited to follow in Kovin's footsteps, slowly and carefully. Teris brought up the rear, keeping an eye to behind them as well as the plants around them.

"I've never seen these get so big!" he declared as he pulled off several fruit from a nearby tree, stuffing them into his gather pouch, which he had slung over his shoulder. The last one he merely bit into, letting the fresh juices stream down his chin. A look of utter joy lit up his face. Noticing the other two, he picked two more, tossing them over to them.

"What is it?" Mitt questioned, frowning down at the red and gold fruit in her hands. She saw it was large and slightly familiar. She finally bit through the skin and smiled as it was far better than any fruit she had eaten before.

"Lunch," Kovin supplied before Teris could speak, as he seemed happy to continue stuffing his face. He bit into his own fruit and smiled as he turned back to finding them a safe path to that water.

"It's like he's vanished again," Garth stated, appearing sorely vexed. Sabin looked disgusted as Torr was frowning.

"Could he be using some of the underground paths?" he ventured. "He might have been learning them as a way to get away from us, or to get closer to us. Most of Hailys was said to be underground and Ryes' stories seem to confirm it. Perhaps there are still paths below that can be used?"

"Or used to come up behind us?" Sabin added. "You might have the right idea there, Torr. Let's backtrack to where we were last sure of his traces and take a very good look around the area." He got nods of agreement from them.

They returned to the spot they could last clearly identify Korman's scent and footprints, and then fanned out looking for not just any further signs of him, but any place where he might easily hide, or get into an underground passage and use it to avoid them. After over a couple of hours of careful searching, Garth found a spot which had a loose panel of metal that had been pulled over what appeared to be stairs leading down into the darkness. Korman's smell and footprints were here, vanishing inside.

"Got it!" he yelled out for the others. In a few minutes they'd rejoined him. "You're right, Torr. He went underground," he stated in a lower voice.

"What a motherless son of a demon!" Sabin declared. "It looks like he has a couple of torches stashed here, too," he pointed out, seeing two lying just inside on the top of the wide stair.

"So, do we face him in territory he's explored and knows, or do we wait for him to surface?" Garth asked.

"I'd like to see what's down there," Torr ventured, "but I'm not eager to meet him there, either."

"Let's make our own torches first," Garth suggested, "and leave his undisturbed. We can carefully explore and if we find him, we'll handle it. Let him think he's undetected and safe down there for a while."

"And wait for him to surface for the challenge?" Sabin asked, his dark eyes gleaming.

"That would be my choice. Still I want to see if we can find out where he's been hiding. I wonder if this is how he found and kept track of Tyra and Ronn?"

"It might be how he did it," Torr replied, frowning again. "It doesn't seem that he's in the area now. Everything's quiet." Garth nodded his head in agreement. They put the plate of metal back in place and went back to camp, noting the area carefully as they left and making sure to eliminate their own traces from the area, too.

"And we're going to do a very thorough search near our own camp, too," Garth stated with fire in his eyes. "He's not going to be able to come and go as he pleases around us!"

"Oh we are going to go through the area as if we were cleaning it up for an Elder Inspection," Sabin promised wholeheartedly. "And fully block him out so he can't come at us sneakily in the middle of the night."

"That's something he's done to others in the Village in the past," Torr said with a low growl in his voice. "My own father was murdered by Korman that way."

"It's not happening ever again," Garth promised. "Somehow we have to fully put a stop to his rampages for all time."

"We can do it together!" Sabin agreed.

Nature

"It's a stream of some sort," Kovin stated, looking puzzled. What lay before them was a wide channel of flowing water that was purposefully structured and precisely controlled by all outward appearances. There was a low wall of a smooth, seamless grey-white stone that defined the channel and more of it was used to create a curved surface down to the water. For the most part, the water's channel was very straight, but sometimes there appeared to be deliberate curves added to it for no apparent reason.

"These people truly like to keep everything in order and obeying their will," Teris agreed. Mitt just huffed her agreement, trying not to laugh.

"How arrogant," she finally added, grinning widely. "How can they think they can control nature in such a way?"

"Well, they're not in control anymore," Teris replied, gesturing to the wild growth all around them with a sweep of his arm. He ran a hand through his dark hair, thinking about it, frowning.

"No matter," Kovin stated. "It runs south and for now we can use it as our guide. The pathway next to it still seems solid from what I can see, so far."

"Let's find a good spot to make camp," Mitt suggested. "It's starting to get late and I want a fire going to keep away the larger animals."

"Me, too," Teris agreed.

"As our lady has ordered, so it shall be done," Kovin teased, grinning with a mock bow to Mitt. She blushed and giggled at his gesture. "Let's get moving." So they headed off, hopeful to reach their destination soon.

Suddenly Teris gave an odd, cut-off cry, causing Kovin and Mitt to suddenly stop and turn. Something had leapt up and hooked claws into his back and backpack and Teris was struggling to get it off and get away; turning this way and that. Mitt snatched up a nearby stick and jumped at it, shouting and then smacked it across its face and open maw. It let Teris go and dropped back as he twisted and moved away from it, as quickly as he could possibly manage. The animal gave a yowling snarl. Teris' face was a mask of pain and he was breathing hard in panic. That alone scared Mitt, but she pulled up her determination, facing off this small monster. It was thin and about half her size with long claws that were at least as long as her fingers. It was covered in a short, thick tawny-yellow fur with reddish tufts of long fur around its head and paws. She didn't know what it usually hunted, but was determined not to be its next dinner.

"It's got nasty fangs and claws," Mitt shouted as Kovin moved up next to her with his spear at the ready. It snarled at her and crouched down as if readying for another leap. "And moves wickedly fast!" she warned.

"Let's keep facing it as we back away," he suggested, signing to her to back off. "We might be in its territory and it could be just letting us know. It might have cubs to protect." He braved a quick glance over his shoulder. "How're you doing, Teris?" he inquired, worrying about his friend. "How badly are you hurt?"

"There's another two trying to come in from the side and behind you," he reported. "They have us surrounded, except for one side. How well can the two of you swim?" he asked. "That stone stream might be our only way out of here."

"Good idea. Let's all three back to the low wall around it and get over it. It's a small obstacle we can put between us and them," Kovin ordered. They carefully edged over to it and as Mitt turned to climb over it, there was a red and tawny flash as one of creatures charged them. Kovin stabbed it ruthlessly with his spear, determined to not let any of them fall to these fast-moving terrors. A loud, harsh cry issued from it as it retreated just as quickly. The red blood dripping from his spear's blade proved he did get it and it was something mortal, after all.

"Teris, move!" he ordered, realizing his friend was still next to his side, appearing torn within as he paused.

"I can't move fast enough," he responded. He turned and Mitt reached for his spear, which he surrendered to her. She was ready to guard his back as he scrambled over the four-foot tall wall. One started to advance but then paused, as if it recognized the danger in her hands. The wounded one was making mewling sounds and limped as it paced behind the other two. Teris took back his spear and Mitt then took Kovin's as he came over the wall to join them.

"Let's move on downstream and see if they follow us," Kovin suggested, knowing they needed to get away from there before looking to see how badly wounded Teris actually was in truth. His backpack looked to have taken the brunt and was torn with long gashes running through the leather. Some of his things inside looked damaged, but they didn't have time to stop and check anything right now. There was blood on it, too, but it didn't seem as if it was flowing from his wounds, as far as he could tell. "Where's your spear, Mitt?" he asked her as they kept a good watch on the animals, as they moved away from them.

"I think I left it leaning against a tree at my last bathroom break," she admitted, embarrassed by her mistake. She still had the stick in her hand but felt so defenseless, as she kept her eyes roving as they walked; checking the water below them and the other side, as well as where they were going. She did not want to be caught unawares.

"That can cost you your life. You need to make a new one tonight. Do you have any spearheads with you?" he asked.

"I should have some that might be small enough for her," Teris volunteered. He stepped over a small fallen tree, which had leaned over the wall and split at the part on top of the wall. The wall still appeared undamaged, which gave him a moment's pause to take a closer look. It appeared as if the weight of the tree itself had caused the split, not from something other than the force of gravity.

"This looks promising for some good wood for you, Mitt," he advised. She stopped to check for a part she could easily break off, not having a hatchet with her, either. She spotted a large limb that was partly under the mass. She tugged at it for a few moments until Teris lent her a hand and it parted with a loud crack. That sudden noise startled several birds and other small nearby animals which fled. One small ground runner flushed one of the tawny stalking hunters, which had hurt Teris. Kovin cast his spear, pinning it solidly. It died quickly. He rushed over the wall, grasped his spear and gave a loud shout, throwing out his arms to further frighten any other nearby hunters. One scampered away, startled, as more of the smaller animals, which all ran at his shout.

"That might throw them off for a little bit," Kovin stated as he came back over the wall. "Since we don't really know how many there are out there, let's put more distance between us."

"Don't go near the water," Mitt suggested, pointing. There was something in it which splashed as it sank back below the surface. "Whatever it was, it just snatched a bird in one chomp from the other side of the channel."

"Why am I not surprised?" Kovin laughed. "Can you hold out for a bit longer?" he asked Teris. He got a terse nod in return. "We'll find a safe place soon," he assured him, then took the lead, now they were past the fallen tree. Mitt held her branch looking at it to get a feel for it as they travelled onward, heading south. She began to strip off the leaves and smaller branches as they went.

"I'm not leaving you behind anywhere," she quietly promised it.

They got back to camp and saw some small, brown and gray furry animals were exploring and examining all their things. They shooed them away, half amused and half unhappy at the unexpected invaders.

"They didn't get into our food, thank goodness," Ardis declared, happy with that small piece of good news.

The pots were scattered, as was their bedding, but everything else still looked fine. One of the storage packs was knocked over and part of the contents had been pulled out, but that looked the worse of it. Ryes went over to check it. One of the ropes stored in the pack had been chewed up a bit and a tarp was pulled about as if it was being investigated as a possible nesting material. She laughed and she pulled everything out and found one small animal was still hiding in it. She held it by the scruff and put her other hand under its hind legs to give it some support while she examined it. Its body was about ten inches long. And she realized it was terrified.

"What is it?" Maren asked, coming closer to get a better look.

"I don't know, other than afraid," Ryes responded. The other two women came closer too.

"Are you just going to let it go? Or keep it for a pet?" Shadd asked, laughing lightly.

"I have an idea. Let me try something," she responded, grinning. She took in a deep breath, then let it out slowly, relaxed and closed her eyes, settling back into a more comfortable squat. She reached out with her inner self to the small creature trying to gently calm it. She felt it relax in her grip and realized it was a female. Then she warned her to keep the rest of her family and herself away from this camp. She imparted that it had hidden dangers, no matter how interesting the new smells were here. She felt her trembling now, so opened her eyes again. Slowly she lowered her to the ground and watched her scamper off.

"That felt strange," Maren told her, shaking his head. "I wanted to run away too!" She laughed at that, shaking her head.

"You weren't the one I wanted to impress fear upon," she replied, still chuckling.

"What did you do?" Ardis asked, curious. She'd felt an uncanny vestige of fear for a few moments, too.

"I tried to convince her to stay away," she replied. "I think she was looking for a safe, secure place to nest." She shrugged then dumped the rest of the contents of the pack out for inspection. "I'd love to have one for a pet, but we don't have the time, nor the room for pets right now."

"That's the truth," Ardis agreed with a sigh. She turned back to getting the bedding sorted out, shook out and back in order. Shadd picked up the pots and other equipment scattered around. Maren checked the stew they had simmering from this morning. It smelled good and most of the water had boiled down now. He set about stirring it and adding a little more water to it again. He started humming a Winterfest song, which got Ryes to chuckling merrily, then joining him by singing it softly aloud as she worked.

Garth, Sabin and Torr arrived back at camp as they were busy cleaning things up. They appeared puzzled at the disarray.

"We had some uninvited guests," Shadd explained as she finished stacking the pots. She had rinsed them out before putting them back on the flat rock they had been storing them upon. There was instant dismay on the men's faces which set the others to laughing.

"Not anything more than a bunch of small tree dweller-like animals," Maren explained, grinning ear-to-ear. "Dinner's just about ready," he added. He was warming up the leftover flat cakes they had made for breakfast on a flat rock next to the cook fire.

"And we have bubblenuts for dessert," Ryes bragged, showing them a bowlful she had emptied out from her gather bag. This news got a round of cheers from the three older men, as it seemed they loved the treat, too.

"What are those sticks and tinder you brought in for, Torr?" Ardis asked, wondering at the armload he set down near their firepit.

"We have a project for all of us to work on tonight," Sabin replied for him.

"Ah, we're making torches so we can go exploring inside the buildings we opened up today?" Shadd asked, appearing happy with the news.

"You opened up some of the old buildings?" Garth asked, suddenly looking unhappy with her report. "They're dangerous," he emphasized. Ryes tugged on his arm, getting him to face her.

"We were not going to sit here all day waiting for our brave adventurers to return," she told him. "We stayed near camp and were looking for some smaller bits of that bright metal that the buildings are made of to bring back to Aric. We'd like to see if he can make us some truly sturdy beltknives from it," she explained.

"The best we got today was two entrances into either two buildings, or different areas of the same one. We weren't sure and they both needed to air out before anyone can go inside to look," Ardis supplied, understanding they needed to let them know they could be responsible explorers, too.

"Oh, what a stench!" Maren declared, nodding his head in agreement. "I'm hoping one night will be enough to clear that foul air out of them."

"The best part is we found a huge bubblenut tree!" Shadd declared, displaying her own handful of the prized nuts. Torr laughed at this, shaking his head in amazement.

"As long as no one was hurt and you are being careful of what's around you at all times," Garth finally advised, frowning in concern. Ryes solemnly met his eyes.

"We're very careful and did keep an alert eye to everything around us. And Maren was glued to my side every moment of the day," she stated clearly for him, hearing the worry in his voice.

"Good!" he replied, then pulled her close to him and wrapped his arms about her and gave her a tight hug, which got her to laughing lightly.

"You're the one who's going to break me," she protested, gasping for breath. He relaxed his arms but held onto her. "What happened out there, today?" she suddenly pressed, feeling he had to have a reason for the odd over-protective attitude.

"We'll talk about it over dinner," Maren butted in before Garth could say another word. "It's finished and I'm going to get Honey, so we can all eat and get things discussed." With that he trotted out of camp, looking glad to finally be relieved of duty for a while.

"Dinner sounds good," Torr stated, grinning as he pulled Shadd into his arms, too. "We missed our lunch today," he admitted.

"Now it sounds truly serious," Ryes said, frowning. "But let's wait for Maren and Honey to return, first." Garth nodded his head at this then kissed her lightly before letting her go.

"After dinner," Sabin agreed, giving Ardis a kiss, too. She smiled her agreement, kissing him back soundly. Torr had his arms around Shadd too, and everyone was feeling a moment of happiness in this wilderness.

They found a covered bridge that had been partly collapsed by a wall leaning into it from the other side of the stream's course. It appeared only that part of the wall existed of what might have once been a building. There had been two chambers in the middle, at opposite sides of the bridge, which might have been gathering or viewing places. There was some dirt and debris, but no animals, nor signs of any dens. There were heavy, metal screens over great window openings in the walls of each of the alcoves and remains of what might have been benches made of a natural stone and wood around the outer walls. They made their camp within these sheltering walls.

"Look at this," Kovin gestured at the side of one of the windows. "The metal and stone are melded so perfectly, as if they were made that way from the start." Teris shook his head at it in disbelief.

"How did they do it?" Teris asked. Kovin had washed out and bandaged his wounds, now that they were in a safe place to camp for the night and had a good-sized fire between them and whatever lurked outside. They'd taken an accounting of all that was left in his pack and salvaged all they could. Now Mitt was trying to fire-harden the shaft of her new spear while munching on her share of dinner.

"If it could be done before, we can find a way to do it again," Kovin stated as he returned to the fire and his dinner.

"Are we going to be building fancy bridges now?" Mitt asked, laughing lightly.

"We are going to be rebuilding Matlowe Village," Kovin informed her, grinning with a fire alighting his eyes. "Can you imagine the things we can accomplish if we could bring some of these building materials back home with us? We can make it as amazing as the great cities that lie to the far east!"

"Well, first you would have to convince the Elders it would be something you could accomplish," she reminded him, her eyes dancing with her inner humor showing in the light of their campfire. Teris huffed a laugh at that, nodding his head. "I'd love to see you bring this bridge over to the Yuri. We could use a good, sturdy bridge to cross it safely. And if this one is still standing after a building collapses on top of it for hundreds of years, I think it's one we could use there, too."

"It would have to be longer," Kovin laughed, "but it would be a start."

"Maybe that's how we win the Elders over? Doing smaller projects at first like a good, sturdy bridge?" Teris suggested, grinning ear-to-ear now, igniting with the inspirations sitting all around them. Mitt laughed, nodding her agreement. "I'd have loved to have seen this city when it stood tall and beautiful. I wonder what it was like in truth? The little bits we see around us are still amazing!" Teris' voice had a ring of wonder that touched the other two. "Those huge towers away to the north... I want to go explore them! Can you imagine building something like that in Matlowe?"

"Let's start out smaller though, first. Let's find our friends and then build our new world together," Kovin suggested. "I'll take first watch while you two get some rest," he added. Mitt checked her haft and decided she had done all she could with it for that night.

"Wake me for second watch," she stated, still smiling over their future plans. She made sure her blankets were still bug free, then snuggled down for the night, her new spear haft beside her and at hand. Teris did the same, starting to feel his pain return, but was too tired to let it keep him awake.

"I'll take the last watch," he said before dropping off.

"Sure," Kovin returned, thinking otherwise. He and Mitt had planned on only making it two watches tonight to allow Teris' body some added rest for healing. He started sketching in a patch of dirt what he thought a bridge across the Yuri should look like, wondering if he would truly get the chance to build it someday?

"So once we figured out how he was getting around unseen, we decided to check around our camp to see if we could find his hidey holes," Garth explained, as he finished up his second torch.

"And?" Ryes and Ardis asked at the same time, then grinned at each other merrily, knowing he was baiting them.

"We found four of them. All of them had stairs leading down below. Two for sure because they had some of his torches cached inside them and one possible and the last one we don't think he's found yet, but we're not taking any chances," Sabin stated, grinning.

"We blocked all four of them in ways we don't think he'll be able to get them opened up without lots of help," Torr continued for them. He pantomimed by ramming his fist into his other palm, with a grim look upon his face as he did it.

"Sure, we're trying to find good ways down to explore and find some useful treasures and you're destroying the better ways down," Maren laughed, having finished his third torch at the same time Ryes finished her third. They were competing again with each other, in their own way. She teasingly stuck her tongue out at him as he smirked at her, both with mischief in their eyes as they grabbed the materials they needed for their next torches. Garth shook his head and sighed. Sabin just shrugged.

"So, what is the plan for tomorrow?" Ryes asked. She paused long enough to look Garth and then Sabin in the eye. Both appeared uncomfortable. She nodded her head, thinking she could understand why.

"How about all of us explore that last one you found leading down?" Maren suggested, pausing since Ryes had stopped her manufacture. "That way we are all standing against Korman instead of just the three of you?"

"No. The plan for tomorrow is Sabin, Torr and I will check out the one we left alone west of here out in the ruins. We will try to figure out how much he is actually down there and where he's going. If we run into him, we'll get back up above and see where it goes. Ryes, Ardis, Shadd and Maren will go ahead and carefully check out one of your openings to see if you can find anything we can actually use. If you need any help, or something happens, get back to camp and we'll be back by lunch time to lend a hand," Garth stated, having come to a decision. There was protest in the eyes of the women and Maren, but no one spoke anything against his plan. He gave them a nod, and then smiled.

"It'll be fine," Sabin assured them. He got murmured assents from the others, then Ryes brought out the large bowl of bubblenuts for everyone to enjoy before bed. That brought out their smiles again, all around.

"We have been following this course for three days, now!" Mitt complained. Teris was a bit feverish so they stayed near the water course as the way was mostly clear and the only danger in wild encounters were in the early morning and evening.

"It's still going south," Kovin returned. "And the buildings remains are further spaced out, as if there was less need for the manic clusters out and away from the city center," he observed. He was half supporting Teris now and leaving Mitt to watch for any immediate dangers.

"Perhaps?" Teris started, the felt Kovin give him a small shake of his head in denial, guessing what he might be about to say.

"No. We are not going to leave you behind," Mitt and Kovin both stated, having heard him try to suggest it for some time now.

"I was going to say we're getting almost to the end. Look at the changes in the channel. We'll have to get out of it before the wall gets too high for any of us to scale," he returned firmly, looking obviously frustrated with them both.

They stopped to take stock of their surroundings fully. They had drifted into a mindless haze with the continuous walking in a very mundane and unchanging area. Now that there were changes being pointed out to them, they could see the differences. The ground underneath their feet was even sloping downward now. And the water was flowing much more swiftly than before. It was amazing to wake up from this numbing nightmare they had been immersed in, all unknowingly.

"How did this happen?" Kovin asked no one in particular.

"You were sleep-walking," Teris teased, grinning. "I think we all were for the last two days."

"Well, now that we're awake, let's get out of this thing!" Mitt declared, feeling she had been less in the haze as the other two. She ran over to the wall, which was now higher than her head. She was going to jump up and hook her hands over the top of the wall when Kovin shouted at her.

"Wait! Let me boost you up, so to get a good look at what's over there first." She nodded her head at this, understanding him instantly. She realized he did have the better idea there, after all. Who knew what lurked over the wall? They hadn't been totally isolated from the wildlife with travelling in the channel. There'd been other smaller encounters, which should have kept them more on their toes. Still, she did not want to run into anything with lots of claws again!

Kovin came over and helped Teris sit down next to the wall, dropped both their backpacks and then stretched for a moment to loosen his muscles. Mitt suppressed a giggle at the look on his face. He ignored her, but was grinning as he laced his fingers to boost her toward the top, so she could see over the wall. She dropped her pack next to theirs and put her foot on top of his laced fingers. She still had her spear in her right hand, just in case. Kovin lifted her upward, supporting her light weight easily.

"Nothing dangerous in sight," she finally stated after taking a good look around. "Be careful with the top of the wall. It looks rough and you could cut your hands," she warned. She pulled herself up on top of the wall, carefully picking where she put her hands and feet. She again surveyed the area nearby, not seeing any obvious dangers.

Kovin grunted as he thought but Teris had pulled over his backpack and tossed him his heavier blanket. He gave him a nod of thanks. "Try this," he suggested, tossing it up to Mitt. She caught it and nodded, getting the idea. Tucking her spear haft under her arm, she quickly folded it into as many thicknesses as she could.

"It will help," she advised. "Ready."

Kovin tossed up her own backpack which she almost dropped before she got a good grip on it, then slung it up on her shoulder. Then Teris grabbed both of their backpacks and put them over his shoulder before Kovin boosted him up, too. He laughed as he got a good grip on the wall, using the padding, and then turned and lowered himself down. By the time he reached the verge on the other side, he was breathing hard as if he had run a distance. His arm and side looked like they were hurting him again, but he picked up his spear, which Mitt tossed down to him after Kovin tossed it up to her. He took over at standing watch. Kovin tossed up his spear to Mitt before launching himself up at the wall. He scrabbled at his hold, but managed to pull himself up on top. He looked around for a few moments before turning and lowering himself down again. Mitt tossed down his spear and Teris' blanket, then Kovin helped her down. Neither of them wanted to risk injury with Teris still in such pain and still now up to full heath after that attack.

"That sounds like a waterfall ahead," Teris said, leaning against the wall, but steadier on his feet. "Let's break for lunch, then go check it out?" he suggested.

"We're probably almost there," Mitt said, smiling. "I saw another big structure like a bridge across but this one was different, when I was up there waiting. It looked about half a day ahead still. It might be where our lake is at."

"Hopefully it'll have a place where we can camp inside again," Kovin stated, hoping. "But lunch sounds like a good idea right now." He knelt down and started sorting through his pack. Mitt kept watch, even if Teris was still standing doing the same.

Carefully picking their way through the rough terrain, they finally reached the end of the channel. It did, indeed empty out into Lake Ever. There was a large building which appeared to control the intensity of the flow of water into the lake and seemed to still be functioning. The door into the building didn't budge when they tried it and Kovin couldn't even get his knife into the jam to use it to pry it due to a protective plate over the point where it latched shut, by the door knob. Mitt began to explore the small stone shelters nearby.

"There're like the ones on the bridge, only on land," she commented as Kovin helped Teris over to the closest one. "Let's use the one just a little further. The screen is intact and somehow I feel safer with it to help keep out the night creatures."

"That does sound good," Teris agreed. Mitt lent a shoulder to him to free up Kovin as she pointed out the one she had like, so far. He trotted over to it, check it out and saw the door was working, which made it better to his eyes, too. Still he went onward and looked into a few others while Mitt and Teris went to the one she originally picked. They waited until he was satisfied and returned.

"We're going to another one. It has two tables and I want to use one to block the door at night," Kovin stated. Both gave him a nod of agreement and followed along at the best pace possible. They came to it and saw it appeared in better shape than the original one Mitt picked. The two simple tables inside called to mind many of the simple tables the villagers had inside their homes. Except these ones appeared to be made of some unknown material, as many things were around them in this place.

"Just a little clean up and it's perfect," Teris supplied as he sat down on one of the built-in seats at a table.

"This table appears to be bolted to the ground," Mitt observed, squatting down to look at the base structure. Kovin scoffed at this, grinning.

"Watch," he invited. He picked up the end of the table nearest to the door and it came free easily. Mitt laughed as she looked over to see the floor substance crumbled and appearing to turn into sand. She stepped over and hefted the other end. It came up too, but with some effort. Still she grinned merrily.

"Never knew I was so strong," she boasted. They moved the table next to the door to have it ready. "Do you think it'll be enough?" she asked, once again serious.

"It'll be all right. And hopefully tomorrow we'll find our friends and be safer," he spoke with confidence. Mitt smiled again, her eyes alighting with delight.

"I can't wait to see Garth's face," she replied. "He's going to be so mad at me!" She laughed lightly.

"That he will," Teris agreed, grinning now. He pulled up his gather pouch and started emptying its contents on the table, after clearing the dirt and debris. "I have the start of dinner. We just need some meat and a good cooking fire," he offered.

"Sounds good," Kovin replied. "Mitt get started on a campfire where the table was set and I'll go see what I can find for our meal." She gave him a nod, doffing her pack and throwing it up on the other end of the remaining table. Kovin picked up his spear again and trotted out the door.

"I have to wonder," Teris commented as Mitt started to clear the area for the fire, but kept the dirt itself for her base element.

"What?" she asked, curiously.

"The Old Ones were strange. They came all the way out here to the lake, to what appears to enjoy their time near nature, yet they locked themselves away from it at the same time," he reasoned. "Why?"

"Probably to keep it at a safe distance?" she replied, smiling. "I'm going to go find some rocks. I'll be right back," she said, giving a nod out the door. "I'll be close by," she added in promise, as she stepped over to the open doorway. He gave her a nod of his head as he took out his beltknife to clean some of his findings.

"I'm not going anywhere," he promised in return, grinning. Mitt nodded as she gripped her spear and then closed the door behind her. She felt she could well understand wanting to keep the wild nature around here at a safe distance, too. She prayed to find her brother and the others soon.

Challenge

After Ryes and Maren took care of the morning chores around the campsite; making very sure their food and important supplies were packed well against small, furry intruders. Ardis had been impatient as she waited for them, while Shadd had been busy with small things she wanted to get done, too. When they were done and Honey was safe in her newly expanded pen, they were ready to head out to explore one of their buildings. They had plenty of newly-made torches to help light their way, too. There were smiles all around as they headed out. It felt like they were starting out on their own adventure. The older men had left earlier, wanting to get a dawn start on their own explorations.

When they arrived, they saw the night's airing out had improved the smell. It wasn't all gone, but was far more tolerable. Ryes had Maren tie off a sturdy rope on one of the immobile girders, which was sticking up through the soil, near the opening. She double-checked the knots to be sure. He had objected when she first started to show him the knot she wanted tied, thinking his strength would be better than her own to secure it well. But now that it was done he studied it closely.

"Where did you learn to tie knots like this?" he asked her, puzzled.

"Tara taught me how to walk a taunt rope and if I was to learn how to walk on one, she reasoned I first needed to learn how to put up the rope, so I would be safe," she explained, grinning at the memories. "Since this is not just me, I wanted to be sure the knots were tight and would hold all of us. Thank you, Maren!" He smiled as he gripped her shoulder, giving her a nod.

"You're welcome," he replied. "Let's get a torch lit and get a look at what's below," he suggested, still a looking a little nervous with this venture. Ryes gave him a nod of assurance. She led him back over to the large opening where Shadd almost fell through yesterday. Ardis was there with a lit torch already in hand.

"Let's drop it in, a little away from where we'll be coming down," she suggested, as she was trying to see what lay below.

"What if something catches fire?" Shadd asked, worried as she frowned.

"We really have no way to hold a torch while going down on a rope," Ryes reasoned, lightly laughing. "I would think if it caught something on fire, we'll just wait for it to burn itself out." That got laughs from the others and nods of agreement. "Here," Ryes said, handing Ardis a second torch. "Light a new one before tossing the other one," she suggested.

Ardis nodded and did so, then gauged it as best she could and tossed down her original torch. It dropped at least twenty-five feet before bouncing a couple of times then came to rest at an odd angle.

"Made it," she breathed out, "but it's not as bright as I would truly want."

"Can you make out anything?" Maren pressed, crowding closer to the edge.

"Not much and what I can see, doesn't appear to make sense from up here," Ardis replied. Ryes had the rope in her hand, but dropped a folded blanket on the edge of the opening to help protect the rope before she lowered it below. "Will it be long enough?" Ardis pressed, sounding worried.

"It'll be fine," Ryes assured her, smiling. "The only thing I can think of why it wouldn't make sense is the horrible forces of destruction which were unleased in the attack. Let's go carefully," she offered.

"Let me go first," Maren stated, his arms crossed and determination in his bearing.

"Why do you get the honor? Ardis and I are the ones who picked this spot!" Shadd protested, a proud grin upon her face. "I'm the one who opened up this building. I should be the first."

As Maren opened his mouth to retort, there was an echoing yowl from far away and below them. They all froze in place as a second one sounded in response. A gust of wind blew around them, as Ryes shivered at the calls.

"What's that?" Shadd asked, "a large predator?"

"A challenge cry," Maren whispered. Something clicked in Ryes' mind.

"They were successful in their hunt already. They found Korman!" she stated. She ran, grabbing her pack and waterskin. Maren rushed to grasp her arm.

"Garth can handle it. Stay here; out of the way. They don't want any of you women getting hurt, especially you with the cubs you carry, Ryes." There was an earnestness in his manner, as his eyes pleaded with her for compliance.

"We have to be there," Ardis insisted, as she picked up her pack, too. She shoved her waterskin back inside and slung it up on her back, daring him with her eyes to stand in the way.

"If anything happens to Garth..." Ryes started, then sighed, her hand went to her beltknife. "Korman will never touch me," she vowed, meeting his eyes.

"You're not going to try to kill him, yourself?" he demanded, shocked.

"No!" Ryes answered, startled. "This is for me." Maren's eyes locked into hers and she knew he was deeply troubled by what she said. Ardis and Shadd stood rooted in astonishment, too.

"No, Ryes. If anything happens to Garth, we'll take care of you and his cubs. You must live, if only for the cubs." There was a note of panic in Maren's voice, as he pleaded with her for sanity.

"I still have to be there, Maren, let me go!" She twisted out of his grip, but he tackled her and pinned her to the ground.

"No, you can't! Those were Garth's orders," he insisted. Ryes struggled for a moment, and then suddenly she had a vivid flash of inner Vision.

She was in pain because her cubs were about to be born. Maren was trying to calm her down, while getting ready to help with their birth. Torr was looking at her with concern, from over Maren's shoulder. But, the pain of the pending birth wasn't what truly troubled her. It was Garth's absence... She needed Garth desperately, and he wasn't there.

The sights, sounds, smells, colors and feelings were there, then gone; just as suddenly as they started. Ryes was left with a clear memory of the Vision. Maren had been caught up in it, too. They looked into each other's eyes, a hundred questions running through their minds but they didn't reach out to speak to each other mind-to-mind in this tense moment. Then, Maren got off her and helped her to her feet. Shaken, Ryes grabbed her pack, cast them a worried look, and then began to descend the knoll. Maren was right behind her. Ardis looked to Shadd, questions in her eyes as they were wondering what happened? They quickly trailed down after them.

They spoke in hushed voices as if they were afraid of disturbing the ghosts of the people who once thrived in this great city. It was a sad tomb, but still a testament to what their ancestors had achieved. Could they ever dare to build a city so great again upon Tayna? But for now they were tracking Korman, who was a threat to all they held dear in their lives now.

"It looks too clear," Sabin stated in a low voice, "he must be setting us up." Garth huffed out a breath and nodded his head.

"I think he got reckless when he found we had blocked his other exits closer to our camp," Torr offered, feeling he was more right. "It didn't look like he checked the one we used to get down here."

"You could be right, Torr," Sabin agreed. "He's confident we'll never find our way down here, much less try to track him here through this maze."

"Here," Garth said, turning around and putting his torch closer to the ground, making sure of the signs he thought he saw. "This is the point where he left the underground." Sabin stepped closer and examined the markings in the dirt, too. He nodded his agreement.

"Yes, it has to be... but how?" He ran his hand over the wall before him, puzzled. It was rough, but still reflected light as if made of a smoother substance. Garth watched the marks his fingers made on the wall and how they stood out on top of the dirt caked on it in places.

"There," he pointed out where it appeared there were more finger gouges into the wall on one side. Torr held his torch over their heads to help add in his light. Sabin dug in his fingers into the same places and pulled. The panel slid smoothly to the side. It was so smooth and fast that he almost fell down from the strength he had applied in his effort. Garth steadied him as he looked through the opening.

"A hidden door," Torr commented as he looked out upon a sunlit clearing before them. "Who would've guessed?"

"Damnable cubs!" They clearly heard Korman shout as he stood up to face them.

"I think he noticed," Sabin commented as Garth handed him his torch and stepped out of the tunnels.

Ryes never knew what guided her through the twisted wreckage of stone and dense vegetation. Dark pits had opened up at her feet, but she never noted them as she wove her way around them. All she knew was that Torr and Sabin were suddenly standing before her. Her sudden appearance with Maren and their ladies right behind her, startled them. Sabin grabbed and held her by her arm, as her eyes began to register the scene before them. On the ground of the small clearing ahead of them lay a bloodied and torn body, which moved feebly. Ryes' heart almost stopped beating when she saw it, then she saw it was Garth who was standing over it.

Garth, too, was scratched and bleeding badly, but there was a fierceness to his stance he never before displayed. Then Ryes noted other things about him. He'd grown a few inches taller, his shoulders were wider and he put on some weight. Not as fat, but muscle. Their long journey had wrought changes in both of them, but Ryes hadn't noted the ones in Garth, because they'd been together through it all. He was standing, still focused on Korman, who was on the ground before him.

"I… withdraw… my claim," Korman finally managed to gasp out, in a feeble voice. Garth stepped away, and then turned to see Sabin restraining Ryes. The bloodlust of the challenge was still pounding in his veins as he strode up to them. His eyes were blazing with pent up anger. Sabin, as if seeing something deadly for the first time in his lifelong friend, quickly released her and stepped back. Ardis and Shadd were shocked at what they saw in him, too. This wasn't the Garth they knew! Maren stood rooted, afraid to move and attract his attention. Torr looked grim, but gave him a nod of his head in understanding.

Without a word, Garth took Ryes' pack from her hands and tossed it in Torr's direction. Then he scooped her up into his arms and headed back the way they'd come. Maren turned to follow them, but Sabin caught his arm and shook his head no.

"But, Garth's injured," he protested.

"Ryes can take care of him," he assured him. "Leave them alone for now." Maren looked defiant, but Sabin said reasonably, "Garth just won a challenge, let him have his prize." Maren's eyes went wide and his lips shaped an "oh" as understanding hit him.

"What do we do with him?" Torr asked, indicating Korman, who was struggling to get up from the ground. Sabin thought a moment, then suggested,

"Maren, you'd better ask if he needs any help from us."

"Why me?" he protested, but already knew the answer.

"Because he's your father," Shadd chided him, frowning at his outburst. She knew there was little affection between them, but this... It still wasn't right.

"Not that he's ever acknowledged it, except to punish me when I was a cub," Maren grumbled, as he dropped his pack and headed toward Korman.

"Sir," he said as politely as he could manage, standing next to him. "Do you need any assistance?" He saw his injuries and was amazed that he hadn't collapsed yet. Korman looked up, startled by his son's offer. He frowned as if struggling to understand what he was offering.

"Not from the likes of you," he finally growled out. He struggled but managed to regain his feet and turned eastward, limping away. It was bad enough that he was defeated so thoroughly, but to have it witnessed by the rest of these young cubs was more than he could bear. He knew he needed tending, but hoped to take care of it, himself. Tanns was another one to face, when he reached home.

"See, I told you," Maren assured the rest, as he returned to retrieve his pack. Sabin shrugged his shoulders as Torr scowled.

"Shouldn't we," Shadd began, but Torr gave her a shake of his head. "But, he needs some basic supplies," she persisted.

"He'd never accept it from us. If you truly feel strongly about it, leave it where you think he might find it; as if you accidently dropped it from your pack," Ardis advised, seeing her friend's concern. Korman needed help, even if he'd never accept anything from them. She met her eyes, and gave her a nod of her head in acknowledgment. They all turned, heading back for their camp.

"What if there's a `sport' because of this?" Maren asked Sabin in a low voice, worried. Sabin shrugged his shoulders.

"I'm sure they'll be able to handle it," he assured him. Maren shook his head at this.

"Garth won't be there. It's going to be OUR problem," he told them. The shock on their faces mirrored his own inner unrest. "Let's go back for some tea and I'll tell you about it," he suggested. Sabin wondered where this information came from? As he walked, he put an arm about Ardis, as they went. She didn't look happy about it either, but it didn't seem quite as unexpected news for her as it was for him. Where had they been and what happened today, he wondered?

Ryes was surprised by and afraid of, Garth's sudden passion. He'd swept off with her in his arms and found a secluded spot near a small rill, which probably fed into the lake. It wasn't too far from their encampment. He'd been gentle, but there'd been a true need in him, which she'd never seen before. Now she lay in his arms as he lightly dozed. She worried about his wounds becoming infected, but was reluctant to wake him. She felt the fire still burned deeply within him. Finally, she let herself relax and began to reach within herself. If she could heal her wound before, then maybe she could heal Garth's wounds?

"Sweet One?" he asked, sounding puzzled, as she reached out to him from within.

She couldn't answer him now that contact had begun. There was a burst of fire along her nerves as their life energies blended. The harmony they shared was there, one which she knew would always exist between them. She reveled in the bonding, savoring it a moment, and then got to work. She didn't have as much energy to draw upon for this venture as she could want to get it fully done. It seemed to take forever to speed up his body's healing. She concentrated upon the worse areas, making sure there'd be few scars. Suddenly she was done and burst free, momentarily exhausted.

"Garth?" she asked, opening her eyes, meeting his. "I did the best I could." He hugged her to him, stroking her hair. The steady sound of his heart beating flooded her with quiet relief. "I didn't even know if I could do it," she admitted in a low voice, shaking. "I tried doing for you what I was doing for myself when fighting Doran. It's sure tiring."

"Oh, Sweet One, what would I ever do without you?" he murmured to her, kissing the top of her head.

"Garth? Ryes?" Maren called out from nearby, startling them. An anger instantly ignited in Garth, surprising her, he face openly showed it.

"It's only Maren," she quietly scolded him. "He's probably worried about you. You were scratched up pretty badly." He stiffened within her embrace. "Let me go talk with him," she offered, trying to calm him down. "I'll reassure him and send him back to camp." He finally let go a breath in surrender.

"Alright. You go. I know it's only Maren, but I can't think clearly now," he admitted, with some effort. She smiled up at him, then grabbed her tunic, undergarment and belt.

"Don't move. I'll be right back," she teased, with a mischievous smile. Garth smiled and then pulled her down for a quick kiss. She sat up and dressed, then stood up and fastened her belt. She found Maren on the other side of some bushes; about a dozen feet away.

"Hi Maren. What do you want?" she asked with a bright smile. A look of relief broke out on his face as he saw her.

"Is Garth all right? He looked pretty bad," he asked, concern etching his young face.

"It looked worse than it was," she told him. "I already took care of it."

"Well, here's dinner, since you missed lunch, and your blankets and pack. Is there anything else you need?" He extended his arm but did not take a step closer. Ryes stepped through the bushes and took the things he had for her gratefully.

"Thanks, we truly appreciate this," she said with a warm smile, then saw his face. "What's wrong?" she asked feeling there was more he wanted to ask of her. He shifted his balance, looking down at his feet for a moment, feeling uncomfortable.

"I was wondering... I mean... have you thought that... because..." he looked up at Ryes, a deep pain evident in his golden-brown eyes. "You're risking a sport," he finally voiced. A moment of silence hovered between them as his words hit like heavy stones in her heart.

"I know, Maren," she admitted in a low voice, "but, there's no helping it." She looked at him in all seriousness. "No cubs of mine will be born deformed, or die because of this," she vowed. Maren realized she meant it, fully. He let go a breath and nodded his head, not looking at her eyes as he tried to compose himself, again. "Well, you'd better get back. We'll join you later," she promised, seeing he was finally relaxing.

"Maren!" A voice suddenly growled out loudly, close to them, causing them both to jump. Sabin came down a game trail, finding them at last. He glared at them. "I told you to stay away! Come on, let's go." His voice carried a note of command. But Garth was suddenly standing on the other side of them, dressed only in his breeches. Ryes quickly stepped between Garth and the others.

"Garth, they're just leaving," she told him soothingly, not liking the gleam in his eyes, nor his fighting stance.

"So, the sorceress has been practicing her arts upon you," Sabin taunted insultingly, noting his almost completely healed scratches. Garth took a step toward him, his face showing his anger. Ryes was torn between her own anger at Sabin for baiting him, and trying to think of a way to distract her mate. Her mind racing, she came up with an answer, but quelled at forcing the issue. Maren was tugging at Sabin's arm, trying to pull him away, but he shrugged him aside as if he were a gnat.

"All you want is what I've got," Garth growled. Sabin took a defiant stance, daring him to charge. Garth was tensing. They were really going to fight! Panic momentarily overcame Ryes as she looked wildly from one to the other. She couldn't let this happen! Something within her knew that once they calmed down, they'd still be the close friends they truly were. He needed Sabin, Maren and Torr, as much as he needed her. She knew it!

"GARTH!" Ryes shouted at him, as he tried to sweep her aside. "Garth, if you take one more step forward... I'll leave and you'll NEVER see me again! I swear it!" Ryes was trembling, but she met the mocking look in his eyes with a fierce determination in her own. Sabin looked at her in surprise! Then Maren, who'd been on the verge of running to enlist Torr's aid, stopped and looked at her in utter shock.

Garth held her eyes, seeing she meant every word. A cold wind from hell blew through his soul as he thought of losing her... Knowing there was only one real choice, he swept her up in his arms and held her to him.

"Never! Sweet One, Never!" he promised, as he turned and carried her back to their secluded spot. Maren released a sigh of relief.

"She meant it. She truly meant it," Sabin voiced quietly, as he looked like he was trying to fathom Ryes' motives.

"Let's get something to eat," Maren suggested with a grin. "Arguments make me hungry." He was relieved she broke it up. He knew she meant it, but knew it'd take a heavy toll upon her to do such a thing. He was glad that Garth still had enough presence of mind to hear her threat and understand what she was saying. He and Sabin were still caught up in the earlier challenge. Once they cooled off and got back some balance and sense, they'd be fine, again.

"Everything makes you hungry, cub," Sabin declared with a knowing grunt and smile, as they turned back to camp. His smile was replaced with a thoughtful look. There was more to Ryes than he thought, but he'd ponder it later.

Later that evening, after Garth had recuperated from most of the effects of the challenge, and they both washed up, they rejoined their friends. Ryes sensed the silence which still hung in the air between Garth and Sabin, but knew time would heal it, too. Torr, Maren, Ardis and Shadd were happy to have them back. With most of the day's events being a touchy subject, there was little said about the campfire and they all sought their blankets early. Ryes was so exhausted, she didn't even know if she bid Garth a goodnight before she dropped off to a deep sleep. She found herself suddenly awakened in the middle of the night by someone gripping her arm. In Shaysa's waning light, she couldn't make out who knelt by her, but Garth was sleeping soundly against her back.

"Ryes," Maren breathed, "I have to talk with you." There was a pleading note to her cousin's voice, which in spite of her exhaustion, she couldn't deny. So, Ryes carefully moved away from Garth and crawled out of their blankets. Maren took her hand, leading her away from the dying fire and the others. She followed, grabbing her belt and tightening her tunic laces. He led her under a great evergreen tree and sat down upon a piece of broken stone, lying beneath it. She sat beside him, wondering what could be so important?

"Ryes," he began quietly, "you truly found our old family gift! You healed Garth!" He looked at her in the dim moonlight. He smiled and shook his head, still in wonder. "I've thought about it and wondered if you can help me find my own Talent? I've been trying to reach it. I felt it stirring earlier when we shared that Vision, so I know it's there. I know I have a Talent and am finally ready to meet it."

"Oh Maren," Ryes returned, shaking her head. "It's not that easy. When my Talents started awakening, it nearly drove me crazy. If Garth hadn't been with me..." Her voice trailed off, wondering anew about it, herself. She realized it had to be her contact with the Stone of Power which finally fully opened her inner floodgates.

"But, you've got Tyra's old bloodline to deal with. I only have whatever Jana had to pass onto us. Please help? It may come in handy later when the cubs are born." Maren grasped her hand, as he pleaded his case and she shivered at the memory of their earlier shared Vision. He had been using a Healing Talent in it; she was sure of it. After the events of the day, Ryes was reluctant to think about on what the future truly held any more.

"All right. If you really have a Talent, I'll help you reach it. But, it's not easy and not without risk to both of us. I think Sabin's headache was our warning. Are you absolutely sure?" Maren nodded his head. She sighed in surrender. "Then, relax while I try to reach it within you." He closed his eyes as he tried to open himself up to her, as Sabin advised the last time they attempted it.

Ryes took a deep breath to relax herself. She felt an uneasiness settle in her stomach as she began to reach within. She had to try for Maren's sake, in spite of the memories she knew from Doran of how very wrong this could go for her; the possibilities were vast. She could only be alert and do her best to help him. Their earlier attempt with Sabin had been a failure, with Sabin commenting that they were too much alike. She wondered about it, but couldn't fathom what he meant. Maybe it was because their Talents were so very different from his? Slowly... carefully... gently... she began to reach out for Maren as she had in a different way to Garth, earlier. The moment of contact suddenly filled her being and an instant of panic at touching someone alien to her, yet familiar, almost caused her to immediately break off. With her heightened senses came a greater intolerance to inner intrusions. Or maybe after her confrontation with Doran, she was more wary? But, she held on and began to become comfortable with Maren.

The deep harmony which existed between her and Garth was lacking, but Maren had a gentleness within, which Ryes found quite reassuring. She realized it would be best if she got busy, so started her inner questing. She thought she knew where to conduct her search, so began to move though his being slowly and carefully. She clearly recalled the cold and ungentle contact she had with Doran and her followers and how afterwards she'd felt almost violated. Doran had no compassion for others; it had died within her ages ago. Ryes would never hurt Maren, if she could help it. He was like a younger brother to her, a brother she was only beginning to know.

Maren's hand, which held hers, trembled in reaction to Ryes' gentle intrusion into his very being. He broke out in a cold sweat. He knew she wouldn't hurt him, but there was still a small doubt, now that the actual contact was established. A part of him wanted her careful probing to stop! Their first encounter had been a far lighter touch. This time she was intruding more deeply; serious about her efforts. He wanted to withdraw, but didn't know how. He finally relaxed all that he could and waited, remembering this was what he had wanted all his life! He knew he could be a real Healer!

After an eternity of searching, Ryes finally found what she sought. She circled it warily, not yet ready to disturb the great, glowing sphere. She had no doubts this was, indeed, Maren's sleeping Talent. It was very powerful to her senses. Something within her responded to it... perhaps they were much alike? Knowing he was barely tolerating her presence, and she gained nothing by delaying, Ryes tentatively reached out and touched it. Explosively, a wild coursing fire filled her, as the pent up energy was released by her touch. Hastily she withdrew, almost in panic, until she held a minimal contact with him. Silently, she urged him to exert control over his Talent, before it overwhelmed him. She knew that if he failed to conquer the wild energies of his awakened Talent, he could suffer insanity; his mind locked away within, for the rest of his life.

A wash of cold fear flowed through his being as Maren suddenly found himself flooded with a raging torrent of great power. Ryes encouraged him to act, to control the flood before it engulfed him. She was there, but wouldn't help him any further. He felt a moment of utter helplessness, of drowning in the wild, unleashed energies, and then a spark of irrational anger arose in him, as he thought that Ryes was withholding her help deliberately. That she might be treating this as a game! That she truly wanted him to fail! With these thoughts, Maren determined to win this game and show her his Talent was as good and as strong as her own!

Ryes was surprised at the anger her cousin suddenly directed toward her. Not understanding and not daring to leave him alone, she kept the contact open, but resisted sending him any more reassurances. If his anger could be used as a goad to force him to conquer his untamed Talent, then she'd straighten the matter out with him later. Sitting upon the broken stone, beneath the evergreen tree with the rustling night breezes tugging at them, Ryes and Maren were unaware of the world around them, concentrating upon his struggle within. Unexpectedly, Ryes was pulled away from Maren and her contact shattered as the pain of a blow across her face struck home. She gasped as the world around her again registered upon her reeling senses. She opened her eyes to see a hulking shape, which Shaysa's light revealed as Sabin, holding her, with a silent snarl upon his lips.

"What've you done to Maren?" he demanded gruffly, shaking her in anger. He'd felt Maren's pain, anguish and anger with Ryes as he reached out to them from within. Numbly, she tried to break free of his grip, but found she was as weak as a puppet on a string. She finally managed to find her voice.

"Sabin let me go, or we could lose him for good!" The note of desperation in her voice caused him to pause a moment, looking into her eyes. She tried to reason with him, again. "Please. Maren wanted me to find his Talent. I can't leave him when he needs me the most!" His face was unreadable. "He could go mad if I'm not there to help him, and you know it!" Ryes finally shouted at him.

"Let her go." A voice grated out from behind them. Ryes couldn't see who it was from the way he was holding her, but there was little doubt in her mind that Garth had arrived on the scene. Sabin quickly released her. She half stumbled, recovering her balance, then turned quickly back to Maren, sitting down beside him. Putting aside her fears for the things happening in the world around her, she plunged willingly into that world which was the inner reality. As if struggling against a swift current, Ryes fought to reach Maren, hoping she wasn't too late and irreparable damage already done. Suddenly, she was almost overwhelmed by the surge of contact. Maren had won, but his anger toward her was fierce.

"Why did you leave me all alone when you knew I needed you?" he sent hotly, his mental voice quite loud and clear.

"Maren, I didn't do it on purpose. Sabin grabbed me. He… he thought I was trying to hurt you, somehow," Ryes thought back to him, apologetically. Maren, not listening, lashed out at her in anger. Ryes, unprepared for the inner attack, felt an instant of intense, hot pain, then shock as the slender link was shattered. She came to herself with the world around her spinning out of control. She threw out her arms helplessly, trying to find an anchor. She was suddenly enveloped by a pair of strong arms.

Maren, realizing what Ryes meant as he released his flood of anger at her, felt the backlash of that blast, knowing he'd hurt her. Guilt and regret tugged at him as he consciously tried to emerge into the real world, again. He opened his eyes to see Ryes falling off the stone, her arms reaching for support. He quickly wrapped his arms around her, pulling her back up next to him. Looking across the small clearing, he saw Sabin and Garth facing each other defiantly with Torr's lanky form standing between them. Shadd and Ardis just arrived, looking surprised at this middle of the night contest.

"Out of the way, Torr," Garth growled darkly, his eyes never leaving Sabin's shadowy form. "It's time I put him in his place."

"The only one to be put in his place will be you, Garth." The menace in Sabin's voice caused a shiver to travel up Maren's spine.

He realized they both truly meant it! For the first time in their lives, they were going to fight a challenge against each other!

Torr realized they were serious - dead serious. He stood steadfastly between them, feeling a moment of indecision. Should he stop them, or let them have what they wanted and get things patched up between them, later? Ardis looked to Shadd, wondering how to break it up?

"It's pointless and you both know it!" Maren shouted out. Ryes stirred in his arms, focusing in on what was happening. She pulled away from him and stood upon unsteady feet.

"Stop it, both of you!" Ardis shouted, a panic starting to blossom in her heart.

"Don't let them fight, Torr, please?" Shadd pleaded, tears now in her eyes.

"Garth! Sabin! There must be an end to this! You two need each other, too much," Ryes pleaded as she came toward them. They both looked at her with hostility in their eyes. They didn't want to let go of their anger. She stepped up next to Torr, turning her head to look at each of them, in turn. She had faced off Doran and won. She had no illusions about winning here!

"You both think you're strong and brave, but you're just stubborn and unforgiving, and acting like a pair of childish cubs," she stated, harshly. "I'll issue THIS CHALLENGE!" She held out a hand to each of them. "I'll set the arena and each of you must prove who's truly the best."

"What do you mean?" Garth demanded.

"A true battle of the wills," she answered with a note of defiance, looking only into Torr's shocked eyes. He stood rooted, barely daring to breathe, seeing something deadly in Ryes' eyes. "Are you both brave enough to face ME?" For a moment there was silence in the small clearing, with only the night breezes moving through the trees around them. Finally, Garth reluctantly stepped forward and reached out his hand to clasp one of hers. Stubbornly, Sabin came forward and took her other hand.

"Now, prove this fighting is necessary to me," Ryes stated quietly, as she reached from within herself toward the both of them, unleashing her power and Talents, fully.

Other Worlds

Garth felt an unexpected shock at her contact, which was so very different from what it had been yesterday afternoon. He suddenly found himself standing alone upon a course, dark rocky ground. There was a sulfurous stench in the air and great amounts of heat rising from numerous, jagged fissures, which ran a random course across the darkened landscape. Nearby was a huge crater with an orange-red and yellow, acrid-smelling pool of molten rock, bubbling restlessly. He stood in shock for several long moments, trying to figure out how he got to this terrifying place.

He surveyed the land about him in utter disbelief. A spasm of coughing shook him and his eyes started tearing from the potent fumes, as they drifted toward him. He finally made out a figure on the opposite side of the great crater. Not knowing what else to do, he began to circle the edge of the crater, trying to avoid some of the denser spouts of foul vapors. Maybe that other person would know where he was? He quickly learned to watch where he put his feet, instead of watching the landscape around him. In some spots the ground beneath was a thin crust and the hot, molten rock seeped up to burn him through his boots. When he judged he'd come about half the distance, he looked up to get his bearings and saw it was Sabin making his way carefully toward him.

"Where, by the north wind, are we?" Sabin demanded, as he approached Garth looking scared.

"I could use a blast from the north wind right now," he returned, cracking a dry smile. "I guess with all this heat, our anger with each other cooled off?" He clasped Sabin on the shoulder. Sabin smiled in return and nodded his head, as he again surveyed the land about them, desperate for a way out. He was sweating profusely now.

"Now what?" he asked, his eyes meeting Garth's with his stark fear showing. As he spoke, the bubbling in the great crater gained in pitch and before their astonished eyes, something began to rise up from within it. A long, tapered, tooth-filled snout appeared, causing them to step backward in surprise. As the reptilian-like creature began to emerge from the molten pool, they backed away from it slowly, hoping the red, pulsing eyes would miss their cautious movements, as they turned to retreat. It appeared at least twice as large as a windracer and small movements in other pools momentarily distracted him as he noted small, other animals running into pools of the rock to hide from it, or dive down in under the molten rocks to escape.

Garth stumbled as he looked back again and almost fell into a large fissure, which opened up next to him. Sabin grabbed his arm to help support him, when they heard the scrabbling of the creature's claws, as it tried to gain purchase on the crater's lip. Not sparing another backward glance, they picked their way quickly across the treacherous ground toward some broken hills, which lay ahead of them.

The chase was a long, drawn-out nightmare. They could barely keep ahead of the monster. Their legs were tiring and they were covered with burns and cuts, as they tripped and stumbled across the broken rock in their haste. They could hear the scraping sound of its claws and the breaking of the crust-like ground under its weight. It was the only thing which slowed it down! There was the occasional blast of intense heat, which reeked of sulfur, which was the creature's fetid breath. Great globs of molten rock dripped from its hide, and even with its great size and fragile ground it tread, it was gaining on them. Their hearts pounded within their chests in utter terror.

Finally, they reached the base of the range of hills and hastily began to ascend them. Sabin, surprisingly agile for his stocky build, climbed quickly and skillfully. He looked down to see Garth below him, picking his handholds more carefully and below Garth, the great, reptile-like monster arrived and began to reach up toward him.

"Look out!" Sabin bellowed, over the creature's horrid wailing. Garth half-turned to look down and lost his balance. He slipped downward several feet before he could even move to help. He now hung just out of its reach, as Sabin eased himself down.

"Grab my hand!" Sabin yelled as he reached toward him. Garth nodded and reached upwards. Just as their hands solidly clasped, the small knob of rock Garth was hanging onto with his other hand broke. A great, lava-filled fissure opened below his feet, and the sudden jolt of Garth's full weight caused Sabin's footing to give way, spilling them both into the fissure...

Expecting a pain-filled death, Garth was shocked when he landed in cold, deep water. His astonishment almost caused him to swallow a lungful of the water. He felt Sabin's hand still clasped his own, as he opened his eyes on a watery world. Then, he recalled that Sabin couldn't even swim! Ryes had taught him, at least. Seeing the light overhead, Garth began to swim toward it, pulling his friend along, hoping it wasn't just the sun's light being reflected off of white sands, which sometimes lined the bottom of deep, clear streams.

Just as his head broke the surface and he inhaled a lungful of sweet-scented air, he felt Sabin's grip relax. In panic, Garth pulled him to the surface and held him, as well as he could, as Sabin was helpless, wracked with a chocking cough for several long moments.

"Where are we?" he questioned hoarsely, at last.

"I wish I knew," Garth returned in a low voice, as he looked around them. There was water as far as he could see, in all directions. There were plants with profuse blooms, floating upon the water, which apparently put out the sweet scent they smelled, but nothing else was to be seen.

"At least it's cooler here," Garth commented at last. Sabin grunted.

"You can't keep both of us on top of the water, forever," he pointed out. He knew it, too. He was fast tiring, already.

"Let's see how stable those water plants are," he suggested as he began to swim toward a promising mass of them, pulling Sabin along with him. Reaching a good-sized clump, he knew a moment's indecision as he realized he'd have to let go of his friend to test the plants. Sabin, realizing this too, reached out and pulled one of the broad-leafed plants over to him.

"It'd take a lot of work to make any kind of raft from these," he stated with distaste, as he shoved the plant he held underwater, noting the tiny bladders beneath, which held the air.

"Do we truly have a choice?" Garth returned with an edge of exhaustion evident in his voice. Sabin was concerned for his friend. He didn't waste the energy to reply, he simply began gathering all the plants he could reach, and tried to weave their vines together as well as he could.

"What do you need, Starman?" a reedy voice piped up, immediately next to them, startling them both. They turned to see a strange face bobbing in the water beside them. It had a gray-blue skin with white around the eyes and mouth. The nose was flat and narrow, it had large, round, blue eyes which sparkled in apparent merriment and the mouth was blue and thin-lipped. As the creature smiled, it showed off its sharply-pointed teeth.

"Have the Starmen truly returned to bring us presents?" Another spoke up from their other side. This one seemed more delicate and might probably be female, but the total lack of hair unnerved Garth. Neither one had any visible hair, only some kind of bony fin atop their heads.

"My friend cannot swim," he told the first comer. "Is there a place I can safely put him?" They blinked in surprise and then giggled in shrill voices.

"Yes, there are dense places of air-plants nearby." He paused a moment, blinking at them. "What kind of present will you give for us to take you there?" he asked. Sabin growled low, under his breath. Garth tightened his arm around him and thought a moment.

"There's something I can give you, but not until we get to this place you spoke of, first," he answered with quiet determination, even as his strength was giving out.

Suddenly, Sabin's weight was lifted from his arms and a pair of strong, skilled arms supported him. They traveled quickly, as if travelling through the water were as easy for them, as striding through a broad field was for him. Garth was surprised to discover the female supported him. There was such strength in her arms that he felt he could've never bested them, if they'd been hostile - even without Sabin to worry about. They were shortly deposited upon a floating mat of dried, dead grasses with shoots of fresh, green grass growing through the old debris.

Garth lay panting for a moment on the strange, bobbing isle. Then, he unsteadily rolled over and sat up to survey his surroundings. His sudden movement didn't affect the isle's own movement, which reassured him a little. Sabin lay next to him and looked a sorry sight with his body hair singed and blackened along his arms and back and tatters of the water plants tangled in his tunic. By the look on his face, the drenching hadn't improved his temper at all.

"A present, as you promised," the high pitched voice pleaded from the water, at the edge of the grassy isle. Garth chuckled softly, nodding his head.

"A small present to pay for two lives, but it's all I have to give," he said as he extended his beltknife, hilt first, to the aqua dweller. He noted, for the first time, that they were wearing ornaments and some colorful water plants, which might serve them as clothing. The male's eyes blinked in surprise as he examined the knife. The blue gems set in the hilt fascinated him and a small pang passed through Garth, as he recalled it was the mate to the one he'd given Ryes. He could make another, but it wouldn't be the same.

"Garth, not your beltknife!" Sabin protested hoarsely. He watched him spend the whole winter season fashioning the hilts for

the two exceptional blades, Old Aric had forged at his request. He
knew it meant a great deal to Garth to give the daintier blade to Ryes
and now he was giving up his in payment for saving their lives!

"It is most beautiful," the water dweller breathed, accepting it,
"I will treasure it always." He and the female sank beneath the water,
leaving them to their fatigue.

"It's worth the price, believe me," he told Sabin, after the
aqua people disappeared. He turned and smiled to his blood-brother,
recalling they'd been about to fight each other only a short time ago.

"You look a sight! I can well imagine I do, too," Sabin sat up
in disgust. He started pulling the plants off, noting the scorched areas
on his body, for the first time. Garth saw he was badly burned in a
few places too, and his boots were blackened. What was that place?
And how had they escaped it to come to this one? They cleaned up as
quickly as they could, noting the water here was undrinkable, being
far too bitter and salty. They wondered how the water people
managed? They weren't hungry yet, so they lay down to finish drying
out.

"I'm sorry that I ever thought you were trying to challenge
me, too," Garth admitted ashamed now of his earlier actions and
mood.

"I'm sorry too. It was like I couldn't help myself, either.
Some part of me wanted to take a chunk out of Korman, and when
you defeated him, I found I was still all worked up. It was like I
wanted to provoke you to help ease those feelings," Sabin admitted,
feeling ashamed, too.

"I think, if it had been you taking on Korman, I would've been
the same," he replied after a few moments of thought. "We're that
close, after all." They both chuckled at this, knowing its truth.

"And poor Maren and Torr tried to get between," Sabin added
and they both laughed some more. "Let's take advantage of this
moment of calm, at least and get some rest."

"No arguments here on that one," Garth agreed, smiling now.

The bright, yellow sun overhead in a blue, cloudless sky and
the gentle bobbing of the isle beneath them, and the sweet smell of
the plants beneath them soon lulled both Garth and Sabin into a light
sleep. It seemed only a moment later when Garth jerked wide awake.
A wind had picked up and there was a bank of dark, storm clouds low
to the horizon, but what had awakened him was a high-pitched,
trilling noise coming low, over the water. He got up on his knees,
looking for the source of the sound, unable to see anything except the

rolling swells and bobbing clumps of plants. He didn't trust the
shifting movement of the raft enough to stand up, so couldn't get any
clear view around them.

"Starman!" a reedy voice sounded behind him. Garth turned
to see the male water dweller bobbing beside their grass isle. "An
okanta hunt is up and we fear the creature comes this way. There is
no time to take you to another safe place, so hang onto the air plants
and we will sing a prayer to Moire of the Deep for your safety." The
hairless, green-blue head vanished beneath the rolling water before
Garth could do little more than draw a breath to ask what an okanta
was. The reedy raft bobbed violently, throwing him down next to a
groggy, surprised Sabin.

"What's happening?" he asked through half a mouthful of
reeds.

"Some kind of hunt comes this way," Garth yelled over the
high-pitched noise. "Hang on and pray!" Sabin buried a hand within
the plants seeking as solid a purchase as possible giving him a nod in
reply.

The wild waves bobbed the small isle higher and lower, the
pitching turning Sabin's complexion green. He rolled away from his
friend and began to heave up what little remained in his stomach.
Garth clamped his own jaws shut and looked over the waves to see a
huge, dark shape break the water nearby. It was gigantic, as big as
one of their houses back in Matlowe. It came up out of the water, and
then dived again with tremendous energy, right in front of their isle.
Garth grabbed for Sabin as the whole isle pitched forward into the
water, following the behemoth down. Water flooded his senses; he
was confused and couldn't find his way back to the surface. Sabin
struggled within his grasp. He knew this was his last moment as his
lungs hungered for air. He exhaled the last of his breath, then...

They found themselves standing in a small corridor. There
were blazing panels of bright light overhead, set into the ceiling. The
beige walls of the corridor were inset with silver rails, which ran their
lengths. The floor was a sturdy-looking metal grating, with darkness
below. The air was sweet, yet seemed stale, but was the perfect
temperature and humidity. And they were both fully dry and their
clothing was clean with everything in place again. Garth was happy
as he put his palm over the pommel of his beltknife.

"Don't just stand there," a voice growled from behind them,
"either get to your stations, or to your cabin." They whirled to see an
older man in a rumpled, but clean uniform with gold braid upon the
sleeves.

"We don't know where we're supposed to be," Garth stated truthfully, bowing his head slightly in acknowledgment of the man's age and apparent rank. He noted with surprise that he and Sabin had no evidence of burns, nor scrapes on either of them.

"Leal!" the officer bellowed. An adolescent cub appeared at his side, coming up from behind him. "Take these passengers to the lounge and tell them to stay put!" Leal saluted with his palm open across his chest and a more formal bow than Garth used, then turned toward his charges and gestured for them to follow him up the long corridor; a mischievous grin upon his face.

"First trip away from home?" he asked Garth, still grinning as he led them on, his quick eyes noting every detail of their dress. "What planet are you from?"

"Yes, it is, and we're from Tayna," he replied, carefully.

"A REAL pair of Foresters? On this ship?" Leal whistled his awe. "I thought you sensitives couldn't stand much contact with normal people?" he asked quickly, as he led them through a pair of heavy, sealing doors and finally into a spacious room with several people sitting, or wandering around, nervously.

"We have kept to ourselves," Sabin responded with an emphasis upon the last word. Leal nodded cheerfully then indicated the room before them.

"Of course, Sirs. We hope to be through the danger zone soon. Just make yourselves comfortable and the Captain says everything's on his credit during the crisis." He looked anxious to be off on his duties, so Garth nodded his dismissal. But, he turned back to them, before the door.

"Maybe, when everything's calm, you can tell me some stories about Tayna?" There was a wistfulness about his young smile. "I've always wanted to see it." Sabin nodded his head and smiled, his eyes catching Garth's with an amused twinkle playing in their orange-gold depths. Leal's grin brightened and his eyes shone as he bowed formally to them, then turned and left.

They turned again to look at the room before them. There was a very plush, colorful carpeting upon the floor and bright, colored chairs grouped around small tables on their left side and before them. To their right was a long sideboard with taller chairs before it, and beyond it was a huge picture of the stars at night. Most everyone's attention was focused upon that great picture, as if they were trying to study it for finer details. Garth turned to Sabin to ask what he thought they should do now, when another young man in a uniform came up and offered to show them to a table. Sabin nodded an affirmative and they were led to a table near to the star picture, but away from the other passengers.

"Can I get you something to drink, or eat, Sirs?" he asked politely. Garth looked to Sabin, feeling rough and out of place.

"A mug of tea," Sabin informed the young man with a quiet air of authority.

"I chose the same," Garth agreed, as he turned toward him for his order. A small, surprised grin flitted across his face, as he bowed to them and left. Sabin leaned closer to Garth, a dark scowl upon his face.

"What kind of test is this? What's Ryes up to?" he demanded in a low growl, recalling this was all an illusion she was controlling.

"I don't know," Garth admitted. "I had the impression, as we were brought here, that she wanted to show us something." He gestured, encompassing the room around them, "What do you see?" Sabin shrugged in response, then sat back and began to study those about them. They were dressed in fragile, frilly clothes which were in a riot of colors and styles, as if birds in mating season, on display. Their hair styles were just as varied and looked ridiculous. And their ears were adorned with jewelry and the fur died and styled with shapes trimmed upon them.

"What truly is a Forester?" he asked quietly, as an afterthought. Garth shrugged.

"Maybe someone who lives in a forest, but who has a further reach?" There was a note of doubt in his reply. Sabin understood it. He didn't understand what they were doing here, and that uncertainty was unsettling. Were these people real, or had they been so at one time? And where did all this come from to begin with, he wondered?

"Ryes already showed us that our fighting was pointless. We've been too close, too long, to ever mean each other harm," Sabin began hesitantly, "and that there are things in the universe which should never be faced alone. What else is there? Where are we?" He held Garth's eyes with a look of quiet entreaty, hoping for an answer which would beat back the helplessness which his uncertainty raised within him. Garth smiled.

"I'm still sorry for ever letting the blood fever come between us," he told him, sincerely. Sabin smiled in return.

"I'm sorry for ever letting it get to me, too," he admitted. As Garth began to respond, the young man returned with a silver tray bearing two steaming ceramic mugs. He set them before them with quiet efficiency and placed three containers on the table between them, as well as a plate of flattened sweetcakes.

"If there's anything else you need Sirs, just let me know," he offered politely as he gave a small bow, then turned and left them alone, again. Garth gratefully inhaled the spicy aroma of the tea, as Sabin curiously investigated the contents of the containers.

"Two are sweeteners and the third a cream," he announced.

Garth carefully sipped the tea and grimaced.

"It needs it, it's bitter," he stated with distaste.

His head came up suddenly as he noticed several of the people in the room got up to stand before the star picture. There was a great deal of tension about them. He saw, for the first time, that there were colored lights moving differently from the star-filled backdrop. They were the focus of attention. As Garth and Sabin watched, another green one flared yellow, then was gone. At this, a gasp went up from more than one throat.

"What does it mean?" Sabin questioned low, under his breath. Garth shook his head in bewilderment, his gaze fixed upon the star picture too, trying to fathom its meaning.

"They'll get us!" a woman sobbed out hysterically, pointing to a small cluster of blue lights stationed away from the actions of the red and green ones. "There's no one between us and them!" An older man next to her caught her up in his arms and held her against his chest to quiet her sobs; a stricken look in his eyes as he tried to reassure her. Other faces about the room held an ashen pallor now.

"We're armed and fast," the young server said loudly into the stillness of the room. There was a look of youthful determination and defiance in his face, which reminded Garth of Maren.

"Attention crew and passengers of the Western Star, please take all necessary precautions to secure yourselves. We will be pulling power away from environmental support, at need, with our present situation. This will be your only warning," a voice spoke loudly from the ceiling, in a commanding tone. Sabin looked surprised as the lights overhead turned from a soft white to a brilliant red - flashing for a few seconds - then settling into a steady, red light. There was a strange sense of motion, as if the room about them had fallen away from them for a few moments. It left them both with queasy stomachs, which took them a moment to control. Most of the people scrambled for chairs when the red light flashed. Now Garth felt, rather than heard, a strange, steady throb beneath them.

His eyes sought his friend's in panic. He saw Sabin's own
terror clearly, so reached out and gripped his hand in sympathy.
Garth forced a smile onto his own face, to reassure him. The other
people in the room seemed relieved by the red lights, motion and
throbbing noise, so it couldn't be as bad as it seemed. His eyes
returned to the picture and he saw that a pair of the blue lights were
moving slowly away from the frenzied activity of the red and green
ones.

"We must be running for safety," Garth commented quietly, a
background buzzing of low voices had started up again. "We must be
one of the blue lights moving off."

"But, it goes so slowly," Sabin returned. He nodded his
agreement as he released his hand. The red and green lights moved
much more swiftly!

"Sirs..." a voice interrupted their quiet contemplations. It
belonged to Leal, who now stood next to their table. "The captain has
extended an invitation for you to join him on the bridge." Garth
opened his mouth to politely refuse, but Sabin was already standing.
He looked at him in puzzlement, as he grinned broadly.

"If you want questions answered, or looking done, it'd be
better to go about it directly. Sitting here..." he gestured to the room
before them, "can gain us little." Garth nodded agreement then rose
to his feet. Sabin gestured for Leal to lead them onward. Leal
nodded his head, smiling tightly. There was a tautness to his stance,
which gave Garth a moment's pause, but he followed Sabin, as a
twinge of concern tugged at his heart. Once out in the corridor and
alone, Leal turned to face them.

"The captain had more in mind than a simple tour, Sirs," he
informed them, a look of panic showing in his eyes. "Is one of you
gifted with a `Talent,' as the old ones say?" Sabin and Garth looked
to each other a moment. Garth felt doubts rising within him.

"I am, but I've had no real training," Sabin volunteered. Leal
relaxed perceptively and grinned cheerfully, again.

"Great! Our Communications Officer's ill and his second
suffered an accident when the emergency began. Some panicky
passengers accosted him in a corridor. We need instructions from the
military command vessel to know where it's safe to retreat. The
equipment should be able to do most of the work for you, so your lack
of training won't be an issue." Sabin smiled and warmed to Leal at
the display of his youthful enthusiasm. He didn't turn to face Garth,
yet. He knew that he'd disapprove of his volunteering. Instead, he
nodded and motioned Leal to lead them onward. Leal turned with
relief and quickly led them through the many, long passages of the

luxury, cruise starship. They entered a bustling control room and were immediately challenged by the First Officer.

"Sir," Leal stated with a bow, "these are the passengers the Captain wanted." He indicated Sabin and Garth behind him.

"The `Specialists'?" There was open doubt in his eyes. "Good. Which of you gentlemen is willing to assist with Communications?" Sabin stepped forward with a nod of his head. The First beckoned him to a chair, set before a confusing board full of lights.

"Have you ever worked a station like this before?" he asked, as he began to change the pattern of the lights with the touch of his fingers upon their surfaces.

"No, I haven't," he admitted, sitting back to let him do his work.

"It's already set up. Just don the headset and contact The Challenger, the fleet command ship, and relay any information they're willing for us to have." He paused as Sabin frowned at the headset he placed in his hands. "It's really quite simple, it only amplifies and directs your mind's natural, telepathic abilities. It's completely safe, I assure you."

Sabin turned, looked up at Garth for a moment as if to say something, then with a shrug, placed the unit upon his head, as he saw others in the room wearing theirs. He closed his eyes and for a moment felt nothing, and then suddenly there was a feeling of exploding forth - of being thrown out far from himself - across the vastness of the void enfolding them. Yet, he was still aware of his body, far behind. The panic which had been released at first, became the wonder which filled him now, as he reached forth and brushed another mind.

"Challenger here. What do you need?" the mind responded.

"A safe lane of retreat. We're on a passenger ship in the way of trouble," Sabin replied in projecting his thought, as if he were talking with another person in the room with him. Usually, he could only do this if he was in direct, physical contact with another Talent, with both their Talents intentionally active!

"Ah, The Western Star, your course should correct to 326-3872 mark point two. Sorry we can't help more; we're a little busy right now. Good luck!" Then the contact was abruptly broken. The sudden cutoff hit Sabin like a blow. He drifted, reaching out blindly to reestablish contact and some anchorage, again. He shuddered as he did, finally, touch something. It was utterly cold, evil and totally

alien. Sabin quickly pulled back and suddenly found himself sitting in
the busy control room, facing the First, Leal and Garth.

"Well, what did they say?" There was a note of impatience in
the First Officer's voice. Sabin shook his head, and then carefully
removed the headset.

"They said `correct to 326-3872 mark point two'," he relayed,
feeling fully drained. "They also said good luck," he told the First's
retreating back. He sat a moment under Garth's concerned gaze,
trying to clear his senses from the reek of that last, cold, alien touch.
Garth clasped his shoulder soundly and winked at Sabin as he spoke,

"Some tour of the bridge, the price is a piece of your hide," he
teased Leal. Leal's grin vanished as he took his ribbing seriously.

"Sir! I apologize, but all our lives are at stake here!" He had
started to bow, when Garth caught his shoulder, with a hearty laugh
and hauled him back up.

"Young one, don't take all of life so seriously," he advised with
a broad grin. "But I'd like a quick look around, if it's all right."

"Of course, of course," Leal replied in relief, gesturing them to
follow. Sabin waved Garth on, still feeling fatigued.

"I'll see it, later. Just let me rest a while." A slight frown
alighted Garth's brow, but he followed Leal, knowing Sabin sometimes
had his moods and would reject any offer of sympathetic concern.

Leal went down the short, narrow corridor the First had
disappeared down earlier. Garth followed, going slowly, hearing
strange sounds ahead. The way this ship moved sometimes
overloaded his senses. Too many strange sounds, smells, ways of
moving and sights, and at times, he could almost swear he felt a light
breeze and other sounds, which were somehow familiar and
comforting in this mad place he was entrapped. Leal entered the
command compartment then stepped aside for Garth to see the room
before him. He stepped into the chamber and stopped in utter
amazement, his heart beating wildly as his senses drank in the sights
before him.

There was a narrow lip, about one and a half paces wide,
which ran the circumference of the room, a railing ran its length,
making it seem a little safer. Wide steps before them descended into
a pit-like center. Everywhere he looked was a confusion of lights and
motion. Back from the center was a small, raised platform. Upon it
was a crescent shaped console of a black light-absorbing material, and
a black, well-padded chair before it. The black was a dark

counterpoint to the screaming lights and colors of the rest of the room.

Standing up from the black chair was a slight, but commanding, older man. He was the calm, assured director who gave focus to the actions of the other people in this room. All heeded his quiet-seeming voice with great respect. Garth, who'd been on the verge of a panicked flight back to Sabin, was filled with awe, seeing the power this one man held. He held command over his people and the actions of this starship with a quiet determination and self-assurance. He didn't need to prove his physical prowess to hold his peoples' respect and attention; he used his mind, heart and wits.

Garth stood, watched and learned of all that his mind could drink in, but suddenly his eyesight was dimming and his ears weren't hearing as well. He strained to bring his senses back into focus, when he realized he felt the night breezes tugging at his unkempt locks. He looked down and saw another hand held one of his own. He looked up into the emerald-green eyes of the one woman he'd fight to keep, for always.

Sabin's eyes met Garth's over Ryes' head with a look which spoke volumes. They did understand each other, after all and would always be the closest of friends. Sabin was no longer jealous of Ryes' intrusion into their lives; she'd become a part of them all. The three stood silently for a few moments, and then Ryes slowly crumpled toward the ground. Garth caught her up in his arms and hugged her close to him. He gave Torr, Maren, Ardis and Shadd a smile as he turned toward the camp with his precious burden.

"What happened? What did she do to you?" Ardis demanded of Sabin, stepping forward; relieved he looked all right. They'd been so silent, for such a long time.

"She took us on three different journeys and taught us a few lessons," he told her. He shook his head. It was unbelievable the power she'd gained in such a short time!

"Are you all right?" Torr asked, as Maren and Shadd crowded closer, too.

"We're both fine," he replied with a chuckle. "And I hope to never get her that mad again!"

"She took her anger out on you?" Maren asked, not believing it'd be something Ryes would do.

"No," he denied, shaking his head in emphasis. "She showed us that OUR anger was pointless and how much we needed each other to survive. She never did anything more scary than put us into situations we couldn't ever have imagined, and left us alone to deal with them, and each other, through it all. She never once struck at us, nor turned her anger against us. What we faced was what we brought in with us. It's hard to describe, even though I still recall every detail, as if it actually happened."

"Well, middle of the night challenges are not what I crave," Torr stated, draping an arm over Shadd's shoulders, pulling her closer to his side. "Let's all get some sleep," he suggested. Sabin smiled and gave him a nod of his head at this.

"How do you feel, Maren?" he asked, suddenly recalling who started this whole thing.

"Exhausted," he told him. "It feels strange with all this pent-up energy loose within me, but I guess I'll get used to it."

"What do you mean?" Shadd asked, wondering.

"Our little Catalyst made another try at helping Maren find his Talent, but when I touched them, all I felt was Maren's anger towards her. I thought she was attacking you," he apologized.

"And I thought she just deserted me, when I needed her the most," he admitted. "I struck out at her, when she tried to reestablish contact. And after all that, she still managed to take you and Garth on that inner journey. No wonder she collapsed! I owe her a big apology."

"Will Ryes be all right?" Ardis asked as they turned towards camp.

"We'll see what she has to say in the morning," Sabin suggested, hoping it hadn't been too much in one night for her.

"Hey, you and Ryes owe us another day off from chores," Shadd teased Maren, grinning.

"It's not our fault that your digging spot collapsed in, so quickly," he returned. "All right, after we take care of Honey, we'll take care of breakfast," he said, giving in.

"Ah, breakfast in bed," Shadd sighed with pleasure, still grinning. She put her arm around Torr's waist as they all turned back to their own campsite.

New Skills

They arrived with the dawn's light, making little noise that would be noted by the sleepy, rising villagers. Taroom and his wife Aylita were in the Village Square with their two children, Hara and Tarro, his sister Chel and her young cub Amarr. They were waiting for the Village Elders to emerge from their homes to greet them. They had all their possessions in a cart pulled by a pair of sturdy windracers. They were tired from their long journey and hopeful that this village could prove to be a good new home to live in, after their weeks on a long road. Even the windracers appeared exhausted.

"Hello and Good Morning," greeted Gann, who had gotten up early and was headed to his parents' home. They'd had a very good hunt yesterday and he'd wanted to share out most of what he'd caught with his family and friends in Matlowe proper. Taroom picked up his head at this greeting and smiled to hear so friendly a voice, so early in the morning. He quickly stood up from the stone bench.

"Good Morning to you, too," he returned, giving him a nod. "Are any of your Elders up yet? We wish to ask for permission to live in Matlowe Village," he requested right away, hoping for help. Gann chuckled.

"The only one I know of who would be up this early in the morning is Rowan. But he lives over by the Yuri. Let me see if anyone else is up yet," he offered. Then he paused, feeling the heavy thump of his hunting bag. He pulled it off his shoulder and opened it up to take out a pair of fat birds from off the top. He offered them to the stranger.

"I was out hunting yesterday. Here, take these and we'll find a way for you to cook them and have a good breakfast, at least," he said. There was shocked delight on the faces of all the travelers at this gift. The man appeared speechless, but grateful.

"Thank you, so very much!" the one woman spoke up, stepping up to take the offered food. "My name is Aylita and my husband is Taroom. Our children are Tarro and Hara and with us is my husband's sister, Chel and her and her son Amarr," she said, introducing them all, with a happy smile.

"I am Gann, one of our village hunters. I'll be right back, as soon as I can find an Elder for you," he promised as he closed his bag and slung it back on his shoulder. He stepped away, thinking he should find anyone but Metta. Maybe Sonta was up and could speak on his behalf? He headed for his home right away.

"I have skills in carpentry," Taroom offered, as Sonta nodded after hearing their story. Rebin, who had heard their whole story, nodded her head in answer, too.

The family had barely surviving a fire that destroyed their home and several others in Riverward. The disaster had taken a heavy toll on the whole town, so they packed up what they managed to salvage and headed off to find a new home. They were not just escaping the sorrow of the family members and friends they had lost, but also the horrible feeling of depression which now hung over their town. Having just had the messenger from Matlowe Village earlier coming through, asking questions and verifying the names on a list of cubs who had been murdered; it reminded them there were other places in the world to live. And if they caught and executed a child killer here, it might be a good place to settle and call home.

"We could help you build a new home, if you truly wish to live here," Sonta finally said, having come to his own decision about this family already. He would settle it later with his father.

"Other than our gardens and the small animals we raise for food, we don't have much to offer," Rebin added, appearing worried, but was still smiling. Taroom laughed at this and gestured around them.

"I see plenty of work to keep me busy for years," he replied. "And I would appreciate help in building a new home for my family. May I use one of the older home spots? They look like they would be easy to tear down and if the foundations are good, they will be easy to build upon again."

A group of the villagers had gathered around to hear and to greet the newcomers to their new home. Then Gann and Rowan led a group of the hunters, coming up from near Yuri who greeted everyone, too. The new arrivals meshed in with the other villagers easily with hugs and greetings exchanged freely.

"Actually, I was thinking it would be better to move you in temporarily near me," Rowan offered, as he stepped up. "That'll give you and the others time to build your new home here in Matlowe well and in no great hurry." Both Sonta and Rebin voiced their immediate agreement with this offered choice. Taroom smiled and nodded, not sure whether it was a good choice, or not. The friendly hunter was here again, all smiles too.

"I am Rowan, one of the Elders, but I live outside of the Village proper. You might find it more comfortable as a place to live while you're building your new home the way you truly want it built," he offered, introducing himself with an amused smile.

"We will accept your offer of shelter," Taroom replied, holding out his hand for Rowan. He nodded as he crossed his palm and gave him a smile. This got a small cheer from the watching villagers.

"My father only wanted you to be ready to be here in the Village Square tonight, after the sun sets, to tell us your tale of your last home. We get little direct news when the Caravaners are away," Sonta told him, appearing more relaxed now.

"We will be back here by sunset," Taroom promised with a nod. The hunters quickly helped the family gather their things once again, and lead them off toward the Yuri.

"It might be a quieter life than what you're used to living," Rowan said, as they walked together.

"We can use quieter," Aylita replied. Taroom's eyes were glued to the walls of the crumbling buildings they passed on the way. "The last few weeks have been filled with too much excitement."

"You can tell us your story after you've all had something to eat," Rowan assured her. "Did you even get a breakfast this morning?" he asked, concerned for the little ones.

"No. But Gahn gave us a two fat birds which we'll greatly enjoy tonight," Taroom told him, grinning and nodding towards Gann. He chuckled.

"It's Gann," he said. "We can have a breakfast-lunch when we get over to our homes and get you settled into one of the empty houses out there."

"Oh, that would be so much trouble," Chel stated, cutting in and looking worried. "We don't want you to bother over us."

"We skipped our own breakfasts, so it's fine and we don't mind sharing," Rowan assured them, pained to see the worry in their faces. They all looked very underfed. The children had clean faces and their clothes appeared clean, but with many patches. Their tiny faces and bodies proclaimed a thinness that Rowan found uncomfortable. Matlowe had a few of years of small harvests, but none of the children here resembled the three perched in their parents' arms. The windracers also appeared to have been well groomed and taken care of, but still they too looked underfed. The parents wore layers of clothing but their arms were thin, as if they had had too many months of thin rations. Taro and Hara both had wild sandy-colored hair that was kept short and deep golden-colored eyes. They would both grow up to be striking, he was sure.

"We have a very supportive community out here. Just lend a hand to help out a little and everything will be fine," Rowan assured them.

"We take care of each other," Minn added, grinning too.

After half an hour of walking through abandoned houses, they came through to a small wooded area. They were keeping to a well-worn path and after another half hour and a couple of bends emerged upon a wide meadow with a large grouping of homes in front of them. The newcomers stopped, dumbfounded.

"These homes are not falling apart!" Taroom declared, a huge grin blossoming across his face, at discovering this hidden wonder.

"This is where the Caravaners winter and where we live," Rowan assured them. "We all take good care of them." He gestured towards the right of the main grouping of the homes. "The ones on that side are up for grabs if you would like to look at them and pick one you like," he offered. "And you can see our fenced off meadow for your windracers to be pastured in and the shelter at that end is actually made for quite a lot of windracers, as you can see."

"There's a store of grains for them in the shelter too, as well as plenty of sweet grasses for them to eat," Kaytas added. "Ryes had plenty for Honey and they kept a store for the Caravaner windracers."

"This is too much," Taroom said, but his hesitation was met with plenty of encouragement and laughter and smiles by the others.

"Community! You can help with our little garden we have out here, or help show us how to better maintain our homes, or help with all the other small things we take care of each day. Being a part of things is all we ask," Gann stated, firm but with a smile lighting up his eyes. The doubts of the newcomers were melting from their faces as the adults all were nodding at this, looking relieved.

"Grandfather! Gann! Leann! Minn! Come on everyone! Breakfast is getting cold and I am starving!" Tennan shouted, appearing exasperated.

"I'm not keeping her waiting!" Kaytas laughed. "Come on!" They all headed quickly onward towards the warm, if insistent invite.

Taroom was counting his blessings as he approached the houses, enjoying the quiet, the soothing sound of the river, and the laughter around him. He was finally home!

The sun was heading down towards sunset. The torches around the perimeter of the Village Circle were already lit and cast a merry glow upon all those gathered. Half of the Elders were already sitting in their chairs on their platform. Most of the Matlowe villagers were gathered and sitting in their accustomed places. There was a buzz of low voices engaged in chatter of the morning's event. Then laughter and louder chatter filled the evening air as the party approached from the Yuri. Greetings and more laughter ensued as friends and families were temporarily reunited.

Rowan hugged and kissed his daughter and fussed over his grandchildren before he finally went over to take his place on the Elder's platform. Metta beckoned him closer for a more private conference.

"What do you really think of them?" he flat-out asked in a low voice, Rowan leaned closer.

"On the surface, so far, they seem an honest family. The only thing that bothered me is they wanted to borrow some things from the Caravaners homes to use for a while, but I discouraged that as the owners are very far away and cannot give, nor deny the request," he told them. "I gave them each blankets I'd made; I even had small ones for the children and all of them were in tears with this simple gift. I think they've been living through very hard times for a very long time." Metta frowned thoughtfully as he thought on this for a few moments.

"Where are they from?" he questioned.

"Riverward. They told us there had been a huge fire at the end of winter, just as the spring thaw had started. It destroyed a large tract of small homes and there'd been some suspicions about the origin of the blaze," he informed him, his mouth a tight line now. "It might have been started by one of the noble sons, who had been out carousing while drunk, as he was quickly hustled out of the town as soon as the investigation lead that way."

"Oh my," Farra said, as Rebin nodded her head, having heard it all earlier. She had already let the other elders know what had been told to her and Sonta this morning.

"Why would a woodworker leave a place that needed to be rebuilt?" Sina asked.

"Taroom said after losing his parents and many of his friends in the fire, he could not work there. It broke his heart, but he had to leave Riverward. Chel lost her husband and his family, so came with her brother. They said they had nothing left there. And after seeing the few possessions they brought out with them, it's nothing but pitiful remnants. Everything is singed, or partly burnt. They looked like they had tried to clean and repair their possessions, but everything still has the stink of a fire clinging to them. I believe them," Rowan assured them.

"So, do you think there will be others?" he pressed. Rowan nodded his head, as did Sonta.

"I don't know how many will travel toward us southwest of their town, but I'm sure with our runners confirming that list for Sabin, they have been reminded we exist. There will be more," Rowan replied.

"What will be do?" Sina asked, looking frightened. Metta nodded at this, and then smiled.

"We will meet them, determine if they are people we would want living among us, and if Rowan and our hunters don't object, we can temporarily settle them near the Yuri until we can all help the ones we allow to stay build new homes and become part of Matlowe," he finally stated, having come to that decision.

"It's a good plan," Rowan stated, in support of the measures. "We'll keep an eye on the newcomers and see if they do prove to be a good fit for Matlowe."

"Thank you, Elder Rowan," Sonta said, gripping his shoulder with a smile of relief alighting his face. "Don't trust too quickly. Not after that Heda monster."

"I won't," he promised. He realized he finally felt like he was fitting back into Matlowe life, too. He missed Ryes as she would be highly amused with this situation.

"Now let's see to this family and what they have to tell us," Metta added, ready to begin now.

"It was horrific! It was days of buildings burning; of lives lost and precious things gone up in smoke all around us. And more importantly, we all lost family and good friends in the great fire. The Elders finally established a camp for those who survived just outside the city wall. It took forever to get permission to go back and look through the ashes for what little we could salvage from our homes and shops," Taroom related in the Village Circle. "We had to prove who we were – even if most of the guards knew us. Each day! It was humiliating to be treated like homeless beggars in our own town."

"Why didn't you stay to help rebuild new homes for all of you?" Metta asked.

"The Elders decided to not build new homes where the old ones were burned down. They planned to put in a greensward there instead. They told us to build new homes outside the city walls. We did start building our homes. But during the night our tools were stolen and we had to pay to get 'new' ones the next morning. We got to where we slept with our tools with us each night. All of the survivors did. People would disappear in the middle of the night, sometimes there were screams, and they were never seen again. They did not patrol our new home area so criminals ran rampant. The Elders turned a deaf ear to our protests, as did the city patrol. We feared for our lives and the lives of our children," Aylita told them, taking her turn.

"It was so hard and so full of sorrow that we finally decided to take what little we had left and leave in the early morning. It broke my heart to leave the town where I was born and raised and where I tried to rescue my parents and friends, but it wasn't my home anymore," Taroom finished for them. Their sorrow, anger and loss were plain to the eyes of everyone around them. It moved the villagers deeply. Metta sighed. The burn scars were clearly seen on the arms and faces of all the adults and two of the children.

"You may stay and build new lives here, if you wish," Metta finally stated. "Rowan has said you've taken a good, sturdy home out near the Yuri. You have the choice of staying out by the Yuri, or rebuilding a new home here in the main village area. Your skills as a carpenter would be very welcome, here, indeed."

Taroom picked up his head and then gave Metta a nod. He took Aylita's hand, gently kissed her knuckles and then turned to look to the faces of all the gathered villagers around them. There were smiles and nods given to them by the others, encouraging them in their decision. He smiled as he turned back to the elders on their platform.

"We will stay. I'll check out the foundations of the fallen buildings. If they are still good, or can be repaired, we'll build our new home here," he replied. "We thank you for this chance. Everywhere we've found good hearts, but here where the old homes have fallen apart is where I need to be to work and earn our living."

"I know your skills are greatly needed here," Metta replied. "Welcome to Matlowe Village. We're a small village and do have our occasional issues, but we do try to work things out so everyone can live in peace." This last statement was met with a variety of cheers, laughter, jeers and astonishment by the villagers. Taroom strode forward and offered his hand to Metta with a big smile upon his face. Metta hesitated for a few heartbeats, then crossed his hand with his own, giving him a return smile, at last. He would have to speak to his little brother about any newcomers later tonight. He wanted no troubles starting up due to him, anymore.

"She's not responding and her skin's cool to the touch," Garth told Sabin in the morning. The worry in his eyes was plain to see. Sabin followed him over to their sleeping spot and knelt down beside her. Ryes' breathing was slow and regular, as if she still slept, but when he nudged her, or picked up her arm, there was no reaction. Her arm was limp.

"Let me try something," he offered. Garth gave him a nod of his head in agreement, so he closed his eyes, took her hand and reached out to her from within. After several long moments he opened his eyes and gently released her hand.

"Well?" Garth pressed, needing to know.

"She's too exhausted to break free of herself," he told him in a low voice. "Her power's there but it's more diffuse. Give her time to rest and keep her warm. She should be all right. She probably just overexerted herself last night," he advised.

"What's wrong?" Maren asked, joining them. He saw Ryes lying still, looking pale and unresponsive.

"She just needs some rest, considering all the work she put in last night," Sabin assured him with a sigh, frowning. He stood back up and stretched. "She was rougher on us than I thought we deserved," he commented, grinning.

"I still feel pretty beat up, too," Garth agreed with a chuckle. "Maren, what was this about some bet you and Ryes made with Shadd and Ardis?" he asked smiling, relieved she was only tired.

"The first team to dig a way into the bubblenut tree's building didn't have to do any camp chores for two days. They got lucky in their choice of spots," he said, looking unhappy with having to do everything by himself. He wasn't sure of Sabin's assessment of her condition and wanted to get a look at Ryes himself, before he'd feel better about things.

"Since she's too tired to even wake up this morning, I'll help you in her stead," Garth volunteered. He felt it was the least he could do for his lady, considering all she did for him yesterday.

"Thanks, Garth. I truly appreciate it," Maren replied, relieved. It wasn't beyond him, just that he knew they'd harass him about the time it'd take him to get everything done, by himself!

"No wonder the four of you were covered with dirt," Sabin chuckled out, with a shake of his head.

"We're hoping to find some smaller samples of the metal those beams are made of, to see if Old Aric could use it to forge some new beltknives for us," he explained. This got surprised expressions from both the older men, as they realized there was far more promise to their playfulness, than just wasting time.

"What an excellent idea!" Garth agreed. "You take care of Honey. I think Ryes was making some comment that she needed more room and wanted to build a bigger pen for her here, too, last night. So, we'll see if she's up for that later this morning. I'll get breakfast started, then let's go see this hole the ladies dug into your building, and if we can find usable pieces of that metal." Maren smiled as he saw Sabin gave him a nod of agreement. Things were back to as they should be now. If only Ryes were awake to see it, too.

"She's STILL asleep?" Maren asked Shadd, as he returned to camp from their dig site. Shadd had been making more torches and set aside her latest one to look up at Maren.

"She hasn't even twitched," she reported, concern etching her face. "Are you sure she's just tired? She should've been up by now!"

"You go ahead and take the others something for lunch. I'll watch over her for a while," he offered, seeing it upset her to see Ryes this way. She smiled as she got up and went to rummage for their trail cakes.

"We're going to have to go hunting tomorrow," she commented, seeing their stores were down.

"I'll say. There's only so many bubblenuts you can stomach in one day," he agreed with a laugh. Shadd laughed with him as she headed off toward the dig site. He put on some fresh water for tea and a smaller pot to make soup. Then, he went to Ryes' side and looked at her from within.

This wasn't just exhaustion; it was the aftereffects from his attack and straining her abilities to the limit with her healing Garth's wounds, then issuing her challenge to Garth and Sabin. Still a little nervous about testing his own, new skills so soon, he went back to the campfire and starting pulling out the ingredients he'd need for his soup. He went over to Ryes' backpack and other packs and rummaged until he found her gather pouch and other supplies. Carefully, he measured in the spices and added the other ingredients, which would help make a nutritious soup for her to drink, with one of the bones he saved from the last bounder they killed. Somehow in the process of creating this soup, he found the courage to set aside his inner fears so that he could deal with helping Ryes come back from the dark place he knew she was captive. He had to use his Talent and knew now he could do it.

As soon as the soup was ready, he took her mug and filled it, then went to her side. He set the mug down and lifted her up out of the blankets, settling her into his lap. He reached within himself, then out to her, tapping his Talent to try to restore her body to what she should normally be. After several long minutes, he felt her feeble movements, as she fought to awaken. He wasn't finished, so continued his work until he knew she felt "right" to him, once more. He opened his eyes to see her eyes open, looking up at him in curiosity.

"What happened?" she asked, having noted it was only the two of them in camp.

"How do you feel?" he returned in question. She grinned up at him and sighed.

"As weak as a newborn," she admitted. He placed her back atop her blankets, then handed her the mug of soup, as she sat up.

"I made this especially for you," he told her. "The others are out exploring our building and looking for treasures." She took the mug, her hands still unsteady, but the smile in her eyes was her old self.

"Darn, I thought the four of us would be first," she teased. "What time is it?" she asked, noting the sun was overhead. He gestured for her to drink, so she sipped it and was delightfully surprised. "This is excellent! So you've become an excellent cook and very Talented Healer, all in one day!" He gave her a shallow bow in response, a small grin upon his face at her compliments.

"It's past lunch and will soon be time for dinner," he admitted. He saw the shocked expression upon her face and it took everything he had to not laugh aloud. "You were closer to dying than I'll ever admit to anyone. Sabin thought you were only tired, but I knew better. It's a good thing you did awaken my Talent, or we would've lost you." She sighed as she knew he was speaking the truth and smiled for him.

"Thanks, Maren. I've no idea how to repay you..."

"You don't owe me anything!" he stated sternly. "I and the others here actually owe you so much more. Now, I want you to sit and drink your soup while I go try my hand at fishing. I think we all deserve something hot and fresh for dinner, and it's the quickest thing I can think of right now. I only hope my skills as a fisherman have improved enough by now."

"Do you want me to help?" she asked. "I should be up for fishing, at least."

"You can come along, but I don't think you'd want to feel them suffocating to death," he dared her. She grimaced at the reminder, but gave him a nod in agreement.

"I'll still need to find a way to distance myself from that again, so I might as well get in some practice," she said. He gave her a nod of his head in understanding, not envying her such a task, and then signed for her to finish her soup. She gulped it down as he fetched his fishing line and hooks, savoring the flavor. Then she dug into her backpack and found a special packet of oily herbs she liked to use to help attract the fish to the hook.

"What's that?" he queried, curious as she waved it at him.

"Usually works better than wigglers on a hook," she replied grinning, as she pulled on her breeches and tightened her laces. She grabbed her boots and fishing equipment, all ready. She still knew she wasn't fully recovered, but there was no way she could lie in bed the whole day! "Where's Honey?" she asked, seeing she was gone.

"Garth and I made her a larger pen, over by the lake. She's a lot happier there with plenty of room to run," he informed her. "Let's go see how she's doing and catch us a decent dinner." She laughed her agreement, following behind him. She'd been out of things; there was no doubt of that!

"Gosh, that smells great!" Ardis commented as they approached the campsite.

They were carrying most of the more interesting things they found inside the bubblenut tree building, leaving behind a pile of other items under some large rocks for tonight. But they had been sadly disappointed when the books they found crumbled to dust at the slightest touch. It wasn't fair that the one thing they needed most still eluded them! Garth felt that somewhere there had to be some knowledge preserved for their use to rebuild their world, once again. They only needed to find it.

"Hmmm, smells like Maren's honoring that bet we made," Shadd added with a light laugh. "Let's get washed up, first," she suggested. She realized they were covered with mud, dust and dirt from their hard day of opening the hole wider and exploring within that oddly canted building.

Ryes had been right; it hadn't needed more than a good airing out. Within had been lots of spaces of varying sizes which they thought had been rooms. There were sheets of hard material that made up many of the walls. It wasn't wood, nor any other substance they knew. But it seemed it was practically indestructible. Other kinds of the material seemed similar but were not as well made. They were brittle and broke easily – sometimes becoming a hazard with the sharp shards. But the shards were not hardy enough to make a usable blade, as they crumbled easily. Then there were lots of smaller objects, which looked useful and sometimes not. They collected many of them, which they brought back outside for further investigation.

"That's a good idea. I wouldn't want to try eating dinner like this," Sabin agreed as Garth chuckled, brushing uselessly at the dirt on the front of his tunic.

"Let's bring Honey back in, too. I'll feel better if she shelters with us at night. There are too many predators about after dark," Garth said. The group turned toward the lake in concert, diverting from their campsite. "And it might be easier to figure out this stuff, if some of the dirt's cleaned off it," Garth speculated, as they walked.

"When Ryes wakes up, she might be able to tell us what these things are, since she was mind-sharing with that ancient witch," Ardis added, then recalled they were trying not to talk about her, so as not to upset Garth any more than he already was. He sighed and nodded his head, the smile wiped off his face as the worry returned. "Sorry," she apologized to him. "I'm sure she's fine by now."

"I'm know Maren's watching over her. He feels responsible since it was his quest for his Talent which sparked things last night. He just couldn't apologize enough to me, today," he related with an almost smile upon his lips.

"Come on, let's hurry. That smells too delicious," Shadd pressed. It did them no good to speculate. If Ryes wasn't any better by now, then they'd have to decide a course of action. They reached the lake and got to work, the sun was almost setting by the time they finished washing. Honey was missing from her new pen, but Garth said he'd see if Maren had brought her back in, before he started looking for her. There were no signs of violence in the area, so they didn't think she had come to harm. And her pen door was closed and secured, so he didn't think she had let herself out. He had to have brought her back in, already. They gathered their things and hurried back to camp.

Seeking Answers

"About time," Maren teased, as he and Ryes were sitting near the fire talking. "We're waiting to eat with you and we're practically starving!"

"You're always eating," Torr returned with a laugh. Garth strode over to her quickly and picked Ryes up, hugging her to him in joy.

"You're all right, Sweet One! I was so worried about you," he declared, happiness filling his heart once more. She laughed as she looked into his honey-colored eyes.

"You can thank Maren. He brought me back when I was too lost to find my own way," she admitted. "And he makes the best soup you're ever tasted," she added with a chuckle.

"Is that your soup we smell, Maren?" Sabin asked, laughing to see his friends so happy, again. It'd been a small miracle.

"No. Ryes and I went fishing, and since there're so many useful plants growing around here, she stuffed them with wild grains and baked them, instead of just frying the fish. So, we all get a special treat for dinner tonight. Will you put her down so we can eat, Garth?" Maren demanded, smiling mischievously. Garth laughed as he put Ryes back on her feet.

"We've got some things we want you to look at later; that you might be able to tell us what they are," Ardis requested. "We've only started looking on the uppermost floor. There're so many rooms and so much stuff, but it's a pity the books turned to dust."

"They did?" Ryes was shocked and disappointed. How were they going to find out how their ancestors lived, if there were no books left to read? She had the borrowed memories of the sleepers, but there wasn't much which was truly practical. The sleepers had taken all the technological wonders around them as accepted everyday things. The ladies had been more concerned with their appearance, friends and various entertainments!

"Unknown items later! Let's eat!" Maren repeated impatiently, as he started passing out loaded plates. This got laughter from the others as they took their plates and sat down. There was still plenty of time to explore their findings later.

"Maren, when are they going to let me explore a little on my own?" Ryes protested with a pout. "There's nothing here to hurt us, now. Korman's well gone!" It was two days after Maren's rescuing her from the darkness and she was chafing at the harsh restrictions Garth had enforced upon her.

"There's still too many large predators roaming about, and what about me?" he asked with a yawn. "Do you think I like being left behind, too?" He lay back upon the sun-warmed stone, feeling sleepy after a good lunch. "Take a nap. Later we'll harass Garth until he gives in and lets us go out with them tomorrow." Ryes smiled at the thought of her and Maren changing Garth's mind. It'd be easier to learn how to fly!

"Ardis and Shadd get to help," she started, still protesting the restriction.

"But they're not carrying cubs, yet," he quipped back, he cracked open an eye to look at her, giving her a nod of his head. He appeared glad she was still sitting on her chosen spot.

She subsided with a sigh of resignation. She knew it wasn't that he didn't understand her urge to explore, but since things were more the way they used to be, it'd be better for all of them if they didn't push it, again. Garth and Sabin decided to explore a few more days, and then choose a direction to head off in what they felt was true. They needed to find a good place to settle before the summer could fully establish itself. So, they'd have plenty of time to set aside stores for the coming winter months. She knew they'd all miss the gentle winter clime of Matlowe soon enough. Maren had let Ryes walk a little away from camp before they had lunch; in hopes it'd mollify her a little. It seemed it wasn't enough.

Even after their short walk, there was an abundance of pent-up, restless energy stirring within Ryes. She wanted to do something more - not take a nap! Maren looked to have dropped off, but she knew all his senses were tuned in upon her movements. Finally, feeling trapped, she settled back against the warm rock wall behind her and closed her eyes in surrender, letting her thoughts drift.

She cast her mind back to that first, short vision she had of Hailys, before the flames and destruction descended upon it in her night visions. She tried to imagine what it'd been like. What did the people look like, before their faces registered their terror?   Who killed so many, so horribly? Couldn't something like Doran's shield barrier placed over the city have saved it? Why hadn't they thought to use something like it? All they had were the sad remnants of a great empire. Didn't Kahmarr care what happened to her outer worlds? Had they merely turned their backs upon Tayna, or were they busy trying to save what lives they could? All Ryes had were more questions and no answers... still.

Her thoughts turned to fathoming her still, largely unknown Talents. Was it the power from the stone which enabled her to stop those weapons as they flew through the air aimed at her, or was it something coming from within her? She hadn't tried to move anything since and knew she didn't have enough focus to attempt it right now. The restlessness within her craved something more. Ryes recalled that short incident where she thought she drifted back through time to the past, outside Doran's valley. Was it an aftereffect of using the stone's power, or something she could do at will? That old guardsman believed it was willed, but only those of Royal blood could wield it. So, how could she do it? She was sure she didn't have any royal blood! Or was her mother truly that close to the throne?

And that was the man her mother ran away from, before. He was really old; older than she could imagine Rowan's own grandfather looking if he'd still been alive. Still, he hadn't seemed bad to look upon, so there must've been other reasons she fled the marriage. At least she and Ronn found each other and some happiness, before their lives were cut off so suddenly. She took his sword when she vanished. Did she still feel something for him after all? Or was there some other reason she took it? And HOW did she do it from beyond the grave? That gave her a small chill up her back.

Time walking... How had she done it in the first place? How far back could she go? Did something like Hailys' terrible, violent destruction hinder it? Slowly, she recreated the memory of the shifting sensation she felt when she accidently projected herself back through time. She brought up all the aspects she experienced as the shifting occurred, then realized the wrenching sensation was real! She was feeling the same reeling surge of power unleashed within, once more. As she settled, she opened her eyes on a very different Hailys.

She sat upon a neatly-manicured, lush, green carpet of grass. Above her was a meticulously-shaped evergreen tree, which gave her cool shade. Behind her rose a gracefully-arched sandstone building with ornate stone carvings gracing its many stories of windows.

"You! Forester!" Ryes, startled, turned to see the irritated speaker. An older woman stood near her, holding a strange implement in one hand. Indignation was plainly written upon her face and in her stance. "If you people don't like our `artificial gardens,' then keep off of them!" Ryes blinked and wondered why her sitting on the grass aggravated this woman so much? This was a garden? Just grass, trees, flowers and bushes? It wouldn't feed anyone, except a bounder! She stood up hesitantly and started to move off in the direction she hoped the gardener came from.

"Ah, pardon me, but where am I?" Ryes asked politely, as she started to go around the woman. Her scowl deepened as she looked at her more closely, as if finding a new biting bug on her arm.

"This is Thesa Hall Library. There're directories at every major cross point," she informed her as she huffed off, muttering something about Foresters under her breath. Ryes stood a moment, looking up at the tall building again, as questions and ideas danced behind her green eyes. She didn't know what a "directory" was, but she'd definitely investigate the ruins of the Thesa Hall Library when she returned to her own time! Her initial fright was replaced with charged excitement. She was in a REAL CITY of her ancestors! A living city in the bloom of its old glory! Ryes was almost dancing as she rounded the front of the structure.

She stopped to gape in astonishment. No wide, packed dirt paths to tread upon here! There was a broad, smooth, stone-paved avenue which ran before the building she stood in front of. And, there were people, so many people... More than triple Matlowe's whole population, in just one glance! She didn't know where to go first. Somewhere here she had to find the answers to some of her questions!

Maren stirred uncomfortably, half awakening from a troubling dream. He listened for a moment while trying to decide to drift back to sleep, or get up and see if Ryes would mind seeing about trapping some fat birds to eat for dinner. There was the sound of the light winds stirring the leaves of the trees around them and of small animals stirring in the grasses, but nothing from Ryes. He opened his eyes and sat up, expecting to see her gone. He was surprised to see her leaning back against a piece of stone wall, looking as if she were sleeping. Something about the way she was breathing didn't look right and there was a strange feeling in the air; a tingling which tugged at his Talent in a strange way. He stood and went to her side.

"Ryes?" he questioned, taking her hand. There was no response. It was akin to when she overexerted herself, yet somehow different. He carried her back to the flat stone he just quit and lay her down, carefully. He then closed his eyes and reached within himself. Once he was centered, he reached out to his cousin from within, trying to figure out what had happened to her this time?

There was power here! It was free and coursing throughout her being. He searched for her within this confusing tide of energy and finally found a link, a lifeline which anchored her to herself. Where was she? He called out to her several times, but the only thing he felt was that she was too busy to answer him. This wasn't right! He quickly withdrew and opened his eyes. There was only one thing he could do. Go and get Garth and Sabin. Maybe between the two of them, they'd be able to bring her back? He feared for Ryes; that thread seemed too fragile. What if she lost her way? He tightened his belt, checked the small clearing for any lurking dangers, and then ran off, knowing where they were planning on working today. There had to be a way to save her!

"So, how long do you think Maren'll be able to keep her out of trouble?" Sabin asked Garth, as they took a break from their explorations. They'd just opened a ground level entry into their third building and were letting the noxious fumes disperse, before going any further. They were in no hurry today and the others were resting, catching their breath and drinking water from their skins. Everyone was covered in dirt already, again.

"We've probably reached her limit by now," he returned with a smile. "Frankly, I thought I'd have a fight on my hands with her this morning. She was really upset over my restricting her from riding Honey, but I don't think all that bouncing about would be good for the cubs." This got a chuckle out of his friend.

"So, what do you think?" Sabin asked, suddenly turning a little more serious.

"A few days to a week at the most," Garth sighed, knowing what he had actually asked. "If we find anything really promising, we'll stay a little longer. Otherwise, we have to find a place to hunker down for the winter and make sure we can provide for our new families. We're all going to be too busy by next spring." He paused a moment and smiled in an odd knowing way, "And I don't think you and Ardis have to wait, anymore," he observed, giving him a nod. Sabin was surprised, not having paid as much attention to this, as he realized he should!

"Are you sure?" he demanded, feeling totally unprepared.

"Ardis looks just like Ryes did that day. Have you even thought of where you're going to go? We'll take care of the hunting, so you two can concentrate upon more important things," he offered. Sabin suddenly grinned as he chuckled.

"How about the other side of our little lake? That way, if any real problems happen, we're not too far from each other," he suggested, thinking upon it.

"What kinds of problems are you expecting?" he returned with a curious look in his eyes. "If anything happens on our side, we'll handle it. I want you concentrating upon Ardis, and don't worry about us."

"With Ryes, I'm beginning to believe almost anything can and will happen," Sabin returned, meeting his eyes, daring him to refute him. Garth realized he did have a point.

"How about, if something happens that's out of our league, I'll send Maren around on Honey to see if you feel like lending a hand?" he countered in surrender, with a smile in his eyes. "Believe me; I don't think you'll be too compelled to help."

"What is it you need help with?" Torr asked, wiping off his hands on a cleaning rag, as he stepped over to join his cousin. Garth shook his head, noting the women were chatting about some plant they just discovered.

"Nothing. Sabin thinks he needs to be close by, in case we need his assistance with any problems Ryes might stir up. Ardis looks ready," he told him. Torr was surprised as he glanced over to look at her, and then turned back to the men.

"Oh, that's why her color's been off today? I thought she might be coming down with a spring cold, or something," he admitted, chagrined. Now he knew what to look for in Shadd. At least with his cousin and friends, he didn't need to worry about getting into any challenges. "So, where're you planning on going?" he asked Sabin.

"Other side of the lake. That place we originally camped, when we got here. I thought it'd be sheltered enough with those small stone houses. Looks like it might rain tomorrow, so it's a good spot."

"How about if we send Maren over on Honey now, to get things set up for you? Then, you and Ardis take a long, leisurely stroll around the lake, tonight?" Garth suggested. "So, if you're pinned down in one spot, because of heavy rains, you won't feel too cramped with having the rest of us practically at your elbow, to cheer you on." Sabin and Torr broke into hearty laughter at this, imagining the scene Garth painted for them.

"What's so funny?" Ardis demanded as she and Shadd looked up to see the men laughing merrily about something. It didn't look as if they were paying them any attention, but she still wondered if they weren't the butt of their humor?

"Ah, just something about Ryes and the cubs," Garth quickly returned. "She's hard enough to get settled down, now," he told them, catching Sabin and Torr's eyes. There were things they liked to discuss among themselves, and the women didn't need to know EVERYTHING! The others were smiling and nodding their heads in understanding. It's what he and Sabin were originally discussing, after a fashion.

"She wasn't too happy with you this morning," Ardis agreed. "But I'm sure once the cubs are born, she won't be as restless as she is now. They're bound to need lots of attention and care."

"I could see her going out to hunt and gather plants, if she only has one cub to cart about," Shadd commented, smiling. "You might have a time tying her down, then," she concurred, as they stepped over to join the men.

"She does have a point, cousin," Torr teased with a smile, gripping his shoulder in sympathy. Garth groaned as he rolled his eyes at this. It was true. If Ryes only had one cub, he'd have his hands full trying to keep track of her!

"When we were talking the other morning, Ryes said she thought it was too early to tell, but still thought it might be two," Ardis volunteered, hoping to ease Garth's mind. "With two it won't be quite as easy to go out for a day of hunting."

"I hope she's right," he commented. "Let's try that last building we opened up, yesterday. It should be aired out, by now. I want to get back and see what she's up to, and maybe get a little hunting in before dinner time," Garth suggested. This got smiles all around, as they each gathered up the interesting things they found so far, today. Their packs had been empty at the start, but were now bulging with their treasures.

"Garth! Torr!" A voice hailed them from further up the valley, between the fallen buildings where they were working. They looked and saw three figures standing atop their bubblenut tree building. Garth waved to them, wondering who they were. They disappeared, as they saw the signal. Sabin's smile turned to a scowl as he recognized the voice.

"Kovin," he breathed, unhappy with his presence. "Of all the times for him to show up! Ardis and I are heading back to camp, right now. I'll see you later," he said as he stepped close to her. "Let's go," he suggested in a low voice. She frowned, uncertain.

"What's the problem?" Ardis returned, wondering what had him so deeply upset, so suddenly. Kovin shouldn't have brought out such a deep reaction in him like this. He looked angry, on the instant.

"I'll tell you on the way," he promised. She threw a puzzled look to Shadd, but went willingly, at his urging.

"What's wrong?" Shadd asked Torr, stepping closer to the remaining men.

"Ardis' time has come," Garth told her. "And you know how Kovin was about her, the last few months we were in Matlowe."

"Ooooh," she agreed, seeing what he meant. "But she doesn't WANT anyone except Sabin. Kovin's just going to have to accept it. It's her right, as it was Ryes', to choose who fathers her cubs," she insisted, starting to look upset. "This stupid challenge thing is going to stop! I wouldn't care if Torr lost a challenge, I'd still mate with him, because he's the one I choose!" She latched onto Torr's arm, looking at the both of them, in all seriousness.

"Now I know why Ryes told Maren that she'd kill herself before she'd ever let anyone else get their hands on her. I feel the same way!" Both men were utterly shocked to hear this declaration out of Shadd. She was so quiet and calm most times, that such heartfelt determination as they now saw in her eyes, was almost impossible to comprehend.

"When did Ryes say that to Maren?" Garth asked, meeting his cousin's eyes, seeing his inner grappling with her devotion to him. No matter what their traditions held.

"When we heard you and Korman calling out your challenge. Maren begged her not to go; that we'd help her with her cubs, no matter what the outcome of the fight. That's when they had that shared Vision, too."

"What Vision?" he pressed, his heart pounding now, worried about her more than ever. Something inside was tugging at him and he didn't know what it was, or where it came from.

113

"Maren told us it was about when Ryes has the cubs. You're not there for some reason, and that's what was causing her the greater pain. She didn't tell you about it?" she asked, worried about it now.

"No," he admitted with a sigh, recalling he was barely rational after that challenge. Kovin, Teris and his younger sister, Mitt, were walking toward them, relief in their eyes. "You knew about this, Torr?" he asked him, needing answers, now.

"We didn't know how reliable it might be and thought she'd tell you about it long before now," he admitted. "I thought she would have shown that Vision to Sabin, at least."

"By the gods, this place is immense! Can you imagine what it must've been like when it was a city?" Teris panted out, as Mitt ran up and wrapped her arms around her brother, laughing merrily. Teris was barely able to walk and practically collapsed down upon a nearby piece of fallen stone wall as he sat. Everyone stepped closer with concern in their eyes. Mitt tugged on Garth's tunic to get his attention.

"It took us too many days, but we finally found you!" she declared, as Garth returned her hug. His heart was still heavy with what Shadd had voiced, and his impulse was to go find Ryes right away! Some inner instinct told him she might be in trouble and he needed to find her, now!

"What're you doing here?" Torr demanded with a laugh, as he clasped hands with both Kovin and Teris, in turn.

"Are you all right, Teris? What happened to you?" Shadd asked, suddenly worried about the condition of her friend.

"I'm better now that we've found you all, at last," he assured her. She unstopped her waterskin and handed it over to him. He took a long drink, looking to need it.

"We came out here to warn you Korman had headed this way and we think is on the hunt for you, Garth. And we decided we had to see the ruins, too. And this short one wouldn't take no for an answer. I'm sure Karr's livid by now," Kovin related with a nod to Garth. He looked upset about something, but it didn't seem to be anything concerning them.

"I already defeated Korman a few days ago and he's gone back to Matlowe. Right now I'd better go find Ryes," he told them, as he released his sister. "Something's not right." Mitt saw he barely noticed her and didn't look happy, at all. What was happening here?

"What do you mean?" Shadd asked, seeing the wild look in his eyes.

"I don't know… Ever since that other night… I just know when something's wrong."

"You may be right. Look, here comes Maren," Torr pointed out. Garth spun, seeing her cousin running toward them, his face saying it all.

"Where's Sabin?" he panted out. "There's something wrong with Ryes and I can't reach her," he admitted, scared.

"He went back to camp. What happened?" Garth demanded.

"We were taking a quick nap and when I awoke, she was too still, again. It's like she's gone deep into herself. This isn't like the other night when she overdid things. There's an immense feeling of power around her now, and something else. I just didn't know how to bring her back," he related, panic in his voice.

"She'll be all right," Garth assured him, meeting his eyes, unconsciously taking command in the same way as he'd seen the ship's captain held it. "But, I need you to get Sabin and we'll go check her, ourselves. Where were you?" he asked calming himself, pulling out their map. Maren looked at it a few moments, and pointed.

"The mound which looks like a sitting windracer, on the south side of it," he told them. "Hey, good to see you Teris, Kovin, but what the heck is Mitt doing out here?" he asked, giving them a quick nod and smile. "Be right back with Sabin," he assured them, having caught his breath. Something about Garth's attitude put him to ease, and he felt better about things with him leading them. He turned and trotted off to their campsite. He suddenly understood why Sabin and Ardis weren't here, with the other men's unexpected presence. Ardis looked different this morning… Maybe, he thought?

But, right now Ryes was more important. He couldn't even trust her to behave long enough, for him to get a quick nap!

Garth put away the map, knowing where it was and went over to help Teris to his feet, once again, supporting his weight to help them all get there faster.

"We'll have Maren take a good look at you as soon as we figure out what's wrong with Ryes," he promised with an apologetic smile. Teris nodded his head at this, but appeared puzzled.

"Maren? Why Maren?" Kovin asked, equally puzzled. Torr, Garth and Shadd laughed at hearing it.

"He's a Healer! He has Talent!" Torr assured them, with a big grin upon his face.

"Maren? Truly?" Mitt shook her head as she voiced her doubt.

"Truly!" Garth replied, then lead them off to where Maren left Ryes.

Ryes stood, utterly astounded, as her senses drank in the bustling scene before her, trying to grapple with the unreality of this place. There were droves of people walking by on both sides of the avenue, all in a great rush. There were large, metal-and-glass pods which traveled above their heads, suspended upon rails, which were supported by flying, graceful arches high overhead. Many faces looked out the windows of the pods to the scene below. Ryes approached the wide walkway noting the neatness and order of the plants in front of this and the other buildings, crowding the area across the avenue. It did grate upon her nerves to see each leaf and flower exactly in place, as if grown by design. She'd rather the natural, chaotic growth of the forest any day!

As she approached, she saw there were friendly nods and greetings exchanged occasionally, but the bustling didn't ease. There were many colors and styles displayed in the hair and clothing of both the men and women. Several noted her in her trail clothes and simple braids, but did nothing, other than give her an occasional nod or small smile. She still wasn't quite sure what a Forester was. Even from the memories of Doran's followers, they knew little, other than a people who lived in the forests, tended the animals and plants, and made sure the visitors obeyed the rules within the preserves. They held the power of the law upon Tayna, but she wondered if they did so in Hailys, itself? They had to be more to them than just caretakers and law enforcers.

She saw the people coming and going from the many buildings. The structures were each as different from one another, as the people themselves. She saw some people using little round boxes with those crystal cylinders Maren found in one of the buildings. Others were talking into something like the headsets they used on that starship, only smaller and much lighter. Still some were watching tiny pictures projected into the air before them, but still managed to avoid running into the other people on the walkways. Surely, they all looked far too busy to ever enjoy this precise order of the greenery

around them! A shadow suddenly loomed before her, startling Ryes.
She looked up to see the smiling face of a tall, thin man dressed in
flashy, colorful clothes. The smile upon his face seemed warm, but
there was ice in his brown eyes and a chill in the air around him.

"Gracious Forester," he began nervously as she looked at him,
puzzled. "I see you're lost. Perhaps you require the services of a
skilled guide?"

"I've no coins to offer you for such a service, even if I needed
it," she hedged, taking a couple of steps back from him, her senses
screaming to put distance between them. She felt he was a predator
of some sort and would not fall prey to him – ever.

"Your card would suffice, lady. Since when would a Forester
bother with money?" he asked, taking a step toward her as he held
out a hand, his eyes narrowing. His smile tightened into an evil
grimace. Suddenly a tall, dark-clad, lithe form intervened between
them, his back to Ryes.

"This gentle lady does not require your services, gaf," a low
voice spoke with derision, coming from behind Ryes. The man froze
at the appearance of the others, now he flashed his smile again, but
stumbled as he started backing away from them. The figure in front
of her made a small, waving gesture with his hand. The smile faded
completely from his face as he turned and ran into the bustling press
of people on the walkway, quickly disappearing.

Ryes' curiosity peaked. Why would such a brash man
suddenly flee in panic from such a small, innocuous gesture? The
dark clad figure turned to face her, as the speaker moved to stand
beside her. She gasped. The eyes of the tall, dark one were the color
of liquid silver; so beautiful, yet they seemed so deadly. He wore a
one piece, skintight, body suit of a light absorbing, black material.
The exposed skin of his arms was very fair, but hairless and almost
white in color. His face was delicate, yet firm, and his hair was jet
black with white streaks running through it, mostly covered by a
hood. Even with the white streaks in his hair, she knew he wasn't old.
His graceful deadliness held Ryes enthralled in wonder; she didn't
even hear when the other person with she spoke to her again.

"You are the lady from the House of Li?" The blue-robed
woman, who'd stood beside her asked. She smiled at her utter
fascination in Hadu's appearance. Ryes blinked, realizing she was
being addressed, but still very reluctant to quit her study of the
person before her. He returned her stare, unblinking.

"Lady Timewalker, please come with us! The city streets are
no place to discuss important matters, and we do have a shuttle to

catch." There was an urgency in her voice. Ryes turned to look at the speaker and realized she knew her, but couldn't quite place her.

"What's a shuttle? And is it very hard to catch?" she asked, thinking of the various birds, fish and small animals she'd hunted, but none had been called a "shuttle." Then an upwelling from the memories borrowed from Doran, revealed the answer as the blue-robed woman gave her an exasperated look, as she sighed.

"No matter. Please come with us now. My name is Adina of the House of Li. I will try to explain as best I can, before your time here expires." She ushered Ryes along with a gesture, being careful not to touch her. The quiet, deadly one fell in behind them. He never made even the slightest sound and for some reason that unnerved her. She felt she was in the presence of a very accomplished hunter!

Questing Back

Ryes looked again at her hand, nervously. It was as if someone were holding it and she thought she could hear Maren's voice calling out to her. With a small sigh, she forced herself to relax. There was so much to see about her, she couldn't leave now! It was all so much brighter and more exciting than the way Doran's memories had painted it, with Adina mostly willing to answer her many questions. They sat in an enclosed car with glass covered windows, granting a clear view of everything outside. It was attached to many more cars, end-to-end, riding upon a cushion of air, on the rail suspended above the bustling, colorful crowds below. Everything moved so fast here!

"Is there anything wrong, Ryes?" Adina asked with concern, noting her uneasiness and the way she had looked at her hand for a few moments. Ryes shook her head and smiled assuredly, trying to look confident in such strange surroundings.

"I'm just not used to so much haste," she explained. "How was it you seem to know me so well, when this is the first I've met you?" Ryes felt her strength beginning to ebb and thought the direct approach might bring the answers more quickly.

"You were foretold to me in a True Dreaming." She waved off a servitor, who offered drinks. "Unfortunately, portions of the dreaming were unclear." She leaned forward conspiratorially, her strong perfume causing Ryes to blink. She wondered at this since she was only present in spirit, not here physically. "It was foretold that you and your son would be my and Hadu's saviors." She indicated her silver-eyed guardian, who calmly stood beside their seats. Ryes already noted that everyone else gave Hadu wide berth, when having to pass him. The danger he represented was either well-known or well-sensed by others.

"But, my cubs are yet unborn," she protested, surprised as she put a hand to her belly. Adina sighed and shook her head.

"There are many mysteries to True Dreaming, but the dreams are never wrong. This one had bothered me so, because on this day I leave Tayna for Kahmarr for good, and will never be returning. I came to verify the fate of your mother Tyra, for my sister Mada. It's sad that she's so young and chose to be so impulsive in her choices. It broke your grandmother's heart, when she heard she had joined Doran's cult," she told her, looking upset about it, herself.

"She didn't join Doran's cult, but only sought temporary shelter at her temple. She eventually will escape and find Ronn, who was… will be her true-mate," Ryes informed her, feeling she deserved to know what happens. She smiled at this, her eyes lighting up and she appeared relieved.

"I did not think she would join that mad woman's followers. Some of their radical views and practices were very disturbing. My, you do look so much like her," she told her. Ryes smiled as she sat back and shrugged her shoulders as myriad questions popped up in her mind. How does she, and a son she has yet to birth, save her great aunt who lived hundreds of year in the past? She glanced up at Hadu and wondered what could beset Aunt Adina which he couldn't handle? Again, there was a feeling as if someone grasped her hand. She looked from her hand to the questions dancing in the Lady Adina's eyes and found no answers to her own, nor solace for her great aunt. The shuttle lurched to a halt and Adina looked up to a sign which lit up above their heads, to tell them which stop this was. She dabbed at her neck with her perfumed scarf, and then looked at Ryes with concern.

"You're fading! You must return, before you lose yourself in time." Ryes looked at her hands, realizing she was becoming translucent.

"How do I do that?" she asked, deeply concerned now.

"Where is your Protector?" Adina questioned anxiously. "Your mother should be with you, at the very least!" Ryes shook her head.

"She can't, and I don't have a protector," she admitted. Her aunt became very agitated at hearing this.

"How far back are you walking, child?"

"I think only a couple hundred years. I was trying to figure out how I Time Walked the first time," she answered. Adina paled at this; her eyes were round in shock.

"Time Walking is not a game, young one. You can lose yourself in time and become nothing more than a spirit which wanders homeless, forever lost, because your body will die if you do not return!" She was scolding and telling her information she needed at the same time. "And so much time has passed? Are you sure it has been so long?" she asked, frowning as she thought about it.

"Come on, if you really believe it's so, then let's get started right now!" Ardis urged Sabin, as they returned to their camp and were emptying out their backpacks next to their sleeping area. "No one else's here and I'm not letting anyone else father my first cub," she told him. He stood rooted in shock as she unlaced her breeches and pulled off her boots. "Nothing formal, just a start for what we'll have plenty of time for, the next several days," she promised as she dropped her breeches. She pulled off her undergarment and saw a staining and knew it was true. She couldn't believe the excitement coursing through her entire being in this moment.

Sabin's heart was hammering as he heard what she said and saw what she was doing. Not here, his inner sense screamed! But, she was stripping off her clothes and he was powerless to move. She saw his fear and excitement, so stepped closer and started undoing his laces for him, smiling teasingly as she did it. He wrapped his arms around her, his blood pounding as a deep moan escaped his lips.

"We have to pack and get out of here," he tried to tell her, but she nibbled upon his ear, as she pulled down his breeches for him.

"Just a quick one for the trail," she invited. "We're not even going to undress all the way for this. You're my first and only love mate, Sabin, and no one's going to take that away from us. Come on be my first for real!" she invited, pulling down his undergarment. He groaned, but gave in, easing her down onto their blankets. He might end up in a challenge over this, but he didn't care right now!

"Sabin!" Maren called as he ran into camp. He didn't see them right away, but heard a commotion and was amazed to see he and Ardis were coupling, right here, in the middle of the day! He stopped in his tracks dumbfounded, unsure if he should stay, or quietly leave them be. But, Ryes needed help... He stood frozen with his uncertainty.

"All right, Maren. What do you need?" Sabin demanded, his arms still around Ardis. Feeling extremely embarrassed, Maren sidled a little closer, but not too close, keeping his eyes averted.

"Garth told me to come get you. Ryes is lost within herself again, but this time it's very different. If there's something I can do by myself, tell me what it is and I'll take care of it. I just couldn't reach her and when I called out to her, it was like she went deep and was too busy to bother listening to me, or to answer."

"At least we had a little time to ourselves," Ardis teased, happy, having enjoyed it, even if it was quick. "You go ahead and I'll get things here packed. I'll be waiting for you," she promised, tugging upon the lower fold of his ear gently with her teeth, sending chills up his spine in reaction. He didn't want to let go of her, but knew they needed to get to a more secluded spot, to finish things more properly, anyway.

"I'll be right back," he vowed, then kissed her passionately before he got up to get dressed, again. He smiled as he saw Maren standing with his back toward them and pointed it out to Ardis. She smiled, nodding her head. It was so like him, to try to afford them some privacy. He wondered why he didn't have the blood anger as he had when Garth had fought Korman? He felt possessive of Ardis, but somehow Maren was not a potential opponent and he had no anger towards him at all. Or perhaps that Challenge of Ryes' had cured him? He quickly pulled back on his clothes and boots, and then clamped a hand upon Maren's shoulder, startling him.

"All ready," he assured him, feeling on top of the world now.

"Great. Let's hurry, so you can get back to Ardis," he replied, still blushing darkly.

"Wait until you find your own lady," Sabin chuckled. "You're not that much younger than Shadd, cub."

"I do have my ideal lady in mind, but have yet to find her," he admitted, sighing wistfully. They left as Ardis began to gather the things they'd need for the next several days. Ryes had been right and her sister dead wrong. The first time for real was the most exciting one, and she couldn't wait to see what the next few days would hold for them. Time alone, together... Yes, that's what they needed the most! She hoped Ryes would be all right. She couldn't wait to tell her and Shadd all about it!

"Ryes!" Garth shouted as he eased Teris down to sit upon a stone slab, almost as worried about him now as he was about his wife. He threw down his pack beside the stone she lay upon. He grasped her hand. She was as unresponsive as the other morning, but this felt very different, just as Maren described it. There was a strange feeling of unleashed power in the air around her. What had happened?

"It doesn't look like anything's been bothering her," Teris observed, looking around the sunny, peaceful clearing. Mitt dropped her pack next to Garth's and looked down at Ryes. Her eyes widened as she realized she looked a little heavier about the middle. Could she already be pregnant? She looked up at her older brother; a thousand questions plagued her mind. But, she saw the anguish in his eyes and knew if she were ever cruel to The Huntress, she'd pay for it in the end, herself.

"What's wrong with her?" she finally asked, biting back on her own disappointment that he seemed to value Ryes more than her, now. Garth met her eyes and smiled, giving her a shake of his head.

"I've no idea. If Maren couldn't reach her, then we'll hope that Sabin has some ideas. This is different than the last time she was like this. Maren brought her out of it, that time."

"Since how does Maren have a Talent?" Kovin demanded, puzzled. "Isn't he a little too old for a Talent to manifest?"

"Apparently, he's not too old. Ryes helped him find it several days ago," Torr replied. "She's a Catalyst, after all," he reminded them.

"It's just that Sabin's had far more experience than either of them. I hope he knows what to do," Shadd added, looking up to Torr. He pulled her closer to his side, giving her a nod of his head in agreement.

"I'm sure that between Sabin and Maren, they'll figure this out," he assured her.

"Garth, are you all right?" Mitt asked, worried for him, too.

"I'll be fine, once Ryes is," he told her, smiling for her again. "Karr's going to have an absolute fit over you running away," he scolded, but truly didn't have the heart for it.

"We had a screaming fight," she admitted with her eyes lowered. "I couldn't take it anymore, so when I heard Kovin and Teris say they were heading out to find the rest of you, I followed them. It wasn't until we crossed that creek, that they noticed me," she admitted, meeting his eyes, mischief in her own. "I'll be old enough to get cubs of my own, next year, or the year after," she stressed, "Karr doesn't have to treat me like a baby!" Garth thought on this a few moments as he looked down at his own, dear lady. Yes, they'd have plenty of room to accommodate his sister in their lives, but he didn't want her trying to bring Ryes any grief, either. He knew her too well. She loved to get her way, one way or another.

"You can stay for now. We expect you to pull your weight,
though. Ryes and I are expecting our cubs to come by the end of the
winter, so I'm asking you to help take care of her. She does enough
things like this, where she manages to get into mischief in one form or
another," he related as he smiled down at her, wishing in his heart
that Sabin and Maren would hurry. "And I need you to help keep her
out of mischief."

"You've got that one right," Sabin agreed, as he appeared at
Garth's side. "Give me a few moments to see. Maren? You come,
too," he advised. If this was something out of his league, it might
take the both of them to bring her back, and he wanted every
advantage he could find. He had Ardis waiting for him, after all.

"Now, listen to me," Adina spoke with some authority, "You
must not play with Time Walking until you get a Protector to help keep
you safe. Tell your Clan Mother and she will see to it." Ryes started
to protest, but her great aunt held her hand up, gesturing her to
silence, sure now that the girl had done it without permission.

"Now do exactly as I say, close your eyes upon this time and
place and concentrate upon feeling your own body around you. Think
of what you are lying upon, the weight of your clothes, your chest
rising and falling as you breathe, the blood rushing through your
body. Think of all of this, very hard." Ryes licked her lips and nodded
agreement, seeing how serious she was about all it.

"I'll try, but what'll I do if..." she started, but Adina cut her off.

"No ifs here! Do it, now!" Ryes nodded her assent and closed
her eyes, forming a picture of her body around her. That sensation of
someone holding onto her hand helped, as she wondered who it was
and why they'd want to keep her hand captive?

"Ryes! Ryes!" she heard Maren and Sabin. She tried to reach
for them, realizing if they were looking for her, she must've been gone
a long time, indeed. She didn't want Garth upset with her over this.
She'd never told him about her first Time Walking adventure.

"I'm here," she called in return, confused as to where they
were; raw power was ebbing and flowing around her. "Where are
you?" she sent in question. "I can't find you!"

"Hold on! Stay calm!" Sabin told her. "Try to imagine your
body around you. FEEL YOURSELF, Ryes!" He was deeply worried.

She was lost in a strange place and he had no idea how to reach her. At least she heard them and was trying to come back to herself.

"I'm trying. But, it's hard to concentrate in here," she returned, feeling herself growing weaker. NO! She couldn't end up lost here! She had Garth and their cubs, yet to be born, to get back to! And she still needed to rescue her Great Aunt Adina and Hadu. She wouldn't abandon them, too!

Sabin suddenly backed out, getting an idea. He opened his eyes as he saw Maren open his, shocked at being yanked out so unexpectedly. He smiled and gave him a nod in encouragement, seeing he was practically in a panic.

"Garth, take out your beltknife," he ordered as he saw the questions in his friend's eyes. Garth did as he bid, handing it to Sabin, but he shook his head no at this. "Now, take Ryes' hand and open it up flat." He did it, still wondering what he was up to. "Next lay your blade flat across her palm. Close your eyes and imagine with every bit of your being that you're cutting down into the palm of her hand with the blade. Picture in your mind the knife biting deep and the blood's welling upwards, as you draw the knife across her palm. If you believe it, it'll give her the incentive to find her way back. We'll never reach her, otherwise. You're the closest one to her. Do it now!" he ordered.

Garth looked puzzled and shocked at this, but closed his eyes and created the picture as clearly as he could within his mind. He saw himself opening Ryes' hand and taking the tip of the blade and biting deep into the palm of her hand, then drawing it towards her wrist. He pictured it in the most exacting detail, as coldly as he could, as if she deserved this severe punishment. Maren looked puzzled at this, wondering if Sabin was right? Could she use this as an anchor to find her way out of that inner maze of power? He practically held his breath as they waited.

"Owww!" Ryes yelled in protest, catching her breath and opening her eyes, suddenly feeling so heavy. She sat up as Garth opened his eyes, a smile immediately upon his lips. She expected to see her hand gashed open, but it was fine with only his knife blade lying across it. He took it back, and then wrapped his arms around her, relieved.

"What was it, this time?" he demanded trying to keep his exasperation from his voice; pulling back to look her in the eyes. She sighed and her shoulders drooped, knowing it was all her own doing, and she'd needlessly upset him again.

"Remember that morning, after we escaped the valley?" she asked, looking up again. She blushed as she saw the others crowding around them. He gave her a nod of his head to continue. "I somehow went backwards into time and was back in Doran's valley. A man was there to claim Tyra from Doran's keeping. She killed him of course, but I prevented her taking his soul to feed upon. It was like I was a spirit, or ghost, and one of the officers, who served under the man who was killed, told me I was Time Walking. I had no idea how I did it, or how to get back, so I concentrated upon you and the next thing I knew, you were asking me what was wrong."

"Yes, I remember," he told her, frowning as he did recall that day too clearly. "I thought she was trying to pull you back to the valley, again." She smiled as she shook her head no.

"I did too, at first," she admitted. "Then I thought it might be an aftereffect from controlling the energy from that power stone. Today, I was too restless and didn't want to take a nap with Maren, so I was thinking about what happened that morning and the next thing I knew, I was in Hailys before it was attacked. You wouldn't believe the people! There were so many people! And everyone was in such a horrible hurry! While I was there, I ran into Tyra's aunt who told me I and our son are supposed to save her and her guardian, Hadu. She was trying to help me return. It scared her to think I was Time Walking so far into the past," she admitted. Garth sighed as Sabin laughed.

"But, did you learn anything USEFUL?" Sabin questioned, wishing he could've gone with her on this time walking! Maybe they could try it together, later? She turned an impish grin toward him.

"I was next to a library. It may be this building here. And there are `directories,' which are small maps to tell people where they are and what buildings are near them, at the larger intersections of their avenues," she informed him. "And those crystal rods that Maren likes, record information within them like books, only Adina said they last far longer."

"Hah! Then we're keeping every crystal rod we find. I was going to use them to make pendants," Maren declared, smiling at this news.

"We need to see if we can make one of their old readers work, so we can extract the information," she warned him. Garth scooped her up, and then set her upon her feet.

"First off, NO more Time Walking!" he ordered, laying down the law. She opened her mouth to protest, but saw the look in his eyes and gave him a nod of her head. "Maybe later, after we get settled in our new home, you, Maren and Sabin can make another try, but not so far back. Yes, there's a lot we need to learn, but not at the cost of losing you and our cubs, Sweet One."

"Right! I've got to get going," Sabin told them smiling, remembering he had a special duty to perform, now. Kovin suddenly stepped in his way, a glare in his eyes.

"What makes you think she wants you?" he dared him, feeling he could guess why he had to rush back to Ardis. There was a scent clinging to his clothing which ignited his own senses, and he wanted her for himself. Sabin growled deep in his throat, ready for this challenge.

"Because she told both Ryes and I that she wanted Sabin and Sabin ONLY!" Shadd shouted at him, pushing her way between them. Ryes was quickly by her side, looking hostile, too. "She saw you before you caught up to the rest of us and chose to go with Sabin, herself. You're not going to take that away from her!"

"It's her right to choose whom she mates with, not yours!" Ryes told him, daring him to try to issue a challenge. "If you're really spoiling for a fight, then I'll give you one you won't ever forget," she promised. This got a reaction out of both Garth and Sabin, which he didn't miss.

"I want to hear it from her!" he demanded, looking angry now.

"Then you will," Ardis shouted back, coming up behind him. She stepped over to join the other women. "I'll have Sabin for my first, and no one else. Even if you could possibly win a challenge against him, I'd still mate with Sabin. He's MY CHOICE!" Kovin stood with confusion and sorrow plainly written in his eyes. The sudden, hard rejection was tearing him apart, but if this was what she insisted upon, what could he do?

"I'll withdraw my claim," he told her, then turned away, leaving, and not caring where he went, feeling deeply torn within.

"We did it!" Shadd declared, bounding in happiness as all three of the women were laughing and hugging each other. Sabin looked to Garth with a puzzled grin upon his face.

"What're we starting here?" he asked his friend, in a low voice.

"Probably something we shouldn't, but who are we to tell them no?" he returned. Torr chuckled in agreement. Mitt saw all this and smiled, liking the idea. The village women had been far too long under Korman's claws, for something like this to not be considered a triumph. It gave her an inner excitement, which couldn't be quelled.

"Come on, husband of mine," Ardis said as she broke free to step up before her prize. "We have some cubs to make." He shrugged his shoulders in surrender at this, smiling.

"Now which is the weaker sex?" he asked Garth as he put an arm around Ardis' shoulders.

"Actually, there's no weaker sex. Each has different strengths, but only together do we have the whole and completeness," Ryes commented grinning, as she and Shadd finally released each other and were watching their friends. This got full agreement and laughter from the rest, as Sabin and Ardis left to collect their things.

"I'll go see if Kovin needs someone to talk to," Torr offered, as Shadd gave him a nod of her head in agreement.

"Maybe it should be the both of us?" she suggested. "I want to explain things to him."

"I want to hear this, so I'll understand it," Teris said, seeing how possessive Shadd was with Torr now. He tried to stand up, but practically fell. Maren was quickly by his side, appearing very concerned now.

"Let me take a look at you, first, Teris," he offered, helping him back up to sit on the stone. He knelt before him and offered him his hands.

"Yes. Let me see you heal," he agreed, an odd smile on his face. "I was told you have Talent now." Maren huffed out a laugh and gave him a nod.

"I do and you're going to get to feel it firsthand, now," he assured him, then closed his eyes and took both of Teris' hands, calling up his Healing. He found the deep injuries and the infections running wild through his body because of them. It took him a while to make sure he once again felt "right" to his inner senses. He opened his eyes seeing the wonder and surprise on Teris' face.

"Maren... I..." his words failed him utterly. He pulled back a lock of hair from his eyes and realized the movement no longer pained him. He jumped up, pulled Maren back to his feet and gave his friend a hug of gratitude as he laughed out his inner happiness.

"You're welcome," Maren replied, happy he had his Talent now. Teris would have died if he hadn't been healed. He nodded in response to Maren.

"Now I'm ready to go with you, Torr. I want to hear about all that's happened to bring these great changes!" he told him, feeling charged. He grabbed his pack and settled it upon his back with ease.

"It's a good idea, if you want to hang out with our little, wild band," Torr agreed with a laugh. He realized he didn't mind Shadd's attitude about being the one to choose whom she mated with. After all, she had the taste to pick him. Maybe Ryes was right? That it was only together they could face off what surprises lay ahead? He, Shadd and Teris all headed off in the direction they saw Kovin go.

"How about getting our spears and going hunting?" Garth suggested to Maren with a friendly cuff on his shoulder. Maren smiled, but shook his head.

"I want to find something lighter, so we can get some of those fat pleip birds, which were feeding near Honey's new pen. A snare's too slow and won't catch as many," he complained. Ryes thought a few moments.

"It's too bad I left that crossbow back at the valley," she told him with a sad sigh.

"What's a cross bow?" Mitt asked, just as Maren was about to speak up, too. Garth looked surprised, but smiled as he realized it had to be that odd contraption she dropped, when she finally reached him next to that flowering tree.

"It fires small quarrels, or darts, about this long," she said, spacing her hands for them. "I recall something from one of Doran's followers about a bow and arrow. It was more primitive and used on hunts here on Tayna, when the hunter wanted to feel close to his prey. The bow's a bent, strong piece of wood with a taunt cord going from end to end, and the arrow's like a dart, only larger, with feathering to help it fly right," she explained, frowning. "Let me get my parchments and I'll try to draw one," she offered.

"Why not do it right here?" Garth asked, handing her a stick and showing her the loose soil near her feet. She grinned and took the stick with a laugh.

"The simpler way is sometimes the best," she agreed as she got down upon her knees, smoothed the dirt and began her drawing, explaining it as she went.

"You're sure it's not supposed to be soft wood?" Maren questioned, wondering after a few minutes of examining her sketches.

"I'm sure and it's better if the wood's dry, not green. It's supposed to give, but not too much. The better the tension in the wood, the farther and better the arrow will fly, I think," she replied. "With practice, you should be able to take a bird from a good distance, even on the wing, as long as you don't try shooting straight up overhead, and get yourself," she reminded him, laughing lightly.

"Is this something from one of those sleepers you talk about?" Garth asked, frowning at where this knowledge came from.

"Yes," she replied. "One was daughter of a hunter here on Tayna and had to help her father make hunting devices," she explained. "There were only a few of her memories shared among them as she... Larin, had to take up being one of the attendants and died in her service to Doran over a hundred years ago. From what they knew of her, I think I would've liked her." The other three looked uncomfortable, but Garth gripped her shoulder and gave her a nod of his head in support.

"Let's find something bigger for today, and then try making some of those bows and erros for tomorrow?" Garth suggested, thinking it'd make a very handy hunting tool.

"That sounds like a good idea," Maren finally agreed. He wanted time to make sure he did this one right! He wanted to be the first to make a good, working bow!

"We'll leave the birds alone and maybe they'll think they're safe, for now," Mitt suggested, smiling. The Huntress was a fount of information when it came to hunting, she recalled. That one trip out had taught them all far more, than they could learn in their lifetimes! But she didn't understand what Ryes was talking about memories and sharing them. It had to be tied to her Talent, she thought.

"We'll probably need some practice first," Ryes suggested, as she smiled at Mitt. "What're you doing all the way out here? Won't your mother be upset?" she asked, concerned.

"My mother said if I was old enough to hunt, I was old enough to look after myself, long ago. Oh, Garth, I forgot," she said, turning back to him. "Mother's pregnant again. Is there any way we can go home before she's due? I'm worried about her," she admitted.

"Do you know when Marla's due?" Maren pressed, stepping closer. There was an urgency in his eyes, as well as worry.

"Not until late fall. I think that's what I heard her tell Karr," she said. There was some relief in Maren's eyes as he sought his friend's.

"As soon as Sabin and Ardis have finished," Garth stated, knowing this was something he needed to take care of, too. "We'll head south and maybe west. Once we find a place to get ourselves established, we'll go to Matlowe and bring them out here." Ryes nodded her agreement, knowing he was right.

"Maren can help Marla," Ryes told Mitt, trying to comfort her. "His Healing Talent is very, very strong."

"As long as we get to her on time," he added, hoping he spoke truly.

"Now, wait a minute," Ryes said, tugging on Garth's backpack. "You're not burdening Honey with all this junk. We're not keeping everything we find here!"

"Why not? She's a strong windracer," he teased, baiting her. He saw the shock in her eyes and laughed. "We found some decent wheels and are planning on making a cart. That way we can load it up and she can pull it more readily," he explained. She sighed in relief.

"Let's go pick up our spears," she reminded him, as she saw the mischief in his eyes. "We still have dinner to catch."

"Anything you say, Sweet One," he said as he wrapped an arm about her and grabbed their packs with his free hand. Maren took them for him, as Mitt hugged herself to his other side, causing them all to laugh. She sighed, happy. Maybe she could get used to Ryes? Her brother had wanted her for as far back as she could remember and was happier than she'd ever seen him, this Time Walking thing aside. It seemed she had a lot of catching up to do to understand them now. And there was nothing being said about sending her back home right away! She was just so happy!

The Pathway

"It looks like some kind of pathway, as if it were an abandoned Caravan road, it's the only wagons that would be large enough to make such tracks," Ryes said, standing back up. The pathway was a pair of deep ruts sunk into the ground, as if something large and heavy made it, going this way more than once. She knew the Caravaners avoided Hailys, so she wondered who it could've been? "It hasn't been used in a lot of years, though. It's not like the paved roads of Hailys, which we found parts of," she stated, turning back to the rest, doubts in her eyes. "What do you think, Garth?"

"It's going the same direction we are," he pointed out the obvious. "The cart's wheels don't exactly match up to it, but it might still make the going easier on Honey. We'll have the cart ride on the ground between them. We should be fine, if it's been a long time since it was last used." Ryes reached over and patted her mare on the neck, smiling with a lot of affection for her.

Honey was so patient with them and let them lead her through the craziest places as they had carefully travelled through the outskirts of Hailys. Ryes had Mitt out with her gathering all the wild grains they could find, the last few days at their original campsite, and bundling some of the finer grasses to use as feed for Honey, when they left on their quest for a new home. It took them ten days to traverse Hailys and come out near the southwest end. Ryes had never appreciated how far north they were before now; when they finally turned back toward Hailys, from the creek and Doran's valley, earlier. Finding this ready-made path had been an added blessing and she looked upon it as a sign of good fortune. They would be soon leaving Hailys far behind! Not without regrets. She mentally promised herself to search for her father and siblings' gravesite when she next got the chance to return. She wanted to find it. And later had a promise to fulfill to her mother, too! She hoped she'd be able to find her without going back to Doran's valley.

"The day's wasting," Sabin reminded them. "Let's find a good place to make camp, before the sun gets much lower." Ryes smiled as she walked back to Garth.

"It runs straight and true, as far as I can see," she agreed. "Once we get camp set, we can go over the maps, again," she offered in hope. Her only real concern was water. They hadn't found much yesterday and nothing today. This land looked too dry, with brown, dried grasses and little promise and the summer heat just getting a good start. But, Garth had become their leader and he decided they should press onward. At least they seemed to have a path now laid out before them.

"Alright," he said, "Let's keep going and find a camp spot with more promise." It looked fairly flat, but it wasn't something he could explain. This way "felt" right and until it felt otherwise, this was the way he'd take them. Ryes quirked a small smile, but fell in beside him as she held Honey's halter and they started walking, again. It wasn't that this journey was tedious; it was that it had finally become mundane to the original party. The three newcomers were having the time of their lives and now the rest of the group felt as if they were "old-timers!" Garth quietly chuckled to himself as he watched Mitt and Teris trying to run down a scatter-chase for fun.

"Nothing we haven't done, ourselves," Ryes commented in a low voice, smiling at their antics. Sabin chuckled at this too, coming up to walk on her other side.

"That's the truth. It's seemed like forever since we left Matlowe," he agreed. "I thought I caught a tusker's scent a few minutes ago. If we can find a good spot to stop, we can go see about tracking it down."

"Sounds like a good plan," Garth agreed. Ryes noted Ardis was trying to catch her eye, so she dropped back to see what she wanted, passing the halter rope to Garth and leaving the men to talk about the things they thought of as important.

"Ryes," Ardis started, then paused blushing. "How soon did you notice?" Ryes grinned, giving her a nod of her head.

"It seemed like it was almost right away. That's how I knew I `caught.' Doesn't it feel strange?" she added.

"It sure does," she returned, relieved. Shadd looked puzzled as she stepped closer.

"What does?" she pressed, needing to know what they were talking about; suspecting that she already knew, but wanted to be sure.

"My tunic's a little snug today and I was worried," Ardis told her in a lowered voice. Ryes chuckled as her eyes shone with her inner humor.

"Garth reminded me that I was the one who wanted lots of cubs, so I'd have to have something to feed them," she related, still amazed at the changes as they happened to her body. "But, there're some days when I feel so slow and sluggish," she admitted. "It's like they've sapped all my energy. I can feel movement now. Like a bunch of flutterwings are loose in my stomach." She laughed lightly, realizing she was feeling their movements again.

"Ah, a cub of my very own," Ardis sighed, happily. She looked like she was feeling charged now.

"No. Yours and Sabin's," Shadd corrected her. "They're going to need both parents to raise them for a while," she reminded her with a chuckle, too. "I can't wait for my time. Poor Torr, I've just about have him worn out, already," she admitted.

"No wonder he looks so tired most times," Ryes teased. Maren tugged on one of Ryes' braids as he stepped up to join the women in their conspiracy. Sometimes they didn't mind it; sometimes they told him to make tracks elsewhere.

"Let me try something, Ardis," he offered, getting an idea.

"What?" she questioned, wondering what he had in mind?

"Trust me?" he dared her, throwing it open for speculation. She looked at him, then to Ryes for a few seconds, and gave him a nod of her head.

"All right," she granted him her permission. He smiled as he closed his eyes, and after a few moments, he placed a hand across her stomach, as they walked. None of the women spoke, not wanting to distract him. After a few seconds more he opened his eyes, smiling merrily as he removed his hand.

"Do you want to know how many and what you'll be having?" he dangled his offer temptingly before her. Ardis blinked in surprised, and then grinned merrily.

"Yes, Maren, of course I want to know," she gave in, almost holding her breath in anticipation.

"You're now carrying two very healthy cubs. Two sons," he informed her, happy to be the bearer of glad tidings. She cried out as she threw her arms about him, hugging him happily. This caused Sabin to turn around with questions in his eyes. Ardis released Maren and trotted to catch up to him, to tell him the happy news. Shadd, Ryes and Maren were laughing as they watched her go. Kovin looked puzzled as he'd been bringing up the rear and hadn't heard the whole exchange. He paced himself a little closer to the others. He realized he did still want to be a real part of this group, too.

"Can you do the same for Ryes?" Shadd asked, hoping this wasn't taxing him too much.

"If she wants me to try," he offered, smiling his triumph, his eyes merry.

"Yes, I'd like to know," she gave in, grinning. Maren stepped closer to her, and then closed his eyes. He reached over and placed his hand upon Ryes' stomach as they walked for a space of time. He suddenly opened his eyes and looked at her, worry in their brown depths.

"There are three healthy ones, but one which will need both of our abilities to help him become `right,'" he spoke to her directly, thought-to-thought, as Sabin taught them, before. "I warned you there was the risk of a sport." He wasn't happy about this, but there was something within him which told him it wasn't beyond them to make things "right" for this small son of hers.

"Anything," she returned in like manner, determined to win this, as with any other challenge thrown her way. "You're my teacher and guide in this," she reminded him, knowing his healing abilities were far greater than her own.

"Reach within and feel it for yourself," he pressed, showing her how. She gasped as she saw it, too.

"Four… my gosh! I'm going to be busy," she marveled. Yes, the wrongness was clear, but he was right. With time and effort, it wasn't beyond them. "Don't tell Garth. I want it to be a surprise," she warned. He withdrew his contact and smiled more genuinely.

"You're right, you're going to be busy," Maren said aloud. Garth had looked back as they were talking without words. He wondered what was wrong? Had the challenge Korman sparked caused their cubs some harm? He tried to be gentle and careful, but it now tore at him. Ryes saw the worry in his eyes and smiled for him.

"Well?" Shadd demanded. They'd been quiet far too long, as if they were talking without words.

"It's a secret," Maren taunted her, grinning. "We want to surprise Garth," he added. Ryes nodded her head, her eyes were happy, as she placed her hand low upon her stomach.

"I think I'd better enjoy all the quiet time I can," she commented. Shadd frowned, puzzling this out, and then she recalled that Ryes' mother had four cubs, according to Rowan. And when Garth and Gann were born, his mother had three, but their last littermate died when they were young. She smiled as she thought this meant at least three, but maybe even as many as four! She'd be busy for sure – either way!

"I can't wait for my turn," she happily sighed.

"You're in such a hurry?" Kovin asked her, chuckling as he stepped closer to the trio. "Don't you want more out of life before you're saddled with cubs?"

"I've wanted my own family since I was a little girl," she admitted, not letting his questions deflate her. "And soon I'll get my chance." He laughed, shaking his head at the thought.

"I only hope you have no regrets about having cubs," he replied. Shadd laughed at this and picked up her stride to catch up to Torr, who was walking in front of the cart, listening to Sabin and Garth.

"Being a woman, truly we have no choice in the matter when the time comes," Ryes told him, thinking about what he said. "I had a life of my own choosing before and will have one I choose to live after they're born. They'll only enrich it." He smiled at this nodding his head, understanding what she meant.

"Exactly," Maren agreed.

"What're you doing?" Maren questioned, as Ryes was sitting so very still. They established their camp and the rest of the men with Shadd and Mitt were out hunting. Ardis was taking a nap, still recovering from the days when she and Sabin got too little sleep, and here was Ryes sitting quietly with her eyes closed. Almost innocent looking to the unknowing eye. But, there was a tingle of power in the air, which teased Maren's heightened senses, so he was investigating it. He was afraid she'd try something dangerous again.

"I'm trying to think fish," she admitted to him in a low voice, keeping her eyes closed. "If there're any fish nearby, I should be able to sense them. I hope," she explained, knowing why he'd be concerned with her using her Talents. It wasn't like he didn't have cause, so she could forgive him in this.

"What?" he questioned merrily, thinking this truly sounded like a waste of a Talent!

"If there's any fish nearby, then there must be water we can drink, too," she reasoned as she sighed and opened her eyes, letting it go. "I know we're heading toward the Yuri River, but it's still too many days away and I'm worried about our water supply. It's been two days out here with no water around!"

"Now that's an idea I hadn't thought of. With your being able to reach out to that viper, a bunch of fish should be easy," he agreed, smiling. "Well, while most the others are gone, I want you to lie down and we'll have another look at that little son of yours," he pressed, feeling it was best to attempt this while they had the time and peace. She smiled, seeing he had a point, so lay down quickly and relaxed. Maren sat next to her, then closed his eyes and reached for his center, anchoring himself, then out to Ryes. She welcomed his contact, as they both reached for and surrounded the one, small cub still growing within her with their combined Talents, effecting repairs and encouraging growth.

Ardis awoke seeing the fire burning cheerfully, then saw Ryes lying down as Maren sat next to her, his hands spread out in the air over her stomach. It was like they were in some kind of inner commune, rather than him just offering prayers for her cubs. She wondered about this. Shadd said they wouldn't tell her how many, but voiced her own speculations based upon their comments, afterwards. Three or four? It was an amazing thought! Garth was acting strange since then, too. He was good at sensing when something was wrong with Ryes, and here she and Maren were, as if they were using their Talents...

She sat up suddenly. AS IF THEY WERE USING THEIR TALENTS! Maybe there was something wrong with the cubs and he was healing them now, to make sure they'd be born all right? She had to admit to herself, she slept better knowing they had a real Healer among them. They were now safer having their cubs out here in the wilderness, than back in Matlowe! She was afraid to disturb them, so sat waiting, hoping for a few words with Ryes, before the rest of their party returned from the hunt.

"There, that should help," Maren said, as he opened his eyes. Ryes opened hers too and smiled up at him.

"Thanks, Maren. I'm going to have to find you more of those sweet tubers you like so much," she teased. He laughed, and then saw Ardis walking over to them.

"What's wrong with the cubs?" she asked straight out, as she sat down with them. "You were healing them, weren't you?" she demanded, concerned.

"It was only one which needed the attention," Ryes breathed out, admitting it to her. "He's fine now, thanks to his gifted second cousin."

"When Korman challenged Garth, he fathered a sport. We were just making sure he had as much chance of being born normally, and at the same time, as his siblings," Maren explained. "You do know you can't free mate for at least two months afterwards, don't you?" he asked, wondering how much these young women did know?

"Oh, yes. My sister warned me of that, long ago," Ardis admitted, blushing. "I'd forgotten about that afternoon," she said, glad she and Sabin were very careful. He'd been so happy and proud that they were going to be having two cubs – just as he foresaw!

"Good. Just make sure Shadd and Mitt know it, too. It's a good thing you women got everything set straight with Kovin and Teris," he grinned as he chuckled. "How old is Mitt?" he suddenly questioned, worried about her, now.

"She's about a year younger than you," Ryes told him. "She has plenty of time to get things straight in her head about whom she wants, or doesn't want. Is she too young for free mating, yet?" she asked, truly not knowing.

"No, she isn't, but I don't think she's ready for anything like that, considering the way she acts!" Maren chuckled at the expression upon Ryes' face. There were times when she asked the craziest questions.

"Are you going to teach her of the joys of free mating?" Ardis teased him, with a light nudge on his shoulder.

"No," he replied in a low voice, looking her in the eye as he spoke. "She's more like my kid sister. That's a terrible thought!" He smiled as he now spoke. Ryes thought she saw something more behind his eyes. She wondered, but wasn't going to ask him about it in front of Ardis. "I'll find my dream lady, and do my best to win her," he related with a heartfelt sigh. Ryes smiled at this, hoping the best for him. Then they heard voices raised as the hunters returned to camp.

"You'll find her, Maren," she encouraged him as she stood up to greet Garth properly. It looked like they brought down two very large bounder bucks with some good-sized prongs upon their heads. She shook her head at this. "I think they're finally learning how to hunt properly," she commented to the others with a wink, then headed toward Garth.

"So, how many?" Ardis whispered, itching to know.

"Don't tell ANYONE, especially Sabin because he'll tell Garth and she wants it to be a surprise," he requested, wanting to hear her promise it, first.

"I won't, I swear," she assured him, understanding.

"Four. Two daughters and two sons, now that their smallest will be as large as the rest, and just as healthy," he admitted, feeling he could trust her.

"Oh my gosh!" she declared in a low voice. "She IS going to be busy and it will be a big surprise for Garth!" They both laughed at this, as they got to their feet.

"Hopefully, he'll only be out on a hunt," Maren added, under his breath, recalling that instant of Vision, still too clearly. Ardis looked at him in surprise for a moment.

"You truly believe it was a real Vision?" she pressed, questions in her eyes.

"Neither Ryes, nor I have any doubts on it being true. It's puzzling out the circumstances of why he's gone that has plagued me," he admitted. "After all, that's four cubs I'll have to deliver with no one to distract her." They both chuckled at that with Ardis nodding her head in agreement.

"We'll be there for her," she assured him, gripping his shoulder for a moment. He nodded his response, finally smiling again.

"Thank you," he replied, looking relieved.

"You never did tell me about your first Time Walking adventure," Garth stated as everyone was sitting around the cook fire feeling full and happy after they ate dinner. Ryes looked over to him, giving him a nod of her head.

"I was so exhausted and only wanted to put distance between us and that valley, at the time," she admitted. "I just forgot about it later."

"So, tell us all this story now," Ardis urged, ready to hear all about it. She had a hide in her hands and she was working on to remove the hair from and hopefully make into something useful. It was still very stiff and would need a lot of work.

"We'd just left the valley and Garth had collected some stones to mark the path down into it with the symbol for death, to hopefully warn others to stay out," she began; falling into a storyteller mode she'd seen her grandfather use all her life. "I was just standing and waiting while he packed everything back up in his pack, when suddenly I was engulfed in what seemed to me a blinding golden light. I felt myself being wrenched out of my own time and cast back into the past and didn't feel I had any control over it at all."

"What did you do?" Mitt asked, amazed. Since she had watched her brother bring her out of the last one, she was sure the first one had been a truly scary experience.

"I thought that after all my efforts to disconnect Doran from the world, she'd found a way to overpower me, anyway," she told them. "But some tall men arrived on some marvelous windracers. They were dressed like soldiers from the stories of old. They announced they were there to rescue Tyra Li."

"Your mother?" Teris asked, astounded.

"Yes, my mother," she affirmed. She told them the whole story of all she had seen, heard and done, leaving nothing out and while they were amazed, they now believed her fully. "And since I'd been in contact with that Stone of Power, I thought it had all happened because of it. Now I'm thinking being in contact with that Stone only activated and released my own Talents for use. I still need to take the time to meet them, if you will." She finished her long tale.

"Once we find our home, we'll have to go back and collect that Stone to keep it from others who'd mean great harm," Sabin suggested. Garth and the other original travelers nodded their heads at this in full agreement.

"Wait, we never heard of this valley before, nor what happened," Kovin protested.

"And what happened when you went into the past in Hailys," Mitt prodded, wanting more, too. Ryes laughed merrily at this. It was finally starting to get dark so she was reluctant to keep them all up too late.

"Just one of the two tales," Garth suggested. "We need to get some sleep tonight."

"All right," she agreed and launched into her visit with her Great Aunt Adina. She didn't want to talk about Doran's dark evil when darkness lay around them now.

"What kind of wagon could've gone down there and back up the other side?" Teris asked, seeing what lay below them. The clear pathway they were following traveled down, across and back out of the wide ravine in front of them. Both the down slope and hill back up were steep inclines and looked to be a lot of work. Still the path ran straight and true as if nature wasn't allowed to get in its way.

"A very sturdy one. Don't they usually have a team of windracers?" Sabin asked Ryes. She didn't look happy as they surveyed the drop below them.

"Yes, with anywhere from four to twelve windracers, depending upon the size of the van," she informed them. "We only have our lone Honey," she reminded them, "This is going to be work for all of us to get it accomplished. It's not that the drop, nor the climb back out are impossible, just that it looks like hard labor. This had better be worth it," she stated, very concerned as she looked to Garth.

"We're still going this way, Garth?" Ardis asked, frowning as she looked to him. He nodded his head, as if his mind was still focused on heading this direction.

"At least we found your water," Maren added.

There was a wide, shallow stream running across the bottom, which looked cool and inviting. It originated from a waterfall, tumbling down near their pathway, off to the right of it about a mile away. The sound of the rushing water was nirvana. And there was a pool which formed downstream from the pathway, and this must be where those fish Ryes sensed last night must live. She said they lay directly ahead of them, but not too far and here they were this morning. The bulbous, underground tubers she found for them yesterday could be squeezed for moisture, but it wasn't anywhere near as satisfying as real, cool water. And it left a strange aftertaste in their mouths which only made them want real water all the more – to rinse it out.

"Ardis, Mitt and Ryes will walk Honey down to the pond; the rest of us will use our ropes to help ease the cart down this slope. First we're going to turn it around, though. I don't want the traces to get damaged as we lower it downhill. Then, after we've rested and had something to eat, we'll help Honey pull it back out, up the other side," Garth decided, thinking this was the best plan, for now.

"I can help with the ropes," Ryes stated, then caught the look in his eyes and sighed her surrender. Ardis looked unhappy with being excluded too, but didn't need more than a raised eyebrow from Sabin to know where any protest she could voice would lead.

"But, Garth," Mitt protested, pouting.

"Not now," he ordered, as he took Ryes' backpack off her shoulders, to dig within for the length of rope he knew she carried. He was glad she insisted they have plenty of rope with them when they set out. Her foresight had saved them several times, already. She took her pack back after he removed the rope. Garth was checking it for wear.

"It might be easier if we unload the cart, and then reload it once we get it up the other side," she suggested reasonably.

"It'll take us forever that way," Kovin protested, thinking. "This was going to be enough work, without having to make several trips back and forth for our things."

"At least a couple of days," Torr agreed, as Garth considered it. "We need to find a good place to settle and soon. I'm not sure if we want to waste time with unloading, carrying and reloading all our things."

"We can do this more quickly with our ropes and backs," Garth decided. He eased his pack off and dug for his own rope. "Go ahead and start walking," he advised Ryes, seeing she was stalling. "We can manage this." She quirked a smile at him, then turned to freeing Honey from her harness. She took her halter and coaxed her down the slope, off of the pathway, just in case. Ardis and Mitt followed in surrender.

"He wasn't even going to let me try to help," Mitt complained as Ryes smiled at her and gave her a nod.

"He's stubborn," she agreed, "but, usually has his reasons." Mitt looked at her curiously.

"That's for sure," Ardis voiced her support. "What I can't figure out is how he's suddenly become our leader, even if none of us ever consciously agreed to it?"

"It's like something's changed within him. Maybe he's become more centered within and knows his mind better, so we just accept

what he says?" Ryes suggested with a laugh and a shake of her head.
"I've no idea why it happened. Maybe when he defeated Korman?"

"Yeah, he's changed a lot! Can I take Honey's rope?" Mitt
asked, wanting to make better friends with the windracer mare, as
she'd seen the way Maren and Ryes handled her before. Ryes
chuckled as she handed it over to Mitt. She grinned as she took it and
extended her hand to Honey to let her get her scent. The mare
nuzzled her hand, accepting the scratches Mitt attempted, as she'd
seen Ryes give her from time-to-time, smiling with a light showing in
her eyes, as she did it.

"She likes you," she commented, as she winked to Ardis, who
was smiling at this display. Ryes glanced back to see them beginning
to ease the cart downhill with the ropes. She thought they were doing
things the harder way, than just unloading it would have been.

"Honey!" Mitt suddenly shouted as the mare, scenting the
water close by, was pulling free of her, trying to run downhill to
quench her thirst, she veered back to the road for a quicker path.
Ryes made a hurried grab for the trailing rope, as she and Mitt were
running to catch the normally, sedate mare, laughing as they ran.
Ardis turned back to see how the others were progressing with their
labor.

"Look out!" Ardis shouted, as she saw one of the ropes break,
and the rest lose their grip upon the remaining one. The laden cart
started a wild, uncontrolled dash for the bottom of the ravine, the
deeper cut of the pathway keeping it fairly straight in its run. Mitt
didn't hear her, but Ryes turned to see it almost on top of Mitt, and
coming quickly for her. A wheel caught Mitt, pulling her under it and
Ryes, in horror, stood rooted to the spot.

"NO!" she shouted, casting her arms out before her.
Suddenly, the cart stopped, as if it had encountered an invisible wall.
Ryes stood there, shaking with sweat beading her forehead. She had
no idea how she accomplished this, but knew she didn't have the
strength to hold it for very long. "Maren, get her out of there!" she
shouted to her cousin, seeing he was closest to Mitt, who now lay
trapped between the front and back wheels. She didn't look too good
and was crying in shock and pain. Maren scrambled to pull her out.

"Get out of the way!" Garth called, seeing Ryes still stood in
the cart's path. She looked to be straining and it was wringing his
heart to see her in such danger. He started running towards them,
right on Maren's heels.

"I can't. I'm fighting Tayna herself, in this," she admitted.
"Hurry Maren! I can't hold it much longer!" She saw he reached Mitt
and quickly had her in his arms, safely out of the way. Ryes released

the cart and threw herself down onto the ground, hoping it'd pass over her, as she curled up tightly into a ball. It rumbled and thundered overhead as the harness roughly caressed her back, then was gone in a cloud of choking dust. Just as she was starting to realize she was still alive, she felt strong hands drag her up to her feet.

"Are you all right?" Garth demanded, fiercely hugging Ryes to him, needing to be sure. She gasped and smiled, tears in her eyes as she coughed.

"I think so. Is Mitt all right?" she asked barely getting anything out with the dust in her throat and his tight arms; still she needed to know. She realized she felt drained, as if she'd been pulling the cart in Honey's stead all day long!

"Maren's working on her right now." She heard someone answer as Garth held her, almost crushing her in his arms. His very real fear still coursing through him, as he watched Maren healing Mitt, hoping she'd be all right, too.

"How did you do that?" Sabin asked, stepping close to see if Ryes was injured. She smiled at him.

"I have no idea," she admitted. "Only that I could use a nap right now. I feel exhausted. Is the cart all right?"

"Garth, she needs to breathe," Sabin chided him as he nudged him with his elbow; seeing how tightly he was holding Ryes. Garth realized this for himself and relaxed his arms. She gave a sigh of relief and nod to Sabin for her small rescue.

"Let's see to Mitt, first," Shadd suggested as Garth let Ryes go, but kept an arm about her, not letting her stray from his side right now. They walked toward Maren, Ardis and Mitt. Torr, Kovin and Teris joined them, all looking very concerned. Ryes saw all their things had been spilled off the cart in its mad race down the slope, and one wheel now lay on the dirt, but most of it looked intact. It'd come to rest three quarters of the way across the stream. Honey had reached the water safely too and was drinking her fill, which worried her too. She shouldn't drink so fast.

"She's going to be fine," Ardis told them, the relief in her voice coming through clearly. Mitt's eyes were open as she smiled up at them, but Maren's eyes were still closed; not quite finished.

"Don't move," Sabin advised her, seeing Mitt looked embarrassed and ready to squirm free with the rest of them now present, as Maren still held her in his arms. After a few more minutes, Maren opened his eyes and smiled down at her.

"There, now you're healed," he assured her, letting her go. Garth gave her a hand up and a hearty hug, as Maren got up and dusted himself off. Both of them were covered in her blood. "I think Ryes has the right idea. Let's unload the cart and carry our things back up the hill. It's a lot safer," he suggested.

"Thanks, cousin," Ryes told him, stepping over to give him a hug in relief. "How're you feeling?" she asked, noting he didn't seem anywhere near as tired as she now felt. He smiled and chuckled merrily.

"Like I've been struck by lightning and can take on all of Tayna," he boasted grandly, spreading out his arms, as if to encompass the world. This got laughter from the others as they each stepped forward to give him their thanks, too.

"This is all my fault," Ryes apologized to Mitt, as she took her turn to give her a hug. "I've spoiled and indulged Honey far too much. She should've never pulled free of you, no matter how thirsty she was."

"No, this is my fault. I should've listened to you, when you said it right the first time. We should've lightened the load, then the ropes would've held just fine," Garth insisted, meeting Ryes' emerald green eyes. "It's a good thing we have you, Sabin and Maren out here with us," he admitted, wondering if he should lead this party, after all? Ryes hugged him, as if sensing his self-doubt.

"The mark of a good leader is admitting when he's wrong," she teased. "And to remember from his mistakes and do better, later." She'd heard Darman tell her this once and seen him practice it, himself, as he led his band of Caravaners. She saw it in Garth and knew, given time, he'd be an excellent leader. He chuckled as he gave her a kiss.

"Let's gather our things, see what's beyond hope of repair, then start hauling it uphill," he told them, feeling in slightly better spirits.

"Let's see about filling our waterskins and getting a good drink of water, too," Ryes added, smiling happily up at him. "And maybe some baths. I feel like I could really use one, now."

"A bath sounds good. I could use one, too, and wash up my clothes," Maren agreed. This evoked another round of laughter and voices raised in comments of concurrence.

"Why don't we wait the bath until we're done with the hauling and just make camp at the top of the other side?" Garth amended; reminding them they still had more work ahead of them. "Let's get busy," he ordered, as he took Ryes' hand and walked back toward the pathway to start picking up the things which were now lying upon the ground.

Ryes pointed and laughed, the others soon saw what she saw. Honey had flopped down into the shallow water by the pathway and was rolling in it, looking joyful.

"I think she's earned her frolic time," Garth said, chuckling at the sight of the windracer enjoying a good bath. "We'll join her soon enough." And with that they all got busy in earnest. The promise of a bath was a great reward.

Stranger in the Wilds

Sabin suddenly sat up, staring off into the gathering darkness. Most of the others were already in their blankets, starting to drop off, but something had alerted him and he knew someone was out there, just beyond their firelight. As Ardis sat up with him, sensing his instant wariness, she saw Garth and Ryes doing so, too. Sabin reached for his spear and stood up, signaling Ardis to stay put. Garth was up and ready, also.

"Who's out there? Show yourself!" he challenged the darkness. After several long minutes, they heard timid footfalls sound as someone approached their camp.

"I smelled your food and saw your fire, but didn't want to bother you, truly," a timid voice spoke as a small woman stepped into the firelight. She carried a sling on her belt, was wearing animal skins neatly stitched together, and had worn sandals upon her feet. She looked about the same age as their own women and they wondered what she was doing out here in the wilderness all alone?

"You're from one of the plains tribes," Ryes stated, coming to her feet and stepping forward. She motioned her closer to their fire. She followed slowly and looked ready to bolt; she seemed afraid. Ryes went over to their dying fire and to the covered pot of bounder stew. She dished some out into her own bowl and offered it to her, as she motioned for her to sit down, as she sat down, herself. The others were now fully awake and curious about this stranger. She saw she looked a bit thin, as if she hadn't had much to eat in a while.

"Thank you," she said, sitting and accepting the offered bowl and spoon, gratefully. "I'm not much of a hunter," she admitted. "My skills lie more in tanning and curing hides, not catching the animals while they're still alive and wearing them!" She spent the next several minutes hungrily eating. Garth and Sabin did a quick reconnaissance of the area, making sure there was no scent, nor trace, of anyone else about them. They weren't taking chances that she might be a distraction for an attack.

"What're you doing way out here, all alone?" Ryes questioned, smiling at how quickly she was eating. It was as if she hadn't had anything for days! The woman handed back the empty bowl noting the rest were now gathered about them; settling upon the not well-cured hides placed on the ground around the fire. They didn't look hostile, just curious. She smiled shakily.

"I truly have no idea. I've been bothered by strange, intense dreams and was going somewhere. Someone wanted me to come to her. She called me her daughter. And then suddenly that inner sense of purpose and direction deserted me. I found myself wandering near here, too close to the great ruins. I know it's a long way back to the plains, but even if I had to return there, I realized I didn't want to go back. I found these tracks and thought if I could find the Caravan wagons which made them, they might take me in, until I could get somewhere new to live. I've heard they're a good people to befriend," she explained.

"It was a woman's voice? In your dreams and in your head?" Ryes questioned sharply, suddenly frowning.

"Yes," she agreed, seeing this upset her greatly, wondering if she should've admitted it. Ryes sighed, relieved, and then grinned happily.

"And it did quit? You don't hear her anymore?" she pressed, needing to be very sure.

"Yes, it stopped very suddenly," she assured her, noting her relief and relaxing again.

"Then I did stop Doran from luring others to become her mindless slaves!" Ryes laughed aloud, jumping up to hug Garth. It made her feel good to know she HAD saved others from that evil valley. He and the rest of their group laughed with her in triumph. Ryes turned back to the stranger, smiling merrily.

"You need to tell us that story about that evil place," Kovin pressed, curious about it now. It seemed it wasn't a summer dream with this stranger having heard some kind of lure, too. Ryes nodded her head at him.

"We haven't truly had the time for me to do so for the three of you, yet," she admitted, "How about tomorrow evening?"

"That sounds good," Teris agreed, smiling. Ryes turned back to their newcomer.

"My name's Ryes and this is our leader, Garth," she introduced him. "And this is Sabin, Ardis, Torr, Shadd, Mitt, Teris, Kovin and Maren. We originally came from Matlowe Village, but have decided to find a new place to call our own, too."

"My name's Raya of the Moondance Tribe," she introduced herself. "I grew up wandering the plains with my family and tribe, so this has been the first time I've wandered anywhere alone."

"Welcome, Raya. You're more than welcome to stay with us, until you find something better," Garth invited her. She smiled and laughed at this, relieved. She watched them the better part of the day, hauling their things and cart up the incline to this side of the ravine. They hadn't seemed a bad group, with lots of joking and smiles exchanged freely. She was relieved she didn't have to wander directionless, all alone anymore.

"You're not alone now," Mitt insisted, grinning.

"Thank you," she replied, meaning it.

"Do you want more stew?" Ryes asked, "Just help yourself. We'll still have plenty left over for breakfast."

"It's really good," she replied in relief, as she saw the others starting to settle back into their blankets. She had her meager ones in her small backpack. She shrugged off the pack and took the refilled bowl with gratitude and a big smile.

"Torr, you take the first watch, and then wake me in a few hours," Garth told him in a low voice, as Ryes was getting Raya another bowl. "Just in case. We have a windracer she could easily take off with, as well as the rest of our supplies." Torr gave him a nod at this, as did Sabin. "I'll take the watch after you."

"And I'll take the watch after you," Sabin volunteered. Garth smiled, giving them both a nod of his head.

"Wake Maren for the last watch," he suggested. Sabin smiled with a huff of a breath.

"Just like old times," he commented. "Feels like we've been on the trail all our lives." He suddenly got a Vision of Raya with her arms around Kovin, smiling up at him. It looked like they were standing outside their new home. So she's with them there.

"It does sometimes, doesn't it?" Garth agreed with a low chuckle, not seeing his friend was having a Vision. Sabin turned for his blankets once more, feeling better about her, now. He'd tell Garth about it tomorrow.

"You can sleep by me," Mitt offered Raya, as she sat with Ryes and the newcomer. Garth wasn't happy with this, but kept it to himself. They had no idea what kind of person this Raya was like, and if she was being drawn by Doran's call, she was a Talent of some sort, in the least. And if she was about the same age as most of their women, her first season would be upon her soon. Maybe this was just what Maren, Kovin and Teris needed, if she'd accept one of them for the mating.

By the time they established camp the next late afternoon, Raya was part of their group in many ways. She was slowly opening up, and learned she could joke with the rest, and was smiling more now than ever in her life. It wasn't that their life on this pathwas easy, but that they didn't let the small things burden their hearts. They were a fresh wind that seemed to free her soul and refresh her spirit.

Raya spent the day trying to work with a couple of the more promising hides. She knew she could save them and make them into something more usable. Ardis was paying close attention to what she was doing and did her best to help out. She noted Ardis had the basic skills, but not much beyond that knowledge. She found herself teaching her as they worked the skins and explaining things to her; surprising herself that she fell into the role so easily. Again, this helped her to feel she could fit in and be a true part of these people.

She told them stories from her life out on the plains and they listened with eager ears, asked strange questions at times, and laughed with her on the funny parts. They tried to see the things she described for them, giving her inner vision shape with her words. Sometimes she felt she succeeded, sometimes she knew she didn't. They didn't understand the concept of the men owning women and being totally in charge of their lives. It was foreign to them and had Raya paying attention to their own interactions within this small group.

As they set up their camp, she played her part and helped like she was one of them. This got further approval from both Garth and Sabin, who hadn't looked at her with doubts dancing in their eyes the whole day, as they had last night. They accepted her fully now, as if she had started out with them from the beginning of their journey. This acceptance had the others more relaxed, too. Soon they had dinner cooking and she got the women to try some of her spice combinations, which were simpler but just as hearty. She loved the variety of the plants and seeds the women had gathered while out on the trail. They were very good with their choices.

And Honey welcomed her skilled attention and gentle care. She saw that Ryes and Honey were very close and that Ryes could speak to the heart of this stout, caring windracer. It was a rare person who could do such a thing - even among her own tribe. The wind, which dwelled deep in the heart of each windracer, rarely whispered to others. Ryes heard hers and understood and gave of her own heart in return. It brought Raya to tears, which were impossible to truly explain. Ryes hugged her, seeming to understand her heart, too.

That evening, as soon as their food was passed out to everyone, the others started asking Ryes for her story about Doran. Raya soon realized this was the one who had called her away from the Moondance Tribe to head off into the wilderness all alone. Her life had been turbulent at the time, so the calling was a welcome event for change.

"This time you're not going to leave anything out," Maren pressed her, looking stern. "We all deserve to know the full tale."

"It was a horrible ordeal and you had glimpses in the nightmares which were visited upon you, too, before we were separated," she pointed out.

"And Sabin and I had a short Vision of you facing her off in a very strange place, while Garth was keeping company with the ghost of your mother," he shot back, starling her and surprising Garth.

"You did?" he asked, looking between Sabin and Maren. The others appeared surprised at this news too, and stated asking questions all at once. Sabin held up his hands to quiet them.

"Maren had some bad nightmare and was about to run off to find you two when we had a shared Vision. Up to then I thought I could only do that with Ryes," he admitted after a few moments, as if he were measuring his words.

"So, let's hear about the root cause of all those strange things and you both can tell us your full tale now," Torr requested.

"To tell this tale so that our newcomers will understand it better, let me start with what was happening when we started having the nightmares after we left Matlowe," she began. She wove it again, after the style her grandfather taught her, getting nods of approval from Maren and Garth at times while she spoke. She left little out this time, telling them of the full blown nightmares they encountered in that evil valley. Of the sad existence of the sleeping handmaidens; of the horrible ending of the one old groundskeeper and the determination of Doran to keep her small kingdom intact and dancing to her own whims. Of the way she destroyed lives, both when she was free and young, and then through the years when she was captive but still a power to be reckoned with and feared. How Doran became a darker and darker being to her very core. Raya was shaking at times and she and Mitt clung to each other, seeing with her words the dangers she faced. When Ryes was through, it was fully dark and they were glad of the comfort afforded by their merry little campfire.

"We will have to go back to get it," Ryes stated. "The Stone of Power cannot stay there to be turned towards evil purpose again," she told them, getting nods of agreement. "And I must go back to free those women, who might find the courage to live again in a new age."

"We'll all go with you and see if we can encourage them to come out of that endless sleep," Shadd avowed, a solemn look in her eyes, as she was shivering at the thought of such evil.

"Maybe your dream lady is there, Maren?" Ardis teased, smiling now. "You said she needed rescue from the cold." He started to refute her, but then paused, frowning.

"I don't know, but I don't think so," he finally replied, blushing. "I feel she's somewhere else. We'll see…" This got a laugh out of Garth and he gripped his shoulder in encouragement.

"You'll find her," he assured him. Maren could only nod. "Now, let's get our watches set and off to bed. It has been a long day!" There were murmured agreements from the rest as they dropped their dirty plates into the wash bucket for the morning. After the full tale of Doran, no one wanted to look for the stream in the dark. They all slept a little closer to the fire this night, too.

"Let's check on your little one," Maren ordered as he found himself stuck in camp, again with Ardis, Ryes and Raya. Ryes smiled in resignation as she gave him a nod of her head.

"What does he mean?" Raya asked her, puzzled, as they were cleaning the tubers Ryes found earlier this morning. They were the sweet ones she favored, herself.

"One of my cubs needed a little help, so he'll be born all right," she related, as Maren helped her to her feet. Raya looked unsure of this. "My cousin's a Healer," she explained. Maren gave her a nod and small bow, as he led Ryes over to her blankets.

"A Healer? A real Healer?" she questioned Ardis with surprise in her voice, turning to see the laughter in her eyes.

"Yes, and a very strong one, too," she assured her. "He completely healed Mitt when the cart ran her over the other day. It's a relief knowing Maren's with us. Shadd's almost due for her first season. So, with the three of us having cubs in the spring, it's a blessing with Maren here to help with their arrival. Have you had your first season?" she asked, suddenly wondering, mentally kicking herself for not thinking to ask before.

"No," she admitted, blushing. "It was the other reason I didn't want to go back to my tribe. I don't like the choices I have for a mate. And I think I'm due very soon," she told her, dropping her voice to a lower level.

"Just before Shadd, then. We've already let the men know that WE choose whom we mate with, and to the four winds with this challenge stuff." Ardis smiled, seeing the shock upon her face at this. "I know the pickings are pretty slim, but with Maren, Teris and Kovin to choose from, I'm sure you'll get some fine cubs." Raya sat for a few minutes, thoughtful about the issue. It was true that the last two days, Kovin and Teris were waiting upon her, hand and foot, but Maren seemed like he wasn't interested. He was friendly, but not attracted to her as if he were courting her.

"Why does Maren act the way he does?" she asked in a low voice, seeing he and Ryes were busy, with her lying down and him sitting beside her; his hands gently upon her stomach. Both had their eyes shut.

"He has some kind of dream woman, whom he says is beckoning to him at night," Ardis told her with a merry laugh. "I asked him how he's supposed to find her all the way out here, and then you just appear. So, now he's sure she will, too."

"Oh," she replied, smiling. So, that left Kovin and Teris as the only unclaimed men. Not bad, considering they both treated her with respect and caring. It'd be a hard choice since she truly didn't know them yet. "What about Mitt?" she pressed, wondering.

"Her season's not due until next year, but Ryes said she thought she and Teris were getting close, like they're thinking of trying free mating. But, we noticed he sure seemed more interested in you, yesterday. So, I don't know. A maybe free mate isn't as good as a woman who might actually choose you for real mating," she teased. "Why don't you talk with them, alone, away from the rest of us and see how they feel about things? You can always try free mating, to see if either one is more suited to you," she offered.

Raya practically reeled with the thought of being fully in control of this aspect of her life! She tried free mating several months ago with Toron, but he was used to bullying others. She found he abused her during it, more than anything else. It took a long time for the bruises and cuts to heal up. She noted Shadd and Torr practically went at it every night, but with Ryes and Ardis carrying cubs, it wasn't safe for them now. But, when would she get the chance to be alone with either Kovin, or Teris? Then she got an idea.

"Maybe, when they get back, I could go fill our waterskins and wash bucket with some fresh water?" she suggested to Ardis. She caught Raya's eyes and got her full meaning.

"This is a wilderness. Maybe one of the men should go with you, just to be sure you're safe," she agreed smiling, chuckling at her ruse. She sure caught onto that fast! She felt more comfortable around her after Sabin told her about his Vision. This was further proof she was fitting in with the rest of them quite well.

"I appreciate your help, very much," Raya told Kovin, as he helped her scrub and rinse out their dinner dishes. With both of them doing the chore, it was done quickly. She'd gone out earlier with Teris to fill their waterskins, but realized he had not felt "true" to her senses, so had not gone beyond normal, friendly banter. Kovin felt different. There was a solidness to him, not just in his body, but his spirit and heart that appealed to her and drew her to him.

Before she knew it, she was close at his side and looking appealingly up into his eyes. He put down the bucket he held and wrapped his arms about her. He was slow and careful as he pulled her into his arms, as if being sure she was willingly welcoming this embrace. She smiled for him and hugged her body to his, wrapping her arms around his neck as she looked up into his soulful, brown eyes.

"I wanted to see what you were like," she started, not sure how to voice it.

"And how was Teris earlier?" he asked, needing to know, feeling the barb of his words, too. He'd seem them laughing as they returned with the newly filled waterskins and wash bucket.

"I don't know. I didn't feel as comfortable with him and never got this close," she admitted, blushing. He smiled at this and leaned down to kiss her gently upon the lips. She then opened up after a few moments, letting her inner passion loose and deepened her kiss back. This ignited him as they kissed and explored each other before free-mating beside the stream. She didn't feel any regrets about her choice and found she couldn't get enough of Kovin, now. He was passionate yet gentle.

"We wanted to let everyone know we're going to try being together," Kovin announced to everyone before they settled down for the night. Raya nodded her head, blushing as she tightly gripped his hand while they stood before the rest.

"That's wonderful!" Ardis declared, standing up and giving Raya and then Kovin a hug. "I'm glad you two are making a go at it." Shadd laughed as she had stepped over and wrapped her arms around the both of them too.

"A fine idea," she agreed, grinning merrily. "It is your choice, Raya?" she pressed, wanting to be sure. Raya nodded her head, a happy smile breaking out as she practically beamed. Ryes laughed and hugged her and Kovin, too.

"I think you've found a good man," she said, as Maren nodded his agreement.

"The best of Matlowe," he added, getting his chance to hug her too. "If you'd like me to check you over, we can do that tomorrow," he advised.

"Maren just likes to make sure all of us are at peak health, all the time, now," Mitt teased. She gave Kovin a hug, then Raya. "Welcome home!" she added to Raya.

"Living with you has been like finding the home I was meant to live in," she agreed. Teris stepped over and hugged Kovin and then Raya.

"It feels like you're always been with us, already," he agreed. "If you need anything, just ask," he urged, his eyes met hers and were clear and steady and she knew he meant it truly.

"Thank you," she replied. She turned to all the others. "Thank you, all!"

"You're welcome," Garth assured her, smiling. He clasped Kovin's hand and gave him a nod. "Better get your sleeping spot picked out," he urged, chuckling. Then he, Sabin and Torr took turns giving her a hug, too.

Kovin gave him a nod and went to get his blankets and pack. Raya put the clean dishes back where they were stored and got her pack and blanket, standing ready for Kovin's decision. After they got settled, Mitt got her blankets and pack, then settled herself down next to Maren. He looked surprised at this bold move.

"What?" he asked with a laugh, surprised.

"I'm not sleeping alone and you're just like one of my brothers," she told him haughtily, then slipped off her boots and snuggled into her blankets. Maren shook his head and shrugged.

"Good night, Sis," he told her, and then turned his back and got into his own bedding and comfortable for the night. He chuckled quietly as he settled, but resisted teasing her tonight.

"SABIN!" He suddenly heard Ryes call out his name as he and Torr were talking, falling further back in the line. He frowned at Torr, but there was a strange note of urgency in her voice.

"Better see what's up," he urged as he saw they stopped and were waiting for him. Teris appeared annoyed, but Garth was amused. He trotted up to the front and saw Ryes standing stock still, staring out at the horizon before them, further down the pathway.

"LOOK!" she prompted him, pointing. He shaded his eyes and cast his gaze where she indicated. He almost stopped breathing as he saw what she saw. He nodded as a broad smile blossomed across his face.

"Yes, that's it!" he assured her, as he grabbed Ardis in joy, dancing with her in a circle. She was laughing at his wild display, as Ryes was laughing too, hugging Garth. "We found it!" Sabin told Ardis and the others, to their dazed wonder, as they gathered closer. He pointed to the far, white tower jutting above the horizon. It was interesting that their pathway seemed to lead straight for it.

"That's it?" Torr questioned as he looked at the strange structure. "It looks like something out of Hailys. What is it?" he asked.

"A tower, which we can use as our watch tower," Ryes explained with a laugh. "You can see for miles from there, Torr Sharp-Eyes."

"It's tall enough," he agreed, noting it wasn't easy to distinguish against the bright sky. "Are you sure no one else is living there?" he questioned, wanting to be very sure before they approached this mystery home of theirs.

"I didn't see anyone, but us in my Vision," Sabin assured him, cuffing him on the shoulder affectionately. Kovin laughed at this, relief in his heart.

"It looks like the end of our road, too," he pointed out the pathway running toward the distant tower. Raya nodded, appearing thoughtful.

"Come on, let's hurry. We can make it by nightfall," Mitt urged, getting excited now that it was in sight.

"No. We want to approach this place by day," Garth decided. "We want to make sure it's ours; free and clear. I don't want to surprise anyone in the night, to be sure." He met everyone's eyes, making sure he had their compliance. "We'll go as far as we can today, then camp for the night and see what the morning brings." He got nods of assent from each of them, glaring most especially at Mitt and Ryes. They'd both been too good, far too long. This got a smile and nod from Ryes, as Mitt gave him her grudging nod of compliance.

Soon they came across a real Caravan road crossing their pathway. The difference was interesting and they could clearly tell theirs had been heavily used, but not in a long time in comparison. Ryes checked it but soon announced no one appeared to have been on the Caravan road since early spring. It was disappointing but still encouraging to have some possible friends passing nearby on occasion.

They continued following the pathway since it did, indeed, run straight toward that distant structure. Garth and Teris were talking about the availability of the land here for cultivation and observations on the supply of water for planting crops, or a garden at least. It was almost at the end of the planting season, but he hoped they'd have something to show for it before the winter came; IF this place was empty and truly theirs for the taking.

Teris knew the land and growing plants. He's been delighted with the seeds Ryes brought with her and with what they gathered from the wild plants at Hailys. He never thought to try to grow a bubblenut tree, but was excited with the idea of the attempt. He had Ryes set aside far more than she thought prudent for the project, but he thought the more available, the better their chances at success. A good, deep stream ran its course parallel to the pathway, the few last days. If it ran near this new home of theirs, they'd be able to tap it for watering their crops and gardens, if the rains proved insufficient for their needs. He saw the deep green of the grasses and plants around them and thought it looked good, even if summer was now in full swing.

As nightfall approached, they set up camp and set their watches, since they were facing a new unknown element in the structure before them. It could be clearly seen now, with a white-painted building supporting it. It looked too small to house them, but Sabin and Ryes had merrily laughed at this; the secret being something they decided to keep, for now. Garth finally got it out of Ryes, as they snuggled down into their blankets for the night. He smiled into the dark as he thought about it.

"That's clever," he agreed. Then realized she was tugging at the lacings of his breeches. "What?" he questioned quietly, wondering.

"Maren thought it'd be all right now," she teased him. "It seems like it's been forever." She grinned mischievously, the firelight danced in her eyes.

"Won't it hurt our cubs?" he asked, worried. She assured him before that between her and Maren, they were going to be healthy and strong. He didn't want to do anything to endanger them but, the thought did have his blood pounding loudly in his ears.

"No, it won't. They'll be fine," she assured him, teasing him by nibbling at the fold of his closest ear. It caused a shiver of excitement to travel up his spine. "So, are you going to pull those off and get a little closer to me, or not?" she dared him. This was all the encouragement he needed.

"Ryes," Maren scolded as she sat with her back to one of their cart wheels, her eyes closed.

"I'm not doing anything - yet," she assured him. "I was just thinking of it." She opened her eyes and glared at him in disgust. "I can't get away with anything around you," she complained. He laughed at this, grinning mischievously.

"Not anymore," he assured her, sitting down next to her. He was now stuck watching Shadd, Ardis, Mitt and Raya, but knew his real chore would be Ryes, because she was bored and had wanted to be with the men to see their new home now; not being stuck here until they declared it safe. The rest of the men had gone ahead to check it out.

"Then, let's try this together," she urged. "I promised Garth I wouldn't try Time Walking again, until we reached our new home. I want to see who made this pathway; why they built this place, and then left it here abandoned."

"And he didn't want you trying anything this dangerous alone, either," Maren finished for her, chuckling at her ruse.

"Come on, it can't be that far back," she pleaded with him, wanting it so very much. "I know this path we've been following is nowhere near as old as Hailys." He sighed, thinking about it. He wanted to see it for himself, too, he had to admit. But, could she take them both back safely and make it possible for their return?

"Ardis?" he suddenly called out. After a few moments she appeared with a puzzled look on her face.

"Give Ryes and I an hour and if we're not awake by then, go get Sabin, please?" he requested, noting Ryes drew in a breath sharply in surprise at this. Ardis didn't look happy with his request, but gave him a nod in understanding.

"If you're sure," she pressed, worried. He gave her a confident nod of his head. Ryes looked startled and happy, all at the same time, so she smiled her encouragement. "Be careful," she warned, feeling it still needed to be voiced.

"We will," he assured her. Ryes nodded, too.

"I'll bring him back safely," she avowed. Then closed her eyes as Maren took her hand and closed his. Both were calling up their Talents to make a firm link between them, first. Mitt watched the exchange, frowning, and then looked up to Ardis.

"What're they doing?" she asked, wondering.

"Remember when Ryes was in trouble at Hailys, when you first arrived?" she reminded her. Mitt gave her a nod at this. "They're going to try it together. I bet to see who lived here, before. It might help us understand why they made this place, then left it," she told her with a sigh.

"It's too bad we can't go along with them," she pouted, as she wondered if she could. Ardis shook her head at this; turning back to her sorting, once more. Mitt saw she was busy, so crept over to Ryes' side and took her other hand and closed her eyes; hoping she could reach them. She just had to try!

Hoomans' Place

There was that now familiar, wrenching sensation from the inside and an immense wash of power being unleashed. It was very different this time, as Maren hung onto her for stability in this maddening chaos, making Ryes realize she was the one in control here. So, she directed them backwards until she detected life coming and going about this place, making it feel very busy. Another joined them, with fear and excitement being projected, as they realized Mitt was with them on their venture. It gave Ryes a moment of panic as she knew Mitt had no Talent, but she also had no way to keep her from following them. There was no helping it now; both she and Maren knew Garth would be unhappy with them all. They could only do their best to make sure she came to no harm. They opened their eyes, finding themselves sitting beside their pathway in the evening, with bright, white lights coming from the tower nearby. There was even a light flashing from the top of the tower; flashing green, yellow and then white. There was a great, dark mass sitting upon the ground on the far side of the tower, which isn't there in their own time. It too was adorned with bright lights that gave them small glimpses of its shape in the gathering darkness.

"Oh my gosh," Mitt declared, still holding onto Ryes' hand, as they stood up together. Ryes was unsure if they should let go of one another, or not, so held onto both of them tightly to help bind them to her.

"Stick together so you're protected by my Talent," she warned aloud, then drew in a breath in wonder. A strange carriage came down the path, running quickly past them, and then braking to a stop before the tower. It looked like someone took one of the shuttle pods from ancient Hailys and put wheels upon it!

"What was that?" Mitt asked; her eyes wide with wonder.

"A shuttle-pod with wheels?" Ryes ventured to voice. "Something like the ones in Hailys, long ago."

"Is there any way you can make it so they can't see us?" Maren asked, hoping they hadn't been spotted, already.

"Maybe, if I will us not to be seen?" she questioned, still not knowing what she was doing with this Time Walking stuff. She closed her eyes for a moment and focused on this thought for a few moments. "Let's go test this first with those people getting out of that wheeled shuttle pod," she suggested, smiling nervous assurance, as she opened her eyes. "If they see us, we can always return home and try another time."

"What've we got to lose? They'll only think of us as ghosts, otherwise? Isn't that what you said?" he pressed, needing to be sure she wouldn't yank them home too soon. He wanted to look around.

"Yes. It's like being a ghost, or spirit," she told him. They started walking toward the shuttle pod. There were two strange, furless men chattering with each other, standing beside the open hatch as they unloaded boxes from the back of the shuttle. They looked like they were Starmen, but with strangely squashed faces and their ears were much smaller and round-shaped. Their eyes were much the same and they had a solid upper lip, which did not detract from their appearances. One did seem to have grown some hair above his lip which made him seem better. They were of the same size as their own men in height with the regular variances in shape and height they knew in their own people. Overall, not an unpleasant looking people. The boxes were strange-looking and had handles and straps on them. It made it easy for them to carry, she mentally noted.

"I don't understand what they're saying," Maren complained. His heart almost jumped out of his chest as he realized these were the same people as his blue-eyed lady!

"I think they're probably speaking their own language," Ryes teased him, smiling. "At least they don't seem to see us standing here, nor hear us speaking," she stated, speaking loudly. They didn't react. They were carrying their cases, walking toward some tall, open doors down in a pit, below the tower and its lights. They followed, curious. Maren looked excited, smiling to himself. Then Ryes recalled his dreams about a blue-eyed woman with blonde hair and wondered. They went in the door right behind them, the lights within almost blinding them after being out in the darkness. Their pair paused to speak with some other people inside the main doors.

There was a long, wide ramp leading down to the entrance. The doors were tall and wide and only partly opened, it seemed. Ryes realized they could drive three Caravan wagons in through the partly opened door and not touch each other, nor the doors. She saw they were panels rolling on tracks. The room within it was vast and went far back. The ceiling was high enough to stack ten large Caravan wagons on top of themselves easily. It reminded her of some of the galleries she'd seen through the borrowed memories of some of the Handmaidens of Hailys, when it was grand and new.

"What is this place?" Mitt asked, astonished as they stood a moment looking around.

"Our new home," Maren replied, grinning. "Let's see what it's like inside," he prompted. Ryes nodded her head, as they stayed right behind their two men. They finished talking with a few other people and were on the move again; they followed them through the interior doors, which were both opened wide. Those were huge doors too, but swung inward. They found themselves in a wide, bustling corridor, with many people coming and going at a great hurry.

"Something's got them upset," Ryes observed. "This seems to have some kind of urgency to it and is nothing like the bustle of Hailys. Their faces appear tense and others are very upset. It's more like when Hailys was on fire and people were fleeing the city."

"Looks that way to me, too," Maren agreed. They continued in the direction their original pair went, feeling strange as people passed right through them, leaving them with an odd, painful sensation as they did so.

"I don't think we should let them do that," Ryes suggested, sounding doubtful, dodging a big man in a rush down the passageway, pulling all three of them up against a wall. Some dark cases blocked the foot traffic away from them.

"Let's go check out some of these rooms here, and get out of their way," Maren concurred, not liking the feeling he got when it happened, either.

"Yes, let's get out of the way!" Mitt urged. They went through two sets of open doors with a short hallway between and found themselves inside a room with a narrow table in the middle of it. A man was treating a woman lying upon it. She appeared very pregnant and had managed to cut open her leg. He was using a small machine to quickly seal the gash closed. This had Maren disturbed, wanting to help, seeing her obvious distress and pain.

"No, Maren. You can't. This is what was in the past, not what is in our own time," Ryes reminded him. "You're just a ghost here, remember? I don't think your Talent would work for you here."

"He's trying not to hurt her," Mitt told him in comfort. "I think with all this rushing and panic, there isn't enough time for him to be more careful."

"They don't have any Healers here," Maren agreed with a heartfelt sigh, still wishing he could help her.

"This might be their version of Healer," Mitt replied. "Maybe they don't have any Talents?" Ryes nodded agreement at this, and then turned them back to the main corridors.

"Let's go see what else is here," Ryes suggested. They eased back out into the corridor, then around a turn. They took several more different corridors to avoid others and to learn and explore where they could, and try to puzzle out some of the odd actions they saw these people doing in some of the rooms. Finally they found themselves in a large room, which was in an area where there were obvious rooms they lived in. There were waste chairs in separate little rooms and curtained stalls here, too. When they looked within one where there was someone singing, they saw a naked woman standing under some falling water in one of them. She was washing her body, then rinsed it and started to soap her hair. Maren was smiling strangely at her, as Ryes thought they'd seen enough.

"Maren," she protested, tugging on his hand to get him to respond.

"I found her," he breathed, raptly, "My dream lady. And she sings while she bathes!"

"But, she's here in the past!" Mitt protested, seeing his infatuation clearly in his face.

"So, how're you supposed to save her, if she's already gone from this place?" Ryes questioned, wondering.

"Maybe, they'll come back?" he suggested, hoping.

"Well, you're not supposed to see her without any clothes on, and not even being introduced," she ordered him, brooking no argument in this matter. "Come on!" She pulled him back out, upset with this strange fixation he had for this furless woman.

"Mitt? Could you give me a hand with this?" Shadd asked, not seeing the young woman about. She, like Ryes, usually managed to find enough trouble on her own and it was best to keep tabs on her whereabouts at all times. She got no response, nor did she suddenly appear out of nowhere to surprise her. This had Shadd puzzled. "Ardis, do you know where Mitt is?" she questioned.

"Mitt?" she asked, and then her eyebrows shot up in surprise. "She couldn't have!" she declared, scrambling to her feet. She quickly rounded the cart to see her holding tightly onto Ryes' other hand, her head resting against her shoulder, as if taking an innocuous, mid-morning nap. Her breath exploded out in exasperation at finding her here.

"What's going on?" Shadd pressed as she stopped, seeing the trio with their eyes closed. It looked too familiar. "Oh no, you knew about this?" she demanded, worried for them.

"Yes, but it was only supposed to be Maren and Ryes. Maren told me that if they weren't awake in an hour's time, to go get Sabin to help. They've only been gone a few minutes," she explained. "Maybe with Mitt in the mix, I ought to get him, anyway?"

"What're they doing?" Raya asked, seeing their concern with the trio taking a nap together, as she followed them.

"Don't you feel it?" Ardis questioned, turning to look her in the eyes, frowning. Raya looked puzzled for a moment, and then suddenly understood, nodding her head in agreement.

"There's some kind of tingling sensation in the air," she stated, doubting her senses. "It feels as if insects are crawling upon my skin, all over. Why do I feel this?"

"If you were hearing Doran's call, you're a Talent. It's what it is and how strong it is, that we don't know. Ryes is a Catalyst and might be able to awaken it within you, if you want it awakened. Sabin once told me that there was such a tremendous feeling of power around Ryes when she's Time Walking that anyone with a Talent would feel it. I was sure you could sense it, if nothing else," Ardis explained.

"Time Walking?" she returned in question, "what's that? It sounds too simple and direct. Could a person truly walk through time?" And she had Talent? She didn't believe it, but this seemed to be proof of the matter in their eyes.

"Literally, they're walking into the past to see who the ones to build this place were, and why they might've left it behind," Ardis replied as Shadd nodded her head, understanding why, as well.

"They want to see if we have a legitimate claim to keep it as our own, or if the original owners will return," Shadd explained to Raya. It was something which needed to be determined, after all. "And Garth did tell her she could Time Walk, if she wasn't alone. It was just that Mitt is the unexpected element here," she added and saw Raya understood what they meant, now.

"How can Mitt do this with them, unless she has a Talent of her own?" Raya questioned, wondering.

"No, she hasn't seemed to carry one, but Sabin said there's so much power unleashed when Ryes does this, that maybe you don't need to have a Talent to Time Walk with her?" Ardis suggested, frowning. "But, I wonder if it'd make getting lost in the past easier, if you had no Talent to help tie your inner self back to your own body?"

"Maybe you'd better get Sabin, after all?" Shadd prompted, feeling it'd be a prudent thing to do now.

"True, I'll go. Just don't touch them," she cautioned, knowing Shadd already knew this warning. Raya nodded her head in response, sinking down to sit before the others as if still puzzling it all out.

"I wish we could understand what they're saying," Mitt complained in exasperation, watching as wheeled carts were loaded with sealed boxes and other containers, and being rushed down the hallways now. Some were being taken to storage areas, some rushed out the door.

"Look, they're storing some of their things, so they must expect to return sometime," Maren said, looking crestfallen at this revelation.

"But, they're not here now. I mean when we're here, so something must've happened to them. Didn't you say those pathways were years old?" Mitt asked Ryes, who was frowning, as she was trying to mouth their words.

"Yes, they're very old," she agreed. "Look at that," she gave a nod of her head to two of their own people, who were dressed in the fashion of the humans and being taken outside under the direction of the woman Maren was obsessed with, who was dressed now, and another, petite brunette. "Maybe the answers to our questions lie there," she suggested.

"You mean to make us visible to them, so you can ask what they know about these people?" Maren demanded. "When are we going to get the chance?" He realized they looked like what plainsmen were said to be. "Are they plainsmen?" he added, noting the look about them like Raya. Ryes gave him a nod in affirmation.

"I think so," she replied. "They're like the plains people in Darman's paintings."

"Let's follow and see if an opportunity comes up," Mitt pressed, wanting to get out of this madcap rushing. Ryes smiled and gave her a nod of her head, seeing she was disturbed about all the haste about them. The three trailed the two women and their charges outside, back into the gathering darkness, across the grassland and up to the dark bulk, sitting upon the ground. They stopped under the smaller lights to talk with a pair of men dressed in uniforms. As they stopped and their attention was focused upon some parchments, Ryes made them visible to the plains people, soliciting a look of shock out of the woman.

"Who are these people here?" Maren questioned directly, knowing they didn't have much time.

"They're called hoomans," the man answered in a low voice. "Who are you?" he asked.

"We're Time Walking, but come from Matlowe Village," Ryes answered. "Why are you here with them and why all this haste?"

"A lady Talent!" the woman gasped, her eyes wide with awe in their depths.

"There's some kind of an emergency. And the only reason we're with them is they captured us to study us. It was very bad for me for a long time, but these two hooman women rescued me from the evil hooman elder, with the power of their own hooman elder to back them." He held up his hands to show they were bound with a strange cord. "They trust Ptan, but not me quite as well. Although, I think the women trust me and must make some show for their own men," he explained.

"Can you save us?" Ptan pleaded, hoping for rescue.

"We're like spirits here. If we can find where they take you, maybe there's a chance," Maren told her, knowing this had to be hard on them. Of all the peoples who lived upon Tayna, the plains people had let go more of technology, than any of the others. Even to shunning the establishment of cities and villages; becoming nomadic wanderers across the vast plains.

"Maren's supposed to save the blonde woman," Mitt put in, smiling impishly, "Maybe when he saves her, we can save you, too?" Maren blushed at this, but nodded his head.

"She's worth saving," he stated steadily, meeting his eyes.

"What's happening?" Mitt questioned, feeling suddenly strange inside.

"It's all right. It's merely time to go back," Ryes told her, trying to calm her. "We'll see what we can do," she offered the plains couple then pulled away, holding onto Maren and Mitt, hearing Sabin's insistent demands. There was that sickening, wrenching feeling, then a settling within themselves; the sensation of feeling the weight of the world and their own bodies, once more. The others seemed surprised at how heavy they suddenly felt, amusing Ryes.

"We were spirits, remember?" she teased them. They realized she was speaking truly.

"And I'm sure we're in trouble," Maren sent to the other two, before the link was finally severed.

"That's probably true," Ryes agreed, saying it aloud, as she opened her eyes seeing Garth kneeling before her. He didn't look as unhappy as the last time, but he wasn't pleased, either.

"They're called hoomans!" Mitt announced, smiling brightly, as she let go of Ryes' hand. "That was fun, can I go again?" she asked her brother.

"Why didn't you return as soon as you noticed Mitt was with you?" he demanded in a low voice. Ryes sighed, but was happy with his self-control.

"We just got there and I didn't know if we could keep her from following again, so I decided to let her stay with us. I kept a tight hold upon her, to make sure," she explained. He sighed and gave her a nod, knowing his sister.

"So, you can take a non-talent with you, too?" Sabin speculated, thinking on this; seeing that Mitt was not only safe, but charged from her adventure. He looked like he was feeling a little jealous, now.

"I didn't know I could, until now," Ryes told him. "You know I'm still learning my skills. I didn't think I could stop the cart the other day. I thought that, in the temple, it was only through the power of the Stone which I was controlling, not that it actually lay within myself."

"So, why did these hoomans leave?" Garth asked her, helping her to stand up, then lending Mitt a hand, as Sabin helped Maren to his feet.

"There was some kind of emergency," she explained, "But the plains people we were asking didn't know exactly what. They were captives of the hoomans, with the man's hands being bound by some kind of strange cord. He said they didn't trust him as much as his wife, Ptan."

"Ptan and Alda?" Raya spoke up suddenly, a strange look in her eyes. "They were from my own tribe. They disappeared many, many years ago; long before I was born. It was told as an old lover's tragedy to the children. They left because his father wanted Ptan and Alda didn't want to fight him. Later, a Visionary saw them eaten by a great metal monster," she explained, looking excited. "So, they truly existed?" She met Ryes' eyes and saw the truth.

"We saw them taking some things with them, but storing the rest in special rooms. There was so much running and haste, that it was hard to determine why all the rushing. There wasn't anything that we could see that was different, other than that massive, dark shadow they were loading their things inside of," Maren told them. "They were taking the plains people in it too, I'm sure."

"If we could've had more time," Ryes started, then caught the look in Sabin's eyes and gave him a nod in understanding. She saw the rest of their band gathered around them, ideas coming to light in their eyes, too.

"Let's show you this new home of ours, which the hoomans left behind for us," Garth offered, smiling. "Then, once we get settled, we can go back into time and see if we can unravel the mysteries these hoomans represent."

"Sounds like a good idea to me," Ryes agreed. Mitt threw her arms around her, giving her a kiss on the cheek, causing Ryes to blush, as Shadd chuckled merrily.

"Thanks for taking me with you," she said, then released her again. "You should see what made these tracks!" she exclaimed to her brother as they turned toward the main door. "It moves very fast on great, dark wheels and people and their things can ride inside of them." Garth chuckled at this, shaking his head.

"Maybe soon," he agreed. "This could be our answer to figuring out how to make the equipment inside operate safely. Some of it looks outrageous and there're obvious signs posted, which Teris thinks warn of danger. There was a red circle around the images with a slash through the middle. We'll all stay for now in the great antechamber between the inside and outside doors, and then try to figure out how to activate what we need, and is safe to run. Yes, Ryes and her Time Walking will serve us well," he said with obvious regard for his wife, smiling. She smiled and nodded her agreement in return.

The outer chamber, which when they were Time Walking had been brightly lit, was dark, yet still had the feeling of being a massive space. Ryes demonstrated how to unlock and open the doors wider for the others, having noted it on their adventure into the past, augmented by a borrowed memory. This simple thing seemed to please Kovin and Garth as they both spent some time playing with the doors while the others organized a camp within the building. The inner doors were solidly locked against their entry and that seemed to frustrate the men.

Near the inner doors were neatly stacked crates, each bearing many labels in a language they did not understand. Torr was going to take one down, but it was locked into place in some manner and would not be dislodged. Ryes pointed to the small discs which were on each side of the cases which touched the others and reasoned they had to be what locked them together. That gave Torr something to try to puzzle out as he was determined to see what was inside of one of them. He was now trying to figure out how to remove one of the discs.

Maren discovered one of their hand lanterns and after playing around with it for a few moments, figured out how to turn it on. Blazingly bright white light emanated from it and practically blinded everyone as he was waving it around in triumph. He figured out how to turn it off and then spent a few moments turning it on and off to be sure he could do it on demand. This pleased everyone that there was something here which they could use and was a very useful tool. Garth and the others set out to explore the huge room and hoped to find more lanterns within it, or other useful things.

While the men were gone exploring, Ryes, Raya and Mitt set up a simple pen for Honey near the underground building entrance. They moved the cart inside and while Ardis and Shadd cleaned the area up and set up a simple camp, Ryes and Mitt went to get fresh water from the nearby stream. Raya was starting a firepit near the top of the ramp. None of them wanted a fire inside the building with possibly suffocating smoke coming from it.

"Look, that's where they get their own fresh water," Ryes pointed out to Mitt after they finished filling their pots, waterskins and buckets. She put hers down and paced further downstream but did not see the outlet. "But I have no idea where their wastewater comes back out here," she added, appearing puzzled.

"Why's that important?" Mitt asked, wondering. Ryes didn't immediately answer but went back out to the intake pipe and out into the water to get a good look at it. She seemed amazed and admiring of the design. She swam back in seemingly satisfied.

"It's important because we don't want to take our drinking water near their waste outlet and end up very sick, or even dying from it," she explained. I wanted to make sure this was the intake, at least, and found it is because it's still working," she stated. "I'll look for the outlet tomorrow, so we'll know for sure where it is located. Just in case." Mitt nodded her head now understanding it better, too.

"It's a good size, so I think it's meant to support quite a lot of people," Ryes said, as she picked up Honey's water bucket and several of the waterskins, slinging those over her shoulder. She grabbed another bucket for their dirty dishes.

"Do you think we'll find a way inside?" she asked as she picked up the pots and the rest of the waterskins, ready to head back in.

"We will," Ryes replied, smiling merrily now. "Why are you in such a hurry?" she asked, curious. "We barely got a chance to look around in there, before."

"I want to take a standing bath under one of those waterfalls. That looked like fun," she returned with a mischievous look in her eyes. Ryes laughed outright, nodding her head in agreement.

"It sure did," she agreed. "Wait until we tell everyone all the things we saw, tonight."

"They won't believe us," she teased, laughing.

"Oh, they will... in time," she returned, her eyes shining. They returned just as the men returned, too.

After half the day of exploring, they turned up a small box of odd items and another two lanterns, which they were happily using. They seemed to expect Ryes to identify the items since she had the memories of the Handmaidens to draw upon. She laughed at this, only shaking her head.

"They were advanced, but not the same as our own people. Their things seem similar, but worked differently," she tried to explain.

"But you have seen ours in operation, so are still the one to look at these," Torr pressed, extending the box to her. She sighed, but accepted it.

"I'll try," she offered.

Ryes sat thinking while the birds were roasting over the fire. Ardis and Shadd were helping Sabin and Torr to construct another simple oven for them to use later, once it cured. Garth, Kovin and Teris were double checking the pen's construction and the rest of the immediate area. Maren was watching her, while occasionally poking the sweet tubers he had roasting, too. He grinned at her, and then shook his head no.

"You're not going to do it, tonight," he told her outright.

"Do what?" she asked, a look of amazement in her eyes. "It was still just a thought," she complained. She gave him a look of exasperation, as he chuckled merrily.

"You're thinking of doing a quick Time Walk to see if you can find out how to open the inner building's doors," he stated. She blushed at this and finally gave him a nod of agreement.

"If I could find the key," she started, then sighed, shook her head in wonder and let the thought go for now. "We think too much alike," she commented. He laughed heartily at this, nodding his head in agreement.

"That we do," he agreed, "which is why I knew what you were thinking as I was thinking the same thing, myself. But with Sabin and Raya sensitive to the power unleashed when you Time Walk, I don't think we could get away with it tonight." She laughed with him merrily at this point, grinning.

"We'll get another chance, yet," she told him, smiling with her eyes alight with mischief.

"What's so funny?" Mitt asked, coming back out from their campsite.

"We just discovered we think too much alike," Maren boasted with a big grin upon his face.

"So, when are we going again?" she pressed, speaking in a low voice as she dropped down to sit between the two. She saw the look that passed between them and frowned. "You're not leaving me out," she told them firmly. Ryes sighed and shook her head, smiling again.

"Truly, we cannot seem to keep you away," she agreed.
Maren laughed. "But not immediately," she warned. "I think Garth
and Sabin want to check things out first."

"You're not exhausted as you were before," Maren observed,
then moved one of the tubers out of the coals to keep it from burning.

"No, I'm not. It could be because it wasn't back as far as in
Hailys," she offered, wondering about it, too. "Or it could be that I'm
getting better at using my Talents. I've been practicing, after all.
And there's something I want to try with everyone tonight, after
dinner. It could be fun, if it works," she teased them, grinning.

"As long as it's not dangerous," Maren returned, giving her a
nod. Mitt was nodding agreement too, but Maren doubted there was
any consideration in her mind for danger.

"Everyone join hands, relax, close your eyes and try to clear
your minds," Ryes instructed, since they were all willing to try
something she wanted to do with them tonight. Once she made sure
they were all holding hands, she clasped Garth's and Maren's hands
and closed her own eyes. She opened up her Mind Voice Talent, now
having found a way to identify it in her own mind and formed up a
pool of their collective thoughts. This alone seemed to charge her
friends. Once she got everyone calmed once again, she shared parts
of what they saw and experienced while Time Walking in this new
home of theirs.

They marveled at the rush and panic of the hoomans and the
immense size of the underground building. Ardis loved the sight of
the tame waterfalls they used to bathe under and the nearness to
their own, small homes. Mitt again relished and shared her memory
of the large shuttle-pod, as Ryes called it, and the apparent ease with
the way it moved and stopped at the command of the hoomans inside
it. Maren shared his frustrations in being helpless to help the hooman
woman, who'd been injured. Sabin and Garth were curious about all
the different rooms in the building and the way some were shut off
from the others with heavier doors. And that there was more than
one level to the inner building. Once they had gone over their short
adventure, Ryes unleased another of her Talents and took them all on
a journey in the here and now.

She pulled them over to experience what it was like to be a
fish swimming in the nearby stream, and then moved them over to
the mind of a small bounder as it was nestling down for the night next
to his mother's soft, furry side. She was lovingly licking his fur as he

dropped off to sleep. Ryes pulled them further upward to the wings of a night-hunting bird, as she soared and searched for prey for her next meal. She then pulled them free and just let them all feel what she'd discovered before, the pulse of life all around them and how they were connected with it all. The heartbeat of Tayna, herself, welcomed them, sheltered them and protected them. Finally she pulled them free and settled all of them safely back within themselves, slowly dissolving the link.

"What was that?" Garth breathed, amazed as he put an arm around her shoulders. Ryes grinned up at him, the firelight dancing in her eyes.

"The last was an expression of a very old Starman Talent called Empath. That's why it's now hard for me to go hunting and take lives," she explained.

"Amazing!" Shadd declared, looking as if she was still trying to grasp it fully. Teris laughed and shook his head. Raya and Kovin were sitting with happy, but stunned looks on their faces, while Torr appeared as if he were still trying to believe it all. Mitt was charged and elated.

"So that was Ptan and Alda," Raya breathed, smiling happily as she hugged Kovin.

"That is what it's like to be an animal? Can you do that with plants, too?" Teris pressed, wonder dancing across his face.

"Not as deep," Ryes admitted, "and it seems best with trees. The bigger and older, the better."

"Can you show me?" he begged, wanting to know now.

"Not tonight," Ardis interrupted, before Ryes could speak. "I'll sleep better tonight not dreaming tree dreams," she scolded, laughing. Most of the rest laughed with her and agreed, too.

"I'm getting a little tired, now," Ryes told him. "We'll try it later, though."

"Thank you, Ryes!" Mitt practically shouted, jumping up and giving her a tight hug in happiness. "That was a great before bedtime adventure!" She laughed and hugged her back, nodding her head in agreement.

"I thought it was something you'd like," she admitted.

"Thanks," Maren agreed, taking a turn at hugging her, as Mitt let her go.

As they were finally going to bed in their new shelter, they all felt more a part of their new home, having felt and seen more of it already. They knew they'd all be safely inside this marvelous place the hoomans had left for them, soon. It didn't feel as big, scary and empty now.

Garth pulled her in close and gave Ryes a kiss, which she returned willingly.

"So, we're finally home. In our own home," he said in a low voice, having felt that deeply from Tayna, herself. He felt she'd lead him here.

"Yes we are," she assured him, feeling truly safe for the first time in a long time. She snuggled down into his arms and fell quickly asleep. Garth grinned as he gently brushed back a lock of hair that had fallen across her face. He kissed her forehead before falling into a deep, welcoming sleep, too.

Settling In

"I like this one," Ardis commented as she sat and brushed out her hair after she, Shadd and Raya had taken a refreshing swim and bath in the nearby stream, downstream from the water intake. They sat around their campfire and were brushing out their hair afterwards. Usually they shared Ryes' brush, but the men had found one last night, which had been left behind by the hoomans. It had a fancy handle with what looked like gold worked into the back and handle in a fanciful design. The bristles looked very new still, so she decided it could be her own brush. Not that she wouldn't share it with the others, but still wanted it to be her own to keep. Shadd laughed and nodded her head.

"I like your soaps," Raya stated, as she pulled out the loose hair from Ryes' brush, to help clean it after using it. They all seemed so fastidious about their possessions, but she found it didn't bother her anymore.

"Ryes made them, but I like them, too," Shadd agreed. "She said she'd teach us how to make them. I hope she'll get a chance, soon."

"Now that we're home, perhaps so," Ardis replied, leaving her dark brown hair loosely tied back today instead of the braids she used on the trails. "I'm still wrapping my mind around what it was like to be a bird flying through the night sky. I had flying dreams all night long and didn't want to get up this morning!" She laughed merrily, still reliving the brief memory.

"I want to do it again, too," Shadd admitted, laughing with delight.

"How amazing are Ryes' Talents," Raya agreed. "How many does she have? It seems so unusual." Shadd and Ardis exchanged a glance for a few seconds, which Raya noted.

"She's like her mother with more than one, but her grandmother was also a Healer. So, do you want Ryes to help your discover your Talent?" Ardis asked, smiling again. Raya fidgeted, turning the brush over in her hand, as if thinking for a few moments.

"I never considered myself a Talent, nor knowing I might have one," she started.

"Do have one," Shadd corrected, grinning as she teased her. Raya looked up and gave her a nervous smile.

"Knowing now that I have one, I'm not sure if I want to meet it," she admitted. "I've heard it's dangerous and you can lose your mind and that scares me!" She cocked her head to the side and gave Shadd a teasing smile in return. "What would you do if you suddenly found out you might have a Talent?" Shadd opened her mouth to give a quick answer, then closed it and frowned.

"That wouldn't be an easy decision," she admitted, finally, blushing. "I think I understand, now."

"No, it's not. So, for now I'm going to go on with my life as if I were Talentless. If something happens where it's important, I'll consider what I'll do then," she finally said, having found the courage to voice what she found in her heart.

"That does sounds like a good idea," Ardis agreed, understanding her thinking, too.

"Hang on tight," Ryes warned, smiling for Garth as he still looked nervous. Sabin was more relaxed as he held her other hand. Maren was staying out of it this time, to act as their timekeeper; to make sure they didn't stay gone too long. And Mitt was sitting on the sidelines too, because she wanted to be the first to hear about their adventures. They were sitting inside the outer room, near their campsite.

"Ready," Garth told her, then realized it'd be easier for them all if he could try to relax. "I don't know, after that last time it was only the three of us," he teased her. She laughed merrily as Sabin chuckled.

"We KNOW to never challenge her, now," he agreed. Maren frowned at this, still curious as to what she did to them? Mitt appeared perplexed. Ryes gave them a confident nod of her head, then closed her eyes, centering herself within; finally she reached out to them both. She began to reach back, that inner lurching wrenching them from their own time and place to one back in time, but nowhere as far back as Hailys. She kept her mind clear of that, as she concentrated upon the hoomans.

"Take us to before their frenzied departure," Garth suggested through their link. So, she drifted back further. They opened their eyes upon the cavernous room they were sitting in when they left, only Maren and Mitt were gone, the lights were on overhead and there was a hooman sitting in a chair in front of the long, thin table, set near the doors. His back was toward them. As before, she willed them not to be seen by the hoomans. They stood up together, as she instructed them earlier.

"We're here... there... then!" Garth happily declared, wanting to step closer to see what the hooman was like, for himself, and what he was doing. Ryes, sensing this, gave him a nod, letting him lead them. He and Sabin practically dragged her over to the machine he was using on the table, their eyes drinking in every little detail.

The hooman was using his fingers to change the screen, using a flat surface set on the table to make the changes. It responded to him readily, then a voice came out of the machine, itself, and he spoke back to it very calmly, as if it was the normal thing to do. Ryes noted he used a particular word to preface what he said, each time he addressed the device. "Com-pew-ter," she thought was what he named it each time he addressed it.

"Come on, there's more to see!" Ryes prompted them, after several long moments where both Sabin and Garth seemed mesmerized by this one small piece of equipment. She craved more!

"We want to see what it should look like, to see if we can find one and make it look like this," Garth explained. "It might explain why nothing in this place works" Ryes sighed in resignation, knowing it could be important. He chuckled at her impatience, and Sabin gave a nod of his head in agreement.

"We need to master their language it seems, to get it to work," Sabin commented.

"He starts everything with `com-pew-ter' when he's talking to the machine. Is this how they address each other, too?" Garth wondered aloud.

"No," Ryes assured him. "From my earlier journey, no one even said the word. It must be linked to this particular machine." She felt sure on this score. Another hooman came into the room from outside, greeting the one already here. He tossed him a shiny, gold disc, gave him a wave, and left, heading into the one open door leading into the main building. The one at the table caught it easily, taking it out of its clear case, inserted it into a slot on the face of the machine and had his eyes glued to the screen. Two tiny lights were flashing for a few moments, and then a series of pictures, obviously taken at Hailys, was displayed upon it.

"They can make pictures on little discs?" Sabin spoke in awe.

"Sort of like the memory rods of our own people in Hailys," Ryes added, seeing the connection now.

"You didn't say they held pictures, too," Garth scolded her, frowning. She shrugged as she smiled.

"You never asked," she reminded him. "We still have to figure out how to get one of the readers to work."

"Yes we do," Sabin agreed, while Garth smiled ruefully. "Okay, show us more," he prompted as he stepped back from the table, looking to Ryes.

She led them in through the open door leading into the wide hallway. It was brightly lit, with few people actually in the corridors. They walked down one after another, seeing the underground building with all the larger access panels open. And they started to explore the different levels, which were tied together by both wide stairways and a mechanical lift. They observed the equipment in operation and how the hoomans conducted themselves around it. They found a library containing hooman books in a whole room crammed with shelves, but there was no way they could read in their language. Still, much of what the hoomans did was mystifying to the trio as they went from room to room.

"What is this place?" Sabin questioned, wondering, as they took a lift back up to the top floor, accompanying one of the hoomans.

"Alda told us they captured him and Ptan to study them. Maybe they're here to study Hailys and anything else they can about us?" Ryes questioned in return. "That's one of the women who had charge of the plains people." She gave a nod of her head, recognizing the dark-haired woman, who was walking down the corridor they arrived upon. The man they came up with waved at her and then turned and went down one of the other passageways.

"Maybe she's going to check upon them, now?" Garth queried, urging Ryes to follow her. She had a case in her hand with one of the gold discs in it. She smiled as she passed another man in the hall, giving him a nod of her head and quick greeting. She looked to have some kind of purpose here, Ryes thought. She led them down the stairs a level and down the corridor away from the living quarters, heading through a small door, acting now as if she didn't want to be seen. She held herself flat against a wall, trying to observe and hear what was around her, before going further. There were voices coming from within the room, but she turned for a small door near them and went quickly inside. They quickly trailed her, drifting through before the door closed quietly behind her.

Inside, she ducked down low as she crept over to a long, mechanized, control table, took her disc out of its box and put it into a slot. Instead of playing pictures, she did something with the controls, and then stepped back from the observation window, still trying to not be seen. Garth and Sabin were shocked at what they saw outside the window.

Alda lay upon a metal table and appeared to be in great pain as three hoomans were tightly grouped together around a smaller, control table. The elder in their midst looked like he was getting great pleasure out of Alda's pain, while the other two appeared uncomfortable but did nothing about it. Then they saw a blonde woman standing to one side. She was very unhappy, but looked powerless to be able to help him, too.

"That's the one Maren's obsessed with," Ryes told them, pointing her out to them.

"Those fatherless monsters," Sabin growled.

"We can't help him; it's what was in the past," Ryes reminded him, holding tightly to his hand. She felt her own heart wringing over this callous abuse.

"What does this other woman do with her disc?" Garth asked.

"Maybe to prove what these ones are doing to Alda?" Ryes conjectured. "After all, he did tell us the two women rescued him with the power of their elder behind them. This might be how their elder came to know the truth?"

"It'd make sense. If she took pictures of what they were doing, without them knowing, then showed it to her elder. He'd have to act upon Alda's behalf, with such proof set before him," Garth said, accepting what Ryes proposed as solid reasoning. "Elders always need things proved out, with no doubt. It could be why this woman in here with us it staying back out of direct sight, too. She was trying to see it for herself, but striving not to be seen, so she can testify as a witness."

They soon finished their work, shutting off the equipment. The two younger men said their good-byes and left out another door. The elder ordered something of the blonde woman and she finally moved to approach Alda. She started removing the pieces of equipment attached to his body, being as gentle as she could.

The elder approached her when her back was turned, then suddenly pulled down her breeches, startling her. He shoved her down on top of the plainsman and slapped her buttocks as he stepped closer. He started to pull down her undergarment, and then suddenly looked upset with her, seeing she was in her season. He pulled her back to her feet and turned her around to face him. He appeared mad at her, instead of acting like he wanted her for mating. He shouted at her and shook her. She snapped back at him, so he slapped her hard across the face. Ryes found it almost impossible to not want to rush out there to batter this man in a like manner, in return. It was everything she could do to hold onto Garth and Sabin, too. She heard a loud gasp from the woman spying upon them. The blonde woman was quietly crying, as she gripped Alda's arm in support. The vicious elder yelled at her more, then turned and left the room, slamming the door behind him.

She stood crying for several long moments, then reached down and straightened up her undergarment and breeches. She wiped at her eyes as she turned and continued to free Alda from the many, painful attachments they inserted into his body. She spoke to him in a kind, gentle voice, with tears still running down her cheeks. The last was a long tube which had been inserted inside his leg. It appeared this procedure pained her as much as him, but she did it as fast as she could, then cleaned and bandaged him quickly. She released the tie down straps, freeing his legs, arms and torso. Next she rolled a smaller, wheeled table next to him and helped him onto it. The other woman stopped the recording, a determined set to her face as she took her disc and put it back in its case. She breathed a vow in a low voice to her friend in the next room then quickly left, making sure no else was in the hallway outside before stepping out.

"Now I know why he told Maren that she deserved rescue," Ryes breathed out with a sigh.

"You're sure they're both saved from this man who delights in giving pain to others?" Sabin pressed, wanting to hear it from her again.

"Yes," Ryes assured him. "It seems with their people, as with our own, there're those who do things for their own, selfish interests only, and those who try their best to help others, no matter how strange to them they would otherwise seem."

"We've seen enough. Let's return," Garth ordered, getting a last look at the control table before them. The blonde woman was wheeling the cart-table out a door on the far side of the room below them. Ryes agreed. She then reached back for herself, linking up with her body again, feeling that lurching of her return, pulling Garth and Sabin easily with her. They opened their eyes to see Maren looking very concerned, but unsure if he should take action, or not.

"You all looked like you were upset about something," he commented to the puzzlement in Ryes' eyes. "I was worried about you." She smiled assurance for him, giving him a nod of her head in understanding as she released both Garth and Sabin's hands.

"We witnessed Alda being abused," she told him, not wanting him to know how his own dream lady was being hurt, too. It'd only cause him distress, which he couldn't do anything about. Sabin looked at her, catching her eyes, seeing why she worded it that way.

"They were running cruel tests upon him, with the one hooman elder getting pleasure from his pain," Garth explained as he stood up and extended a hand to his lady.

"He said the two women freed him from something. It must be what he was talking about," Mitt stated, jumping to her feet, then helped Maren up. Sabin stood too and moved over to the machine's table as it still sat near the one wall near the main door inward. They had ignored it before as they couldn't move the objects off of it. He picked up a small, clear case with one of the discs inside, which was still sitting on it - forgotten.

"I'm going to try this one," he stated as he put it in the slot on the machine face, like he saw before. The tiny lights lit up, as in the past and the screen came alive, displaying a hooman talking, as if addressing whoever was watching him.

"Com-pew-ter," Ryes said. Suddenly, the whole board lit up with many lights and the light panels overhead came on, making Maren take a step back, almost blinded. Mitt yelled out happily at being able to see the whole cavernous room again. A voice filled the air, as it replied to her address. She smiled back to Garth, her eyes lighting up. "Now all we need to do is learn their language, so we can understand it and respond correctly."

"Then that's what you get to do," he told her, finding an inspiration to keep her out of trouble. "You showed us a small room with a bigger machine in it and lots of panels that looked out all over this building and outside of it last night. Maybe, if we can reach it, it might be able to teach you?" Ryes looked surprised, but gave him a nod in response, thinking it was a great idea. He and Sabin examined the pattern of lights, noting the differences to each other in low voices. After a few minutes, the machine repeated its request as the disc finished and popped back out of its slot. Sabin returned it to its case and closed it, a speculative look in his eyes.

Ryes stepped over to a panel in the wall beside the main door. She grinned back over her shoulder to the others, and then gave it her full attention.

"Com-pew-ter," she told it distinctly. It responded to her in a slightly different sounding voice and then after a few moments, the wall made noises and the door responded with a noise of its own. She tugged on the handle and it opened up easily. "Thank you, com-pew-ter," she told it as she noted the lights in the corridors came on now, too.

"You found the key!" Maren declared. The others had come running, having heard Mitt's shout and stood in shock at seeing how vast the room was and how small their cart appeared now inside it.

"You found our way into our home," Garth stated, then stepped over to her and wrapped his arms around her, giving her a happy kiss. She was grinning up at him when he finished.

"Let's go find our own, new rooms," she suggested, pulling him in through the open doorway. He didn't resist and laughed as he scooped her up in his arms, bolding leading them all inside now.

"We could pull the cart in here and not touch either side of the doorway," Kovin observed, grinning. He put an arm around Raya, laughing happily.

"I want to find those waste chairs and waterfalls!" Mitt declared, running inside behind Ryes and Garth.

Ryes got Garth to put her down on her feet and then rushed ahead to the small room where all the screens were set as a part of a massive control center. She thought this door would be locked, but it opened readily at her touch, which surprised her. She stopped to see that all the screens were coming to life now and that the com-pew-ter, which had more than one access set of controls, appeared ready for her.

"I don't know what to tell our com-pew-ter," she commented, waving her hand at it, looking to Sabin and Garth as they crowded into the room behind her. They chuckled, but shook their heads as running feet could be heard coming down the hallway, outside the door.

"You did it! The air's moving inside and even if it's a little musty, it's fresher," Mitt told them. "And the lights are on everywhere." The smile upon her face was reassurance they were getting somewhere.

"I appoint you the keeper of the com-pew-ter," Garth told Ryes with a smile, placing a hand upon each of her shoulders. "It seems to like you." The men left while laughing about it. Ryes stood looking toward the machine with her hands spread out in entreaty.

"Com-pew-ter, we're going to have to learn to understand each other," she told it smiling, pulling out the chair before its table.

She sat down and looked at the pattern of the lights and saw the screens start to come to life. There was a roving picture of the land around the tower. She caught sight of Honey in her pen, just outside the doors. Everything was just like it was in that brief flash of Vision she and Sabin had. This will be their watch room for approaching dangers.

"All I ask is a place to stay for all of us this coming winter, so we can have our cubs in peace and safety," she told it, feeling very small. One screen showed a view of the various hallways and she caught a shot of Garth and Sabin talking with the others, excitedly. Now they could move their things inside to the inner rooms. She hoped she'd be adequate to this task Garth set before her. It'd mean more trips into the past, to get to know their way of thinking and speech patterns, at least. That was the one thing that had her charged.

"We may have started late, but we have better rainfall here, than back in Matlowe, so the grains and gardens are coming in beautifully," Teris told Garth, as they sat down to dinner in the room Ryes said was set aside for the purpose. They'd been living in their new home for over a month now.

This room was far bigger than their small band needed, but with the tables and chairs, it proved a good gathering place, too. They set up the seats they usually used with small blankets on the seats. Ardis found some table coverings so they placed them on the tables to give the room some colors. The white walls would be next, but Ryes wasn't ready to being, still deciding what to paint. She found a machine that could create paints for them and they were painting their sleeping rooms different colors, enjoying the change from the plain white walls.

There were cooking machines in the adjoining room, which had been a delight and trial to learn to use. But, they did learn and their meals were consistently well prepared, now. The freezer and cold keeper were the most amazing machines in the kitchen. They already contained foods, which from the cold keeper had to be trashed and it cleaned out, but from the freezer were still able to be defrosted and consumed. After sampling several hooman foods, they decided the flavors of their own meats were far better, so they trashed the human meats, too, and were now hunting to stock the freezer back up. The other amazing machine was the trash disposal. Ryes insisted upon it being properly done and she was right. Anything placed within it was quickly disposed of, with nothing to bury. Teris insisted they save the kitchen food scraps, so as to build a mulch pile, to make fertilizer for their gardens and crops. So now they had a covered bucket where they put their food scraps for Teris. He picked it up each morning and was quite happy with their contributions.

They'd also found and cleared out a "specimen" freezer in one of the normally closed rooms. They discovered the sad remains of dozens of the peoples of Tayna having been apparently slaughtered and some dismembered for their studies, including Starmen. That had been a sad large pyre to attend for a few days. But they did grant them prayers for their souls and respect in the end. It tainted all their views of these hoomans and they were now not so sure they wanted to meet them if they returned. Ryes still felt it was not the way most of the people conducted themselves, nor approved of it, from what she observed during her trips into the past.

"We've finally gotten some of the bubblenut seeds to sprout. Once they're larger, we'll move them to a more suitable location with good spacing, so they won't crowd each other," Shadd added, smiling with pride.

"We wouldn't want their roots growing down into this place," Torr reminded her, smiling. She nodded in response, having already considered it and thought of a good place for them as they matured a little more.

"As soon as Kovin and Raya return, we'll see about trying to catch some of those wild windracers we saw yesterday," Garth said. "So we don't have to have Ryes scare us with trying to give us wild rides in that shuttle pod of hers!" he teased as she blushed.

"I'm getting better at controlling it," she protested. "Just ask Maren," she prompted, giving her cousin a nudge with her knee. He laughed with a nod of his head.

"She's learning to handle it better and even managed to get it into its top gear this morning. We made it to Hailys in half her normal time," he bragged.

"That was too fast for me!" Ardis protested, rolling her eyes in emphasis. This got chuckles from around the table.

"It was great!" Mitt declared with a laugh. "Ryes is a real good driver." She now considered her officially her sister and far more fun to be around than her own, older sister; even if most times she had to work harder than Karr ever made her do. With Ryes, it wasn't labor, but fun exploration and new lessons. The food and plants they gathered, while Maren explored the buildings, were important to everyone here. Her memories of Matlowe were quickly fading.

"Why don't we use the shuttle pod to drive to Matlowe, to get our families?" Ryes questioned. "We can use the old caravan road and it'd be much quicker than using windracers."

"We don't know the road as well," Garth replied. "Even if we drove parallel to the Yuri, it might not be able to make it. I'd rather catch the windracers and use them. And I don't want the villagers in Matlowe to fully know all the things we now have and can use."

"It'll take time to break them in," she protested, knowing he didn't want her anywhere near the Village since she was beginning to display the signs of her pregnancy, more clearly.

"That's all right," Torr assured her, chuckling. "We'll manage it."

"How about the flying machine?" she pressed, then caught the look in Garth's eyes and subsided.

No one thought the thing would work, much less let her try it! They had discovered lots of different vehicles in a huge "garage" at the far end of the complex. There were different sizes of the wheeled shuttle pods and other interesting wheeled vehicles. The flyers looked crazy and easy, so they pulled out a smaller one to examine in the daylight. The computer named it a helicopter. It now sat outside where she, Maren and Mitt put it, under its cover, which they found and pulled out from the garage, setting it near Honey's pen. She sighed as she turned back to her excellent dinner. They were learning her recipes, too well and had some great new innovations of their own added in.

"So, are you two finished in Hailys?" Sabin asked.

"There's one more area we needed to sweep first, then I think so," Ryes told him, smiling again. "Unless Maren's found something too interesting?" she questioned, raising an eyebrow as she looked at him.

"There's one building I still need to finish collecting the crystals from, and then I'll wait until the worse of the summer heat's past. It's hot enough already," he added, smiling. "I'm glad of the lightweight tunics and breeches the humans were so kind to leave behind. That and the computer which controls the temperature inside this underground building, so it was never too hot, nor too cold. The waterfalls, while far different from baths, are warm and relaxing after a hard day's work. It's a miracle as far as I'm concerned and I fully appreciate it!"

"All right, one more trip out, then you lend a hand to things around here," Garth ordered them.

"I'm going, too," Mitt insisted, "after all, I'm supposed to help look after Ryes." He smiled and gave her a nod of his head. He wasn't going to admit that they sometimes got more done when she was away with Ryes and Maren, than when she was here, underfoot.

"If you say so," Ryes agreed with a sigh. Tending gardens wasn't what she craved. The forests were a little too far, unless she could use a shuttle pod to reach them. After she was laughingly showing Garth the human pictures of people raising "chickens" and "turkeys" in pens, he had them out gathering their own birds to raise as food and for their eggs. There was a large, wire-mesh covered cage being constructed next to Honey's pen. She didn't look forward to having to care for mindless birds, kept in a cage. Maren had teased her about becoming as "domestic," as the birds they were raising!

"What was this morning's language lesson?" Shadd questioned Ryes, breaking into her inner contemplations. She looked unhappy about something.

"It was about horses. They're larger windracers than ours. Very leggy and more fragile, I think. But, it looks like they could easily outrun our animals. They're amazing," she admitted.

"So what did you learn about their horses?" Garth asked, smiling, wondering if she'd show him these pictures, too?

"They're raised on grasses and grains, like our Honey. They have more than one stomach and the humans have to be careful about how much and what they feed them, or it can cause colic and kill them. They use different types of gear for the different kinds of jobs they have the horses doing, just as Darman showed me long ago. They have to carefully tend to their hooves and put metal shoes on them, so they are not in pain when they walk, like Honey. They look to fill the same function as our own windracers do here."

"Too bad they didn't leave any of those behind in storage," Teris commented, smiling, "A taller windracer? It's possible, given time… Like plants," he said, feeling their traits could be selected and bred. "What did you call these people? You and Maren are saying it differently, now."

"Human. It's what they call themselves. Hooman was what the plains people called them. But, since it's their own name, it's human," she explained, smiling at his prompt, glad someone noticed.

"Hueman, Hooman, not much difference," Sabin teased, smiling. Ryes shook her head at this and sighed.

"We truly should be able to get a few things right. After all, what if they ever come back? I shouldn't be the only one around here who can speak their language," she pressed. Sabin gave her a nod at this, then looked to Ardis.

"Want to take your language lessons in the afternoon, since Ryes takes hers in the morning?" he asked, thinking it'd get her inside, out of the heat of the day, and was less work than the gardens, with their cubs growing within her, obviously now.

"Hey, why not you?" she pressed, protesting. "You need to learn it too!"

"Torr can take them with you," Garth decided. "The rest of us will start when we can figure out a schedule which the com-pew-ter will accept. Ryes, you need to arrange this with the com-pew-ter," he suggested.

"Computer," Ryes corrected him. She smiled as she wondered at this. She wanted to learn their writing and numbers more and was getting farming lessons! It was frustrating her and she was going to have to sit down with the darned machine and get this problem ironed out. Let the others laugh at the humans chasing chickens, she was going to figure out how to make a computer of her own, someday. Maybe this called for another trip into the past? Somehow she had to find the key!

Promises Kept

Maren awoke, realizing the sun was setting. He and Mitt had lain down for a nap late in the afternoon, as Ryes was still gathering her seeds and plants. He hadn't meant to sleep so long! He sat up and looked around for his cousin, worried. Then he saw her, sitting nearby, watching the sunset with a wistful look in her eyes. Relief flooded his system and he relaxed once more. He smiled as he eased himself out of the shuttle, trying not to disturb Mitt. He climbed the rock and sat down next to her.

"You know, Maren, the one thing I never did was find the grave of my father and siblings," Ryes commented in a low voice to him, with a smile, welcoming his company. He recalled her watching the sunset from atop the Village Mound, when they returned from their first hunt together. She'd said she was bidding them a goodnight.

"Do you know where in Hailys they were living?" he asked, wondering about it, himself. "Rowan had found it, so maybe it was more on the southeast side of the city; something more towards Matlowe?"

"No, he never told me," she sighed, and stood up to return home. She'd get yelled at enough, with them being out so late. "I'll have to try finding it, later," she told him as he stood, too. "I never appreciated how huge this city must've been and we're only on the surface. The below part was supposed to be far more vast."

"We'll get our chance to look again, soon," he assured her. But, suddenly Ryes put a hand to his arm, gripping it tightly. He saw she wasn't looking at him, but something else. He turned, wondering what could have her behaving this way, when he saw a blue-white figure dressed in a flowing gown of light. His breath caught in his throat as she approached them. He was afraid to move.

"What's that?" They heard Mitt ask loudly, as she watched from the front seat of the shuttle. She must've just awoken. Ryes jumped down from her rocky perch to stand and face her mother's spirit. She heard Maren scrambling down right behind her.

"Who is this?" Tyra questioned, as Mitt ran over next to Maren, feeling that if Ryes was unafraid, then it couldn't be too bad. "And this?" she added, with a smile.

"This is Tann's oldest son, Maren," Ryes indicated him, in introduction. "And this is Garth's younger sister, Mitt. What can I do for you, Mother?" she asked in return, sensing she had a purpose this evening.

"Tann's son," she sighed as she put a palm out toward him. "Yes, he carries the Healing Talent as strongly as Ronn. Watch over him and take care of your cousin, Ryes," she warned with a smile. "He's a precious treasure!"

"Father was a Healer?" she questioned surprised, mirroring the shock in Maren's eyes.

"Yes. His Talent came late to him, but in plenty of time for you and your siblings' birth. He made it a joy, instead of what it would have been otherwise. I see your own first cubs are well upon their way, now," she added, in comment.

"Yes, they should be born toward the end of the winter," she told her, blushing. "Grandmother," she added, teasing with a big smile playing upon her lips. Tyra laughed lightly at this, joy filling her spirit, making her brighter and more clearly seen. They laughed with her.

"Do you recall that you owe me a small favor?" she finally asked, smiling merrily. Ryes nodded her head, remembering it well.

"Whatever you might require," she offered. Maren already knew Garth had agreed to this, but Mitt was surprised, wondering. She kept her peace, not wanting the attention of such a strong spirit.

"It's not truly difficult. Do you still wear the necklace Rowan gave you, before you left Matlowe?" she asked. Ryes knew what she meant and pulled it out from under her T-shirt, knowing it had to be some kind of family heirloom. It flashed and glittered in the last rays of the fading sunlight, with the medallion still depending from the priceless chain.

"Yes, that is it!" Tyra exclaimed happily. "It was a gift from my father, Tair, who was of House Clenons and your other grandfather. He gave it to me, right before I left home for Tayna. He wasn't happy with my grandmother's plans to wed me at age sixteen to a man who was as old as my great-grandmother, so helped with my escape," she explained. "My strength is fading, so more family history later. Please follow me."

She turned and led them through the nearby ruins, then straight across an open field. After a half-hour's brisk travel, they came to the remains of a lone building. It's great, white-and-pink marble tumbled about, but several arches still stood. Behind the arches was a small clearing and within the middle of the clearing was a mound, with carefully placed pieces of broken stone forming the same symbol as the medallion displayed.

"Here is where Ronn, Rayan, little Tair and Tian lay in their final rest," Tyra stated, although Ryes could already guess. "Here is where I should be, also. Instead, my grave is on the outskirts of Matlowe." She turned to face Ryes, Maren and Mitt with determination in her eyes. "All I ask is for you to someday bring my remains to lie here with Ronn's. For now, I ask you to leave the necklace under the stones until you can accomplish the task I require. When it is done, keep the necklace, but leave the medallion. It is the seal of the House of Li and should stay with me. You will have to have your own made at some time."

"This I will surely promise, with, or without the elders' approval," Ryes vowed. She slipped off the necklace. Mitt saw it was breathtaking. Maren lifted several of the stones for her, and then replaced them exactly, after she had set the necklace in a protected place that would be beneath them.

"My thanks, my little Ryes," Tyra said, then faded out. The mist, which had surrounded her, sank toward the ground, enshrouding the stones for a few moments before vanishing.

"Oh my," Mitt breathed out, feeling finally able to do so, now that Tyra's spirit was gone. "That was TRULY HER?" she asked, still doubting her senses. Ryes turned and smiled for her, giving her a nod of her head.

"Yes, it was. Now, we'd better get back, or they'll be trying to figure out how to operate that flyer all by themselves," she commented with a chuckle at the image it brought to mind.

"Garth's not going to let us out like this, ever again," Maren agreed with a laugh. "Wait until we get back and tell them!"

"They won't believe us," Mitt warned, looking gloomy.

"Garth will. He's already met Tyra," Ryes assured her, draping an arm around her shoulders. "Let's hurry!"

"Oh, no," Maren groaned. "Now you get to practice driving the shuttle at night!"

"Actually, I was thinking of letting you get in some more practice," she teased, mischief in her green eyes.

"It'll take us two days to get back, if he's driving," Mitt protested, smiling to see the look upon Maren's face.

"Hey, that's not funny," he returned, "I only believe in being careful!" This elicited laughter from the women, as they headed back the way they came.

A thunderous sound shook the ground, bringing the villagers spilling out of their homes and out onto the main path, in the early morning hours. Fear was in their eyes. It was far too early in the year for the Caravans to be returning! As they stood gaping, uncertain what to do, Garth rounded the knoll, riding astride a windracer. Next to him was Sabin, with Torr, Teris, and Kovin behind them. Maren brought up the rear. They had with them more than a dozen windracers, with some of them carrying packs of supplies.

"Sabin! Sabin!" Lixi called out smiling happily, wanting to run to her uncle, but her mother was restraining her. They pulled their windracers to a halt and started to dismount, all smiles. Their families were in shock at the changes they saw before them and were hesitant to approach these confident, young men, whom they thought they once knew.

"Garth!" Jons called out as she flew to his arms with a merry laugh. "What took you so long?" she scolded loudly, then, "Where's Ryes and Mitt? Are they all right?" she whispered loudly in his ear, her small face suddenly concerned. He chuckled as he gave her a kiss.

"Yes, they're both fine and back in our new home," he assured her, as Glyn and Gann approached with smiles of relief in their eyes.

"Glad to see you made it back!" Gann shouted, pounding him on the shoulder, relief in his heart. Karr was right behind them, holding tiny Kala upon her shoulder.

"Where's Mitt?" she demanded, anger in her yellow eyes.

"With Ryes and the other women, back in our new home," he told her, refusing to let her temper get to him anymore.

"You're not coming back to Matlowe now?" Garvin asked, stepping forward with his arm around Marla. A big smile broke out upon Garth's face as he stepped over to hug and kiss his parents, shifting Jons as he still held her in his arms.

"No," he informed them. "I came back to bring you out there to live with us." Garvin looked surprised as he saw his son was serious. Marla had tears in her eyes.

"I don't know how good I'll be with riding a windracer, like this," she said. Her gravid condition was very obvious to them all.

"Maren!" Garth called out, seeing everyone was surrounded by their families, happily greeting their return. Maren pulled away from his mother to see what Garth needed.

"Oh," he said as he saw him indicating Marla. "Let me see?" he offered, stepping over, extending his hand as he smiled for her permission. She looked doubtful, but gave him a nod of her head. Maren closed his eyes for a few moments, then reached over and touched her stomach. He stood still for a very long time. Garth was worried, hoping it wasn't beyond his abilities. Finally, he opened his eyes with a sigh.

"Well?" he demanded, needing to know.

"This is going to take several sessions," he told him. "I've laid the groundwork, but she should be born as healthy and spunky as Mitt, when I finish with her," he assured him. "Let's see about getting those carts assembled," he added as a reminder.

"Maren, you're a Healer, now?" Gann demanded in utter shock. He smiled, nodded and gave him a grand bow.

"Ryes awoke my Talent and it's come in handy," he told him, as he heard Tanns' gasp from behind him.

"You can Heal?" his mother demanded, shocked.

"Just as Ronn could," he assured her.

"How would you know THAT? Ronn wasn't a Healer!" she scolded, not happy with his attitude.

"Tyra's ghost told me, herself, that his own Healing Talent awoke late, but in time for Ryes and her siblings to be born. She said he made their birth a joy."

"I've spoken with Tyra's ghost," Garth defended his friend, seeing Karr and Tanns about to cut loose on him for such a tale. "She wants us to remove her remains from Matlowe and bury her with Ronn and their cubs." His calm voice and the steady, determined look in his eyes showed them this was something they both believed firmly.

"What're you doing back in Matlowe?" Metta demanded, stepping forward to talk with the cubs. "It hasn't been six months for Sabin, yet!"

"We only came to collect our families, Metta. None of us is staying here and we promise Sabin will be gone well before sundown," Garth informed him, still in command.

Karr stood back, hearing his voice and noting his stance for the first time. He'd changed in many ways, and she wasn't sure if she liked what she saw before her. This was no longer a younger brother she could order about. Old Metta stood in shock to be so addressed, but Garth turned to the rest of his men, ignoring them both.

"Let's get the carts assembled and a head count of who'll be going and who won't. Now!" he ordered. He set Jons upon his own windracer and gave her a wink. "Could you watch him for me? He's not as docile as Honey, but he'll mind you, if you remember how to ride." She smiled grandly as she took the reins he handed her, and then he went to get his tools out of his saddlebag, as Ryes called it. At his order, the rest of the men gathered their supplies and see to doing what they set out to accomplish today. It was why they camped out in the forest near Matlowe last night and came in early this morning, so they'd have plenty of time to assemble the carts and get their families clear of the Village.

"I'll go see about Rowan," Maren offered, in a low voice, as Garth gave him a nod of his head. They promised Ryes to pack him up and move him out, no matter how loudly he protested.

"Why don't you stay?" Karr demanded loudly, catching his eye. He snorted out a laugh and shook his head no.

"Why should I? There's nothing here I want, other than my family. Ryes and I have cubs on the way; due to be born toward the end of the winter. We have our grains growing, a garden thriving and Shadd even got some bubblenut tree sprouts started. There's plenty of game to hunt and we're trying to learn how to raise our own birds in cages for eggs and food. We have windracers and plenty of room to run them in. We have showers, waste chairs and more comforts than you could imagine. What does Matlowe have to offer any of us?" he demanded, having spoken loud enough for everyone around them to hear him clearly. All activity stopped for a few seconds as those who came with Garth agreed wholeheartedly, and those who were still living in Matlowe pondered what he said. Karr looked upset.

"I'm not going! We have to get ready for the winter and at
least there'll be fewer mouths to feed with the bunch of you gone!"
she practically screamed at him, then turned upon her heel and
stomped off home with Kala starting to cry.

"I couldn't even talk her into moving near the river," Glyn
commented with a heavy sigh, as they watched her go. "She's such a
stubborn woman."

"Are you sure we won't be a burden on you?" Garvin asked,
"I'm not good at anything beyond gardening and weaving simple
cloth, anymore." Garth chucked.

"We already have the freezer filled with enough meat to last
the whole of Matlowe through the winter. Ryes was scolding us for
over hunting the area. We'll have plenty," he assured him, clasping
his father's shoulder in understanding as he smiled. "And there's
running water. Waterfalls called showers, instead of bath tubs, and
we have waste chairs. There'll be room for your loom and we'll be
sheltered from the winter storms. There're even some new games
we're learning. Torr and Kovin's favorite is called chess. I think you'll
like that one, too."

"It sounds wonderful," Marla agreed. "Let's see what we truly
need to take and what can stay behind," she suggested to her
husband. He chuckled and gave his son a nod of his head, then
turned to help his wife.

"You know I can't leave Karr, Glyn and the cubs alone," Gann
reminded his brother, sadly. "But, Mitt's all right?" he pressed.

"She's doing just fine and we're even working her harder than
Karr ever could. She doesn't mind it, `cause she knows this is for her
and her future cubs, too," he assured him.

"I know I'm going to be in trouble for this, but I want you to
take Jons with you when you leave. Karr's going to probably throw
me out for a few days, but I'd rather see her safe with you, than
chance another cub killer without Ryes around to protect the cubs.
There's a restlessness in the land this year and we've already had two
families and three couples move into Matlowe from the lands to the
east. When was the last time that's happened?" Glyn questioned.
The shock in Garth's eyes said it all.

"They moved into vacant homes next to Rowan and have been
good people," Gann added. "I guess the runners with those lists have
reminded folk that Matlowe still exists. Things must really be bad for
families to journey out here for a better living. But, Glyn's right, with
the good, sometimes come the bad. That's why the drive to make
them settle out toward the Yuri. There've been other wanderers,

without families, but they don't usually stay too long and we don't encourage them to stay, either. Not after that child killer." He gestured across the Village Circle. "See the proof? They're building a new home here from the foundation of one of the fallen ones," he said drawing their eyes to the newly erected walls.

Garth realized it was something they hadn't thought of, nor discussed. The possibility of having others coming to beg them for shelter. They'd taken Raya in, but since they encountered her upon the road, they hadn't thought of her in such a light. She and Kovin were still having their ups and downs, but she was happy for the most part; especially being the one to choose whom of the unattached men she wanted to mate with. He just didn't know about total strangers moving in with them, yet.

"I hope they don't get word about us. We'd have to look anyone over very carefully, before admitting them to our little community. We allowed Raya, from one of the plains tribes, to live with us because we found her on the road. She mated to Kovin a few weeks ago and it took. Maren said she's going to have two cubs. She's quiet, but has been willing to learn and has taken over managing the kitchen," he told them, then chuckled. "We haven't even named our new home, yet!"

"It sounds like it should be called Paradise," Gann told him, laughing at this. "How're Shadd and Ardis doing?"

"Ardis is due a few weeks after Ryes. She and Sabin have two cubs on the way. Shadd and Torr just finished mating, right before we left for Matlowe, so Maren hasn't had the time to check her, yet. Torr was telling us that this trip is a time of rest for him. I guess Shadd was pretty demanding," he told him, smiling.

"She sure was!" Torr agreed with a broad smile, stepping over to hear what the men were discussing.

"How many cubs are you and Ryes expecting?" Glyn asked, just noting he hadn't mentioned it, yet.

"I don't know. Ryes and Maren are keeping it a secret. I know a son for sure and she keeps saying cubs, so I don't know if it's two or three. Ryes said it's going to be a surprise," he admitted.

"Oh it'll be that for sure," Maren agreed with a laugh, having returned with Rowan and Tennan.

"We've got some carts to finish," Torr reminded them. Garth saw they had one of the steel frames finished and were ready to add the wheels. They had rolls of lightweight material which was sturdy and used to form the walls and bottom of the carts, themselves. They only brought out enough kits to make four carts and the tools they'd need. The humans had been a very resourceful people!

"Right," Garth agreed, then turned to his wife's grandfather with a smile. "Are you ready for a trip to your new home?" he asked. "Ryes is not letting me back in, unless you're with me," he informed him. Rowan chuckled surprised, and yet not so, to hear this from Garth.

"Will there be room for my loom?" he questioned, knowing this was serious.

"She told me it better be with us, also," he related with a laugh. Maren laughed with him, nodding his head in agreement.

"She meant it," Maren verified for him. "Tennan's coming, too." Garth gave him a nod, expecting it.

"Make sure of what you truly can't live without and what can be stored here for a while, or given away. If there's time, we'll make another trip back, before the winter storms hit," he told them. "Got to lend a hand," he said as he turned to their cart assembly project. "We can talk while we work," he suggested, waving them along.

"What's a huuman?" Rowan asked as he followed in his footsteps. Garth chuckled as he tried to think of a way to explain them!

The light at the top of the tower mast could be clearly seen, flashing its white, green and yellow beams into the darkness. Ryes couldn't convince the computer that they didn't need them, so they remained on all the time.

"Why the lights?" Rowan questioned, wondering.

"It's so flyers won't crash into the tower at night, and it indicates this is a good place for them to land. Ryes can't convince the computer that we don't use any of the flyers and no one else on Tayna has any that we know of, but it's even more stubborn than she is at times, and it refuses to turn them off. If we can see the lights, they can probably see us from the computer room," Garth informed him, smiling into the darkness, resisting the urge to wave to Ryes, knowing she'd be making sure it was them at the very least.

Suddenly, there came a strange noise in the air and a whirlwind of dust and small debris being tossed up into the darkness near them. Lights came on, shining down upon them from above, as Garth shaded his eyes wondering what it was? Maren was laughing and waving his arms. The lights started to settle toward the ground, kicking up more dust, then the engine cut down to a lower noise level.

"Want to bet Ryes found out how to fly a flyer?" Maren shouted to him over the noise, as Garth already figured it out. The windracers were nervous, but Kovin, Teris, Sabin and Torr quickly had them quieted down. Two figures ran over to them from the flyer. Both of them ran straight for him.

"Took you long enough!" Mitt scolded as Ryes just kissed him, happily.

"I thought I told you, you weren't allowed to use the flyer," he scolded Ryes, in return. She laughed lightly and shook her head.

"I let Mitt operate it. She's a good pilot," she bragged, then let go of him to hug and kiss her grandfather. "We couldn't wait!" she admitted smiling, overjoyed to see Rowan again. He noted her stomach with a merry chuckle, as she blushed.

"Jons!" Mitt shouted, seeing her with her parents. "Mother, Father," she added, letting go of Garth to get hugs and kisses from her dear family.

"We have room for four others to ride in the back," Ryes told Garth. "We can make several trips, but it's up to you." He thought on what she was offering, knowing the village folk weren't used to the rough road they had traveled, even in the comfort of a cart.

"Why don't you fly back Jons, my parents and Rowan, then return in a large shuttle and we'll load up the rest. I'm sure it'll be easier for them to endure, than flying." He smiled as she gave a nod of her head in agreement. "Then the rest of us can return in the morning with the windracers and their things loaded on the carts," he decided, feeling better about this wild idea of his mate's. It'd be a fast introduction into what they lived with from day-to-day, now. It wasn't like they hadn't tried to warn the villagers on the way here.

"As you command," she teased. "Come on, Jons, you get to fly," she said, then stopped with a funny look upon her face. "Oh my, I guess I do know how to do that now and can teach the cubs, when they get older. Sabin wouldn't have believed this, months ago!"

"No I wouldn't have," he agreed with a laugh, having heard what they discussed. "Now, you're going to have to give both Garth and I lessons in flying," he sighed out.

"It's really easy," Mitt assured him. "Come on, let's get everyone who's going, inside the flyer, so we can hurry back with a shuttle to get the rest," she ordered.

"Grandfather, it's too bad it's night time. You'd love to see what everything looks like during the day," Ryes told him. He shook his head.

"The only thing I want to see are those lovely cubs you'll be having before long." He beamed as he patted her stomach. He thought she was too big already for only two cubs. Ryes laughed as she hugged him again, and turned him toward the flyer. "You're sure this is safe?" he pressed. She laughed again.

"Perfectly safe," she assured him. "And Honey's gotten so used to it now; she doesn't even flick an ear at it, anymore." This got a chuckle out of Rowan, as they reached the flyer. She opened the back door and helped him up. Then, she helped Marla and Garvin up, as Mitt put Jons in. "You have to strap in," she told them, indicating the straps attached to the seats. Mitt jumped up to show them how, making sure everyone was secure. Ryes closed the back door, then she and Mitt boarded through their front doors and strapped in, too. Mitt powered it back up to full and took off, the machine lifting effortlessly.

"You know Garth's going to yell at us for this," she warned, in a low voice. Ryes grinned, mischief in her eyes.

"Nothing we haven't weathered, yet. He'll get used to it, too," she assured her with a laugh. Marla smiled at this, her eyes lighting up in humor. Garth did have his hands full with the two of them conspiring.

Once they had everyone gathered in their dining hall and well fed, the following evening, Garth stood and called everyone's attention. After several long moments the gathering finally quieted down and mostly gave him their attention. He smiled at this, knowing he wasn't an elder to command a higher level of respect. But he knew he would earn it, yet. He was learning!

"It's been brought to my attention that we have been negligent in naming our new home," he started, getting nods of agreement from around his own table. "I'm presenting our choices so far," he added then looked down at the list in his hand, which he could now read clearly. "New Matlowe, Bounderland, Winterhaven, New

Hailys and Human Abode. I would like to put the choice of the names to a vote, but first does anyone else want to contribute a new name?"

"How about Wonder Town?" Garvin called out, laughing.

"I would think you would call it The Burrow, since it's underground and goes deep," Tennan called out, grinning.

"We get to name our own home?" Jons asked loudly of Marla as she was snuggled in next to her. Rand sat with Rein nearby and laughed too. The hall was instantly filled with loud laughter and discussion, as this was something entirely new. They got to be the long-forgotten ancestors who gave their new home its name! After several long minutes, order was restored and the new villagers were ready for some serious voting.

"Take out the Human Abode," Rowan demanded. "None of us are humans and we don't intend to become humans." Garth gave him a nod of agreement while Torr groaned, having wanted that one.

"Not New Matlowe," Rein stated flatly with a disgusted look on her face. "We left Matlowe behind us!"

"And with Hailys being destroyed so horribly; I don't want such a thing to happen here," Maren asserted, speaking out on that one, too.

"So we're down to Wonder Town, The Burrow, Bounderland and Winterhaven," Garth stated. There were nods around at the other tables in agreement. "Let's put it to a vote," he suggested. "For Wonder Town," he said and counted only two hands in the air. "For The Burrow," he added next, getting a few hands. "Bounderland?" he asked and only got two hands. "And finally Winterhaven?" he called out, getting more hands than the others. Laughter filled the air as the gathering realized they had named their new home and they were its founders.

Ryes smiled happily; glad her favorite of the suggestions had won.

"It's the only way to find it without days of running all over the countryside on foot or in a rover," Ryes insisted, trying to sound reasonable.

"She has a point, son," Garvin said, siding with Ryes, much to the frustration of his oldest son.

"He just doesn't like the height," Mitt teased as Maren laughed in agreement.

"That's not it," he returned, then smiled at Ryes. "I promised that next time up, I'd finish our flying lesson and take the stick myself." Ryes' face was lit up in humor, giving a nod of her head in confirmation.

"Then we must go up! We wouldn't want to keep our best pilot on the ground," Sabin teased, gripping him on the shoulder. Suddenly, Sabin had flash of Vision of the two of them sitting in another, larger cockpit than the tiny flyer's. Garth caught it too, wonder in his eyes. Maybe he saw it because of his closeness to Ryes? But, yes, this did feel right after all, he thought. It was a huge machine and many of their friends and family were nearby, cheering them on, then it was gone.

"Since you're never wrong, I think I'd better finish my flying lessons," he gave in with a sigh. The rest were puzzled, wanting to know more, but he turned to leave instead of explaining. They went out to the flyer.

Garth took the pilot's chair. Ryes took the copilot's seat. Maren, Sabin, Torr and Mitt piled into the back, strapping in quickly and were ready. Garth started his systems check, with Ryes only having to queue him in a few times. He finally took the stick, brought up the engine speed to full throttle, then lifted upwards. At Ryes' prompting, he began his flight toward Hailys. It was incredibly fast, but he realized if his ancestors could fly great ships between the stars, he could handle this small human machine. Ryes gave him encouragement and small reminders from time-to-time when he needed them, but she was proud of the way he relaxed and quickly took control of the craft, as if he flew every day!

"We were around here when Tyra appeared," Ryes pointed out the rock where she and Maren watched the sunset. "She took us off that way."

"It's white and pink stone," Maren pitched in from the back, recognizing the spot they were hovering over.

"Wait a moment," Torr warned them. "Can you take this thing higher?" he requested, seeing something out his window and wanting a better view.

"What is it?" Garth asked, as he started them on a gentle ascent, straight up.

"What's that?" Sabin agreed, now seeing what Torr saw. "Get a look toward the middle of Hailys!" They turned their attention that way and Ryes gasped. Without being prompted, Garth turned the air vehicle and headed toward it.

It was a darkness in the bright green carpet of life covering the shattered buildings. As they approached, it became apparent that it was actually a huge pit, which extended miles across and even deeper into the heart of the underground city, than it was wide. The plants were growing down into the cavernous opening, wherever there was purchase for their roots. They hovered over the center for several long minutes; everyone quiet as they tried to grasp what forces, unleashed, could've done this destruction. Ryes recalled the thunder, fire and terror from her nightmare months ago.

"What did this?" Mitt finally breathed in question.

"The humans call it a bomb," Ryes replied. "There're several in storage in Winterhaven, but they're under a special seal, which can only be opened by two people. The `base commander,' or the `head of research,'" she added. "From what the computer showed me, none of the ones there can destroy this vast an area, not even if used all together."

"No one can get them out?" Sabin demanded.

"No one I know," she assured him, twisting around to look him in his eyes. She noted the dark look in Garth's eyes, too.

"Good. They can't do this by themselves, can they?" Garth pressed, needing to be very sure now. He didn't know there were such dangerous machines in storage there! What else could be there which could harm them, he wondered?

"I asked the computer about it. It said there're many `safe guards' to prevent it from happening," Ryes told him. "If you want, you can ask it, yourself."

"Let's hope it spoke truly," Torr commented, still boggled with this scene of destruction. Garth took the helicopter down into the crater slowly, carefully, giving them all an appreciation of how vast Hailys had been, below the surface. On some levels, great galleries opened up, which looked to stretch miles inward, away from them. Ryes turned on the lights they used for flying at night, illuminating the many floors as they descended past them.

"Like insects in a hive," Maren commented in a low voice.

"But, Winterhaven lies underground," Mitt pointed out, "and we're nothing like insects! Not to mention it was built by the humans, so it may be what people do, when they build great cities?"

"Repeating what our ancestors started?" Sabin questioned.

"Tayna was a hunting preserve, so they may have built underground so as not to disturb the land above. If Hailys was supposed to be the greatest city, what of any of the other cities on Tayna? We need to find them, to see if we can recover any of our ancestor's technology and make it ours, again."

"You mean there might even be underground buildings below Matlowe?" Maren asked, wondering for the first time about it. This got a gasp of surprise out of the others as they considered it for the first time, too.

"Who knows? There very well might be," Sabin conjectured. "None of us ever considered it possible, before. There must be clues to the other cities, somewhere."

"They're locked in those crystals. There must be something like our human's computer here, with a way to get at the information we require. We only need to find it," Ryes suggested.

"You tell us where to start looking," Garth invited, gesturing to the scene outside. "At least with this, we have a new way to explore the city, without immediate concern of that death dust. If the plants and animals can live in here, we can start our investigations here. Let's go find Ronn's grave," he suggested, as Ryes sighed at the magnitude of the task before them.

"It's time for another journey back to Hailys' past. My great aunt might have some suggestions." Silence reigned in the flyer, as they gently rose up into the sunlight, once more. Garth shut off the exterior lights himself, seeing how she turned them on.

"You're not going alone," Sabin reminded her.

"I don't know if I can take anyone back that far without danger to the both of us," she stated, unwilling to risk more than herself in such a venture.

"You're not being given a choice," Garth ordered her, as he flew back to their original position. "Where to from here?"

"Head southwest," Maren advised, seeing Ryes looking unhappy and not paying attention to them. She finally sighed, giving Garth a nod of her head. A small smile was all that marked his acknowledgment of victory.

"After the burial," she told him, surrendering.

"There, that place with the arches," Mitt called out. As they came over the clearing, they could clearly see the medallion's symbol copied in broken pieces of stone.

"That's it," Ryes affirmed. Garth set the landmarks into his mind, and then turned the flyer toward home, crossing the empty land between very quickly. In a very short time they were back and landing once again.

"This sure makes the world seem smaller," he commented with a smile, as he set the machine down upon its small, marked landing spot. He started his shutdown systems check, not needing Ryes' prompting this time.

"Let's see about burying Tyra properly, in all due honor," Maren suggested as he took off his straps.

"We're going to need two of those shuttles," Torr observed.

"Land rovers," Ryes corrected him, but then smiled. "Ahhhh, why not? We'll just call them shuttles because that's us! We don't need to stick to the human way," she laughed out merrily.

"That's right! They're long gone, so what should it really matter?" Sabin agreed. Maren smiled as he nodded his head. He wasn't too sure about this. His lady was still with him at night. They were now holding onto each other, experiencing the differences between them. Something told him that he'd see her someday; that this wasn't just created from his imagination out of boredom.

"Maren, you drive the second shuttle," Garth told him. "You have more experience than Torr." He smiled at this, giving him a nod of his head in confirmation.

"I'll let Torr get in some more time behind the wheel on our way back," he suggested, nudging him in the side as he did.

"Wait, I don't want people screaming in fright all the way home," Torr protested with a laugh.

"We all need more practice with these machines," Sabin told them. "So, if there's ever a need, any of us could handle them."

"Even the elders, but the young cubs are still too young to reach the controls, properly," Garth agreed. "That's the plan." He got out of his restraining straps, turning to face the rest. "So, this is officially our flyer number one and the wheeled vehicles are our shuttles. It does sound better than `helicopter' and `land rover,'" he added, giving Ryes a smile. He went around and helped her down.

Two hours later, still well before noon, two shuttles departed to bring Tyra Li's body to lie with her true-mate, Ronn, as she willed it. Everyone except Teris, who volunteered to watch things while they were gone, were loaded into the vehicles, as they took the road to Hailys. The ravine crossing had the newly-arrived villagers astounded with how smoothly and quickly they crossed it in these amazing, frightening machines. Garth turned off their established path to veer toward the west, skirting around the ruins until they came to the correct clearing. Rowan gasped as he recognized the graceful stone arches.

"This is the spot," he affirmed, as Garth smiled. Once he'd been somewhere, he never had a problem finding his way back. They exited the shuttles, and gathered at the mound to pay their respects to Ronn and his three cubs. All the stones were carefully removed. The necklace still lay upon the soil, beneath them. Ryes picked it up and held it as the men continued working. They dug up the wrapped bodies and set them to allow the addition of Tyra's. They deepened the hole. Then they escorted the box containing her body from the back of the shuttle to the gravesite. The box was opened and they gently put her in next to Ronn, with their three, tiny cubs between them. Ryes placed the medallion atop Tyra's shroud, as she wished. Prayers were offered for their souls, and then more for those lost in the destruction of Hailys. They buried them and replaced the stones, exactly as they'd been before disturbing them.

They washed up and had lunch under the arches, enjoying the fading warmth of summer. Then they drove to another area and showed the ruins of Hailys to their dear friends and family, letting them get a small glimpse of what their ancestors left behind. As the older cubs ran and played around them, they walked through the plant-covered stone and tried to imagine what it'd been like. Ryes tried to tell them of the great scores of people and their constant need for haste, so very like the humans she thought. She described the tall buildings and what they looked like. She told them of the neatly kept gardens around the buildings, as if plants could be grown and shaped by will alone. She told them of the shuttles and other marvels, like doors which opened by just standing before them, or the readers, or the headset music and message holders. They laughed, striving to see the pictures she painted for them with her descriptions, but couldn't truly understand half of what she described. She finally shrugged and gave up. The human technology would have to do for now, as at least it still worked! They headed back for Winterhaven. Back to the home they now called their own.

Questing

"Garth, do I HAVE to weed the garden?" Spann questioned, catching him as he was leaving out the main door. "I don't feel like it, today," he confessed to the curiosity in his eyes.

"Do we HAVE to do everything Ryes tells us?" Mason added, wanting to get in his own say. "How come she's suddenly one who runs things? She's always been just the Huntress before, and would run off into the woods if you said `boo!'" There was a sudden ignition of anger in Garth's eyes, which he realized he'd never seen before, in his whole life. Mason took a small step back, wanting to get further away, but felt unable to move further.

"Ryes is MY WIFE and is second to me in heading this new colony of ours," he informed them in an even voice, taking the pains to keep his ire out of it. "She tries to rotate and assign chores as fairly as possible, taking over that task for me. Of course, you could clean out the bird cages today, if you'd rather. I'm sure Minn would gladly trade tasks with you," he offered, smiling tightly. Spann sighed, shaking his head no, fully chastised.

"I'll head straight out to the gardens," he offered, donning one of the straw hats the women had made for working outside in the summer sun. He knew better than to cross Garth, having learned how strong he was when they were children, and it appeared as if he'd grown larger and stronger since leaving Matlowe.

"You'll do as Ryes says, unless there's an important reason for not taking on a task," Sabin added, realizing they were still having problems getting the newcomers settled into their way of life. "Even I have to follow her assignments."

"She outranks you, Sabin?" Mason chuckled out, not believing it! Sabin nodded his head in response, realizing Ryes didn't grind upon his senses as some of the Matlowe elders had, before. And she usually had he and Garth teamed, unless it was something vital.

"She's fair and tries to accommodate us," Sana spoke up, backing her littermate as she stepped forward. "She's not one to shove others into things. I don't mind it." She'd stood back listening, realizing the reason things were so different here was that Garth,

Ryes and Sabin were the leaders and did the chores, too. "In Matlowe, the elders sat and told us all what to do, spending their days drinking, eating and talking. Even Rowan had duties to perform - beyond his weaving. They expect everyone here to pitch in and help keep things running smoothly. So just get used to it, Mason, or go back to Matlowe." With this she donned her own hat and went outside to help gather the ripening fruits, which were ready for picking, today. She knew Fane was safe under her mother's care.

"I'll stay here in Winterhaven," he answered her retreating back, resigned. "It's better and far more comfortable than my hut back in Matlowe." Garth took a step closer to Mason, recalling something else he wanted to mention to him, while he had the chance.

"Stay away from Mitt," he warned in a low voice. "She doesn't need you around her." This gave him pause as he met his eyes. He'd forgotten the night before, in the hallway... They'd only run into each other accidently, and he hadn't realized he had his arms about her right away. It had seemed so natural. The little girl was grown up and ready for free-mating!

"It was an accident," he assured him, smiling. "But she's getting older fast and I don't see any reason for not courting her, if she doesn't object." He heard that she'd spent the night with Teris once, but hadn't since. Maybe he'd get a chance for some fun, too, he wondered? Still he wanted cubs of his own and waiting a year for Mitt would suit him just fine. Garth seemed to guess what he was thinking and practically growled at this. Mason froze, realizing he was walking a fragile rope bridge, now.

"I will have the final approval of who courts her, or not," he coldly stated. "She's MY LITTLE SISTER." Sabin chuckled at this, nodding his head in agreement.

"Then you'd better keep an eye to whom she spends the night with," Mason dared to return, shaking as Sabin's humor broke him from the trance. He quickly snatched his hat and hurried out the door, a chill still travelling up his back. Somehow, he vowed, he'd find a way to win Mitt over. Garth couldn't watch her all the time! He saw his older half-brother, Minn, cleaning out the bird cages outside and smiled. The gardens were far better, after all.

"Need a break?" Mitt asked Minn, as she saw he just finished the third bird pen. He turned and smiled at her, seeing she had a tall, ice-filled glass of golden liquid in her hands. He hoped it was for him, since Seena had collected the eggs he gathered earlier and had yet to return with something cool for him to drink, as promised.

"I could use one," he returned. She grinned as she handed him the glass, understanding this wasn't one of the more pleasant chores around Winterhaven.

"I thought you might," she agreed with a smile. "Ryes and I regularly clean out these pens and I'm relieved you're here to help with the task."

"Thank you," he replied, after half-draining the glass with a long, parch-relieving draw. "This is tea on ice?" he questioned, thinking it tasted so different than when it was hot, yet was still pleasant upon the tongue. Mitt nodded her head, still smiling.

"Yes, it is. It's one of Ryes' ideas, since we have an ice making machine here. I believe it was the way the humans served up their version of tea," she explained. "Let's go over to the shade in the flyer bays. I'm taking a short break, too." He nodded his head, grateful for the chance to cool off for a few minutes. The summer may be fading, but the god Kember was still exerting his power, giving the days a far stronger sun than he was used to. He trailed after Mitt, realizing he needed to clean up a bit, too. Only one cage left and he could do what he wanted for the rest of the day once it was finished. It was why he didn't object to being assigned the task. This way he could finish his chores early in the morning and help Kovin explore some of the more hidden recesses in this underground structure. They found some woodworking tools in a place they thought might be a workshop for wood, as Aric's workshop back in Matlowe was for shaping metals. It was an exciting discovery!

"I realized I was getting too frustrated with trying to figure out a problem with the one flyer. It's not running right and I'm not sure if I fully understand the instructions the computer gave Ryes for me to use, to fix it. It's like it's almost right, but there's something else missing," she explained, "As if something inside of me is telling me there's something not right. And if I could find a way to feel it out from within, I could fix it the way it should be." She motioned him over to the sink, so he could wash up, recalling the way she felt from long exposure. He appeared grateful, quickly taking advantage of this opportunity. The soaps here were nicely scented, as the ones the Caravaners sold in the winter months.

"Maybe you should ask Ryes to have the computer take another look at your flyer again? Maybe it missed something, which you sense?" he suggested, looking about the neat machines and equipment stored in this great chamber. Across on the opposite side was the garage for storing and maintaining the shuttles, but those

doors were sealed today. Mitt sighed as she nodded her head, having
gotten to where she believed that had to be the answer, herself. It
was nice to have it confirmed. She opened her thermal container and
topped off Minn's glass, then her own. She was glad she thought of
bringing it out with her this morning.

"I think you're right. I'll ask Ryes to check on it after lunch,"
she replied, then met Minn's eyes with mischief in her own. "I heard
you and Kovin found some kind of wood shop? You used to carve the
most interesting things," she prompted, hoping he'd tell her, himself.
He chuckled as he sat down upon a waiting chair. He took another
long pull from his glass, and met her eyes with his humor in his own.

"Nothing stays secret around here," he commented, shaking
his head in wonder.

"It's a small group," she reminded him, not wanting to remind
him of the cameras watching them, everywhere, all the time.

"I heard about you and Teris," he began, recalling Garth's
unease with being reminded about her being old enough for free-
mating, now. "Don't you think you ought to go a little slower? I don't
think Garth's too happy about it." She made a face with his reminding
her of Teris. He was sounding like her cousin Torr!

"He was a mistake. He's somehow gotten it into his head that
we should be breeding for our Talents, to make them stronger. What
does he KNOW? He doesn't have Talent! He wasn't interested in ME,
just what my bloodline might bring to any cubs he thought he could
father on me! It was disgusting and I was glad when he finished his
grunting and shoving," she related, suddenly speaking out about it
with anger in her voice. She never intended to tell anyone about the
experience and couldn't believe she'd had blurted it out! Minn was
quiet for a few moments - taking it in.

"It's too bad your first time turned out so horrible. Was he
rough on you?" he asked in sympathy, shocked she'd told him so
much about it. Mitt laughed lightly, shaking her head no, recovering a
little.

"He wasn't my first. Actually, it was one of the Caravaners, a
few weeks after last Winterfest. His name is Ponti. He's older than
me, but was far more gentle than Teris, and he treated me like I was
someone special," she admitted, blushing a dark gold and grinning at
the memory. "I never dared to let on to Gann, Garth, or Karr, but we
met each other every day, in the woods, for a while."

"So, are you waiting for him to return?" he prompted, thinking
she didn't seem the type to run off with a Caravaner; especially now
that Korman was defeated. Mitt shook her head no.

"A Caravan woman named Mella came into season and asked him to be her husband, so he accepted. It was fun while it lasted and Ponti did give me some nice gifts before they left. Still, I'm starting to think ahead. With my being given the choice, it's even harder. I want the best father possible for my cubs and the best husband for myself," she explained. Suddenly, she got an inspiration and sat down in Minn's lap, shocking him anew.

"Want me to help you finish with the last coop, then WE can give it a try?" she requested, her eyes merry as she realized she was half teasing and half serious. She wondered what kind of mate someone like Minn might make? Ponti taught her that older was not always a bad idea.

"You have a whole year to do your choosing, Mitt," he reminded her, realizing he was sorely tempted with her in his arms. Suddenly their lips were together and a passion rose up from within as they kissed. Mitt was clinging to him, as his arms held her tightly, forgetting the glass of tea in his hand, as it dropped to the floor, still undamaged and spilling the remaining contents. "Your brothers are going to kill me," he breathed out, realizing where they were going with this, now. Whether, or not it would remain so with them, when it came time for her mating, would be in Aletagga's hands. This was now and he needed her, as much as she seemed to need him. Mitt laughed lightly, shaking her head no.

"I'll defend you from them," she promised, then returned to kissing him. The birds could wait a few minutes more...

The next morning Ryes, Sabin, Maren, Garth and Mason flew back out to Hailys. Ryes tried to remember where she'd been when she left her Great Aunt Adina, far in Hailys' past. She recalled the name of the stop she was waiting to be announced. After looking at directory after directory, they found one which was still intact enough to show some of the names. Montcliff was listed, so they went toward it and discovered it was just west of the great crater. It fascinated Mason, who'd never seen it before, but Garth cautioned him to stay away. They'd get their chance to explore it, later. He found a good spot to land, in a nearby clearing. They walked over to the area closest to the shuttle stop from the past.

"I have a million questions," she admitted to Garth, flutter-wings loose in her stomach at the thought of taking Sabin back with her. "How will I remember to ask the right ones? What if she gets impatient with me?"

"You'll be fine, and you'll have Sabin with you to help," he assured her, smiling down into her green eyes as she sat upon a tumbled, stone wall. "Only an hour at the most," he cautioned. At the best estimate from before, she'd been gone almost four hours! They didn't want her getting lost, again! Sabin was accompanying her, while Maren was going to monitor them, so he could tell if there were any difficulties and try to get them out. Garth was standing by, in case he needed to use more drastic measures to remind them they had bodies to return to. Mason kept a sharp eye to what lay around them in case any of the larger animals, which lived and hunted here, took an interest in them. He had his bow at the ready.

"I'll be right back," she teased, smiling, seeing he wasn't happy with having to let her go without him.

"You be careful. Both of you," he scolded with a smile, but the look in his eyes was serious and he meant it.

"We will," Sabin assured him, then gave Ryes a nod of his head. He wasn't bothered by Garth's warning. He settled back and closed his eyes. Ryes did the same, then reached over and clasped Sabin's hand. There came that familiar lurching and inner wrenching sensation, only worse than the shorter trips she was now allowed to take alone to watch the humans. She concentrated upon her Aunt Adina's face, then opened her eyes, feeling they'd arrived. She heard Sabin's loud gasp as he saw the constantly moving masses of people before them. Ryes searched, and then saw her great aunt and Hadu stepping off one of the shuttles.

"Aunt Adina!" she called and waved to them. There was surprise in her eyes, but they came straight over, easily spotting them even in this crowd.

"I see you have discarded those simple, Forester clothes," she commented, then smiled in greeting. She wanted so much to give her a hug and kiss, but knew it'd only disrupt her life-force energy. "Is this your mate?" she asked, smiling at Sabin. Ryes laughed and blushed at this, shaking her head no.

"I'd like you to meet Sabin. He's another Talent and blood-brother to my husband, Garth. Sabin, I'd like you to meet my Great Aunt Adina and her guardian, Hadu," she introduced them. Sabin, like she'd been before, was fully absorbed in his study of Hadu's appearance, barely breathing. There was an aura of intense danger about him.

"We have an hour before our connection to the starport, so let us find a quieter place to sit and talk, my dear." There was more confidence in Ryes, which she liked. She was more pregnant than before, so still had yet to have her children. As her eyes spotted a table near to their next shuttle, she asked, "How is your mother, dear?"

"We finally got to bury her with Ronn and the rest of my siblings, here in the outskirts of Hailys," she informed her. "There's so much I was still trying to grasp the last time, that I never got the chance to tell you some of what's happened through the years," she apologized. Adina turned a shocked look her way, but realized she was right. She had assumed Tyra still lived, but it now made sense why she hadn't been there to monitor Ryes' last Time Walking effort.

"Come, both of you," she ordered, as she led them to the table.

"I got to thinking," Ryes started, keeping a firm grip upon Sabin's hand, as they crossed the crowded concourse. People always made way for Hadu, so they didn't have to worry about others bumping into them, accidently. "You have a short time here, in the past, while I have much more time, in my own time. So, somehow I should be able to give birth to that son, who's supposed to help me, and figure out how to save both you and Hadu."

"You are absolutely correct," she replied as she took her seat. Sabin let Ryes sit, then sat on the outside, wanting to make sure she'd be safe from harm, too. Hadu's presence aside, he still didn't know anything about these people and this place.

"I can't believe this is Hailys," Sabin told her, with a smile and a small chuckle. She laughed lightly at this.

"What is Hailys like in your time? Less crowded?" Adina asked, "Is it was any less during the off-season?"

"It was destroyed by an unknown enemy, who came out of the dark of the stars. It was an unexpected attack and in our time there's only tumbled stone from the great buildings and a carpet of green plants covering everything," Sabin replied, meeting her eyes squarely to see her reaction.

"Do you know when it happened?" she returned, getting a disquieted feeling in the pit of her stomach. Perhaps this was what Ryes was supposed to save them from? She couldn't think of anything else which could so endanger them here.

"That has to be it!" Ryes gasped out, "The attack upon Tayna! Is there any way you could get to a starship shield barrier? Could something like that help you survive the thunder and terror?" Ryes hope was clearly reflected in her face. Adina looked at her strangely.

"Those are not made to carry in a pocket," she informed her, then frowned. "There are still starships in your time?"

"No, but Doran of that valley of death uses one to keep safe a stone of power, which her women stole for her. I thought if she could get one, you might be able to, also," she apologized.

"One of the Greater Power Stones?" Adina gasped out, looking pale at this. "In the hands of such evil!" She saw shock and fear in her eyes, which did not assure Ryes. She knew some knowledge of Doran, after investigating her and her cult here on Tayna and the thought of her having so much power at her disposal sent a chill up her back.

"She can't control it anymore. I took that ability away from her; hopefully for good. We'll set up a way to keep a check on things there; to make sure, when we get the time. Right now, we're busy getting ready for the winter, living in an installation the humans built, to study us and Hailys. We're having problems trying to salvage our old technology. Maren's been collecting every crystal rod he can find, but there're no working readers."

"Do you know if there's some kind of computer, or machine which stores knowledge and can operate other machines, here in Hailys?" Sabin asked, taking his lead from Ryes. Adina sat back for a moment with a sigh and a small smile as she observed these two for a few moments, thinking. Yes, there was much here. They needed knowledge to rebuild their world apparently, but she had no idea what a "hueman" was.

"Do not these huemans object to your moving in with them?" she questioned. "And what of Kahmarr? Do they not try to help you reclaim what used to be yours?"

"We've no idea if Kahmarr still exists," Ryes told her in a low voice, looking troubled. "The humans left years ago because of some battles they were having with another people, which moved into our area of space. The computer had no knowledge of Kahmarr, saying the humans had not explored in that region of space."

"How do you know these huemans were not fighting us, the Star People?" she pressed, wondering.

"According to their computer, they know their enemy. They are darkness and evil, shaped like nightmares and I wondered if it was the same people who destroyed Hailys, before? But, we're new to the computer and it still studies us, even as we live under its protection."

"How do you know where Kahmarr lies?" she suddenly demanded, seeing a hole in her story, "if you have no starships to go there?"

"There are great maps carved into the cliff faces of Berrals. One is a star map, but it's two dimensional. Darman, a caravan elder, had a copy of the map, which he gave to me long ago. I showed it to the computer and we have an idea where it lies, but not exactly," she admitted, smiling. "I wish we could find some of our old starships, or a computer of our ancestors."

"I would think starships would be easy. The starport lies west of Hailys, if it still exists. But super numerators are harder. If the city is totally destroyed, as you have said, then there would be little hope of getting one to work, even if you found it. Is there some way you could use the hueman's computer to read the memory rods? They are very basic and simple, with storage and retrieval being done with light, I believe. Is this not right, Hadu?" she asked, looking up to his comforting presence. Kahmarr gone? It was an incredible horror, which couldn't be true! What of the other colony worlds?

"Yes," he replied, never once glancing down to them, but keeping an eye to everything else around them. His voice, like his eyes, glided smooth as silver and sounded just as deadly. It gave Ryes the chills. This appeared to give Sabin ideas.

"Could we use the human's computer and equipment to build a reader capable of retrieving the information stored on those rods?" he asked Ryes. She shrugged.

"Now remember, not all memory rods are worthwhile. Many will contain useless junk. You must find some of the greater repositories, like the libraries," she cautioned, noting they hung upon her every word.

"We found the Thesa Hall Library," Ryes told her, smiling. "The rods, which were salvageable, are safely stored in boxes in Winterhaven. Can light damage them?" she asked.

"Not regular sunlight," she sighed, thinking. There was so much. "Our shuttle is due very soon. I do not recall what Thesa Hall would contain," she admitted. "It might be useful; it might not. The ones to search for will be Rantook, or Caspian libraries," she advised. "You had better go for now. I will think on this and see if I can come up with any better answers for your questions the next time we meet." Ryes smiled, giving her a nod of her head.

"I'll be trying to figure out a way to help the two of you, too," she assured her in return. Adina smiled at this, liking this young woman. The young man with her seemed a little rough, but he was sharp and not unmannered.

"We will be waiting," she promised. Ryes closed her eyes and searched for herself once more, pulling Sabin back with her. She kept a tight hold upon him. The wrenching, lurching motion hit them both hard, but after a few moments they could both feel the incredible weight of their own bodies and the effort of having to settle back into themselves.

"You're back on time!" Maren practically shouted through his light inner linking with the two of them.

"Of course," Sabin assured him, returning his joy, adding in his own sense of relief. The linkage dissolved and they opened their eyes on the world around them, again.

"You're all right?" Garth asked, relief in his eyes as he knelt down and took Ryes' hands into his own. They were now cold. She smiled brightly for him and laughed.

"Yes, we're fine," she assured him.

"I don't know about that Hadu. What is he?" Sabin asked, frowning, recalling the subtle deadliness which enshrouded him. "Everything about him put me on alert!"

"His full name is Hadu-ramashan and his people are called Demmias. He was born on a colony world called Kesper. He not only looks deadly, but I fully believe he is, if you were foolish enough to challenge someone like him," Ryes informed him. "I'd never heard him speak before and that once was enough for me!" Chills still traveled up her spine as she recalled his voice. Garth laughed at this, hugging her to him. She grabbed him, holding on tightly, trying to suppress another shiver.

"And you're supposed to save him?" Garth questioned, merrily.

"As long as he's on our side," Sabin stated, "I don't think we'd ever have to fear anyone, ever again," he assured him.

"There's a starport, where the starships come and go, west of Hailys," Ryes told him, pulling away to look into Garth's eyes. "But as far as a computer is concerned, Aunt Adina doesn't think one would work after such a terrible destruction and long time. She suggests that we use the human machines to see if we can get them to extract the information we need." Garth thought on this, giving her a nod of his head.

"It'll be our winter project," he told her, feeling it might give them plenty to do this coming winter, when the snows would lock them into Winterhaven.

"We also must find both Rantook and Caspian libraries for the memory rods we need. She said most of the rest contain useless junk," Sabin told him. "Let's see if that directory has them listed, and then get home before it gets too late," he suggested. Garth chuckled at this, in full agreement.

They spent most of the day tracking down a usable directory, but now it was getting late, faster. The starport would have to wait for later, as would those libraries.

It ended up taking two teams over three weeks to find and retrieve all the memory rods from the libraries in Hailys. Finally, realizing they didn't have enough room to store the containers of rods in the room next to the human library, they opened up one of the sealed rooms and moved them all into the spacious room, which they weren't going to be using for anything anytime soon. There were plenty of large, fixed chairs facing a raised platform at the far end; the chairs were higher up and on small tiers cascading down to the bottom platform. It was clearly the focus of this room.

"This place is enormous with plenty of room," Torr commented as he and Kovin were storing the last of the boxes against one of the walls near the main doors. "I wonder what they used it for?"

"Ryes said the computer labeled it a multi-purpose room. And just to let you know, I have no idea what that meant, either," Maren replied, laughing at the last. There were so many mysteries in this new home of theirs.

"It looks like a grand place to watch entertainments," Kovin commented, standing and looking down into the main chamber. A railing ran about the top of the main floor behind the top row of chairs. He gripped it as he looked about. Soft carpeting was underfoot everywhere. And several sets of stairs went all the way down to make getting to a lower seat easy.

"You could easily fit hundreds of people in here," Maren breathed out, as ideas danced in his eyes.

"And in comfort," Torr added. "Better than the Village Circle."

"We can call this our Village Circle," Maren replied, grinning. He got approval from the others before they all left the room.

"Ryes, quick!" Shadd gasped out with urgency, trying to catch her breath after running down the hall. Ryes was sitting at the computer console, working on a project which Neil assigned her. After meeting him and visiting him several times a week, she now had lots of homework, as he called it, to catch up on. She looked up puzzled, but saw the panic in her eyes.

"There is an individual in the kitchen area in need of emergency treatment," the computer intoned in English, displaying the picture on the main screen so she could see the situation.

"Raya?" she questioned, seeing her huddled and crying in a corner.

"How did you know?" Shadd demanded, frowning, then saw what Ryes pointed out on the screen.

"Computer, thank you. I'll return to finish this, once I've seen what's needed for Raya," she told the machine.

"Program is saved and stored," it intoned, then shunted to standby mode. Ryes gave it a nod as she got out of the chair and hurried to the kitchen with Shadd.

"It watches us all the time," she commented, concerned as they ran. Ryes laughed merrily.

"Only in the public areas inside and outside. I think the humans didn't trust each other very well. There's no way to turn off the cameras, so it's just another thing we have to put up with; the bad and bizarre along with the good and comfortable." Shadd gave her a nod of agreement, as they encountered Mitt just inside the kitchen door, looking panicked.

"She keeps yelling at us to stop it," she told Ryes, "and she's holding her head like it's hurting her."

"Go wake up Maren. I know he hasn't had much sleep since he had last watch last night, but this sounds like something for his expertise." Mitt gave her a nod and ran out the door. Shadd and Ryes rushed over to the corner where Raya was crying.

"It's all right," Ryes assured her in a low, soothing voice, as she knelt down next to the plainswoman. Raya had her hands over her ears and was rocking forward and back as she cried. Ryes went to pull her up, so she could hold her in comfort, but as her hands touched her, she knew her inner power had been unleashed. She drew in a deep breath in surprise. She immediately centered herself, knowing this could only be handled through her Talent, and then reached out to the stricken woman from within.

"Ryes?" she questioned, lost and alone in this mysterious torrent of power and voices she couldn't shut out. She felt like she was drowning as she couldn't escape that whirling torrent of pure energy, which threatened to shred her very being.

"Yes, it's me, Raya. You must exert control over your Talent, before it consumes you," she encouraged her. She projected that she was here to help support her, but the real work still lay in her own hands.

"What do I do?" she questioned, starting to panic. Her fears were nothing in the face of this madness!

"First calm down," Maren sent to her, with assurance that he was here to help, too. "Then remember this is your life and YOU CONTROL YOUR TALENT, not the other way around. You survived for weeks with little food, or water, alone in the wilderness. Are you going to let this defeat you?" he demanded with a little more of an edge. She started to pull away from him, but realized she couldn't escape neither Maren, nor Ryes here.

"You've never seemed like a person to turn and run from her problems," Ryes agreed. Raya realized they were right. She wasn't a coward and she wasn't going to let this unfolding within herself conquer her now. She turned back and wrestled with her inner power, until it obeyed her will and fused to become one with her being. Ryes laughed in happiness at her success, as Maren was relieved.

"You did it!" Maren declared, joyfully.

"But what's my Talent?" Raya queried, wondering.

"You hear the thoughts of others without physical contact, which Sabin, Maren and I require, along with having our Talents already in use. That would be Mind Voice. It might be handy to know if someone was speaking the truth in an important situation, but I wouldn't abuse poor Kovin with it, too much," she advised, teasing her.

"You may be like Ryes with more than one ability. Just don't worry. You'll know how to use your Talent, when you need it the most," Maren assured her, showing her the view he had when Ryes stopped the cart from killing Mitt, now months ago. "She didn't know she could do that, until she needed it."

"It's a good thing you were there to heal Mitt," Ryes added, recalling that disaster, too clearly.

"If I can hear thoughts, can I project them?" Raya asked.

"I don't know. Try with one of us first," Ryes offered, then withdrew from contact. She opened her eyes to see Shadd, Ardis, Tennan and Mitt looking worried, so she smiled for them.

"Ryes, can you hear me?" Raya shouted within her head, without moving her lips.

"Yes, but you need to speak more softly," she advised her aloud, as she put a hand to her own head in pain. She unconsciously brought her Healing Talent up to ease it.

"Sorry," she apologized aloud with a smile, as she and Maren opened their eyes, too. "I didn't realize how strong it can be. I can shut out the others, now that I've figured it out." Maren helped her to her feet as Ryes got to hers on her own, rejecting the hand Ardis offered her. She was walking on the treadmill in the gym now, several times a week, to keep her legs in shape. Garth wasn't happy with this, afraid she'd hurt the cubs, but Maren assured him it was good for her.

"What was the problem?" Shadd asked; glad to see them happy, once more.

"Raya's Talent bloomed and she had to let it know she was the boss, not it," Ryes said, as Raya blushed and gave her a nod.

"Ryes," a voice overhead sounded, startling the others in the kitchen with her. She chuckled as she looked up to a camera.

"Computer, what's the problem?" she asked it in Dolbith.

"There seems to be some trouble starting," it informed her, also speaking Dolbith, amazing the rest of her friends. It displayed a view from one of the outside tower cameras, projecting it into the air before them. It showed a band of riders descending upon what was obviously their hunting party, with their spears being leveled as weapons. The smile melted from her face as she saw the attack.

"Mitt, you go up in the flyer, while Maren and I take a shuttle. Stay out of their range, but use the loudspeaker to see if you can scare their windracers. Play some of that loud, human music; that should do it. Maybe between the two of us, we can show them not to pick on our menfolk." Mitt gave her a nod, then rushed for the door.

"Wait, I'm going with you," Raya told her, throwing down her oven mitt. "Ardis, sorry," she apologized as she glanced back to her friend.

"Not to worry. I'll get Rein or Sana to help me finish up with the baking," she assured her as she waved her on her way. "Just bring Sabin home safe and sound."

"We will!" Mitt replied, grinning before disappearing.

"Computer, hold down the fort while we're gone," Ryes advised, recalling Monty using this phrase, whenever he left it alone to handle matters.

"Affirmative," it responded. Maren was already trotting for the door, as Ryes hurried to catch up. An all-out attack? What could be the problem? Her heart pounded, worrying about Garth and the others.

Judgement

"I think we have enough birds to last us until the spring after next year's spring," Torr commented to Garth with a chuckle, as they headed home with their cages in one of the small carts. They only had one of the windracers out today to pull the cart for them. They felt it did them all good to walk and enjoy the outdoors, as much as possible.

"We've got to get the rest of those inner stalls and cages finished for when the winter winds and snows hit. I know the computer isn't happy with the idea, but unless it wants to let us clear out one of those lab chambers, the anteroom will have to do for our windracers and birds," Sabin added, thinking of the few things they still needed to finish, before the cold set in. Garth chuckled at this, giving him a nod of his head.

"It's too bad that starport was only an empty crater, but at least we found the libraries," he commented. "It'll be something if we can figure out a way to read all those memory rods we have stored, this winter. At least it'll be a project to keep Ryes and Mitt busy with," he chuckled as Sabin and Kovin agreed, laughing, too.

"Who's that?" Torr asked, pointing to eight riders coming toward them at a full gallop.

"They've got their spears leveled. I don't think they mean to be friendly," Garth observed, taking his hunting bow and restringing it. He saw the other men doing the same. "Let's let them know they don't scare us," he added. They stood ready, standing between the riders and the cart, arrows notched and ready to fly. The riders saw them standing alert and ready, so Toron signaled a halt.

"This is our land," he shouted to the strangers.

"This land belongs to us," Garth returned, keeping his voice and hand steady. "We know where the plains people roam and you're far outside of your tribal markers." They consulted Raya about the matter long ago, when she was learning to drive a shuttle. She took them to the range of the plainsmen, pointing out their boundary markers. Perhaps it was time to put out boundary markers of their own, so they'd know they meant business?

"We seek a woman of ours who went astray," Gleds shouted, not recognizing the strange weapons they held, pointed in their direction. They looked like tiny spears, but how could they actually do much damage with their small, slender size, he wondered?

"Raya's my wife and mate," Kovin told him with a low growl in his throat. "She chose me because she wanted me," he added, knowing they could never, truly, appreciate what he was saying.

"She's mine to do with as I please," Toron told them, kicking his windracer hard in the sides, to run this insolent man down. Garth fired his arrow into the ground at the stallion's feet. The animal reared up, but didn't throw his rider. Garth had a new arrow notched before Toron had control of his mount, once more. The other riders appeared uncertain, waiting for their leader to make his move first, but fear was in their eyes.

"She does what she wants to do. She knew where you were and chose to stay with us. She picked Kovin because he was whom she wanted. You can turn around and leave, or my next arrow will end your life," Garth threatened, seeing he was ready to cast his spear. Suddenly there was a loud racket from above them, as the small flyer swooped in towards the plainsmen. There was a loud, blaring sound coming from it and Garth had to repress a smile, as they all realized who it had to be above them.

With the noise, dust and wind coming down suddenly from above, the windracers of the plainsmen started to buck and bolt, their riders losing control. Three of the riders were thrown, but managed to catch their mounts before they ran off. Their own windracer stood patiently with his cart load, but the birds loudly protested the commotion; their squawking was loud and distracting.

"Watch their leader," Garth warned, keeping his eyes upon him as he finally forced his stallion to his will, cruelly beating the animal, and charged them. The one who'd spoken out before also got his mount under control and charged with his leader. Then, a shuttle was skidding to a halt between them and the plainsmen, its horn blaring. This caused the leader's windracer to throw him to the ground, and then it galloped off, following the others as they were running back to the open plains. Garth saw the other man, still upon his mount, casting his spear at the shuttle's window and his wife. His anger ignited as he loosed his arrow, aiming straight and true.

The flyer landed, as Maren threw open his door and jumped out. The plainsman was clutching at the arrow, as it protruded from his chest, falling off his windracer. They noted that the spear had failed to break the window, and Ryes was shocked, but safe. Sabin and Garth were quickly beside the downed leader, as Maren rushed to

the other man's side. He had a hard time breathing with the arrow
buried deep in his body.

"Don't move," Sabin threatened, aiming straight down at the
man. Garth took his spear and broke its fire-hardened shaft over his
leg in absolute fury. Their captive was just as furious and surprised at
his display of strength. A snarl of fury painted his face as he
remained upon the ground.

"Maren, you don't have to heal him. He tried to kill Ryes,"
Garth ordered, seeing he was removing the arrow, bent and working
on him. Maren heard, but couldn't not heal the man. It now drove
him in a way he knew he'd never explain. Garth saw Raya and Mitt
leave the flyer, heading straight towards them, rage evident upon
Raya's face.

"How DARE you ever think you had the right to come looking
for me, Toron!" she screamed at the leader with her fists balled as if
ready to strike him, "I'm NOT your PROPERTY and when I tell Old
Dyan what you just did, you'll be lucky if he only hangs you upon the
Wailing Rocks, as an example to others!"

"It's all right, Raya," Kovin told her, seeing how this man's
presence upset her like she'd never been since they met. What could
he have done to her, he wondered? She saw Kovin was all right and
ran to him, grabbing him and kissing him in relief, as he wrapped his
arms around her, smiling.

"I was so afraid he was going to hurt you," she admitted,
tears in her eyes now, "Garth, my advice to you would be to take him
back as a prisoner to Old Dyan, the leader of the Moondance Tribe,
and tell him his hunting party had better watch their boundary
markers a little more closely. It's a sacred trust, which all the tribes
hold with honor. Even if our little settlement isn't a plains tribe
domain, our rights will be upheld, unless outright war is ever
declared."

"Are you all right?" Ryes asked Garth, seeing Mitt had joined
them, too. He nodded his head to this, not taking his eyes off this
viper, Toron.

"A WOMAN rode that flying thing?" Toron breathed out,
shocked and disgusted. "I was defeated by women!"

"Why not? She's a good pilot," Ryes told him, her eyes
narrowing. He looked dangerous. She looked back to Garth. "Should
we check to see what's on his mind?" she asked. Raya suddenly
turned in Kovin's arms, realizing she should've already done that!
This Talent had just been hatched within her and she'd no idea how or
when to use it, yet.

"Raya, what's wrong?" Kovin asked, seeing her eyes were shadowed.

"I just found my Talent. Ryes and Maren saved me from it taking over my mind. I can hear other's thoughts if I choose to listen in, now," she whispered to Kovin, hugging herself close to the warmth of his body. She realized she was still feeling cold from the aftereffects of the ordeal.

"Not now. Wait until Garth needs to know for sure. Don't let Toron know what you can do," Kovin advised, seeing how much she hated this man. It must be akin to Korman challenging Garth for Ryes when they were in Hailys. He just didn't want to let her go.

"Get one of those special binding cords from the shuttle," Garth ordered Ryes. She went and opened the back, getting out two of the heavy ones she saw the humans use on Alda. Only the cutters could remove them. She brought them out to Garth. Garth and Torr pulled him to his feet and bound his arms together tightly behind his back. "Mitt?" he asked next, quickly getting her attention. She was watching Maren work on the other man.

"Yes?" she asked.

"Fly up and check to see where the other riders are. If they're on their way back to the plains, go on in and get the flyer stowed away. If they're not, tell us over the radio and we'll take it from there," he ordered, then smiled at her. "Thanks," he added, giving her a nod of his head. A bright smile blossomed upon her face at this. She gave him a thumbs up, as Ryes showed them the humans using it as a hand sign of approval, then trotted off to her waiting, flying machine.

As Sabin and Torr held Toron, Garth strode over to the shuttle and opened the door. He took up the mic and depressed the small switch on its side.

"Computer, please relay," he ordered in English, as Ryes taught him.

"Relay open," it intoned in response.

"This is Garth. As soon as we return, there'll be a meeting to discuss establishing our boundaries with the plains tribes. Everyone will meet in the dining hall." With this he released the button.

"It's all clear, Garth. The riders are heading home, very quickly," Mitt reported, having heard his broadcast, too.

"Thanks, Mitt. Go on back," he ordered her, then resettled the mic in its holder on the dashboard. "Torr, could you blindfold him?" he asked, thinking the less he knew about them, the better.

"Garth, we'll walk back with the cart," Kovin volunteered, his arm still around Raya.

"Thanks Kovin, go ahead," he told him, smiling to see the two of them happy over the outcome of this encounter. They walked off, leading the patient windracer. Ryes was beside him, now holding the second man's spear.

"He threw this with full force," she commented in a low voice, "at least we know a little of what this thing will stand up to." Garth sighed as he wrapped his arms about her.

"Your luck's still holding out," he teased. "I think, even if it had gone through the window, it would've merely skewed down the length of the dashboard. But, it was still much too close as far as I'm concerned," he admitted as he gave her a kiss, relieved she was all right. "The next time grab more men to help out," he suggested in a low voice. She smiled impishly.

"What, and let them think I'm helpless?" she volleyed in return, mischief in her eyes.

"Let's get back and see about getting things settled," he said, releasing her. He turned to see if Maren was finished and saw his eyes were open once more. "Sabin," he ordered, pointing to their second prisoner.

"Wait, Garth!" Maren protested, standing up and helping the plainsman to his feet. "He's not a bad person, truly. I'll vouch for him," he pleaded, with a hand still upon his patient's arm. Garth sighed, unhappy with this turn. He knew it wasn't a question of Maren's loyalty, just an example of his loving kindness. He wouldn't be who he was, otherwise.

"He still gets his hands bound and will be blindfolded, until we determine exactly where his heart truly lies," he decided. Maren didn't look happy, but gave him over to Sabin, who bound his hands in front, instead of behind, as with the other one. He took the second blindfold Torr made and tied it over his eyes. Garth motioned for them to get into the shuttle, then took the driver's wheel, himself. Ryes smiled as she and Maren took the seat beside him.

"Well, it was a nice day," she commented, as they drove back to Winterhaven.

"Stow the leader in the finished cage," Garth ordered, as they finally entered the anteroom between the inner and outer doors of Winterhaven. "When we need him for questioning, we'll bring him in."

"What do we do with him?" Torr questioned, indicating the man Maren had healed.

"He comes with us. I need to know a few things, first." He saw his father standing in the inner doorway. He signaled him to stay put until Sabin had their prisoner secured, then they headed toward the inner doors.

"The outer doors sealed right after Ryes and Maren left. We couldn't go out, nor could anyone else come in," he informed him with a puzzled look. Garth smiled at this, giving him a nod of his head. "We just released the locks by talking with the computer, seeing the doors were sealed, as they'd never been before. There were strange ports open on the side of the tower building, which sealed again, once we assured the computer we were fine."

"I gave it to understand there was a chance for violence and the computer took steps to ensure that everyone inside would remain safe, until we returned and assured it we prevailed," she explained. "At least we now know how to take steps like that, if we ever need to," she chuckled, relieved.

"Let's get the meeting started," Sabin suggested, having put their main prisoner away in the solidly-built cage. He used an extra cord to bind his feet, as well. He could see him straining at his bonds, but to no avail.

They went through the doors, Torr hauling the other prisoner along indifferently. Maren looked distressed to Ryes' eyes, so she gave him a smile and a nod, to let him know that she'd make sure he was heard, at least. They went down the halls to the dining room. The room was very changed from what it looked like when they first moved in. They'd hung decorative artwork upon the walls, placed colorful cloths upon the plain, metal tables and rearranged them to give more of a sense of community. Warm rugs were on the floor, making it feel more like home. Almost everyone was here; already seated, discussing the day's events so far, with fresh mugs of tea in hand, both hot and iced. The voices quieted as they entered the room, going to one of the empty tables to sit and wait for the stragglers.

"We're waiting for Raya and Kovin. Is Minn on watch, now?" Garth asked Ardis. She gave him a nod and smile, then jumped up as a small bell sounded. She was joined by Seena, as they rushed to pull the fresh bread out of the oven. Its delightful odor soon filled the room, reminding them it was almost time for dinner. Lixi ran over to Sabin, wanting to be picked up. He chuckled as he complied, placing her upon his knee, so she could watch the proceedings. Kovin and Raya soon entered and took seats, as Ardis and Seena rejoined the group.

"Minn won't be left out," Ryes assured Garth. He gave her a nod, realizing he could watch them on the screens from the computer room. He stood up and faced the people who now depended upon him.

"As we were returning from our hunt, we were accosted by eight mounted riders with spears held at the ready," Garth told the assembly, "We were ready with our bows if needed, but waited to see what they'd do, first. The leader, Toron?" he questioned, looking to Raya for confirmation. She gave him a nod of her head at this. "Demanded we give Raya over for his use, even after Kovin told him they were mated. They tried to charge us, but our very resourceful ladies intervened upon our behalf and drove most of the attackers away. The leader fell from his mount, but this one cast his spear at the shuttle and Ryes. I shot him with an arrow, but Maren healed him, bringing him back to health. Maren vouches for him, but I'd like to put Raya's new Talent to the test, first. Raya?" Garth requested, inviting her to stand.

"Yes, Garth?" she asked, then at his nod, she stepped closer to the prisoner and closed her eyes. She reached out to him, gently touching his mind. It was akin to running her fingers through Kovin's hair, before she braided it for him in the morning. It was silky and soft, gentle and yielding. After a few moments, she withdrew and opened her eyes.

"What's his name?" he asked.

"His name's Gleds," she replied, her hand lightly upon his shoulder, "But I already knew this answer, even without my Talent."

"What're they doing here?" he questioned.

"They've seen the lights on our tower for months and finally decided to see what was worth raiding here. Old Dyan denied Toron permission for this, but he decided to go ahead and do it, thinking we'd be ignorant of tribal law. Gleds mentioned me because he was trying to save Toron from his folly, as I was the only legitimate excuse they'd have for riding outside of the Moondance Tribal grounds. He didn't actually expect that I'd be living here and mated," she explained.

Gleds sat, wanting to see what was happening. Who were these people? It scared him that the sweet, little Raya he knew, now wielded such great power! He recalled Toron brutally using her before, and had been ashamed, but powerless to stop him. When she ran away, he well understood and his heart hadn't been in it when Toron demanded they search for her, months ago.

"Did he truly mean to kill Ryes?" Garth pressed, dead serious about the matter, now.

"No. He was aiming for the wheeled, metal monster, which had unexpectedly attacked them. He didn't even see Ryes, until after his spear was cast. It surprised him, as did your arrow suddenly in his chest. He's not a cruel man, Garth, but then I knew that from when I was a cub. His mind and heart are good, just as Maren asserted," she finished. Garth sighed at this, knowing he couldn't punish him, if all she said were true.

"You may cut him loose," he ordered. Torr stood with the cutter in hand, ready, but Maren stood and extended his hand to Torr, asking with his eyes for the honor. He smiled as he passed them to his friend, giving his own cousin a nod of his head before sitting back down next to Shadd, Rand and Rein. Maren cut the cording loose from his hands and helped Gleds pull off the blindfold, smiling to see the bewildered look in his eyes. He recognized him and gave him a smile and a nod in response.

"Thank you, Great Healer! You saved my life," Gleds told him, bowing to Maren more formally. This got him to blushing. "And to you lady Raya," he added, bowing to her, too. This got cheers and laughter from the others about the room. "I'd never have harmed the lady Ryes, if I'd known she was the one controlling such a great, metal beast. And I thank you, Sir," he told Garth. "Your justice is as swift as your tiny spears, straight and true." Garth smiled at this, then gave him a nod of his head.

"Garth," Raya spoke out, taking a stride away from Gleds, so she could face him more fully. "I'd like to withdraw from having to read Toron's mind, if possible. I couldn't be free from prejudice in his case, as I was a victim of his abuse in the past."

"I could try," Ryes offered, not looking forward to it, either. Garth considered his wife and Raya, then realized Ryes had a rod of solid steel at the core of her being. He doubted Raya was as tough as she.

"If you could do this for me?" he requested. "If nothing else, I know you can control any confrontation in ways he could never begin to imagine," he reminded her. She smiled at this, knowing he spoke the truth. Sabin chuckled, nodding his head in agreement. Raya took her seat next to Kovin, smiling for him.

"You're going to HAVE to show me what you did to them that night," Maren scolded her, as he helped Gleds to a seat next to him at the table. She smiled mischievously as she laughed lightly.

"I don't want to give you nightmares, which might last the rest of your life," she teased in return. This got puzzled looks from most of the others in the room, not having heard the story of the challenge, yet. It was one the three participants kept close to their hearts, even still.

"Sabin and Garth were going to fight a challenge and wouldn't listen to anyone, but Ryes took them up with a challenge within, of her own making. They haven't even given each other a cross look, since," Ardis explained to Seena. "He won't ever talk about it, but it had to be something very powerful, from the way he still acts."

"Come on, Garth, tell us what happened?" Mitt demanded, curious about it, now. It'd been hinted at from time-to-time, but no one spoke about it, otherwise. Rowan looked disturbed, but was curious, too. What had she done to them, he wondered?

"Not now, Mitt. We have to question Toron," he reminded her. Ryes pulled an extra folding chair over, next to the other one, as Torr and Mason went to get the prisoner.

"Maybe after dinner?" Ryes asked, looking to Garth for permission. "After all, a telling doesn't carry the power the actual experience held," she teased, smiling. Sabin groaned, recalling the details too well, even now!

"We'll see," Garth replied, inwardly agreeing with Sabin's groan. Torr and Mason appeared with their prisoner in tow.

"Whatever that traitor told you was a lie!" Toron shouted out to the room, as he was brought before them. Mason thrust him down onto the flimsy chair.

"He didn't give us one word of testimony," Garth returned in a level voice. "We don't work that way here," he assured him, smiling to himself as he did. It was fully the truth, after all.

"I'm not telling you anything, either!" Toron shouted, turning his head toward Garth's voice.

"Ryes," he said, giving her a nod. She sighed, closed her eyes centering herself. Torr and Mason stood ready, in case he tried to hurt her in any way, but neither dared touch them right now.

    She laid her hand upon Toron's shoulder, reaching out to him
from within. This man's heart was more beast than true man's, and it
repulsed her to have to delve into his heart and soul for the answers
they needed. He lay like a vicious creature, trapped and helpless
before her power, as she lightly sifted through his memories. What he
did to Raya angered her and he thought to strike at her, seeing it as a
sign of weakness. But her response left him as helpless as a child,
crying in terror. When she gathered what she needed, she withdrew,
upset that she'd let him draw her out enough to strike back so hard.
She let herself believe she had more control than that, but now knew
otherwise. Next time she'd be far more careful. She opened her eyes
and saw fear in the eyes of the villagers. There was nothing she could
do about it, but hoped they'd come to realize she wasn't a brutal
person, who hurt others casually.

    "He fully intended to murder and take whatever he found
here, that he could carry off. He thought what he couldn't hide from
Dyan, he would gift to him; thinking to bribe, or buy his way out of
being punished. He's gotten away with it before and considered us
just another notch upon his stick," she told Garth with a sigh, focusing
only upon him. Garth gave her a nod and smile of support. They'd
seen the outward signs of their inner battle. Toron had snarled and
growled, then suddenly cried out in pain and shock, then that turned
into a whimpering and crying, as if he were a child. Ryes' face had
remained calm and resolute through it all, but Garth noted the
villagers were upset over the display.

    "Thank you, my wife," he replied, reminding them of the value
she held for him. She got up from the chair and returned to her seat
next to him. "Raya, do you still believe this Dyan would punish him, if
he's let him get away with it in the past?" he asked. Raya's face was
as white as new snow as she turned toward Garth.

    "I saw what he's done," she breathed, standing back up. "I
watched what he tried to do to Ryes and what she did to him in return
for his attack. He deserved it! Yes, he's done many ugly things
before, which I'm sure Dyan has no idea of how truly brutal he's
become." She paused a moment blushing darkly, now knowing what
Toron had thought and felt as he beat and raped her long ago when
she approached him for a try at free mating. "The choice is up to you.
Kill him now, returning his body to Dyan and making a treaty with the
Moondance Tribe, or press Dyan for his sense of justice and return
him to his charge, hoping he'll punish Toron for his transgressions.
Toron won't rest until he kills us all now, whether or not Old Dyan
supports him." She sat down, seeking comfort in Kovin's arms,
knowing she had a long way to go before she'd be as capable as Ryes
when handling such malicious violence.

"It's all lies!" Toron declared, tears still streaming down his face.

"Remove the prisoner," Garth ordered. He tried to struggle, but Torr and Mason held him securely. They left the room with him, quickly, even though he was shouting and struggling against their hold. Sabin set Lixi down and came over to kneel beside Ryes' chair.

"Show me," he requested, needing to see this man's heart, as she and Raya saw it, to fully understand how grave their danger lay.

"Me, too," Garth added, smiling as he sat down next to her, again. She sighed, then gave them a nod, smiling. She closed her eyes, centering herself once more. She reached out and extended her hands to them both.

"I'm NOT missing this!" Mitt whispered to Marla as she quickly shifted over to grab onto her brother's shoulder, closing her eyes, too. Kovin got up and placed his hand over Sabin's, closing his eyes, needing to know what he'd done to his precious wife.

"Can they just do that?" Marla asked Rowan, unsure about this matter. Rowan looked uncertain.

"I don't know," he replied as he got up and joined them, putting his hand over Garth's. The images and feelings sent through shocked him, but he stayed, reveling in the sensations of their minds and hearts joined, in trying to understand this danger, which had come into their midst. Torr and Mason returned, seeing them in commune.

"The direct method is usually the best," Torr commented, wondering if he should see it for himself? Mason didn't understand what he meant, so returned to his seat, waiting with the rest. Torr decided to get it out of them, later. Maren was quietly talking with Gleds, trying to find an understanding in another way. He knew he could always badger Ryes into showing him, later. Tennan looked unhappy with him seating this complete stranger between them. After several long moments, their eyes opened and there was a grimness upon the men's faces. Mitt was as shocked as Raya had been, but like Ryes, she had a solid, inner core. So, she sat back and analyzed what she learned. Ryes was tired by the time they finished, feeling more ready for a nap, than dinner. Everyone returned to their seats as Garth stood up.

"We'll take Toron to Old Dyan of the Moondance Tribe to see if justice still exists in this world. We'll establish an understanding of where our land lies and maybe even get a treaty of some sort written. If this man is released and allowed to raid again, his life is forfeit here. He's to be killed on sight, from that point onward," Garth told the assembly. "Gleds, you're given the option of staying here with us, or returning to your own people. You have until Sabin and I are ready to leave, to make your decision," he offered.

"Thank you, Sir Garth," Gleds replied, standing up and bowing to him, again.

"You're welcome here," he replied, smiling, at last. "Let's eat," he suggested. This got a happy response, as several people stood to bring out the bowls and trays, which were ready and waiting. Ryes stood, but Garth restrained her. "You sit, Sweet One, and I'll go help," he told her in a low voice, knowing she was drained.

"But," she started, but sat down, seeing the look in his eyes. As he left the table, Mitt knelt beside her chair.

"We're going to have to make sure Raya understands we'd NEVER let anyone do something like that to her, again," she whispered. Ryes looked at her, knowing what she meant. She'd only been young and curious about free mating!

"Not as long as any of us lives and breathes," she vowed in agreement. "We'll talk with her later," she assured her.

"I'll go help," Mitt offered, standing up, smiling once more. She disappeared quickly into the kitchen.

Low voices in the room started discussing this turn of events and Ryes noted smiles were once again cast her way, which she returned. Ryes noted Rowan looking toward her, smiling encouragement. She smiled in return, letting Toron's violence go. It did her no good to dwell upon what he'd done to others in the past, now. They could only work to protect those they held dear, to the best of their abilities.

"I'm glad you didn't choose to end his life here," Maren stated as he took a seat. Shadd nodded agreement, while Torr appeared thoughtful. Sabin was frowning, appearing as if he didn't want to be reminded of his own banishment from Matlowe.

"At some point in the future we might have to take that as a serious consideration," Torr stated.

"We'll have to establish our own set of governing laws to live by," Ryes said, as they met quietly in a "conference room" after dinner.   Most of the rest were off doing their own evening pursuits elsewhere in Winterhaven.

"We could just load him up in the flyer and get him out to his tribal elder in a few hours," Kovin suggested. "We'd probably beat the hunting party back to their encampment," he added chuckling.

"We're not taking anything of obvious advanced technology with us," Garth asserted. "We're going to ride out on windracers. I don't want to be overpowered and our things stolen and in the hands of someone who could cause some real harm. Like Toron."

"That sounds about right," Sabin agreed, nodding his head. Ardis put a hand upon his arm, wanting to hold onto him as she dared to ask what was on her mind.

"Who's going?" she asked aloud, her heart pounding loudly in her own ears.

The others shifted and looked at each other around the room. Each uncomfortable with having to voice their willingness to go, or stay behind. All except Garth, who gave Ardis a nod of his head, having already made up his mind in this matter. His gaze was steady as he met each of his friends' eyes, trying to assure them with his confidence.

"I'm leading the team and will be going out to settle this matter with Dyan, Chief of the Moondance Tribe," Garth assured them all in a gentle voice. Ryes deeply blushed, gave him a nod in return, then jumped to her feet and quickly left the room. Her immediate exit gave the rest pause, having not expected such a thing from her. It didn't disturb Garth, to all outward appearances. The rest remained in their seats.

"You can't go alone," Raya spoke up into the silence, in a low voice. "I'll go with you as they're my people and I can help you reason with them." Garth shook his head in response.

"We need you here, Raya. I don't know how long I'll be gone, but I feel you would be safest if you remain protected here in Winterhaven," he told her. Kovin looked relieved to hear it. "I want all the women to remain here, away from any possible abuse or contests of ownership," he stated.

"They don't think of women the same way we do," Torr agreed with a nod. "Do you want me along, cousin?" he pressed.

"No, I need you to keep everyone safe here, Torr," Garth replied with a grin. "You can keep your far-seeing eyes trained upon any enemies that might come stalking our small village. If any of those stragglers come out of the east, I want you to make sure they continue on down the road." Torr huffed a laugh at this and nodded his head.

"And what if there are some good ones among them?" he asked, grinning, "how will I know the ones we'll want to keep?"

"You'll have Raya and Ryes here to help with that. I think Ryes has Mind Voice too, but hasn't practiced it enough to learn how to use it properly," Garth advised with a sad smile. "She plays more with that computer than tries to work with her Talents lately."

"I'll go with you," Rowan volunteered, finding his voice as he met Garth's eyes. Garth shook his head in answer.

"You don't need to sleep upon the cold, hard ground ever," he replied. "It would be a dishonor to treat you so, Elder Rowan. You deserve so much more. When we can meet them with our marvelous machines, then you can come and show them our great wisdom and a better way of living." Their eyes met for several long heartbeats, then Rowan gave him a small bow of his head in agreement. Maren sighed in relief.

"As you wish," he said with a heavy sigh. Garth chuckled.

"There's still so much out in the world," he replied, "you'll get your chance to plant your feet in new places yet," he promised. Rowan smiled, giving in at last. Ryes burst back into the room. She had her folded up map and something else in her hands and a smile of triumph upon her face.

"What'd I miss?" she asked as she went back to her seat.

"Grandfather isn't being allowed to go," Maren informed her, grinning.

"Good," she replied, nodding her head in agreement. "I'm going to need some advice when these little ones come and if anything happened to him out there, they'd be deprived of a wonderful Great-grandfather!" she asserted, grinning as she looked at Rowan. He laughed, nodding his head.

"I'm going," Sabin spoke up in a voice that brooked no arguments. Heads turned his way as Ardis closed her eyes, as if she had guessed it from the start. A tear glistened in the corner of her right eye.

"The two of us are all that we need to take that snake home," Garth said before more could volunteer. "I want the rest of you here to protect our new home. And Mitt, no tracking and following us this time!" She met his eyes with a big grin.

"Why walk when I can fly?" she teased. Merry laughter ran about the room, breaking the somber mood. Ryes held up the other item she had brought back with her. It was curious and shaped like a small shield with a large, well-made pin attached to the back, so it could be worn. It had many symbols painted on it and was bound by a silver cord across it. Rowan recognized it and gave her a nod of approval. Raya looked surprised and appeared relieved at seeing it.

"What?" Garth started, having never seen it before.

"This is a Badge of Passage," she explained, "it was given to me a couple of years ago by Darman and Rinna to use if I ever decided to leave Matlowe Village before my time came. It grants the wearer protection from tribal laws for both the plainsmen and the mountain dwellers. Wearing this would make you an honored guest and so you'd have to behave in an honorable manner in return," she added as she handed it to her husband. "It will help keep you both safe."

"And commands respect," Raya added, "among all of the tribes. They're very rare."

"And if the bearer is harmed, it would spark a deadly war," Rowan stated. "It's a very serious matter. No one wins a war with the Caravaners."

"Thank you," Sabin said before Garth could. Ryes gave him a nod then unfolded her map. Everyone saw she now had Winterhaven marked clearly on it.

"Raya, can you help me determine the best way to your tribe's camp?" She gave her a nod, trying to decipher the huge parchment before her. Ryes pointed to her head with a nod and she quickly realized what she meant so called up her Talent and the both of them got busy with laying out their plans. Seeing the others in the room were appearing frustrated being left out, she gently extended her Talent and enfolded them into the map discussion. This almost visibly charged everyone in the room, to be openly included.

"You want to catch them before they journey to the winter camp," she suggested, and shared her memories openly with her new family. She surprised herself with the way she looked upon her former family now, feeling they were backwards in many ways.

Departure

"I'll be back, long before our cubs are born," Garth promised. Marla had given birth yesterday morning to his youngest sister, Myran, and now he could hardly wait to hold his own cubs!

"You'd better," she scolded, still feeling chills from that Vision she and Maren had shared, what now seemed so long ago. She had her arms wrapped around him, not wanting to let go. Sabin gave Garth a nod, as he finally gave Ardis a last kiss, then released her to mount his windracer, whom he now called Spur. Garth kissed Ryes a last time and let her go, too. He mounted his own windracer, Pacer. He took up the halter of their third windracer, which carried their supplies and a dragging litter with a still-bound Toron lying upon it. He wore the blindfold, even if it was a week later, now. They didn't plan upon removing it until they were well clear of Winterhaven. They waved their farewell, then left to fulfill this task they knew they needed to accomplish, as their friends and families' voices were raised in bidding them a safe journey.

"They'll be back," Maren projected to Ryes, as he threw his arm around her shoulders, so only she could hear him, having prepared himself as she was saying her final good-byes to Garth. He then showed her the Vision Sabin shared with him, of he and Garth sitting in a great cockpit, surrounded by very, complicated-looking controls. She smiled up at him, her eyes lighting up, feeling much better about it, now.

"And we know Sabin's never wrong!" she sent to him, in return. Raya snooped in on their small exchange, smiling. She knew they could feel her presence and shut her out if they wanted to, but they knew she needed the practice. They both agreed, better them, than anyone else.

"Garth's still not the pilot Mitt is," she told them aloud. Mitt heard her and frowned, wondering why she'd say such a thing? What were they discussing?

"What's Garth going to fly?" she demanded, stepping before the both of them, blocking them.

"It looks big," Ryes told her, as she broke away from Maren, feeling much better. "So, he won't be back for the cubs, but will for other events," she sighed. "Are you sure you didn't tell him how many I'm having?" she demanded, suddenly recalling he might have a reason to stay away for a few months.

"NO, I promise I didn't tell!" Maren laughed as he backed away from his cousin, playfully holding up his hands before him, as if she were going to hit him for his insolence.

"Okay, how many is she going to have?" Garvin asked, wanting this big secret out, now.

"Four," Maren informed all of them. "He's really going to be busy when he returns," he assured everyone.

"Maren!" she shouted exasperated, blushing a dark gold. There was laughter as she chased him back inside.

"Oh my, so many," Marla gasped, shocked. Rowan chuckled at this, somehow not too surprised.

"Ryes was one of four," he told them. "Maybe it runs in Tyra's family?" he ventured.

"That's right. There were three tiny shrouds in the grave with Ronn," Shadd added, recalling the burial.

"We did have three for our second," Garvin reminded his dear wife. He had sired Karr, Garth, Gann, Githan, Mitt and tiny Myran. Githan had died of a fever when very young, and her other three births had been single cubs, only. The times Korman got to Marla never took, much to their relief. Marla smiled up to her husband's happy face, giving him a nod. She held Myran close to her breast, so proud of her newest daughter.

"We may yet have another in a few years," she teased. "So, you'd better watch out, man of mine." She wasn't quite past her bearing years and hoped, with Maren's help, they'd have at least one more cub. Garvin laughed as he hugged her and turned for the doors inside, an arm about her shoulders.

"We'll worry about that, when it comes," he sagely advised. Rowan chuckled as he walked behind them, sorely missing Jana.

"It looks like it might rain later today," Shadd told Torr as he looked at her strangely. "What?" she questioned.

"I'm relieved we're only going to have one!" he teased. She swung at him too, then wrapped her arms about him in a tight embrace.

"I'm glad you're staying here with me," she returned with a sigh. She felt sorry for Ryes and Ardis, knowing the next few days were going to be rough for them.

"There're times when I think Sabin and Garth are attached at the hip," Ardis sighed out, stepping over to walk beside them. They seemed closer than brothers and she'd finally gotten to the point where she could accept it. "But Sabin did show me a Vision he had. He'll be back in time for these two. So, sometime between the time Ryes has hers and I have mine," she told them. She also recalled the one he saw years ago, of them watching their four cubs play in a field of flowers, near a row of bubblenut trees. Shadd replanted the tree sprouts near the creek, so they'd have plenty of water and room to grow. She smiled to herself as she looked across to the field before the trees. Yes, this was the right place... Seena gasped, wondering at this.

"You're sure?" she pressed. Ardis looked to her, smiling.

"Yes. He hasn't been wrong, yet," she bragged in return.

"No, he hasn't," she agreed as she picked up her granddaughter, Lixi. "Time for your writing lesson," she told her, smiling. Lixi made a face at this.

"Sabin said I HAVE to, if I want to fly like Mitt, someday," she gave in.

"Ah, I'd better get the flyer inside its hangar, before it rains," Mitt suddenly spoke up, recalling her responsibilities.

"I'll give you a hand," Mason offered, smiling. She returned the smile and gave him a nod in gratitude.

"Thanks," she replied, turning back for her machine. Garth acknowledged she was in charge of the flyers, while Ryes and Maren were in charge of the shuttles. She felt proud to be given such an honor, so young, before everyone else here in Winterhaven. And she was the one who now taught the rest their flying lessons. She truly felt this was her place, where she'd been meant to be and would be all the rest of her life.

The End of Book Two

And a small treat... a peek at book 3 of the Adventures of Ryes and Garth

The Winds of Change

Return

They rode, tracking those who'd been part of Toron's raiding party, as they returned home. There were some signs of the riders trying to hide their trail, but as they neared their home territory, there were no further attempts. Once they were in Moondance Tribal territory, they removed the blindfold and left their prisoner blinking against the bright sunlight.

"I'm an important man in my tribe!" Toron warned them, shouting. He saw he was tied down to a sled they had tied behind one of their windracers.

"So important they're all out looking for him and just happened to miss us, out in the open, heading their way," Sabin commented, as he snickered to Garth. Garth smiled, giving him a nod of his head in agreement.

"After what we saw, I'd almost rather have Korman hanging around, than him," he agreed. He knew he had his days when he'd rather tear and shred the frustrating machines the humans kindly left behind for them, but then, he had Ryes to cajole him into letting go of his frustrations and approaching his problems from another angle. He knew, as long as she were his, he'd never sink to the level of this Toron. He missed her terribly already and they'd only been gone a few days. The lenoon soup she packed for them had been such a blessing with the chill from the rain their first day out, but then, Ryes always looked out for him. He wanted this chore done as quickly, as possible. They had cubs on the way and he vowed to himself to be there for their birth, no matter what Maren said he and Ryes saw. He and Sabin could be out hunting, after all.

"I don't know. Korman can be pretty brutal to the women, if the mood's on him," Sabin commented, "I'd rather they both party in hell together, away from all decent people." Garth chuckled at this, giving him a nod of his head in agreement, breaking free of his inner contemplations.

"Let's check the map," he suggested, since they decided to take a lunch break and let their mounts rest in the shade of an old, gnarled tree. They had a copy of one of the human, aerial, reconnaissance map of the area they were travelling. They'd overlaid their own markings, so they had a more complete picture of what lay around them. Before they left, they made sure Ryes, Torr and Mitt knew their route, so they'd keep a watch for their return. He made sure his sister didn't try to follow them in the flyer. He didn't want it to be an accepted sight. He'd rather use it as the women had, to help add fright to any who chose to oppose them. The plains tribes were still an unknown element. If they couldn't reach an agreeable understanding, they might need every minute advantage they had within reach of their claws.

"I'm hungry, too!" Toron complained.

"After we eat, then we'll feed you," Sabin reminded him patiently, as he'd done so, for the last few days. If he didn't get this small reassurance, he'd keep up the yelling until either they answered him, or stuffed a rag into his mouth. He was tired of the man and hoped to find his encampment soon. Garth studied the map, checking the compass, to make sure they were still headed in the right direction. It should be either later today or maybe by tomorrow morning, by Raya's estimation of where the tribe camped this time of year. They'd be setting up for their great hunt of the large, plains animals they used for food, getting ready for the winter months. Menna, the harvest moon, would soon be in the right setting for their semiannual, Great Gathering, so they had to get there, before they left the area, entirely for the event.

After they ate and the windracers had gotten their fill of fresh water and grass, they filled their waterskins, then stripped down Toron and bathed him, as well as themselves in the cold, swift-moving stream. Toron protested loudly, so Garth shoved him underwater for a few moments, to remind him who was truly in control. He pulled him back up, chuckling to see the panic in his eyes, as he was coughing and choking.

"Don't you know this is extremely unhealthy?" Toron demanded, sputtering and gasping for air. He was indignant with being made to bathe. "It not spring, yet!"

"The stench coming off your hide's unhealthy," Garth told him. They brought out soap and scrubbed him down thoroughly, then got busy with themselves. They washed their clothes and blankets, then set everything out for the warmth of the afternoon sun to dry. Both Garth and Sabin felt much better, now that they were clean once more. Toron sat and glared at them, glad there weren't any breezes to give him a chill. At least his lunch was still warm. He noted that while they had brought their hunting weapons, they didn't use them, anymore. Raya, or Gleds, must've warned them about hunting upon Moondance Tribal lands, without the head elder's permission.

"Where did you get that Badge of Passage?" he finally demanded, wanting to know this, at least. "They're not given out lightly, and this one came from Dara, the great chief elder of all the plains tribes, making it being handed out extremely rare!"

"If you must know, it belongs to my wife," Garth said, as he fingered the very, distinctive badge he worn upon his left shoulder. "She's held in some esteem," he told him smiling, seeing it made him nervous to see him wearing it. Ryes gave it to him, telling him it was for free passage through the plains tribes' territory. It was given to her by Darman, himself, in case she should ever decide to leave Matlowe for the wider world. The only one who could deny her leave was the head elder of all the plainsmen, Dara, and he was a close friend of Darman's. He carried letters from both Darman and Ryes. Darman's was to remind Dara and of the value he placed in the person he'd given this token to, and Ryes' letter explained as to why her husband carried the Badge in her stead.

"How could she know Dara?" he challenged. Garth and Sabin merely laughed at this, as they started packing their now, dry clothing and supplies away.

"Ryes knows much of the world. More than any of the three of us," Sabin said, giving Garth a nod of his head at this. Their contest with her had been more than enough proof for his purposes.

"Get back on the litter," Garth ordered. Toron hesitated, knowing that if he tried to run off, they'd merely ride him down. He stepped over reluctantly, hating this more than anything else. They tied him down again, and then mounted up to continue their journey.

"I only see two of them," Sabin breathed to Garth as they set upon their windracers.

"That's all I saw. Perhaps they'll come out and give us an escort in soon?" Garth cast his eyes upon the horizon, back from where they'd come. He knew if he called for help, Ryes and Mitt would be out very quickly in the flyer, but he refused to take that step until absolutely necessary. He kept the computer's gift of the emergency transmitter, safely in his coat pocket.

"It shouldn't be too much longer, now," Sabin returned. "Let's see how far they intend to let us go." With this, he kicked Spur into motion, mischief in his eyes as he glanced back.

"Not fair!" Garth protested, as he nudged Pacer in the ribs, urging him to catch up. It wasn't fun for Toron, tied to the litter as he was, when the two of them got playful, but Garth suspected Sabin did this to get back at him for being the way he was, too. They galloped for a few minutes, and then slowed to a walk once more. The mare pulling the litter caught up to them, Toron yelling at them for their recklessness. They laughed at this, paying him no attention at all. Their two escorts, at a distance, had become four.

As they topped a gentle rise, they saw a party of swift riders coming toward them at a fast gallop. They stopped their mounts, waiting for them. None had their spears leveled in their direction, which Garth thought was a good sign. About a dozen riders broke into a circuit of their small knoll, riding around them in a circle, as two of their leaders came forward to speak with them, directly. Sabin noted they saw the Badge upon Garth's shoulder and noted their attitude was one of respect. The riders stopped, facing them.

"What do you seek in the territory of the Moondance Tribe Traveler?" the older one asked Garth.

"To speak with the elder known as Dyan," he replied. "We have messages to deliver to him from Gleds and Raya." He didn't mention Toron's presence. He didn't need to. He saw none of the tribesmen tried to approach to cut him loose, nor even to talk with him. Curiously, Toron was quiet for a change, not even demanding his release. The other riders stopped their mounts, facing them from all sides. They held their spears pointed straight upwards, butts grounded within the carriers made for them, upon their saddles.

"Come, guest Travelers," the spokesman invited, then turned and led them forward, toward the camp. It was as reported. One bearing a Badge of Passage looked to be seeking them out with Toron as a prisoner. This promised to be an interesting evening.

For more books, check my website: